THE HOLY SAIL

THE HOLY SAIL

Abdulaziz Al-Mahmoud

Translated by Karim Traboulsi

مؤسسة قطر
Qatar Foundation

دار بلومزبري - مؤسسة قطر للنشر
BLOOMSBURY
QATAR FOUNDATION
PUBLISHING

Arabic edition first published in 2014 as *Al-Shiraa' Al-Moqaddas* by

Bloomsbury Qatar Foundation Publishing
P O Box 5825
Doha, Qatar

www.bqfp.com.qa

BLOOMSBURY and the Diana logo are
trademarks of Bloomsbury Publishing Plc

QATAR FOUNDATION and the QF logo
are trademarks of Qatar Foundation

British Library Cataloguing-in-Publication Data
A catalogue record for this book is available from the British Library.

ISBN: PB: 978-9-9271-0167-0
eBook: 978-9-9271-0168-7

2 4 6 8 10 9 7 5 3 1

Typeset by Newgen Knowledge Works (P) Ltd., Chennai, India
Printed and bound in Great Britain by CPI
Group (UK) Ltd, Croydon CR0 4YY

To find out more about our authors and books visit www.bqfp.
com.qa. Here you will find extracts, author interviews, details of
forthcoming events and the option to sign up for our newsletters.

Author's Note

I HAVE LONG BEEN INTRIGUED by the period of time between the late fifteenth and early sixteenth centuries. Many major events took place during those fateful decades, not only in the Near East but in the rest of the world as well. Ultimately, it was the moment of history that ushered the Near East into a dark age just as Europe emerged from its own.

In the final decades of the fifteenth century, Europe sent its fleets to discover the world and take control of maritime trade routes. Christopher Columbus eventually reached the New World, the Portuguese circumnavigated the Cape of Good Hope, and the powerhouses of Europe began to close ranks against the Ottomans. At the same time, the Islamic world, which, unlike Europe, had enjoyed a great deal of religious tolerance and coexistence, was going into decline. In 1508, the Portuguese fleet reached the shores of the Arabian Gulf, setting off a chain of events that led to the demise of the Jabrid sultanate, then the most formidable power in Arabia. The Jabrids fiercely resisted the Portuguese invasion, but were eventually defeated, thus ending their reign. The Mamluk sultanate in Egypt, a militaristic state that dominated the Muslim world for centuries, collapsed at the hands of the emerging Ottoman Empire in the Battle of Marj Dabiq. The Ottoman Sultan Selim became the new Muslim caliph, after the last Abbasid caliph handed over his seal and the Prophet's cloak, officially recognising him as his successor. Istanbul became the capital of the Islamic world.

This period may be well chronicled in Western records, but in the Arab world it is obscure and inaccurately described, vague and neglected in academic books, despite the commendable efforts of some academics to gather as much information as possible about this historically significant era.

I have relied on Arab and Western references to set the historical background of this novel; some of the works I am most indebted to are listed in the bibliography. I was keen to use characters who were actual historical figures, and honour their role in the events described in the novel. My aim was to link these events together and to revive figures who have been forgotten over time or who have been overlooked by historians in light of the successive tumultuous events that followed.

Cast of Characters

Kingdom of Portugal

Manuel: king's brother-in-law and confidant
Mr Rodrigo: king's private doctor and astronomer
Moses: renowned cartographer
Pêro da Covilhã: diplomat and explorer
Afonso de Paiva: diplomat and explorer
Afonso de Albuquerque: general
Miguel Ferreira: Albuquerque's aide
António Correia: military commander
Lourenço de Almeida: military commander
Francisco Álvares: priest

Sultanate of Egypt

Sultan Qaitbay
Al-Nasser Mohammed: son of Sultan Qaitbay
Qansouh al-Ghawri: amir
Hussein al-Kurdi: Mamluk army officer
Suleiman: Mamluk officer and Hussein's best friend
Jaafar: waiter

Jabrid Sultanate

Sultan Muqrin bin Zamel al-Jabri

Nasser: Sultan Muqrin's cousin
Ghurair bin Rahhal: vizier
Jawhar: Nasser's slave
Jamal al-Din Tazi: religious scholar

Kingdom of Hormuz

Turan Shah: King
Maqsoud, Shahabuddin, Salghur and Vays: sons of Turan Shah
Khawaja Attar: vizier
Halima: Attar's daughter
Farah: Halima's maid

Yemen

Sultan Amer al-Taheri
Murjan al-Zaferi: emir of Aden

India

Zamorin of Calicut
Qasimul Haq: Zamorin's most senior adviser
Si al-Tayeb: son-in-law of Qasimul Haq
Malik Ayaz: king of Diu and environs

Ottoman Empire

Sultan Selim

Persia

Shah Ismail

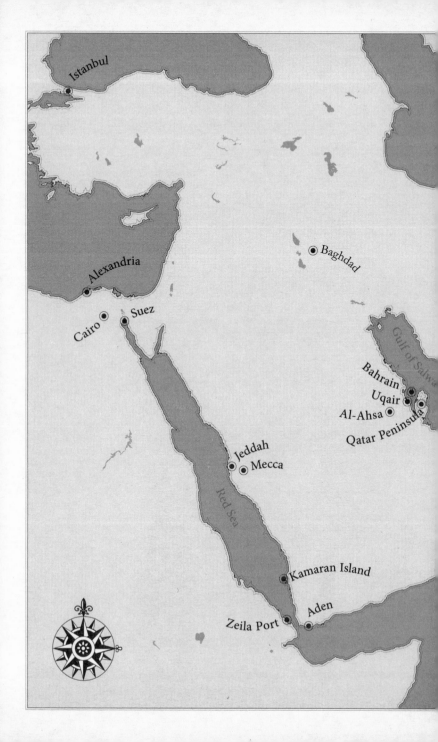

Qeshm Island
Hormuz Island
Debal
Khor Fakkan
Muscat
Kuryat
Diu
Goa
Arabian Sea
Calicut

– 1 –

Lisbon, Portugal

December 1486 AD

As NIGHT FELL, LISBON´S main road grew crowded with the poor and wretched unable to find shelter from the bitter cold. They piled rubbish on the pavements, set it on fire and gathered around its warmth. From time to time, children emerged from these haphazard congregations to chase after passers-by they spotted from afar, pulling at the people's garments and begging for money while pointing to their mouths or rubbing their bellies to crudely signal their hunger: the harsh cold, the merciless wind and the relentless rain afforded them little chance to speak.

It was a filthy road, like many of the roads and alleyways of a city hit by extreme financial hardship. Drawn into protracted wars with neighbouring Spain, and embroiled in costly campaigns in North Africa, Portugal had depleted its coffers to the point where a shortage of precious metals left it unable to mint its own currency. Poverty and crime were on the rise, and many people had to abandon their farms and villages in search of safety in cities that they soon overcrowded.

In such conditions, crimes of all kinds abounded. City dwellers started barricading their homes and concealing their wealth, and avoided many roads and alleys after dark. They no longer that their property, or indeed their lives, were safe, as more and more corpses turned up in the morning outside homes or on the roads, looted of their belongings and stripped bare. This sight became familiar, and soon people found it hard to differentiate between dead bodies and piles of waste: both often had things worth stealing. Even once-honourable people experienced the bitter taste of poverty and joined robbers in scavenging for anything of value. Trust vanished, to be replaced by fear of one another, and many turned into recluses in their attempt to cling to life and stay out of harm's way.

Two men appeared from afar, dressed in heavy robes with conical hoods that resembled the mitres worn by Catholic bishops. They passed quickly among the destitute street dwellers who had covered themselves with every torn and ramshackle rag they could find. The urchins noticed the two men and gathered around them, crying and begging for money. The duo ignored the children completely and continued onward against the wind that was now sprinkling ice-cold water in their faces – to which they appeared immune and indifferent. The two men had no time to stop and look at anything around them. If they had examined the faces of the children for even a few seconds, they would have seen their frosty red noses; they would have seen them biting their lips to hold back the pain from their empty stomachs. But who had the time to pay attention to all this? The pair kept their gaze on the road and their expressionless faces did not betray their nervousness. As their pace quickened, their panting produced a fog which rose from both sides of their cheeks. They were trying to get away as quickly as possible. The children had by now given up on trying to attract their attention, and returned to the makeshift fire pits and what little warmth they provided.

The two men continued along the main street for some time, and then turned right into a dark alleyway. It appeared to be faintly lit, less filthy, and otherwise deserted as if off limits to humans. The pair drew their shoulders together instinctively, reaching out for a sense of security that had been lacking throughout their trip across the city. They started moving quickly again with more forceful strides, urged on by the sound of their footsteps that the walls around them echoed back after a small delay. It felt as though there was an army of ghosts on their trail.

They inspected their surroundings, unsure of how they should feel in this eerie place. Should the sudden absence of any trace of humans make them feel safe or should it make them feel cautious and afraid? But they did not give the matter much more thought, and continued walking until they reached the cul-de-sac at the end of the alleyway. There was a stone wall there, to the left of which stood a large wooden door, cut through by a small hatch and a ring-shaped knocker hanging above it.

One of the men, the taller and bigger of the pair, used the ring handle to knock on the door, making a jarring noise that reverberated throughout the alleyway. The man knocked again, with more urgency, and the noise was even more cacophonous, merging with the echo of the previous knock that the alleyway had only confined and concentrated; not even the loud, brisk wind could mask it. The cold would show them no mercy if they did not go inside soon.

Finally, two eyes finally peered through the hatch, and a hoarse voice that sounded as if it had come from the depths of hell uttered three words: 'The Holy Sail.'

'It is heading *e-e-east*,' the taller man answered in a melodious voice, his body shaking and his tongue and lips made heavy from the cold.

The hatch closed and the door opened with a strange squeak. The pair entered quickly and the door was closed again.

Inside, the guard raised the lantern he was carrying to their faces. The men were now rubbing their hands together to get warm. The guard scrutinised their faces before he said, in the same coarse voice, 'Follow me.'

They looked around them and found themselves in the courtyard of a Moorish house. It was painted white, and was clean, well lit and beautifully designed. At the centre of its marvellous garden stood a fountain. The entrances and balconies were decorated with large arches adorned with spectacular engravings. The house resembled many other homes whose Moorish owners had left abruptly, melting one day into the darkness, never to return.

The guard crossed the courtyard to the other side, passing by the fountain. The two men exchanged quick apprehensive glances, before turning their gaze to the man leading the way. They had no idea why they had been summoned here. The soft purling sound of the water brought them a bit of reassurance. The man stopped in front of another door; he knocked before he entered, followed by his two guests, who began removing their hoods in a mechanical manner.

Candles in the corners lit the room. In the middle stood a rectangular table where three people sat, and it seemed from their garments that they were noblemen as far removed from the destitution outside the house as one could imagine. The appearance of these noblemen did nothing to assuage the two men's fear. Moses, the host, stood and extended his arms in a welcoming gesture. As he moved, a large silver cross hanging from his neck flickered.

'Welcome, dear guests! We've been waiting for you. Forgive us for summoning you on a cold night like this. Permit me to introduce you to these gentlemen.'

He pointed to the first, a nobleman dressed in expensive velvet garments; a hat of a matching material and colour, with a long feather affixed to its top, sat on the table in front of him. 'This is the noble Manuel, the king's brother-in-law and confidant.'

The two men bowed in a gesture of respect. Moses then continued, 'This man sitting next to me is Mr Rodrigo, the king's private doctor and a renowned astronomer.'

Retaining the same smile he had received his guests with, Moses said, 'I asked you to come to this house in disguise so that no one may recognise you. This house is the secret location for our meetings, and I hope that it will remain that – a secret.'

He looked the two men in the eyes, as though waiting for them to respond and reassure him that they had understood his intent.

The taller of the two men said, 'The location of the house will remain secret, sir. We promise it.'

Moses looked somewhat reassured, and he invited them to sit down. They sat quietly, and waited for him to explain why he had summoned them.

Moses did not delay; addressing the men sitting at the table, he said, 'Gentlemen, allow me to introduce my two dear friends.'

He turned to the two guests. 'Master Pêro da Covilhã,' he announced, pointing at the larger man, 'and Master Afonso de Paiva. I trust these men completely. They have been chosen for this mission because they speak Arabic fluently, and it is impossible to tell them apart from Arabs by their dialect and appearance. They know me as I know them, and I believe you have heard of Master Covilhã before, haven't you?'

'Yes, I know Master Covilhã, but then who doesn't? I have met him several times at the king's palace, where he is a well-known figure,' said the nobleman Manuel, talking to Moses as though Covilhã were not standing right in front of him. 'But let us get started. We don't want to leave this place at midnight. It's very cold tonight.' There was more than a touch of impatience in his voice.

Moses ignored him with a broad smile. 'Sir, let me offer you and the guests some of my fine wine. They are still rubbing their hands. The cold seems to have penetrated all the way to their bones. A glass of strong wine will do well to make them feel a little warmer.'

Manuel nodded. Moses stood and brought wine for Covilhã and Paiva, who sat silently and awkwardly, conscious that they were being scrutinised by the other men round the table. Moses sat back down and started sipping the drink from his own cup quietly. He then set his gaze on Manuel, and waited for him to begin.

Manuel ignored his glass of wine and reached for a parchment in front of him showing the most up-to-date map of the known world. He looked in the eyes of the other guests sharply for several seconds, before saying, 'Gentlemen, everything said here is to be taken in confidence. Leaking information outside these walls could cost us all our lives, so I once again stress the secrecy of our conversation and the information we shall disclose to you.'

Manuel glanced again at the map and continued. Europe had been cut off from the rest of the world after the Ottomans seized Constantinople in 1453, making it impossible to learn what was going on in the East, he reminded the guests. After Constantinople was conquered, the Ottomans changed its name to Istanbul. The Venetians had concluded agreements with the Ottomans, allowing them to control trade from the Muslim ports to Europe; they could now transport shipments of spice from the ports of Tripoli, Beirut and Alexandria to Europe, and sell them at high prices, depriving others of this lucrative trade. 'If we don't break this monopoly, we will die a slow death. Our coffers have been depleted and our people live in destitution. If we do nothing, we will find ourselves begging the kings of Europe for money,' Manuel said. 'And here we are still using the currency of our enemies, the Moors. It's unbelievable.'

Manuel paused for a few seconds, fiddling with the feather attached to the hat in front of him, trying to calm himself. 'We do not even have enough to mint our own currency!' He said this angrily as if those he was addressing were responsible.

Manuel continued, 'We know that there are sea routes between India, the source of all spices, and Arab lands. They alone control those routes, and monopolise their secrets and ports. We have obtained some information from our informants, who were able to penetrate deep into Persia and India. But this information remains muddled and unclear.'

Manuel adjusted himself in his seat, took a deep breath, and then said, 'Regardless, it would be difficult to do anything about the current situation. The Ottoman presence in

7

Constantinople may prevent us from obtaining the information we want, and keep us from moving toward those spots. We know little about what is going on behind that solid Muslim wall.'

Manuel raised his finger to Covilhã and Paiva's faces, after pausing for a moment, and said, 'But we believe there is another route that could take us to India. We are not sure but we have a good hunch. Your mission is to verify the information we have.

'The password that Moses gave you before the meeting, which you used to get the guard to open the door when you arrived, is the password you shall use to identify all our agents in the Muslim countries. Remember it but never, ever write it down. Yes, the Holy Sail is heading east. In recent years we have been working in utmost secrecy to gather as much information as possible about the spice trade between India and Arab lands, and from there to Europe. We believe there could be a sea route that circumvents this, around Africa.'

The nobleman then tapped with his finger on the African continent on the map. The expression on his face changed. 'Our ships have secretly reached West Africa. We believe there is a route that circumvents that continent all the way to India, but we cannot send our sailors and our ships to uncharted parts of the world. We need to know the ports, where they can re-supply, the wind patterns, the sea levels and the currents. And we are suffering mutinies on the ships, because the sailors are not accustomed to such long distances for long periods of time. We must find a foothold along the coasts of Africa.'

He spoke quickly, expecting his audience to immediately grasp what he was saying. 'We have asked our captains to put up a large cross in each place they stop, so that our sailors will sense that God is with them wherever they may go. They have planted these crosses throughout the western coast of Africa, but distances soon grew too long, and the sailors have become more and more restless. We don't know when our ships will be able to head east.'

Manuel sank back into his chair, blinking rapidly, and began to tell the story of a Catholic friar from Venice named Mauro, who several years earlier had made a large map of the world that was almost four cubits wide. Fra Mauro put into the map all the information he had obtained from Italian merchants who travelled to those lands, including descriptions from a Venetian who had settled in India where he married and had children. When the merchant decided to return home, he stopped in Cairo along the way. There, his wife and two children died from a plague, after which the man worked for several years as an interpreter for the sultan, before he could raise enough money to pay for his journey back. When he finally returned, he went to the Pope with all the information he had. The Pope then asked Fra Mauro to add this information to the map he was already working on.

'All that has been collected over the years was put into making that map – let's call it the Venerable Mauro map – which we paid a lot of gold to acquire. What interests us most are the ports that it describes in East Africa and southern Arabia, since it is from those ports in particular that ships sail to India, and come back loaded with all kinds of goods. Getting to these ports and learning more about them would make it easier for us to send ships to India via Africa.'

Manuel then slammed his hand on the table to draw everyone's attention. 'Your aim, gentlemen, is to reach India and

9

learn about the types of spices, their prices and the trade routes they travel through, not to mention the patterns of winds and ocean currents, the religions of the peoples that inhabit those lands, and the ports that the Arab merchants use. We must become acquainted with those ports, because they will become our bases too. It is important for you to fully succeed in this mission and return with the most accurate information possible. If successful, the king promises you many rewards and titles, and you will have done your kingdom a great service.'

The nobleman paused again. Everyone thought he had finished talking, and Covilhã and Paiva were too stunned by the enormity of the task ahead of them to be able to respond. Moses found this a good opportunity to send a message through Manuel, in the hope that it might reach some powerful ears at the king's court.

He said quickly, addressing Covilhã and Paiva, 'Gentlemen, as Jews we have special connections in most countries of the world. I have written to our friends in Constantinople, Alexandria, Cairo, Damascus, Baghdad, Beirut and Rhodes, informing them of your arrival. Every friend we have in those ports will point you to a friend of his in the other ports, so that you will never feel cut off from the world. All you have to do is utter "the Holy Sail" and if you hear someone reply, "It is heading east," then know that this person is familiar with your mission, and will give you all the help you will need.'

Manuel frowned before he resumed talking, as though he had not heard Moses. 'We have a strong ally in Africa, who is awaiting our arrival impatiently. His name is Prester John, and he is a Christian king who rules a vast kingdom there.

He has a strong army that can defeat the kingdoms of the Mohammedans. All we have to do is reach him and unite our forces. I sometimes feel as though he talks to me, asking me to come and help him.'

Manuel stared into emptiness, as though he had forgotten others were present. 'Do you know that when we find Prester John's kingdom, we could control the world, spread Christianity and get rid of all heretics?'

Suddenly he remembered that all those who were with him in the room were heretics in the eyes of Christians. A sly look came to his eyes, as he hastened to add, 'It is strange that our mutual interests have overcome our religious differences, isn't it? I know that you are all Jews, but that does not matter as long as we are all serving the king.'

Shifting his gaze to the silver cross that Moses was wearing around his neck, he said, 'Before the shimmer of money, faith fades, Master Moses. That cross you wear will do nothing for you and neither will the letter you carry around in your pocket, which says you are under the king's protection.'

Covilhã was busy scribbling down what Manuel had said earlier, and had not paid attention to this last comment. After he finished writing, Covilhã asked, 'But sir, we have no idea what lies in the world beyond Rhodes. Do you have a map showing the cities and ports that we must travel to?'

This was Moses's cue. He stood up from his chair and went towards a shelf crammed with stacks of scrolls. He carefully retrieved one, loosened the tie on the scroll and unrolled it on the table.

'This is a replica of the Venerable Mauro map. If you notice here,' Moses pointed with his finger to the bottom right corner of the map, 'there is a list of cities that we want you to go to, and identify their locations on the map accurately. The Venerable Mauro did not put these cities on the map very clearly, and relied on what he had heard from others.'

Covilhã tried to read the names, but could not pronounce the exotic spelling combinations.

Moses, seeing his confusion, smiled. 'Don't strain yourself too much; they are all foreign names. I tried to decipher them, but could only read Sofala, Hormuz and Aden. For the rest, you will need time to learn how to read them.'

Moses moved his finger, looking for a certain point on the map. When he got to Alexandria, he pressed his finger on the location and said, 'I can't see very well. Is this Alexandria?'

'Yes, that's it,' Covilhã answered.

Moses moved his finger again, until he reached what looked like the mouth of the Arabian Gulf. 'Here you will find a small island called Hormuz. Do you see it? I cannot see as well as I used to, I'm afraid.'

Covilhã squinted as he scanned the map. Then he found it. 'Yes, there it is.'

'Hear me well, Covilhã. We have almost no connections beyond the Mediterranean. We could not find anyone who could give you a helping hand there. I am in contact with the chief rabbi of Alexandria, whom I consider a dear friend even though we have never had the opportunity to meet. We have worked together in trade as each other's agents. He told me that he knew *Khawaja** Attar, a vizier* from Hormuz. He will give you a letter addressed to him once you arrive in Alexandria. At the very least, the vizier will be a good source of information, and might connect you to his partners in India

12

or in the other ports. You will need to forge such relationships when you are alone in those faraway places.'

Moses rolled up the map and gave it to Covilhã. At this point, Manuel felt that he had to end the meeting. 'Hear me out, gentlemen. You will take this copy of the map with you, and you will treat it as a treasure. You must mark each city on the map, and gather as much information as you can about them. Our goal is to circumnavigate Africa and reach India to take control of the spice trade. You have two years to return. If you do not, we shall consider you deserters, and the crown shall seize all your properties. Your families will also be handed over to the Inquisition.'

He rested his arms on the table and continued. 'Until you return, we will give your relatives letters protecting them from the Inquisition, so that you may rest assured while on your mission. Now go, and prepare to leave, we do not have much time.'

Covilhã and Paiva knew that turning their families over to the Inquisition meant they would be tortured to death in an unimaginable manner. Blood rushed to their faces as they were gripped by horror at the prospect, but it was clear that the matter was not up for discussion. Paiva, who had been silent throughout the meeting, tried to defuse the tension. He wanted the meeting to end on a cordial note, rather than with this menacing threat.

'We will do what we can, sir. We hope that the king will be pleased with us, for all that we have is at His Majesty's disposal.'

But Paiva's words fell on deaf ears, and failed to alter Manuel's demeanour as he gestured to them to leave.

– 2 –

Alexandria, Egypt

H USSEIN AL-KURDI ENTERED THE port in Alexandria on foot, leading his horse behind him. He stopped to look at the ships unloading their cargoes down into the wharves. He took pleasure in watching the sea, in watching the movement of boats and people, and he often came here, to the docks, when something troubled him.

He approached the edge of a wharf, stroking the neck of his horse. The horse swished its tail and whinnied happily, and drew its head closer to its master's shoulder, as though asking for more.

Hussein was dressed in his best robes. He wore a small turban and flowing black trousers decorated on both sides with gilded threads. He had similar embroidery on his waistcoat, which he wore over a white shirt. He had a dagger around his waist, and carried a curved Mamluk* sword suspended from his shoulder. Hussein always dressed immaculately whenever he left the citadel; after all, he was an Amir* of One Hundred, a rank he had not attained easily, which was perhaps why he felt he now had every right to show himself off.

Hussein had been born in a village near a river, whose name and location he no longer remembered. He knew it was somewhere in the mountains of Kurdistan, because his former master had told him so; this was how he became known as Hussein al-Kurdi – *Hussein the Kurd*.

His village had been poor and tiny, and the few homes there were built from rocks quarried from the mountainside. When the sky lit up with lightning and thunder, the villagers shared what little food and firewood they had. Hussein remembered how much he enjoyed playing in the mud after the rain with his friends, and running to the cold river at the bottom of the village to wash their dirty clothes and bodies. His mother always cautioned him against going there alone. The last time he disobeyed her, he found a hand grabbing him from behind and covering his mouth. The fading image of his village, as he screamed and tried to free himself from his captor, begging to be allowed to go back, would forever be engraved in his memory.

First, as he followed his captor, he did not know where he was going. Many days passed in which he suffered hunger and exhaustion – eating leaves, drinking filthy water and sleeping out in the open – until they reached a huge city that he had never seen or heard of before. He was told the city was called Aleppo. He had clutched at his captor's clothes and begun to cry. He had never seen so many people swarming in one place before.

He lived in Aleppo for several years, learning the Quran and the *hadiths** of the Prophet, and various arts of combat. Soon enough, he grew into a strong and tough boy. He was twelve when his master took him to Cairo. The city seemed too big, too crowded and too unpleasant to young Hussein. He had travelled along dusty, sandy roads, across crowded markets and between camel caravans loaded with all kinds of goods. He then had to cross a large stone bridge over streaming water; it

15

was nothing like the luscious green land he had left behind. He then saw a high hill at the top of which rested a mighty citadel.

He climbed up the hill and entered the building along with his master and a large number of children of different ages. The citadel was teeming with soldiers, who started laughing and exchanging jokes with his master, as he pointed at Hussein and the others. The boy did not understand what he was doing there. An ugly, burly man came in and ordered the children to undress, then examined them one by one, ordering them to open their mouths.

Hussein could still remember how the man stuck his dirty finger in his mouth to make sure his teeth were in good shape, and how he pressed down on his tongue several times and ordered him to fill his chest with air, before he punched it hard. Young Hussein did not quite understand what the man wanted from him, but he was afraid to cry and disgrace himself in front of his peers in the process. He suppressed a scream that nearly escaped from his lungs, as the man continued his examination, in the manner of someone buying an animal for slaughter. The brute grabbed Hussein's arm and bent it in all directions. Then, signalling that he was now done, he smacked the boy's head and ordered him to join one of two rows further behind.

The brute then took out a purse and tossed it to the boy's master, who opened it and counted the dinars inside before he shook hands with the man. Hussein knew then that he had a new owner.

A sudden tap on the shoulder brought Hussein back to the present. 'How are you, Hussein? Poring over the sea, as usual?'

'Suleiman! I didn't expect to see you today.'

'I was supposed to leave for Cairo with my amir but he has postponed his trip. Come with me, we will get a bite to eat. I'm starving.'

But before Hussein turned around, something caught his eye. 'Wait a moment, Suleiman. Do you see those Venetian merchants on that ship moored over there? Look at the incredible way they dress, though I don't know how they can fit themselves into those tight trousers or how they can bear wearing them. Look at their stilettos; they're almost as thin as needles. What I wouldn't give to accompany them on their way back. I want to see the world, Suleiman. I've never seen Venice or any other city beyond this sea. I love the sea but I have only seen it from a distance, and never truly experienced what it is like.'

Suleiman replied with his usual sarcasm. 'I don't understand your obsession with the sea, Hussein. It's like a beautiful woman; you know it may be risky to get too close, and yet your instinct compels you to do it anyway. That's the sea for you; you know how dangerous it can be, but you would love to try it all the same.'

A caravan entered the port, its great rumbling echoing throughout the place. There were hundreds of camels laden with spices arriving from India via the Suez, belonging to the Karimi Guild, a mysterious group of merchants who monopolised trade from Aden all the way to Suez. The Red Sea was almost their private property, and they were often the sultan's partners in business. All this set the shadowy Guild apart from other merchants, as the Karimis developed their special practices, jargon and communication networks, making it difficult for an outsider to learn their secrets. But they, like their

Venetian partners, always paid their duties to the port, and that was all that mattered to the harbourmaster, who turned a blind eye to the mess the caravans usually made throughout their stay.

In the inn nearby, Hussein and Suleiman sat at their favourite table under the shade of a fig tree. The waiter there knew them well, perhaps too well. He was a large man who had a crooked shoulder – the right one was noticeably lower than the left – and who walked with a slight limp. He had once served in the army, but suffered a serious injury in battle, which left him unfit for service. He was subsequently discharged, and ended up working in the inn. He had known Hussein and Suleiman for many years; they liked his banter and he enjoyed teasing them.

'If it isn't the two generals, the *atabegs**! Welcome, welcome, delighted to see you here! I hope your pockets are lined with cash today, because I haven't had a single decent tip all morning. Has everyone become stingy? I hope you will prove me wrong.' He moved his face closer to Suleiman's, pretending to analyse it. 'I don't see any sign of magnanimity in this face today. Maybe your face will turn out better than your friend's, Hussein!'

The waiter's laughter roared. Hussein gave him a broad smile. '*Atabeg*, no less? Are you trying to get us executed, Jaafar? We are only ordinary amirs, and we would like it if things stayed that way for a while.'

As Jaafar wiped the table, he spoke quietly, stressing every syllable, in a suddenly serious tone. 'You will be Amirs of One Hundred, then Amirs of One Thousand, then you will become *atabegs*. Someone will then kill you or you will kill someone. That's how things always work in Cairo.'

18

'But we're in Alexandria, my man,' Suleiman replied, turning an inspecting gaze towards Jaafar's massive belly. 'Have you not noticed that you started talking too much ever since you retired from the army? I think that paunch of yours is where all the chatter must come from. It's bigger than the paunch of any *atabeg* I know. Now go and bring us the best food you have before I draft you back into the army with us.'

As Jaafar gave a hearty guffaw, his abdomen wobbled. 'Even if you should appoint me an *atabeg* in your army I would still decline. You people enjoy hatching plots against one another,' he said. 'By the way, I'm going to start calling the innkeeper by that title. Maybe someone will kill him and rid us of His Irksomeness. He asks us to work all day, and then makes us clean the inn until everything is shiny. God, I hate the man. I thought I was done polishing things after I left the army, but no. There we used to polish our weapons and helmets, and clean our horses, and here we have to polish the kitchen, the cutlery and the boss's rotten bald head.'

The waiter left to get the food. Suleiman looked at Hussein, who now seemed distracted. 'What are you thinking about, my friend?'

Hussein was pensive by nature, and he rarely opened up to anyone other than Suleiman, his friend since childhood. But as he started talking, Suleiman felt he already knew what Hussein was going to say.

'I'm thinking about the mess we're in. The never-ending rows among the bands of slave soldiers and the comrades-in-arms have become unbearable. All those rebellions in the countryside, in the sultan's forts, and with the foreign mercenaries make it impossible for the country to be stable. Were it not for the spice trade, we would have been finished.'

Hussein noticed a bird as it landed on a branch nearby and waited to hear it chirp, his eyes still on the bird. 'The state's finances are in ruins, and yet Sultan Qaitbay has been spending much of the money he extorts from the merchants to fortify his castles and buy more slave soldiers. But for what reason? Did you know he has not paid the army's wages for three months running? Even the sultan's *khasikis**, his bodyguards and cupbearers, are complaining.'

He turned away from the bird and looked at Suleiman. 'Or how about his monopoly of the spice trade with India? Why is the sultan interfering in everything and not leaving the market alone? One Karimi merchant told me that the Guild might stop trading in Alexandria because the sultan cooperates with them sometimes, only to increase duties on them at other times. Recently, the sultan issued a decree banning Karimi merchants from selling their goods in Jeddah or any other port on the Red Sea. Can you believe it? Why would the sultan bar his own partners from trading?'

Jaafar returned with their plates, which he placed promptly in front of them, before he asked loudly, 'Would you like anything else, *Atabeg* Hussein and *Atabeg* Suleiman?'

Jaafar followed his gibe with another boisterous laugh that sent his belly dancing up and down. Hussein and Suleiman decided to ignore him.

Suleiman grinned at Hussein. He was used to hearing him speak his mind. 'Slow down, Hussein. You still have the habit of thinking about everything under the sun all at once. Can't you set yourself some priorities, man? You will kill yourself seeing only the downside in everything around you.'

Hussein was incensed by the comment. 'I wish I could be as heartless as you are, Suleiman, but I'm not. I see disaster coming and I can't keep silent about it. Everything around us is in a miserable state: trade, the government and the army. Tell me, for God's sake, what do *you* think about what is happening?'

Suleiman felt that he had to offer some response. This was his last day before he left for Cairo with his master, and he did not want to upset his friend. Suleiman's face took on a serious expression, and he looked around to make sure no one was eavesdropping.

He whispered, 'Ever since he became sultan, Qaitbay has been living in a state of permanent anxiety. He's afraid of the Portuguese, afraid of the Ottomans and afraid of the Safavids all at the same time.

'That's why you find him monopolising any successful trade – and then he destroys it with his greed – so he can finance the army and send it to Syria to fight the Turkic kingdoms there, or dispatch campaigns to the Ottomans' borders to let them know the area is his and warn them not to come any closer. If he had been serious about fighting the Portuguese, he would have sent his fleet to assist the Andalusians. They still send delegations to camp outside his palace, while their letters have been piling up on the desk of his vizier.'

He dipped a morsel of bread into the dish in front of him before he proclaimed, 'It's all a right mess, my friend!'

Preoccupied with his thoughts, Hussein had not yet touched his food. 'And can you believe that the Portuguese are attempting to reach India by circumnavigating Africa, behind our backs? If they pull it off, they would be able to enter Egypt via the Nile!'

Suleiman frowned. 'Who told you that?'

'A Venetian merchant who was recently in Alexandria.'

'Is this possible?'

Hussein looked toward the sea again before he said, 'What's stopping them is the huge distance from Portugal to the southernmost point in Africa. Whenever they send a ship, a mutiny erupts on board, forcing it to return.'

Suleiman waved his hand over his food, chasing the flies away, before he dipped his bread again into the plate. 'If the distance between Portugal and the outmost point in Africa is too great, then why should we be concerned? They will die of hunger and thirst before they ever get there.'

Hussein adjusted his turban away from his forehead. 'But what if they succeed in their mission? Just imagine what could happen!'

Suleiman replied, chewing his food quickly, 'They won't succeed, and nothing will happen. Even if they did, we will fight them like we fought many other enemies. We will erect a great chain between the banks of the Nile to stop their ships from sailing upriver. We will fight them in the south before they get to Cairo.

Hussein held his hand to his forehead, trying to calm himself. 'How will we fight them? It would be the end of Egypt and the end of the world!'

Suleiman stopped chewing his food. 'The end of the world? Says who? Have you read about it in the Quran or in the *hadiths* of the Prophet? Please don't talk about something you are not certain of. I know your faith has its ups and downs, depending on your mood and whim, but you are in a bad state and you are over-thinking.' He paused, and suddenly seemed hesitant. 'You need to be careful about what you say.'

Hussein smiled. This was what he liked about his friend Suleiman; he put up with him, his temperament and his almost never-ending questions. He laid his hand on Suleiman's shoulder and said, 'Eat, my friend. You won't find food like this in Cairo tomorrow.'

At this point, a group of soldiers burst into the inn. Their leader spoke to Jaafar briefly before the posse went upstairs.

A commotion ensued, and Jaafar hurried up to find out what was happening. Moments later, the soldiers came back down carrying a large chest, some luxurious garments and bundles tied up in strings.

Hussein called out for Jaafar. 'What was this racket? Who were those soldiers?'

This time Jaafar did not smile. He said, 'Those bastards were sent by the harbourmaster to deal with two merchants from Morocco who didn't pay their port duties. They said they would pay within two days after they arrived, after they sold some of their goods, but unfortunately they fell ill and couldn't go out for the past few days. So the harbourmaster sent his goons to confiscate their merchandise, and the two frail men – dear me – couldn't do anything but scream!'

'How do they survive and pay for their food and drink if they are so unwell?' Suleiman asked in surprise.

'It's odd. After they arrived on a boat from Rhodes, they checked in at the inn and paid me only for two nights. One of them asked me the whereabouts of the synagogue in Alexandria, though they don't look Jewish. They have a Moroccan accent and Muslim names. Strange, isn't it? Anyway, I reckoned maybe they had a message for the rabbi there. The rabbi is like the caretaker of this entire sultanate and many merchants ask about him or vice versa.'

Jaafar did not want to stop talking. By virtue of his work, he had a lot of gossip on the guests of the inn. 'The rabbi came here a few days later and paid me a week's worth of lodging and food for the pair, and asked me to serve them a special diet and look after them as best as I could.'

Suddenly remembering something, Jaafar slapped himself on the head. 'They asked me just now to go and find the rabbi. They want him to plead with the harbourmaster to return their belongings. I must hurry. He's paying me a lot of money these days, unusual for him.'

After a moment of silence, he turned towards them, and said loudly, 'It would be unusual for you too.'

– 3 –

Al-Uqair, Eastern Arabian Peninsula

T HE BRIGHT, FULLY FORMED disk in the sky gave the water a silvery lustre. It was a gorgeously moonlit night, its quiet interrupted only by the subdued voices of the sailors. They spoke almost in murmurs, trying not to disturb their sleeping colleagues. The fires they had lit on board their ships were starting to die down. It was nearly midnight, and the gently rocking sea would not allow them to resist sleep for much longer.

One of the sailors lifted his head, alerted to the sound of a ship approaching from afar, propelled by eight oars hitting the water in impressive harmony. But the sailor quickly lost interest, put his head back on his makeshift pillow and slept.

The boat glided quietly between the anchored ships until it reached the port. A whistle blew and the oars were lifted and then quickly drawn inside. A man jumped from the deck onto the pier and tied the boat to a post. Minutes later, a group of men disembarked from the ship. They spoke to one another briefly before they disappeared up a path leading to a palm forest nearby.

On the dawn of the third day after the ship's arrival, the *majlis** of Sultan Muqrin bin Zamel al-Jabri was buzzing with visitors. The *majlis* sat in the middle of a large farmstead in Al-Ahsa. Caravans carrying all sorts of goods from India,

China, Iraq, Persia and Yemen were parked outside. Throngs of people filled the entrance to the sultan's estate, chatting away in a multitude of languages. The place had become a bazaar of sorts, frequented on a daily basis by those wishing to see the exotic wonders it had to offer.

In front of the farm's gates a group of slaves, all wearing the same uniform, stood in two lines facing one another. Tightly gripping their long swords – the tips of which were touching the ground – they watched the people entering and leaving. Their demeanour was unwelcoming, as their eyes scoured the premises, meaning to prevent any undesirable folk from slipping in. Because of these cruel eyes, perhaps, many poor folk gathered outside the door, not daring to enter yet hoping someone charitable would come out and give them money.

Under the branches of fruit trees that had gracefully come together to create shade, carpets and cushions were laid for the sultan and his guests. A stream flowed along to the right of the *majlis*, originating from a nearby spring. Fish were swimming in the cool and sweet water, trying very hard to overcome the current. No one was allowed to get too close to the sultan's favourite place, where he came to swim on hot days.

Sultan Muqrin sat in the centre of the *majlis*, as usual, his legs stretched out. The fifty-year-old man had a light brown complexion and long braided hair that reached his shoulders. The sultan wore an embroidered *ghutra** wrapped with a circlet of plaited cloth, making it appear like a large turban. He had a thick, fist-long, salt-and-pepper beard, and was dressed in a long cotton shirt with wide sleeves that almost touched the ground when he stood up.

26

An Indian merchant sat opposite the sultan. He wore the turban typical of Banyan* merchants. The turban had a tail that hung down to his lower back and it spread outwards from the top in a fan-like fashion. The merchant seemed tense as he showcased his wares to the sultan, arranged neatly in front of him: jewels made from onyxes, diamonds and rubies; marvellously engraved rings; gilded Indian swords; daggers inlaid with diamonds; and curled-toed shoes interlaced with golden threads.

The sultan had become used to being presented with such merchandise and had learned not to look too impressed – even when he was – to ensure he always secured the best price. When he liked a certain item, he would pick it up, inspect it thoroughly between his hands and then pass it on to his vizier, Ghurair bin Rahhal. When the sultan wanted to go ahead and buy an item, he left it to Bin Rahhal to bargain with the merchants. He paid either in cash or in pearls, a commodity the sultan monopolised in the area stretching between Bahrain, eastern Qatar and the Omani coast.

On occasions such as these, the sultan's guests took great pleasure in getting a peek at the precious goods on display. People who sat close to him were envied for being able to listen in on the conversations and examine the coveted items first-hand. These articles were not easy to move between ports and required many provisions to be transported. Only the Indian Banyan merchants could manage such a feat, with their intricate network of relations with local rulers, harbourmasters and even the pirates infesting the seas.

There was now a hoard of sundry artefacts in front of Bin Rahhal. He reached out and took hold of a ring studded with precious stones, and held it up to the merchant. 'How much for this ring, Banyan?'

The Banyan merchant, by virtue of his experience, sensed a deal was in the offing. However, he had to be very delicate about naming his price, because he did not want to appear greedy, but at the same time he wanted to maximise his profit. 'Consider it a gift to the sultan from his humble servant, the poor merchant standing before him.'

Everyone laughed at this expression, which they had heard many times in varying versions from Indian merchants.

Ghurair bin Rahhal was not a gullible man, easily fooled by such flattery. He had come to Al-Ahsa with his father from Najd when he was fifteen years old. His father found work in the palace, teaching the Quran and Arabic to the children of Sultan Ajwad, Sultan Muqrin's brother. Bin Rahhal was nimble and tactful, and after his father's death, he was raised in the palace as one of the sultan's children. Over time, he became a close companion and counsellor to Sultan Muqrin, despite their twenty-year age difference.

Bin Rahhal was a handsome man. He had a piercing look that could almost see through people. He applied kohl to his eyes every day, which made his gaze that much more mysterious and intense. He was tall and had long plaited hair. He worked in trade, shuttling around the ports of eastern Arabia and travelling to India on many occasions.

Bin Rahhal gave the man a knowing smile. 'Come on then, tell me, how much for the ring?' he asked.

'One thousand dinars, sir.'

As was his custom in matters such as this, Bin Rahhal made a dramatic frown, squinting at the man opposite him. 'What? A thousand dinars? Too much!'

The Banyan started sweating. He pressed his palms together and brought them close to his face. 'I swear by all that is sacred to me, this is the right price, sir. I am willing to dip my fingers into boiling oil to prove it.'

The sultan was listening to the discussion, although he appeared preoccupied with something else. 'Boiling oil? Can you enlighten me, Bin Rahhal?'

Bin Rahhal loved to tell strange stories to the sultan, and the sultan enjoyed listening to them. 'They have an odd custom in India, Your Grace,' the vizier said. He told the sultan of one of his visits to Calicut, when he had seen authorities bring forward a man accused of committing a crime. He had been placed in front of a pot of boiling oil and ordered to plunge his forefinger and middle finger in the oil for a few seconds. The fingers were then wrapped in a cloth, which was sealed with wax. They imprisoned the man for three days. 'I didn't stay long enough to know the outcome of the ordeal,' Bin Rahhal said. 'But usually after three days have passed, the enforcers meet again and open the sealed wrap: if the fingers have fused together, the accused is found guilty, and if they have remained separated, then the accused is found innocent.'

Bin Rahhal had extended his right hand and made an incomplete fist, without the index and middle finger, to illustrate the encounter to the sultan. He continued, 'And let me tell you, Your Grace, the man's screams did not suggest his fingers were going to come out unscathed.'

The sultan gave a boisterous laugh and, glancing at the Banyan, said, 'Shall we bring some boiling oil? Or will you reconsider your price?'

At this point, the Banyan merchant knelt before the sultan and said emphatically, 'I will do as you please, Your

Grace, but believe me, this is the price this precious ring deserves!'

Bin Rahhal examined the ring again, more thoroughly this time. Made of pure gold, its shank alone was as thick as his little finger. A magnificent diamond centre stone sat on top, guarded on both sides by two intricately engraved demi-lions. The remainder of the ring was decorated with small diamonds that gave the band extra weight and complemented the masterpiece.

A guard entered through the door, and whispered something to the bodyguard standing behind the sultan. Moments later, the bodyguard came and knelt beside the sultan and gave him the message. The sultan nodded his head and signalled to the Banyan merchant to leave. But then, in the manner of someone who had suddenly remembered something, he said, 'Buy the ring from him, Bin Rahhal. We shall gift it to the caliph* in Egypt.'

The sultan's bodyguard gestured to everyone in the *majlis* to leave, except for Bin Rahhal, who stayed close to the sultan.

The sultan, addressing his bodyguard, then commanded, 'Bring in the messenger.'

The Hormuzi messenger entered the room and walked to where the sultan was sitting. The messenger's face was gloomy as though he was bearing bad news. He stood in front of the sultan, sat on his knees and bowed his head slightly. The messenger then leaned over and kissed the sultan's right hand. 'Peace be upon you, Great Sultan.'

The sultan was used to receiving many visitors, yet a visit by a messenger from the kingdom of Hormuz was always for a very important reason. Though the sultan paid tributes to the kingdom, he was in fact independent from it and did not

30

have to consult with the king of Hormuz over anything. As the sultan thought of this, he became even more curious as to the purpose of the messenger's call.

'And peace be upon you too, messenger. How was your journey here?'

'It was clear sailing, Great Sultan, but as soon as we approached Bahrain, the wind died away. We had to row to reach Al-Uqair, and by God's grace we had come in a military ship equipped with eight oars. Otherwise, we would have been stranded there until the wind blew again.'

As was the custom for the noblemen of Hormuz, the messenger wore fine linen garments, which India was famous for making. His robes consisted of a mid-calf-length tunic and trousers ornamented with gold trim near the ankles. He wore a turban wrapped in a somewhat unusual manner, with chains of gold and silver attached to its front. The messenger had a silken cummerbund around his waist, in the middle of which was sheathed a small dagger of pure silver.

The Hormuzis were skilled traders and had a powerful fleet. Though Arabic was the official language of the palace, they also had their own dialect, which was a mixture of Arabic, Persian and Hindi. The Hormuzis were mostly Shafi'i Muslims, though there were minorities of Christians, Hindus and pagans in their kingdom.

The servants brought snacks and refreshments to the sultan and his guest. They did this instinctively, knowing the exact moment they should do what pleased the sultan, before he even said anything.

The messenger finished drinking a glass of date juice and reclined into a pillow nearby, feeling a little better for having quenched his thirst. By now it was midday. Temperatures usually rose around this time, and unsurprisingly, the sultan noticed beads of sweat running down both sides of the man's face. He looked tense.

The sultan grabbed a hand fan made from palm fronds, and started waving it back and forth to cool his face. He handed one to the messenger, who immediately put it to use.

The sultan said to his guest, 'When the wind dies out, messenger, we must move it ourselves, like anything else.'

The sultan wanted to know the reason for this sudden visit, but he did not want to broach the subject too crudely. As was customary among Arabs, he started by making general conversation. 'What is the weather like in Hormuz?' he asked.

'Hot and very humid, Your Grace. It's not much different from here, but water there is scarce and our land is arid. If trade were not so prosperous, we would be unable to live on the island. We build our homes from cob, and dig under their foundations to create underground rooms that remain cooler in the heat. We use these in the summer and the rest of our homes when temperatures start cooling down.'

'What do you do about the scarcity of water then?'

'We have set aside ships whose only purpose is to fetch water from the island of Jesm, which the Persians call Qeshm. We store it in underground tanks that our soldiers guard day and night. The water is apportioned to households according to their needs. Water is a precious commodity for us, unlike here. I've seen fresh water everywhere since I arrived in Al-Ahsa.'

'And how is trade in the kingdom?'

'As prosperous as ever, Your Grace. Merchants like to stop in Hormuz for a number of reasons. We have a robust system for the protection of trade; we have many warehouses built close to the port; we deal in all currencies used by traders in all known ports; and our merchants have agents in Zanj, India, China, Persia and Yemen. Hardly anything goes unsold in Hormuz, and our currency never loses its value, because there are always people buying everything on offer there.'

'What about Hormuz's possessions in Oman?'

'Oman pays its taxes and sends us dates and dried fruits. The wealthy of Hormuz go there to buy orchards. Oman is every-thing for us, but the conflicts between its emirs* have almost consumed us. They are constantly fighting one another, and only quieten down in the summer when it is too hot and too humid to march and fight.'

The messenger paused, hesitant about what he would say next. 'The rulers of Oman use your men sometimes in their attacks against each other, as Your Grace must know.'

The expression on the sultan's face changed and he lowered his gaze. 'I have heard of this and I have checked. They are indeed our men, but they are far from us and we do not know what happens there until long after it has happened. I replaced the commander of the Jabrid army there nearly a year ago, and it is my understanding that he is not taking part in the conflicts there, correct?'

The messenger responded quickly, 'He is, Your Grace. Temptations there are too hard to resist. The orchards and bounty in Oman trump anyone's loyalty, no matter how strong. It's all about money.'

The sultan felt that he should spend no further time in these side discussions. 'And now you will tell me the purpose of your visit, messenger. I hope you bring good news.'

The messenger had been waiting for this moment. He bowed his head slightly and said, 'I am on a special mission, Your Grace, which cannot wait. This is why I am in your glorious *majlis*!'

– 4 –

Aden, Yemen

A T DAWN, A COMMERCIAL ship arriving from Suez docked at the port of Aden. A number of merchants, including two who looked like they were from Morocco, debarked. The pair brought down a number of pots containing honey and other goods. None of their fellow passengers bade them farewell; they had not made many friends among the other merchants, and had spent their journey in self-imposed isolation.

As the sun rose, Covilhã and Paiva, still in their Moroccan garb, were able to see the port in all its glory. Located at the mouth of the Red Sea, it stood in a naturally fortified bay that could accommodate hundreds of ships from all corners of the earth. The city walls and its main gate were visible from where the two men stood, rocky barren hills standing guard closely behind.

The port's topography naturally protected it from the monsoon winds, with small ships and large ships allocated separate berthing areas. The port of Aden was well organised and well managed; taxes on incoming goods were calculated on the spot, as soon as cargoes were offloaded, without delay.

A horde of porters gathered around Covilhã and Paiva, offering their services. After tough negotiations, the men were able to rent three donkeys to carry their goods to an inn located just beyond the main gate, alongside the city wall.

They were surrounded by a mass of people of all races and nationalities – Europeans, Persians, Arabs, Zanj and Chinese – matched in their variety by the breathtaking mosaic of their garments. The pair were fascinated by the sheer amount of spices on sale, which had been brought to the port on board ships from the East.

Covilhã and Paiva made detailed queries about storage facilities, prices, ports of origin, the taxes levied on goods and the currencies used in the trade, before they decided to retire to the inn to rest. The information they had gathered in a few hours was already priceless, and they were keen to write it all down.

Aden was scorching hot. From sunrise to sunset, people in the city did their best to avoid the sun's cruel reach. Yet to Covilhã and Paiva's surprise, the city was open and diverse, its markets rich and tantalising. And, unlike in Portugal, they did not notice any military presence around them. Even the officials in charge of the port and of helping merchants with their problems looked no different from other people, save for a special pin they wore on their turbans. People gladly obeyed the decisions of these men, who were appointed by the emir.

They learned that the spices made their way from the west coast of India to the ports in the region, including Aden. Once there, the spices were resold to other merchants, who had bigger ships. The ships were then used to carry the precious haul to Jeddah, Suez and the lands of the Zanj.

These spice merchants were known as the Karimis or Makarims, depending on the dialect used. In the beginning,

36

their speciality was cardamom, but they eventually started trading in all types of spices. The Karimi Guild grew into a formidable trading empire, which had close ties to the sultans and emirs ruling over many ports – some even said the Karimis were the business partners of the Mamluk sultan. From those ports, caravans transported the spices through deserts or jungles in the hinterlands, doubling their prices along the way.

Covilhã and Paiva also learned about a wealthy kingdom to the east of Aden called Hormuz. The kingdom of Hormuz – they heard – had many warehouses storing goods, including large quantities of imported spices. This brought back to their minds what Moses had told them about Vizier *Khawaja* Attar, and they prayed in their hearts that Hormuz was the same kingdom Moses had pointed out to them on the map. The information they got from Moses was not quite accurate, and the map was not very clear, so they hoped against hope that the information they had gathered would pan out.

Yet what they learned was not easy to process. Many factors controlled trade networks in the region. First, there were the sultans, who ruled the ports. Second, there were the trade links and bonds of kinship they had with one another. Then there were the services the ports offered to entice merchants and attract more business and, by extension, more tax revenues.

Almost every religion was represented in the ports Covilhã and Paiva had travelled to: Islam, Christianity, Hinduism, Judaism and paganism. Mosques, churches and synagogues stood side by side, and respect among the adherents of different religions was almost a tradition that no one dared break. From what they observed, trade partnerships were rarely based on religion; nay, merchants often sought out partners from a different land and religion to access new markets.

The Portuguese pair did not come from a religiously toler-ant society. It was somewhat of a culture shock for them to see this much tolerance and absence of reservation in the way people dealt with each other. They could not quite compre-hend what they saw or find a logical reason for why no partic-ular religion lorded over the others. How could people of different religions coexist and work together? Why did the Muslims not coerce others to join their faith as the Inquisition had done in Spain and Portugal?

Their room at the inn overlooked a deserted, filthy alley. They made sure the door was tightly closed, and that no prying eyes were in the vicinity of the window. Confident they were alone, Covilhã opened a sealed container and took out the parchment Moses had given him at their meeting in Lisbon, and marked the location of Aden on the southern tip of the Arabian Peninsula along the eastern approach to the Red Sea. In the right-hand margin of the map the names of other ports – including Sofala, Mombasa, Hormuz and Calicut – were written. Covilhã would locate each and mark them on the map as well. He had already crossed out Aden from the list, and wrote down all the bits of information he and Paiva had gathered at the port.

They slept for the rest of the day. In the evening, they decided to have dinner at a nearby restaurant, which served Indian, Chinese and Swahili dishes, cuisines catering to all tastes.

As they entered, the first thing they noticed was the fragrant aroma of spices that filled the air. Dressed in a variety of robes and speaking in different tongues, the patrons sitting at the tables were as diverse as the crowd of people Covilhã and Paiva had seen at the port. Their first meal out in Aden was a unique experience. The entire port seemed to be eating there. Miraculously, the waiter was even louder than the chattering clientele. When people finished their food, he brought them a mysterious bitter black beverage, which they drank eagerly, without interrupting their conversations. Covilhã and Paiva could not find out what the drink was, but it had a soothing, appetising smell.

After they left the restaurant, they walked past a mosque not far from the port. Curious, they decided to explore it and see what was inside. In Portugal, Moorish mosques had been converted into churches and their original features obliterated, but here the mosques were teeming with life. Covilhã tried to convince a hesitant Paiva to go in with him. In the end, Covilhã pulled him by his robes and they went inside.

They took their shoes off near the door and held them in their hands as others were doing. Several religious lessons were taking place at the same time, each led by a sheikh surrounded by a circle of worshippers; everyone sat on mats made from colourful palm fronds, moving their bodies harmoniously forward and backward, just as the Jews did when they recited the Torah.

The voices in the mosque merged into a drone, which sounded to Covilhã like a great swarming of bees. A melodious tune suddenly overpowered the hum, and made Paiva stand and listen carefully. The call to prayer followed, and the two men decided to leave the mosque quickly.

On their way out, Covilhã and Paiva noticed that the worshippers, who were also a very diverse crowd, were flocking to the mosque of their own accord. No one was coercing them to go to the mosque, unlike in Portugal, where a priest would usually stand outside the church on Sunday morning, haranguing passers-by to enter. As people crammed themselves into the church against their will, they rarely listened to the sermons, instead preoccupying themselves in side conversations, or in keeping their hungry children quiet, or in scratching at their skin, which probably had not been touched by water for months. For the entire mass, their eyes would be set on the door, waiting for it to open so they could leave.

Here, people performed their ablutions and washed with water before they went to the mosque, all of their own free will.

In the evening, they finally decided to do what they had agreed to do before they set off on their journey. Aden was where the pair would split up, Paiva sailing across to the coast of Africa, in search of Prester John's court, and Covilhã continuing on to Muscat and further east.

Covilhã studied his map for a moment; he was hesitant to broach the subject of the difficulties they were likely to face in the days and weeks to come. He knew how nervous his younger companion was about what lay ahead. 'When you get to the port of Zeila, you will have reached the outskirts of Prester John's kingdom. When you're there, make your queries carefully. You might have to travel a long distance to get to him, but when you do, give him this message.'

Paiva grabbed the scroll wrapped in a silk ribbon and sealed with red wax, and examined it anxiously. 'What if I can't find the kingdom? What should I do then? As you know, Portuguese ships brought many scouts to search for this kingdom along the coast of Africa, none of whom have returned! That land is clearly very dangerous, or there are beasts there that prey on humans. Otherwise, why did all those scouts disappear without a trace?'

Paiva's face and demeanour were like a child's as he voiced his objections. Covilhã, accustomed to accommodating Paiva's concerns, spoke to him in an avuncular manner. 'I'm aware of your misgivings, Paiva, but we must learn something, anything, about the kingdom that everyone in Portugal believes exists, at least for the sake of the nobleman Manuel, who is obsessed with Prester John. I – like you – am not sure Prester John or his kingdom even exists, but we have to find some answers nevertheless.'

The two men discussed the rumours circulating in Europe that a wealthy Christian king by the name of Prester John ruled vast lands and commanded a strong army that he used to fight the Muslims. Many legends had been woven about him and the vast amounts of gold in his possession, but no one had ever seen him, and no one knew the exact location of his wealthy kingdom.

Covilhã brought his face closer to Paiva and continued, 'Remember our families. They're waiting for us to return and save them from the Inquisition and those who look down on us because of our faith. If the king honours and rewards us as we have been promised then we shall be safe from the treachery of fate. Remember that, my friend.'

Covilhã took his eyes off his companion for a few moments. There was nothing else to look at in the room save for the small window overlooking the alleyway. He carried on, 'We will meet a year from now in Alexandria, in this same month – August.'

Paiva lifted his gaze from the letter to Covilhã's face, and with an air of sorrow said, 'What will you do?'

'I will travel to the port of Muscat,' Covilhã replied. 'From there, I shall go to Hormuz and then to Calicut, the city the

Venetian merchant Niccolò de' Conti mentioned to the Pope. I think I might also look for Sofala.'

As Covilhã spoke, his eyes seemed unfocused. Then, remembering something, he said, 'The rabbi in Alexandria gave us a message to a vizier named *Khawaja* Attar in the kingdom of Hormuz, which he said was not too far from here. The vizier might assist me in my mission. He is the only person this side of the world that I can go to. I pray he receives me well. I have started feeling like a stranger in these lands.'

He exhaled deeply, taking stock of the magnitude of the task entrusted to him. 'Sofala could also be of significance. I was told it is somewhere along the east coast of Africa, but where exactly, I do not know! Manuel also wants to learn more about it.'

Covilhã looked at the container that housed the secret map before he continued. 'Thank the Lord that we were able to recover our goods from the harbourmaster in Alexandria. If the rabbi had not paid the duties and got them back, our mission would have ended before it even began.'

Pointing at the goods that were with them in the room, he then said, 'Take with you half of the goods we brought with us. This will be your insurance policy during your journey. You must sell as much as you need to cover your expenses, but you must also factor in the journey back. It's fine if you want to trade what you have if you think this would earn you enough profits.'

Paiva's eyes twitched and his voice was that of a man who felt he was about to march into certain death. 'I am afraid, Covilhã. Should I be risking my life for the sake of a legend? We may never meet again or return home, all for the sake of one maniac's obsession!'

Covilhã put his hand on his friend's shoulder and spoke with more conviction than he felt. 'Don't worry. We will meet again. Remember, our future and the future of our people in Portugal depend on us succeeding in our mission. The state of the Jews in Portugal is tragic, but if we succeed, we might start being treated like citizens equal to the Christians. Think of the cross hanging from Moses's neck: though this wise man is close to the king, he has to wear a cross to avoid being harassed because of his faith. I have seen with my own eyes an *auto-da-fé* where five men and two women were burned alive – two Jews from Beja and five Muslims from Alhama. It was a sight I do not wish to see again.'

Covilhã's gaze drifted away as he spoke to Paiva. He was trying to peer into the unknown trials and tribulations that awaited them. Their missions were not easy. Even failing was not easy.

The next day, the pair started playing their roles as merchants, selling their goods and buying others, which they then sold again. They made thorough investigations at the port about the currencies used in trading; the points of origin for the goods traded and how much they were priced there; how long they stayed in the sea; who owned the ships; how shipping costs were estimated; and what risks were involved, and other matters they needed for their report.

Several days into their stay in Aden, they decided to visit the rabbi in the city. The innkeeper told them the man lived near the synagogue in the Jewish quarter. Covilhã and Paiva made their way through the alleyways leading to their destination. They got lost several times, each time stopping to ask for directions. Aden's alleys were mazelike, and reminded them of the Arab cities they had seen in Spain and Portugal: they must

43

have started out as little more than makeshift paths carved out by people's footsteps until they became passageways and arteries.

They were now close to the Jewish quarter. A young boy wearing a multicoloured *kippah* ran out towards them. Two small, barely visible side locks of hair flowed down from under the dirty cap. The boy wore a tattered *izar** reaching to his small knees. The rest of his body was bare. The boy cried out, 'Do you seek the rabbi?'

Covilhã smiled. 'How did you know?'

'Many merchants who come here ask for him. There isn't much in the Jewish quarter worth seeing other than him. He's an important man, but you're going to have to pay me if you want me to show you where he lives.'

'Fine, we will pay!'

The boy marched them to a mud-plastered stone building, which had a small door beneath a faded drawing of the Star of David. The boy went in ahead of them and then asked them to follow. They hesitated a little before Paiva caught sight of the Jewish symbol and pointed it out to Covilhã, who in turn felt reassured. They followed the boy inside.

The interior of the building was dark and it took a few moments for their eyes to adjust. They heard faint humming and saw the rabbi standing opposite a wall, reading from a scroll he was holding in his hands. A large prayer shawl with striped and knitted edges was draped around his neck and shoulders.

The boy came up behind the rabbi and pulled his cloak to get his attention.

'What do you want, boy? Have I not told you not to disturb me when I'm praying? Go away, go, you little pest!'

The boy was obviously used to the rabbi's temper; he stood there and did not budge. He pointed toward the two guests, and then went back to Covilhã, stretching his palm out flat. Covilhã handed him a coin, which the boy kissed and touched to his forehead in a gesture of gratitude, before he placed it under his cap and left.

The rabbi finished his prayers and then greeted the two men warmly, asking them to sit with him in the synagogue.

Covilhã decided to try his luck with the rabbi. Without any introductions, he said, 'The Holy Sail!'

The rabbi frowned in confusion, as though expecting Covilhã to finish his sentence. An awkward moment of silence followed. The rabbi then said, 'What happened to the holy sail? What holy sail?'

Covilhã knew that the rabbi had no idea whatsoever about their mission, and understood that he and Paiva had to be careful but, at the same time, try to extract as much information from him as possible.

The rabbi was a treasure trove of information. He became very forthcoming once they told him they were Jewish Moroccan merchants who were solely interested in making profit before travelling back home. But the rabbi also started complaining about financial hardship, and asked Covilhã and Paiva to donate to the ageing synagogue, which he said was on the verge of collapsing from disrepair.

Like all other people, Jews, the rabbi explained, left for other countries when they became better off, and many Jewish merchants ended up in India, Egypt and Palestine. 'It's also the weather. It's too hot here, most people can't bear it.'

Covilhã was curious about how Jews lived in this part of the world. 'Does anyone harass you here, Rabbi?'

Feeling warm, the rabbi removed his prayer shawl and folded it in a ritualistic, neat manner, and put it on a shelf next to a pile of scrolls. 'No, not at all,' he replied. 'No one harasses us. As you can see, we are part of the people here. We dress the same and eat the same. Some Jews work at the palace. The emir trusts us thanks to our good education and connections.'

The rabbi sighed and then continued, 'But the problem we have is that our people are emigrating. The climate here is unbearable in the summer. Around a month ago, a Jewish family left to India for good. If things carry on like this, we might disappear from Yemen altogether, and only elderly people like me will be left, merely because they can't leave.'

The rabbi explained to Covilhã the Jewish community's role in commerce in Yemen, and told him about some Jewish tribes that lived in isolation in the highlands, which he had not been able to visit as frequently as he had done before. To Covilhã's surprise, the rabbi said he was working hard to prevent marriages between Jews and Muslims.

'But why would you stop them marrying, Rabbi?' Covilhã asked, with his usual pragmatism.

The rabbi waved his hand in front of Covilhã's face, as if throwing something at him to get his attention. 'We have beautiful young women that many young Muslims would like nothing better than to wed. But if we let those women marry outside their community, the Jewish faith would be lost! I am trying my best to prevent this intermixing, which will be harmful in the long run. But believe me, it's very difficult. Love stories in this country are too many; it's as if the Yemenites were born to love!'

Covilhã stood up and gestured to Paiva. The two men then bade the rabbi farewell and left.

Several days passed. By now, they had gathered a mountain of information. Covilhã and Paiva stood at the port of Aden, saying goodbye to one another. Paiva had to board a ship manned by an African captain and crew to take him to his destination on the African coast. Then, a few days later, Covilhã would be going to board an Arab ship, which would take him to Muscat.

Covilhã embraced his friend tightly. He said, 'We will meet in Alexandria in August a year from now. If anything happens, you must write a letter to our friend in Alexandria informing him of your situation, and I will do the same. Now go, my friend!'

Paiva reluctantly boarded the ship, and turned to wave silently to his friend who was still on the pier. Moments later, noises echoed from inside the ship. Ropes dropped from the top of the mast, and the sail filled with wind. The ship began to move westward.

Covilhã sat down and watched the ship carrying his friend as it sailed further away. He wiped the sweat from his face with the tail of his turban.

He thought back to the mountain village near the Spanish border where he had been born and his tireless efforts to recover his family fortune, which had consisted of a farm located at the foot of a hill overlooking a secluded green valley. His elderly father had sobbed as he told Covilhã that the farm had been confiscated by order of the king because Jews and Muslims no longer had the right to own property. Covilhã had not understood why the farm was taken from them, and how worshipping the Lord in a different way could cause such pain. Why would the king intervene between people and the god they worshipped? Covilhã had decided afterwards to get close to the centre of power; if power was the cause of the disaster that befell him and his family, then why should he not be close to it and benefit from it? He had put a cross around his neck and made for Lisbon.

He ultimately became an interpreter at the court of the Portuguese king, and used his language skills to get closer and closer to the king himself, learning Arabic and Latin and French, in addition to the Portuguese and Castilian that he already knew. He once served as representative of the king of Portugal on a mission to rescue Prince Fernando, the king's brother who had been captured at the Battle of Tangier. Not long after that, he worked as a spy for the king in the court of the king of Castile to identify his opponents. The king staged a bloodbath after Covilhã sent him a list of people conspiring against him. This was a pivotal moment in his career, following which he became close to the king and part of his retinue.

Aden's intense heat brought him back to the present. He glanced toward Paiva's ship, now barely visible in the distance, and leaving a broad wake in its trail.

– 5 –

Alexandria, Egypt

Hussein al-Kurdi lay on his bed in the fort. His gaze was fixed on the ceiling. A light breeze blew in from the window. As was his wont, his mind was crowded with too many thoughts: the endless battles between the Mamluks and the Ottomans; the collapse of trade in Alexandria; the rampant poverty, corruption and violent crime. The road between Cairo and Alexandria was no longer safe, conflict was raging between top Mamluk leaders, and people fleeing from the countryside were now pouring into the cities – all because of bad decisions made by the sultan or his entourage to raise money and buy loyalties by any means.

Hussein shuffled out of bed and looked out the window. He spotted an empty nest a dove had started building several days ago. He stuck out his hand and pushed it into the ground below; he hated it when birds built their nests near his window.

Hussein was torn. He abhorred corruption, weakness and bad governance, which he saw as the main causes of the sultanate's sins, failures and divisions. These matters preoccupied him almost constantly, but he was unsure of how they should best be dealt with or resolved. He felt the rise of a strong leader

49

to power would change all this, but he began to despair about seeing this happen in his lifetime.

For Hussein, weakness equated to death, which was why he reacted harshly towards the weak in general. That included the doves that came to his window, which to him were pathetically fragile creatures that did not deserve to live.

Hussein did not have many friends. Not many people could tolerate him and his non-stop grumbling over the dismal situation. Only Suleiman knew how to deal with him and accommodate him. Without Suleiman, he felt lost and lonely, and sometimes angry and incomprehensibly violent. He scanned the road in front of the fort. Not long ago, it would have been crawling with caravans travelling from Suez, and carrying goods from India and China. Where were they now? How did the road become so deserted and miserable? Who was responsible for all this? Where was the sultanate headed?

Disorganised ideas shifted in his head in rapid succession. There were so many things that needed fixing, but he was ultimately only a junior officer in the Mamluk army. All he could do was follow orders without thinking twice. 'Curse these ranks we hold,' he muttered to himself. 'They are just meant to tell us our place in the pecking order, and what proportion of our brains we must not use.'

Suleiman had sailed away with a large campaign to fight pirates near Rhodes; Hussein missed him terribly. His mind was teeming with worries and concerns that he wanted to tell Suleiman about, the only person in the world who would listen to him and his complaints.

Suleiman had not changed much since they were teenagers. He had always been witty and sarcastic, laughing at everyone and everything, and finding a joke in every situtaion. Everyone loved him for his big heart and good nature.

'Oh Suleiman, where are you?' Hussein sighed.

As adolescents living in the Mamluk barracks, the older boys used to humiliate and beat them for no reason. In those days, he wished he were older and bigger so he could fight back; he hated being weak. He remembered the time the older boys beat Suleiman so severely and left him crying for hours. He could not bear to see his friend sobbing. He took a small knife from his pocket and put it in Suleiman's hand, and told him to stab one of the older children who attacked them as a matter of habit. When Suleiman refused, Hussein took the knife back and stabbed the boy in his thigh. It was the first time he had stood up for himself. Afterwards, the other boys understood that Hussein's anger was fierce and his wrath cruel, and they avoided him, fearing his reaction. Since that time, Hussein glorified might and loathed weakness.

He could no longer bear to stay in that depressing room. He put his clothes on and left, taking the stairs down to the courtyard of the fort where new slave soldiers were training. He felt sorry for them; they must have endured much pain and anguish on their way here. He did not want to remember his own story again, and cried out to the groom to bring his horse.

Hussein heard someone calling his name. It was the chief of the guards at the fort who was running towards him. 'The amir demands your urgent presence,' he shouted out to Hussein, panting.

'Why? What happened?'

'His Highness is going to Cairo and wants you to be with him. Something seems to have happened at the palace there.

Clearly it is serious, because the amir ordered preparations to be made for a long sojourn, and wants all commanders to be with him without exception, including you.'

The road from Alexandria to Cairo straddled picturesque stretches of farmland. Over the years, palm trees had been planted on both sides, and now served travellers, providing them with shade and dates. There were many inns along the way, built by Mamluk amirs and the sheikhs of Sufi orders, offering food and lodging for their guests. The entire roadside was almost a charitable endowment to travellers, with the inns, kitchens and planted trees serving all those passing by, free of charge for those in need.

The convoy of Qansouh al-Ghawri, the amir, included twenty camels laden with baggage. Fifty fully armed and armoured horsemen escorted it and mules carrying sundry cooking wares followed closely behind. A company of penurious Sufis trailed the caravan as well; they usually followed Mamluk amirs when they travelled, to take advantage of their magnanimity.

Ghawri rode at the front of his horsemen, his most trusted officers, including Hussein, riding behind him. Hussein turned to Amir al-Ghawri, and was able to see part of his face. The amir had a distinctive long white beard. Though life's trials and ordeals had left their mark on his face, and age – he was well into his sixties – had bent his back, he still retained a commanding presence. He had served as a commander of a military detach-ment in Syria and a Mamluk chamberlain in Aleppo, before he returned to Alexandria, retiring from politics.

The amir was not a talkative man. He kept his eyes fixed on the road ahead, issuing orders from time to time to his officers and aides in a quiet, confident voice. There was something about him that made Hussein gravitate towards him, but he was not quite sure what it was. Had a solid sense of loyalty to his master been ingrained in him during his training? Was it the paternal way Ghawri always treated him? Or was it the charity he showed the poor often and generously? Hussein held him in a higher regard than the sultan himself, who was squandering the realm's resources, abusing the populace and stealing from the funds of public endowments.

Hussein desperately wished that his master would decide to contend for the throne to set everything right. But Ghawri seemed content with merely watching the power struggle from a distance without taking part. That had been his decision since he returned from Aleppo, and he had not changed his mind.

When the cavalcade reached Cairo, it was received by a band of flautists and musicians beating on cymbals and drums, announcing the amir's arrival. Ghawri and his party cut their way through the crowds into the sultan's castle, which then closed its gates in the face of the interlopers following the convoy. At the main courtyard in the castle, the travel-weary riders dismounted and adjusted their garments before entering the sultan's court.

Hussein was not pleased with what was happening. He did not know why the amir and his entourage had come to Cairo, and did not dare to ask. Coming to the capital with the amir was no reason to celebrate; Hussein preferred Alexandria, and the noise the waves made, the smell of the sea, and the sight of the sailboats there. Cairo would deprive him of all that.

The band was still playing outside, as though declaring that glad tidings were to be expected shortly. Amir al-Ghawri entered the sultan's hall followed by his delegation. Sultan Qaitbay and the senior members of his court stood for Ghawri. Even the *khasiki** slaves stood up in the back; the amir commanded great respect in the palace, thanks to the services he had done for the sultanate and also because he was disinterested in the official titles and positions that had been offered to him.

By the end of the meeting, the sultan had appointed Amir al-Ghawri as his *dawadar**, the Bearer of the Sultan's Inkstand, the sovereign's vizier and spokesperson. From that moment, Hussein realised that life as he knew it in Alexandria would never be the same again. His master had become an executive of the sultan's court in Cairo, and Hussein was now expected to be at his side there. He realised that he quickly had to get used to this bustling metropolis, which he had disliked ever since he was a boy.

Time in the Cairene court passed quickly. Not long after their arrival, Sultan Qaitbay fell gravely ill and soon passed away. He was succeeded by his son, al-Nasser Mohammed. The new sultan tried his best to improve relations with the Ottomans and put an end to the armed conflict that had raged with them under his father's rule, though sporadic scuffles continued between their armies along the borders.

At first, Hussein thought things would improve with the accession of Qaitbay's son. The new sultan launched several campaigns to supress rebellions by the Bedouins in the countryside and to crack down on bandits. However, things – as Hussein saw them – became more and more complicated after that, especially with reports coming from merchants saying that the Portuguese had reached India. The Egyptians did not understand how the Portuguese had pulled off that feat, and rumours spread that they had found a secret route and would soon appear in the Nile coming from the south.

People wavered between outrage and disbelief. Then after a period of time, fear of a Portuguese invasion gave way to jokes told first by the hashish-fiends in Cairo. They were a common sight in the alleyways, smoking and laughing so loudly that everyone in the vicinity could hear them. At night, those roars of laughter were all too familiar – and irksome – for the somnolent residents of the city as they tried to sleep.

Hussein was pining for his friend Suleiman. Pirates in Rhodes had captured Suleiman after he was wounded in battle. The Ottomans paid a ransom to get him and other prisoners released, and took him to Turkey. But Hussein did not know his exact whereabouts, and had no way to get to him or find out what had happened to him since; all he could do was wait. He would let out a frustrated sigh before muttering his usual refrain to himself, 'Where are you, Suleiman?'

As time passed, the convoys of the Karimi Guild stopped coming to Suez and Alexandria. Revenues dwindled, the state's coffers emptied and social unrest spiralled gradually out of control. Bedouin uprisings returned to the countryside with a vengeance, and bandits were now so brazen that they were raiding Cairo markets in broad daylight. The Hajj pilgrimage had stopped too as highwaymen now did not spare even the women and children travelling with the Hajj convoys.

People revolted and there were many disturbances. Discord grew between Mamluk amirs and there was little security to be found outside the sultan's palace. Hussein felt things were fast approaching total disaster if nothing was done to alter the current trajectory of events. He had despaired of any attempts for reform by now and, again, all he could say to himself when such thoughts overwhelmed him was, 'Where are you, Suleiman?'

On one sleepless night – now a frequent occurrence – Hussein's train of doomed thoughts was once again debilitating him. He punched his pillow with his fist, trying to adjust its form, as though blaming it for his insomnia. He struck it again, having no other way to vent his anger and frustration. He threw his head on the pillow, trying to close his eyes and clear his mind, in the hope of getting some sleep. But he kept tossing and turning in his bed, without managing to drift off.

At midnight, he was roused from his haunted slumber by voices and loud sounds coming from the courtyard of the palace. He could make out horses whinnying and the clanging of swords. He was now wide awake, anxious that a conspiracy was – yet again – unfolding at the palace and wondering who the victim was this time.

A servant knocked on his door. 'The amir wants you in the sultan's hall, now and without delay!'

He splashed water on his face quickly, put on his turban and made himself as presentable as possible under the circumstances. He hung his sword over his shoulder and scurried to the sultan's hall. When he got there, he saw that all the soldiers, bodyguards, amirs and the *atabeg* had gathered, and spotted Amir al-Ghawri sitting on the right side of the hall. At the centre of the hall sat the Abbasid Caliph al-Mustamsik and the four chief judges in their large ceremonial turbans.

Hussein walked quietly towards Ghawri. He nodded to Ghawri and then took up his place behind his master. One of the amirs stood in the middle of the hall, addressing those present.

'What should we do then? The country is in turmoil and the treasury is empty. Our armies fighting the Ottomans in Syria have not received their wages for months. Uprisings in the countryside have forced peasants to flee to the city, only for them to be ambushed by bandits on the way. Our servants are being lynched in the streets of Cairo, because people see us in them.'

Another amir suddenly stood up and interrupted him. 'Who is the cause of all this? Isn't it the sultan, who has fled and left the throne without warning?' He pointed to the empty chair at the top of the hall and continued. 'This throne has become vacant. No one wants to shoulder the responsibility. This tedious debating will lead us nowhere. Let us decide who should assume the throne right here and right now.'

At the other end of the hall, an amir stood and cried out at the top of his lungs, 'Yes! Appoint whomever you want so you can kill him as usual when you decide you want to replace one sultan with another! How will the new sultan govern if you are going to meddle in every decision he makes, and draw your swords against him when he does something you do not like?'

The amir made a dismissive gesture as he headed for the door, and said, 'I will ride to Fayoum. I will let you choose a puppet sultan by yourselves. If you agree on someone do let me know.' He paused and then, looking at them with utter contempt, exclaimed, 'Something is rotten in Cairo! I cannot bear it, nor can it bear me!'

The hall reverberated with loud, angry voices. Swords were unsheathed and everyone felt that a catastrophe was about to take place. Hussein looked to his master anxiously. He now understood why Ghawri ran away from politics whenever political intrigue came too close for comfort.

57

Abruptly, an amir approached Ghawri. He grabbed the back of his palm, which Ghawri was resting on the armrest of his chair, and held it high. 'Let us elect Amir al-Ghawri as the sultan of Egypt, gentlemen, and I think you will agree this is the most sensible choice,' the other amir proclaimed, looking straight into Ghawri's eyes as though imploring him not to object.

Ghawri was caught completely off guard. To him, this was nothing less than a death sentence. He had only come because all Mamluk amirs were here, but he had never wanted or even thought about sitting on the sultanate's throne. In a trembling voice, he said, 'I do not accept this!' Ghawri stood briskly and repeated loudly, 'I do not accept this at all.'

He sat back down. His cheeks were flushed and his face was red with emotion. Pandemonium ensued as the amirs and *atabeg* pleaded with Ghawri to accept the appointment. They drew their swords and raised them above his head in a dramatic attempt to persuade him.

The Mamluk leaders present were not overly fond of Ghawri, but they wanted a malleable figure to serve as a front through which they could wield their power, to blame when mistakes piled up and to use as a scapegoat if the masses rebelled and demanded the sultan's head.

Ghawri asked them to sheath their swords before he said, 'We all know that what the amir of Fayoum said was true. You change sultans like you change your clothes, and I, with God as my witness, have no interest in becoming sultan. So spare me all of this, I beg you!'

'We will not accept anyone else!' they all started shouting at once. 'You must sit on the throne. Long live Sultan al-Ghawri!'

Hussein's lips moved as if in silent prayer, 'Please accept, sir!' He then glanced at his master in anticipation. Whatever he decided next, it would determine Hussein's future.

Amir al-Ghawri gave a deep sigh and looked to the ground. There was an awkward moment of silence. Ghawri then spoke slowly and sternly. 'If you want to remove me all you have to do is ask me, not slay me. I want you to swear on this now, in front of me.'

Hussein had not expected Ghawri to accept the appointment, but when he did, Hussein felt he was about to faint. He knew that the sultanship was the most hazardous job in the sultanate, the sultan not unlike a sheep being fattened for slaughter. Yet it was also the post where a sovereign could fix things if he understood how to manage his people and his subjects, so Hussein hoped his master would have the skill to repair what the Mamluk amirs had broken before him. He struggled to keep his wrathful fist from striking the heads of some of those present, though he was reassured that he would be able to influence Ghawri by dint of their close relationship.

The commotion in the hall died down. Ghawri was invested as sultan. Celebrations for his coronation began soon thereafter, and the new sultan became preoccupied with receiving well-wishers.

Hussein left the palace. As he thought about what had happened, he found himself amazed by the wondrous things that transpired in Egypt. His master's title had now become Sultan Abu al-Nasser Qansouh al-Ghawri, Sultan of the Two Seas and the Two Lands. A grand title indeed, he thought to himself, though it could also be a death sentence. Were the Mamluk amirs going to abide by their oath not to kill him in cold blood like they had done with his predecessors? Perhaps, but Hussein was not so sure.

Leaving the castle that night was the only thing he could do. His master alone was able to deal with the new developments, and set things in motion to remedy the nation's ailments. There were many resources, tactics and levers of power that the sultan was going to have to use shrewdly to assert his authority over these people.

Hussein, wearing casual clothes this time, walked around the streets surrounding the castle. He wanted to mingle with people and listen in on their conversations, after his long isolation between the silent walls of the stone palace. It was the last night of Ramadan, and people were making eager preparations for Eid on the following day. Poor and ordinary folk revered and enjoyed this feast the most, and used the occasion to forget the misery, destitution and injustice surrounding them on every side. The rich and powerful, meanwhile, were busy springing at each others' throats and stabbing one another in the back.

The muezzin's voice rose out gently from the minaret of a mosque Hussein was walking past. The melody echoed through the alleyways, which were filled with the aroma of barbecued meat and sweets. People began to enter the mosque, handing over their shoes to a boy at the door whose job was to store them away from thieves. These days, even cheap, worn-out shoes were stolen.

Hussein was not religious. He only attended Friday prayers with Ghawri for the sole purpose of letting the public know the amir did not miss his prayers and to deny them any more pretexts to rebel against him. But Hussein had not abandoned prayer completely, either. From time to time, he had bouts of faith that made him pray sporadically. He also found it heart-warming whenever Ghawri distributed money among the poor Sufis; he did not have a cold heart after all, but it needed some patching, as the Sufi sheikh who was always outside the fort in Alexandria had told him once. Hussein had not quite understood what that meant, but he imagined his heart as a tattered cloth that needed to be mended like the Sufis did with their ragged garments.

He took his shoes off outside the door, gave them to the boy and went inside the mosque.

After prayers, the imam stood holding a staff and began preaching to the crowd. 'People! Woe to the Arabs for evil is approaching! Woe to the Arabs for evil is approaching!'

The sheikh's eyes bulged and his staff vibrated in tandem with his body. Hussein looked around at the other worshippers, waiting for someone to explain to him what was going on, but everyone looked as confused as he was.

A voice from the back rows called out. 'What happened? What evil has approached, my sheikh?'

The imam did not answer immediately, and continued to repeat his cryptic warning until he felt they were finally ready to hear the story. Then he said in a quieter voice, 'Woe to the Arabs for evil is approaching! A Frankish* ship has been spotted in the Abyssinian Sea. They have breached the dam of Dhul-Qarnayn* and are now at the gates of Mecca and Medina!'

6

Al-Ahsa, Eastern Arabian Peninsula

T HE HORMUZI MESSENGER LEANED on a pillow and looked Sultan Muqrin straight in the eyes before he started speaking. 'Your Grace, I think you are aware of the conflicts taking place in our kingdom between the members of the royal family. A king hardly sits on the throne before he is killed or deposed. The kingdom has suffered greatly from such struggles, and lost a lot of blood and treasure.' Turan Shah, the king of Hormuz, had died recently and left four sons: Maqsoud, Shahabuddin, Salghur and Vays. A bitter struggle had erupted between the sons over the throne.

The messenger breathed out and hunched over himself, making him appear smaller than he actually was. He glanced at the palm trees in front of him and then continued. 'Maqsoud succeeded his father first, but Shahabuddin did not let him rule for long. He deposed him and sat on the throne for a few months, before he was ousted in turn by Salghur. Vays then overthrew him, and he remains the ruler of Hormuz.

'The spiral of violence is almost never ending. Before I came here, I visited Sheikh Suleiman bin Salman al-Nabahani in Oman, who is Salghur's father-in-law. But he could not promise us anything because he is preoccupied with another battle. Salghur feels that Suleiman has betrayed him because he has not backed him in this struggle, and has vowed to take revenge on him when the opportunity arises.'

The sultan was listening to the messenger intently. When he finished, the sultan said, 'I have heard of all these conflicts among the king's sons but I thought things had settled down after Vays ascended the throne. Tell me, what was the childhood of the four men like? Who raised them?'

The messenger replied, 'They all grew up in their father's palace. But he made a mistake when he put each one under the care of a different tutor. These tutors imparted their rivalries into the young princes. Disputes between them started early on, and the father could hardly resolve one before another erupted. At the time, he was not aware that the problem was not the children, but rather the tutors he had not chosen so well.'

The sultan smiled faintly, and then remarked, 'This is a problem in many royal palaces. In our palace, we tried to avoid this by appointing one educator for all children. We have chosen a trustworthy man because we know it will be he who shapes and moulds their minds.'

The sultan paused and then said, 'I don't know why kings always make the same mistakes!' After another moment of silence, he asked, 'So who sent you then if it's not the king?'

The messenger adjusted his sitting position. 'I am here at the behest of my master, Vizier *Khawaja* Attar. He ordered me to come here to ask you help restore Salghur to the throne.'

The sultan chased away a fly that had landed on his forehead. He shook his head in thought before he asked, 'Why does Attar want to bring back Salghur? Why him out of the four rivals?'

It seemed that the messenger was prepared for this particular question. 'He is the wisest of the sons in the view of my master. If he is reinstated, then Hormuz could restore its lost glory. My master has pinned his hopes on him to restore stability to the kingdom, because the current situation is going in a bad direction. Vays wants to wage war with you to consolidate his power and plunder Bahrain and Al-Ahsa. If that happens, we will all lose. Vays is a reckless young man who does not understand the consequences of his actions, and he is surrounded by inexperienced advisers.'

'How long will you be staying with us in Al-Ahsa?'

'A few days, Your Grace. Then I will return with your answer to *Khawaja* Attar, who is waiting for me anxiously.'

Sultan Muqrin knew that the matter at hand required knowledge of the positions of the other powers surrounding Hormuz. 'How are your relations with Persia in light of these conflicts?'

'Persia is also unstable. There is a bitter struggle between the Ağ Qoyunlu* and the Safavids. The country is in chaos. We do not know who will ultimately prevail, though some merchants told us recently the Safavids have won a few battles. I believe they will remain preoccupied with consolidating their gains in the north for some time. They have no armies in the south. We tried to contact them for the same purpose, but they did not respond to us. We are not too keen on them, Your Grace, so we did not contact them again.'

The messenger then fell silent, seemingly reluctant to say anything else. The sultan did not like the messenger's silence, and wanted to know more. He asked, 'Why is that?'

'Your Grace, the Safavids have beliefs that are foreign to us. They have forced people to convert to their faith. Some refugees and merchants have told us of massacres in some of the areas controlled by the Qizilbash*. They force people to do unspeakable things and, if they refuse, they slaughter them and pile their bodies in the roads and alleys. In the evening, they gather the corpses and set them on fire in public squares.'

The messenger paused, visualising the holocaust in his head. He then murmured, 'The mere thought of them near our kingdom makes us fear for its future.'

The sultan wished to keep the conversation focused, lest he misunderstand the messenger or vice versa. 'So you are saying that Vays dethroned Salghur, and that *Khawaja* Attar wants to restore Salghur to the throne. You have contacted the Omanis but they did not help you, and the Safavids but they did not respond, and hence you came here to ask me to help. Have I understood correctly?'

'Indeed, Your Grace. As I mentioned earlier, restoring Salghur to the throne will benefit both sides, yours and ours. Salghur was raised by Vizier *Khawaja* Attar, and the vizier, through the authority the king would grant him, can improve conditions in the kingdom, rehabilitate its trade and—'

The sultan interrupted him with a sudden question. 'Do you have any idea how serious your request is?'

'Yes, Your Grace, but if Vays survives on the throne, he will be a danger to us all.'

The sultan smiled, impressed by the messenger's answer. The messenger had linked the fate of Hormuz to that of the Jabrid sultanate, a shrewd political move to be sure. The sultan picked up his fan again and started waving it in front of his face. When the servants saw this, they brought a bowl filled with cold water and a folded cloth. The sultan wet it and wiped his face to cool it, and invited the messenger to do the same. It was very hot and humid now.

'Where is Attar now?'

'He's serving as Vays's vizier. The new king needs him to rule the kingdom temporarily. He has been the de facto ruler since the father died but not after Vays ascended the throne. Vays does not let him do as he pleases, and has started pulling the rug from under his feet. Now, he summons him to the palace only when it's absolutely necessary. *Khawaja* Attar feels he is no longer in control of the kingdom, which has become the plaything of King Vays and his courtiers. They will destroy everything that our forefathers built.'

The sultan understood now that the real struggle was not between Salghur and his brothers, but between Attar and the current king. Still, the sultan thought, this was an opportunity that he should use to his advantage as much as possible.

'Where do the rulers of Oman's ports stand on this? Do you not fear they might secede?'

The messenger answered in a quiet voice, as he wiped his face with the soaked cloth. 'That's not a big problem, Your Grace. Some of the rulers of the ports are loyal to *Khawaja* Attar. Some are semi-independent to begin with, such as Suleiman al-Nabahani. They know we can discipline them after we regain our strength. If your forces in the Omani hinterland make even a small move, you will see how those rulers will come submissively to us asking for our protection. This is the law of life: the people of the coast have been weakened by luxury, but the people of the desert and the mountains are cut from tougher cloth.'

The sultan came from a strong Bedouin clan, and the messenger's response pleased him. 'Very well. You can go and rest now. I shall give you my response in a few days.'

Bin Rahhal, still fiddling with the Indian merchant's ring, was shocked by what he had heard. He had not expected the kingdom of Hormuz to ask the sultan of the Jabrids for assistance. After all, this was the kingdom that controlled vast swathes of the western coast of the Gulf, and the kingdom whose fleet controlled the entrance to the Gulf and all the trade routes there.

Sultan Muqrin stood up and walked towards a shaded stream nearby, carried away by his thoughts. He was Sultan Muqrin bin Zamel al-Jabri, leader of the Jabrid tribe, which controlled all the areas between Basra and Oman, and between the Gulf coast and the edges of Najd. The sultan had a formidable military force under his command that could strike terror in the hearts of his enemies; his powerful navy was rivalled only by the fleet of the kingdom of Hormuz. The sultan paid an annual tribute to the kingdom to avoid antagonising it, lest it stop his merchant ships from sailing in and out of the Gulf. For the past few years, the sultan had tried his best to avoid tension with Hormuz. With all this in mind, it was surprising that the kingdom had now come to ask for his help. How should he act? How could he turn the situation to his advantage? And what if he failed in restoring Salghur to the throne?

The sultan was aware that he had many enemies: the tribes rebelling against him in Najd; Rashid bin Mughamis, emir of Basra, who was waiting for any opportunity to pounce on the Jabrid sultanate; the emirs of the Omani coast, who were loyal to the king of Hormuz, but who did not want the Jabrid army to be too close to them. These emirs were his enemies, and an obstacle to his ambition to establish trading posts on the Omani coast.

The servants brought dates on plates made from palm leaves, which they placed in front of him. The sultan took a date and put in his mouth, then spat out its seed as though he did not like its taste.

Bin Rahhal remained in the *majlis*, ready to be summoned by the sultan at any moment. The sultan lifted his robes and dipped his feet in the running water – a habit he had retained from childhood. He then gestured to Bin Rahhal to approach.

'Bin Rahhal, I want you to think with me about this. If we succeed in restoring Salghur to the throne, we would not have to pay taxes to Hormuz any more. Our influence could extend to the Omani coast. But if we fail, Hormuz would smother our trade and blockade our ships, and we would lose our trade with India and the coast of Africa.'

The sultan removed his turban and laid it by his side, then said in an ominous tone, 'We could lose our entire kingdom. It is a big decision that could cost us a lot.'

Bin Rahhal was not yet ready to express his opinion on such an important matter. He wanted to consider all angles before he said anything to the sultan. Things were truly complicated and any defeat – no matter how small – could tempt the tribes around Al-Ahsa to attack. After all, although on the surface they showed allegiance to Sultan Muqrin, the loyalty of the leaders of those tribes was motivated by the presence of a military force protecting the sultan. In the absence of this force, or in the event it was weakened, their fealty would turn into belligerence.

'It is a tricky decision indeed, Your Grace. Let us take a few days to gather information to make an informed decision. We can make queries with the help of our merchants who travel frequently to Hormuz. We can also gather some information about the situation in Persia, since it is possible the Persians would intervene if they are not as preoccupied with their battles in the north as we think.'

The sultan stared at a school of small fish swimming in the stream. Bin Rahhal sensed that the sultan had already made up his mind and was just waiting for the right time to declare it.

'Do that, Bin Rahhal. As you heard me tell the messenger, I will give him my reply in the coming days. He is waiting for my decision before he returns to Attar.'

A servant approached and informed the sultan that another messenger, this time from the Bahmani kingdom in India, was requesting permission to see him.

'Where is he now?'

'Outside, Your Grace.'

'Let him in.'

As the two men returned to the *majlis*, the sultan turned to his vizier and said, 'Stay with us, Bin Rahhal.'

The messenger entered the hall and presented himself to the sultan. He greeted him in impeccable Arabic, and the sultan asked him to sit.

The messenger started speaking as soon as he sat down. 'I have come representing my master, Imad al-Din Mahmoud, vizier of the Bahmani kingdom in India. He sends you his greetings and sincere wishes for good luck and constant victory.'

The messenger reached for something in his pocket and then pulled out a gilded cylinder inscribed with magnificent calligraphies of Quranic verses, and handed it to the sultan.

The sultan opened the cylinder and took out a sealed parchment. He read it carefully and then gave it to Bin Rahhal, his eyes still on the messenger. 'Send back my greetings to Vizier Imad al-Din Mahmoud. Tell him we would be pleased to cooperate with him in any way he wishes. Now you shall be a guest at my palace, where you can rest after your tiring journey. We will speak over dinner.'

The messenger stood up and signalled to one of his companions to come forward. The servant brought a small chest decorated with inscriptions and verses from the Quran and placed it in front of the messenger. The Bahmani man opened the chest slowly and took out a dagger, which he then handed to the sultan. 'My master asks that you deliver this gift to the caliph of the Muslims. He considers this to be in your safekeeping until the caliph receives it.'

Sultan Muqrin took the dagger and brought it closer to his eyes, admiring its intricacies. It was a marvellously crafted piece, the likes of which he had never seen before. Its sheath was made of silver engraved with pure gold, adorned with seven large ruby stones. Its handle was of equally astounding craftsmanship and beauty, and was decorated with agates and diamonds; a golden chain in the shape of small miniature arms connected to one another linked the two sides of the sheath.

The sultan turned the dagger over between his hands for some time, before he passed it to Bin Rahhal to examine. The vizier unsheathed the dagger, revealing a blade fantastically decorated with interlacing engravings and gemstones, as astonishing and unique as the rest of the masterpiece. Bin Rahhal returned the dagger to the sultan, who took one more look before he replaced it in its casing. 'We shall deliver it to the caliph, God willing, though it is a heavy onus, messenger.'

The messenger smiled and said, 'Great Sultan, my master ordered this dagger to be made from jewels belonging to his mother and his wife and others he had obtained during his conquests. We do not have the naval experience you have to sail to Egypt, and the vizier believes you are the best person to deliver the gift on our behalf. He will remember this solemn favour for as long as he lives and he will pray for you.'

'We will see that it is delivered, messenger, God willing.'

The sultan turned again to Bin Rahhal and asked him to look after his guest.

The messenger left the hall, saying loud prayers for the sultan.

The sultan paused, preoccupied by his thoughts. He then resumed the conversation with Bin Rahhal that had been interrupted by the messenger's arrival. 'Send a message to my uncle Zamel in Salwa. Ask him to prepare as many ships and men as he can, and do the same with the emir of Julfar. Let us see how well prepared we are for something like this.'

The sultan noticed the ring that was still in Bin Rahhal's hand. He gave him the chest containing the dagger and said, 'Pay the Banyan for the ring. It is magnificent. Put it with the dagger in the chest and keep them somewhere safe. We shall send them to the caliph in Cairo, after we have completed our mission. Now, you must start preparing yourself for the campaign that you shall lead to Hormuz.'

7

The Arabian Gulf

T HE SHIP CARRYING COVILHÃ sailed from Aden to Muscat, a city overlooking a clear blue sea, which he had heard much about. A flotilla of anchored ships floated flamboyantly opposite the coast, and together with the whitish homes along the shore, they gave the place a unique sense of beauty. The homes were in fact reminiscent of the Moorish buildings in the mountain villages of Portugal. A large mosque in the centre was set like a gemstone in the middle of the necklace formed by the rocky black mountains surrounding the city. Muscat's skyline was dominated by its palm trees, which intermingled with wind-catchers and mosque minarets, creating a colourful assortment that contrasted with the dark complexion of the mountains. The city looked not unlike a Persian carpet rolled out over a rocky ground.

Covilhã contemplated the scene in front of him for a few minutes. It was his first visit to Muscat, which, like the other ports along the coast, paid taxes to the king of Hormuz; Muscat's ruler was the brother-in-law of the deceased king. Covilhã decided he should visit Hormuz; he was carrying a message to its vizier from the rabbi in Alexandria, which he thought should make his mission there easier.

The Alexandrian rabbi had not met the Hormuzi vizier before, but the rabbi did business with the Karimi merchants who had strong and intricate relations in most of the region's ports; it was the Karimis who recommended *Khawaja* Attar to the rabbi. Politicians and clerics seemed to have a knack for trade, and though they disagreed on most matters, Covilhã thought smilingly, money won their unanimous approval.

The distance between Muscat and Hormuz was not great. Ships traversed the sea between the two cities very frequently, which explained the large number of ships sailing in both directions; it was a maritime thoroughfare that was active throughout the year.

When Covilhã reached Hormuz, his ship dropped anchor to the west of the island. Hormuz's topography resembled a water drop tapering at the top. To the east of the island lay the large port that received ships from India and China. In the west, there was a smaller port for ships travelling from other ports in the Gulf. The city stretched from port to port, while the south of the island was covered by palm groves, water reservoirs and some rocky, barren hills.

In the port, he saw many oared military vessels, the smallest of which had eight oars and the largest of which had twenty. From that port, ships sailed to the rest of the ports on the west coast of the Gulf, or monitored the movement of ships entering and leaving, especially those trying to avoid paying their duties.

Covilhã immediately noticed how clean and well organised the city was. Its alleys were covered by large tarps hanging between opposing balconies to protect pedestrians from the sun. The merchants, residents and shops of Hormuz looked affluent. They obviously liked to show off their luxurious possessions, whether at the entrances of their businesses and homes, or on their balconies. As he walked around, he felt he was in an oriental bazaar, and could not conceal how impressed he was with what he saw.

In some wealthy districts of the city, Covilhã saw that locals had laid large carpets outside their homes for people to walk on, in a gesture meant to highlight their own affluence. Servants carrying refreshments stood on street corners serving people date juice or soaked aromatic herbs.

The city had special inns paid for by merchants to feed and shelter poor people and travellers. Covilhã noticed that most of the food sold in the markets had been imported from Persia, India or Oman. The island, as he was told, had little water, which actually had to be brought in from the nearby island of Qeshm. Hormuz's land was not suitable for cultivation either, save for some palm trees, sidra trees and tamarisks in the south. Water was a very precious commodity and people were skilled at conserving it, storing it and even flavouring it with rose water.

The city was divided into neighbourhoods straddled by broad streets, which all merged into one main street over-looking the sea and linking the two ports. This was where all celebrations, festivals and royal occasions took place, as the king's palace overlooked the street directly.

Hormuz's streets were beautifully paved and tidy. There were special areas for street vendors selling barbecued meats and fish, and foods of all kinds and flavours. The delicious smell of their spices filled the streets. As he explored the city further, Covilhã did not spot any beggars or destitute poor people. When they left their shops, the merchants took no other measures than covering their merchandise with sheets, unconcerned about securing them; there was hardly any theft on the island.

Khawaja Attar's palace stood not far from the inn where Covilhã was staying. If Covilhã had looked out his window, he would have seen Attar sitting on the veranda of his seaside estate, enjoying the spring-like weather while the curtains, which barely blocked sunlight, danced with the northerly breeze. The balcony was Attar's favourite spot in the house. He liked to sit there facing the sea, contemplating its deep blue infinity. He also liked to sit alone, and his daughter, Halima, knew not to disturb him in his solitude.

Today, however, she decided to do just that. She took her shoes off quietly near the door, and tiptoed her way to where he was sitting. She kissed his hand and sat on the floor near his feet.

Attar gave her a look of paternal affection. She was his only daughter. Halima had grown and, at seventeen, she was already a young woman of exceptional beauty. Tall and svelte, she had a light brown complexion and charming, lustrous eyes that almost sparkled. She had long black hair, which was plaited so well that it pulled her scalp back a few inches. This made her eyes look wider and slightly elongated, adding an exotic tinge to her beauty. She liked to push her long black plait in front of her right shoulder and twiddle it with her fingers.

Attar looked straight into his daughter's eyes when he spoke to her. Her eyes reminded him of his wife, who had passed away several years ago; Halima was now everything to him, the centre of his world and his happiness. He placed his hand on her head unconsciously, praying to God to bless her and protect her, before he returned his gaze to the sea.

75

Halima's eyes followed her father's. 'What's on your mind, Father?'

Attar did not take his eyes off the horizon. After a while, he looked at her and said, 'I don't want to upset you, my love. But you know things in our kingdom are not well.'

Her expression changed. 'Yes, I know. You have been like this since Vays dethroned Salghur. I know how fond of Salghur you are because you raised him, but he is no longer king; Vays is. So let's accept that because there's nothing else we can do.'

Attar stood up and walked to the edge of the balcony. He leaned over with half of his body sticking out, his posture suggesting he felt deeply troubled by the *fait accompli* his daughter just described. He remained motionless for a few minutes. Halima came and stood by his side, leaning over in the same manner. He felt he had to share his thoughts with his daughter.

'I have sent a messenger to the Jabrid sultan in Al-Ahsa, to ask him to intervene with his army on Salghur's side. I'm expecting the messenger to return any time now.'

Halima looked shocked. 'I think you know what that means, Father! Those people could take over our kingdom or ask a lot of money in return. Have you thought about that? They are Bedouin brutes and—'

Her father interrupted her with his quiet voice. 'I have thought about all of this. But there is no other way. If Vays stays on the throne, this means that Hormuz could lose control over its trade in the Gulf because of his foolishness. People already hate him. Hormuz would lose its possessions across the sea. With the Jabrids, we might find a compromise that satisfies both sides.'

Attar returned to his chair. Halima followed him and sat across from her father. She took one of his legs and put it on her lap and started kneading it as she often did. She knew it helped soothe him.

Attar gave her a smile. Her questions were now more difficult and intelligent than ever before, and he had to find convincing answers. He said, 'I have sought the Jabrid sultan because I could not find anyone else, Halima. Everyone wants our money but none of our problems, which I believe we have to deal with on our own.'

He paused, looked at the sky, and then continued. 'We live in obvious affluence. Our trade is prosperous, at least so far, and we have been able to avoid our enemies by paying them off.' Then he struck the armrest with his fist, as though a scorpion had bitten him. 'Our foolish kings will ruin everything with their senseless quarrels!'

Attar returned his gaze to his daughter. 'True, the Jabrids are brutish Bedouins. But we have so far not been at war with them. We have a good relationship with them, and they pay their taxes to Hormuz. But I know this could all change as soon as they realise the state we're in.'

He gave his daughter an affectionate look. 'Halima, half of the blood in your veins is Arab, not much different from the blood running in Sultan Muqrin's veins. In our city different races have mixed, Arabs, Persians, Indians and Balochi. We intermarried and became a unified people whose allegiance is to the king. But I don't know to which king this allegiance should be now!'

He said his last sentence in a tone that suggested he wanted to put an end to the conversation. Halima moved her father's foot away from her lap and lifted the other one up, trying her best to help him relax. 'But you didn't answer my question, Father. What do you expect the Jabrids to ask in return?'

He reacted as though hearing the question for the first time. He shook his head and bit his lip. 'I don't know, Halima, I sent a messenger to Sultan Muqrin asking him to intervene. The messenger will soon return with his answer. I don't know what he will ask in return, but I hope it won't be something we cannot provide.'

They were interrupted by the procession of the king on his way to the palace. Halima put down her father's feet and ran towards the balcony.

Attar was taken aback by his daughter's inquisitiveness. 'Haven't you tired of seeing the procession yet?'

Halima continued to watch the procession. 'Yes, I'm sick of seeing it. It no longer arouses my curiosity like it did when I was little. But it tells me so much. For instance, it tells me who the new vizier is, who the dignitaries visiting the kingdom are, and who the king's new favourites are. There are so many things you can learn by just watching the procession.'

Halima knew what the procession looked like by heart. It had not changed since the new king had taken the throne several months earlier.

Usually, a camel-mounted escort in a dark red uniform led the procession, beating on two large marching drums. Another drummer followed with four smaller instruments, in front of two bearers each carrying the flag of the kingdom of Hormuz. Two cavaliers rode behind them on stout horses that had been plumped up deliberately. The riders each held a staff bearing the ornate silver standard of the monarchy. Trailing them closely were two cymbalists and four trumpeters.

Servants in expensive robes marched next, directly ahead of the king. The king rode on a grey Arabian horse with a gilded saddle and reins. Long, colourful feathers stuck out from its head.

The king wore a dark red robe, interspersed with green and gold threads. Underneath he wore an embroidered shirt with matching trousers. A fabric girdle around his waist held a jewelled dagger; his turban was made from Persian silk and decorated with golden trim.

The procession and its blare passed in front of the homes by the seaside, reminding the public who the new king was. Halima shook her head as she watched the rear of the procession, then turned to her father.

'I don't know what fate has in store for us, my dear girl,' he said absentmindedly. 'I don't feel reassured.'

She sat in front of him and put her hands on his knees. 'I have always known you as an optimist, Father. Are you also afraid of the Jabrids?'

'If the Sultan of Jabrid agrees to help us, then there will be a price that we would have to pay. I don't know what he will ask from us, but if we remain under this king it will end in disaster for everyone anyway!'

A servant entered the room abruptly and interrupted the vizier. 'Your Excellency, there is someone here to meet you.'

'Who is it? Has the messenger returned from Al-Ahsa?'

The servant answered quietly, 'No, sir. It seems from his appearance that he is an Arab merchant travelling from faraway lands. I'm not familiar with his accent or the way he is dressed. He says he has an important message for you.'

Halima asked to remain with her father in his *majlis* to see this strange visitor, and her father obliged.

Covilhã entered dressed in Moroccan robes. He greeted the vizier courteously, bowing in a slightly exaggerated manner. Covilhã could not help but glance at Halima, whose beauty immediately captivated him. He bowed to her before quickly turning his gaze back to the vizier.

The vizier noticed Covilhã's odd style of greeting. He had not seen it with the Arabs from the Peninsula before. He enquired about his country of origin.

'Your Excellency, I am a merchant from Morocco. I passed through Alexandria on my way to India, where I was given a letter addressed to you.' Covilhã gave the vizier the letter with both of his hands in a theatrical gesture of veneration, while resisting the urge to peek again at Halima.

'Please, sit down.'

Covilhã sat focusing his sight on the vizier, studying his face and reaction as he read the message.

Silence reigned over the room until Attar spoke. 'This letter is from my friend the rabbi of Alexandria. He asked me to help you on your trip to India, and to keep nothing from you. Clearly he holds you in the highest regard. Will you tell me more about yourself? What is the situation like in Morocco?'

Covilhã knew that the rabbi in Alexandria traded in spices with Attar, but he did not want to declare it. It doesn't matter, Covilhã thought, at least he wouldn't feel alone now. He said, 'Our kingdom is at war with Portugal and Spain, Your Excellency. We now trade with the East rather than the West. Our coasts come under frequent attack from the north, and people are grumbling about these endless conflicts.'

The vizier gave Covilhã a strange smile, before he said, 'The world is no longer as safe as it used to be, my Moroccan friend!'

Attar turned to his daughter, pointing at her. 'This is my daughter, Halima. She has not yet travelled outside our kingdom, but she likes to know what's going on in the rest of the world.'

Covilhã smiled. This was his chance to take a good look at her and admire her beauty. He said, 'I will be happy to answer any questions. I have travelled far and wide, and have many stories to tell, but I would like to know more about your kingdom first, Your Excellency.'

Attar smiled again and said, 'It would seem we are going to tell each other many stories. Very well, I'll start.

'Ancient Hormuz was located on the Persian coast. It was a small forgotten village when a Yemeni sheikh called Mohammed Koub arrived. The sheikh started opening up prospects for the locals to trade, and encouraged them to do business with India and China in the east, and the African coast in the west. He took advantage of the seasonal winds that blow in the summer from the west to the east, making them ideal for ships sailing to India and China; and in the winter from the east to the west, which are ideal for ships travelling from China and India to the Gulf and Africa.'

Attar explained the wind patterns with the help of hand gestures, as though there were a large invisible map floating in the air. 'As the years passed, this village prospered and became a large, wealthy city. Sheikh Mohammed minted his own coin, which he called the "dirham". He became known as Sheikh Mohammed Dirham Koub.

'In 1301 in the Frankish calendar, the Mongols attacked Hormuz and destroyed many parts of it. The king decided to abandon the city and move to the island of Jirun, which was a few thousand cubits away from the coast. This is the location of our present kingdom.'

Halima saw there was an opportunity here to ask Covilhã a question. 'What do you trade in exactly?'

'I trade in everything, my lady. But I found that trading in spices was the most lucrative. I was told in Aden that I could sell one consignment of spices in Alexandria at ten times the price I pay in Calicut, sometimes twenty if sailing conditions are rough.'

Attar interrupted. 'Don't believe everything you hear. Most merchants do not tell the truth. They are envious of one another, and consider everything they know a secret that no one else must know. If they have to divulge something, they first distort it and stretch it until it becomes wildly inaccurate.' He then asked, 'Do you know anyone in India? I will give you a letter to some of my acquaintances there so they can help you in your business. Clearly you are a newcomer.'

Covilhã raised his hand to his forehead then to his chest, and said, 'I am deeply grateful for your generosity and courtesy, Your Excellency.'

The vizier's face changed suddenly. 'We have received news that the Portuguese have reached Yemen and the coast of India. Have you heard anything about this?'

Blood rushed to Covilhã's face. He had not expected Portuguese ships to arrive here so soon. He had kept the Portuguese plans secret even from the people closest to him, but clearly ports kept no secrets. 'Are you saying they arrived in India? I was in Aden nearly two weeks ago and heard nothing about it! Are your certain, Your Excellency?'

Attar replied plaintively, 'I heard that they've burned a ship called the *Maryam* near the Indian coast. The boat was carrying pilgrims back home. It was a tragedy that all sailors have

82

been talking about on our shores, but people forget quickly on this side of the world.'

Covilhã was still struggling to believe the news. 'You are sure the Portuguese have arrived there?'

'Yes, definitely. Some in India are hopeful about their arrival, because they pay more for the spices than other merchants. Some kings in India have even agreed for the Portuguese to establish their trading forts on their territories.'

Covilhã tried not to appear too keen. 'Why did no one talk about them at the ports?'

Halima replied this time. She said, 'You must know that there are many ships that come from all around the world to trade in spices, and pass through our seas. Portuguese merchant ships would not draw too much attention.'

Covilhã whispered to himself, 'I hope this remains the case.'

– 8 –

Cairo, Egypt

HUSSEIN SPURRED HIS HORSE after emerging from the gates of the castle in the direction of Muqattam Mountain, galloping the animal towards the edge of a cliff where he liked to go to watch Cairo from up high and afar. Once there, he tethered his horse and dismounted, contemplating a city he neither loved nor liked, but where he was now forced to live. Cairo to Hussein would always be the troublesome, noisy city he first encountered many years earlier. It did not help that this was also the place where his captor had sold him into slavery for a fistful of dirhams.

He listened attentively to the noises around him: his horse chewing dried plants nearby, and the rustling of the wind as it blew over the edge of the mountain, making a sad whistling sound. He heard the echo of the *azan* coming from a mosque at the edge of the desert. The call to prayer brought back many memories, the most recent of which was what happened that night when he heard the imam yelling at the worshippers, 'Woe to the Arabs for evil is approaching!'

It was many days ago that Hussein had heard the imam's speech. It had distracted him from the big Eid celebrations. He remembered the sheikh's expressions as he spoke about a massacre that had taken place at sea and his strange, cryptic shouts of 'Woe to the Arabs!' Hussein had waited until the cleric finished his speech to try to get an explanation. The people's shouts and cries of 'God is great!' made it impossible for Hussein to hear anything, and even now, the noise and pandemonium still clouded the way he remembered the episode.

When the sheikh was finally alone, Hussein went towards him to ask him about what had happened. The imam's eyes were tearful, his face pale and his voice hoarsened by emotion. He dried his eyes with the edge of his sleeve.

The imam told Hussein how, several months earlier, a ship called the *Maryam* left the port of Jeddah, with 300 Muslims on board – women, children and elderly people. After they performed their pilgrimage, on their way back to India, Portuguese ships attacked them. The Portuguese boarded their boat and stole the money and cargo it carried. They sliced off the fingers of the women and stole their jewels. They then took the girls and boys that they liked. They cut off the hands of the ship's captain and crew before throwing them into the sea. 'And as if that were still not enough, they put the rest of the women and elderly in the belly of the ship and burned them alive. The Portuguese watched as their victims drowned in their fiery grave. They did it all in front of the Indian coast, as the victims' loved ones watched the massacre helplessly,' he said.

The sheikh started crying bitterly. He wiped his tears with his sleeve again, before he continued. 'That ship was not their only victim. They have destroyed and burned many ships at the mouth of the Red Sea. They take pleasure in severing limbs and burning people alive. We don't know from which pit of hell those demons have come, but our sultans must set aside their differences and unite to repel this enemy.'

The cleric asked Hussein to help him lean against a column in the mosque; standing for all that time had exhausted him. Hussein felt compassion for the sheikh; he had different concerns than those of the Mamluk amirs and also those of ordinary people, but the sheikh empathised with their worries. Hussein felt that the man spoke for him, and he had listened to him carefully.

Hussein slipped in and out of his memories, recollecting what the sheikh at the mosque had told him. 'The Portuguese ships reached India. They seized the ports there and barred Muslims from trading. Spice convoys stopped coming, money ran out and poverty spread. I believe this is only the beginning and that the worst is yet to come.'

The sheikh had wiped his eyes with the tail of his turban and said in a weepy voice, 'Some of the Muslim kings have sent messengers asking Caliph al-Mustamsik to intervene and protect them.' The sheikh bowed his head slightly and added, in a sorrowful voice, 'I think they're unaware of our actual situation. They don't know the real state of our poor caliph, and how the Mamluk amirs manipulate him. They don't know that his power holds no sway beyond the quarters of his harem.'

The sheikh summoned his strength and took a deep breath. 'We are in deep trouble, the extent of which only God knows. We no longer know how to make a living. We don't know how we can do our pilgrimage or travel. All roads are dangerous. Even Cairo's alleys have become a haven for killers, thugs and bandits, without our rulers lifting a finger to do anything about it. All they care about is money and keeping Egypt's riches for themselves.'

That night, Hussein had noticed some people trying to leave the mosque, fearing they would be punished for listening to the bold imam. These days, crimes such as banditry and theft were not as serious as daring to speak about public money and the corruption of the sultans and amirs. Many outspoken imams had been found dead or disappeared from their homes after giving audacious sermons. Clearly, the amirs knew how much people hated them, but they did not want them to say it out loud. They insisted on repressing all those sentiments or driving them underground, though it was hard to imagine this would change anything.

Hussein had seen many people clapping and cheering when the sultans' processions marched in front of them, only to spit on the floor in contempt and shout obscenities at them after they passed. Did the sultans know about this? Hussein realised that they probably did, but that they did not care.

He felt as if a lightning bolt had struck him that day, after his encounter with the sheikh at the mosque. 'Did what he described really happen?' he asked himself. If so, when and how did the Portuguese manage to get behind their backs? Would they enter Cairo via the Nile as he had heard before? Were they the Gog and Magog he had heard so many stories about in the mosques? Were these signs of the Day of Judgement that he was seeing?

A chill went down his spine. He wished Suleiman were there to hear all this. 'Where is he now?' he wondered. He was in dire need for his friend to dispel his fears in these turbulent times.

At sunset, Hussein got on his horse and set off back to the castle. He reached it at dawn, as the roosters were crowing and the guards were just returning from their night shifts. Hussein went to his room, put on his uniform and walked to the sultan's court, trying to get there before it became crowded.

He did not have to wait for long before he was allowed to enter. When the sultan saw him, he smiled at him as usual; Hussein was like a son to the new ruler. Hussein did not waste time on pleasantries; the familiarity between the two men was strong enough for Hussein to get straight to the point.

Hussein spoke. 'Cairo abounds with rumours that the Portuguese have breached the Dam of Dhul-Qarnayn, and that they are at the gates of Mecca and Medina and could enter Cairo at any time. Have you heard of this, Your Grace?'

'Yes, I have, my son. I asked our representative in Suez to investigate the matter and send back whatever information he can get as soon as possible.'

A servant entered, announcing that breakfast was now ready. Sultan al-Ghawri patted Hussein on the shoulder and invited him to eat. Hussein was not hungry, but he thought this would be a good opportunity to continue speaking to his master away from the din of the court and its demanding guests.

Ghawri sat on a cotton cushion opposite a copper plate containing a variety of foods, and ordered Hussein to sit across from him. It was a simple meal. Hussein was tempted by a dish of fava beans soaked in olive oil. He was hoping Ghawri had a plan to confront the Portuguese, but the sultan was quiet as usual, and was preoccupied with his food as though Hussein were not there.

Hussein said, as he looked at the mini-banquet, 'Your Grace. A few days ago I was at the grand mosque near the castle. I saw with my own eyes how angry and frustrated the people were. I fear these could be the signs of an imminent revolution. People can no longer cope with all the calamities thrust upon them from every direction. But the Portuguese incursion has become their primary concern. We must do something about

88

it. As the custodian of the Two Holy Mosques, you are required to defend them, and the people look to you for leadership in these turbulent times.'

Ghawri continued to chew his food quietly, then drank from a jar that was sitting to his right. The sultan ordered the servants to clear the table and bring the wash pots.

A servant brought a long ewer that had a neck resembling that of an ostrich and a spherical metallic saucer, which he placed under Ghawri's hands. He poured water from the ewer then gave the sultan a cotton towel to wipe his hands.

Ghawri signalled to Hussein to follow him, and walked back to the court. He sat silently.

Hussein was a little annoyed. Although he was accustomed to Ghawri's way of thinking and talking, he felt that the situation was too urgent for this. Something quick had to be done to halt whatever the Portuguese were plotting.

Suddenly, Ghawri spoke. 'Can we defeat them, Hussein?'

Hussein did not expect such a question. His eyes met his master's, as though querying him about how serious the question was. He gulped and his colour changed, before he replied, 'As you know, Your Grace, we do not have a large fleet that can sail on the high seas. We have neglected shipbuilding for too long, and no longer have skilled shipwrights. It is hard to bring back this craft. I don't think we have what it takes to do anything!'

Hussein continued tensely. 'When you neglect something important that you didn't need at one time, you lose it completely and do not have it when you desperately need it.'

Ghawri sighed deeply. Hussein knew he had struck a painful chord in his master. Ghawri enunciated his words calmly, carefully weighing every word. 'Ever since I heard those rumours,

Hussein, I have been thinking along those lines. I have reached out to the Ottoman sultan asking him to send material to help us build ships, and he promised he would. I also contacted Venice for the same purpose. If the Portuguese succeed in their plans, the Venetians stand to lose, and vice versa. I think we should take advantage of their concerns about the future of their trade.'

Ghawri spoke like a seasoned politician who knew what he wanted, unlike Hussein, who was clouded by his youthful enthusiasm.

The sultan shook off the breadcrumbs that had stuck to his clothes then said, 'We have allowed our relationship with the Ottomans to strain for too long. We are going to need their help now to build a fleet. This is always our problem. We fight among ourselves, then when a common threat emerges we close ranks; when the threat is over, we go back to infighting. I hope this doesn't happen with the Ottomans.'

Ghawri's tone suddenly changed. 'Go to Suez now. I will send you all the help I can get. You must begin building ships, and then lead the fleet to fight the Portuguese. I appoint you the admiral of our fleet, effective immediately.'

Ghawri waved his hand in a mechanical way, as though pushing the air away. 'Go now. You have a difficult mission to accomplish in a short space of time.'

Hussein travelled to Suez to personally oversee preparations and construction of the fleet. He felt he had a huge responsibility that he must now fulfil in the best way possible.

His mission consumed his time and energy. Every day, he would go to the shipyard before sunrise and not leave until sunset. Hussein succeeded in inspiring the workers; he told them they were facing a great challenge and a sacred mission that must not fail. In a few months, Suez became a hive of unrelenting activity. This was a boon to businesses in the city, which expanded with the influx of craftsmen from Cairo and other regions of Egypt.

Everyone worked tirelessly. Sultan al-Ghawri fulfilled his promises and sent them all the tools and guidance he received from the Ottomans and the Venetians. Convoy after convoy came carrying timber, iron, copper, gunpowder, tar, ropes and all other supplies needed for shipbuilding. In less than a year, Suez was turned into a naval powerhouse. Ships were then launched one after the other, amid cheers from the sailors and shipwrights.

On the promised day that the fleet was set to sail to defend the shores of Islamdom, Hussein sat near Sultan al-Ghawri, who was attending the ceremony in person and was keen to portray himself as defender of the lands of the Muslims. Ghawri had the ability to emotionally manipulate people. On the one hand, he sent his soldiers to kill his opponents, and on the other hand, he cultivated his appearance as a religious man intent on preserving the lives and livelihoods of Muslims.

His presence today would firmly root this image in the minds of his people. Present with him were also the high-ranking Mamluk amirs, *atabegs*, and Amirs of One Thousand, wearing their best uniforms and accessories. It was a memorable day that everyone made sure they attended, especially the four chief judges, the caliph and the ambassadors of the other kingdoms.

The officials sat under a large tent erected by the seaside near the port. Beautiful lanterns hung from the tent, and around it, the *khasikis* belonging to the sultan and the amirs present stood guard. Cavalrymen wearing distinctive uniforms were lined up next to the tent.

Hussein approached Sultan al-Ghawri to explain to him the details of the ship-launching ceremony, which he had personally overseen to ensure it would dazzle the audience. The sultan smiled; he was already impressed by what he saw. Hussein was encouraged and took this as a sign the sultan believed his mission had been a success, at least in the first phase.

The sultan raised his hand to allow for the ceremony to begin. The cavalrymen marched in front of the tent in perfect sync, followed by the Sultani Mamluk brigade, then the musketeers brigade consisting of Turkic and African soldiers, and then the *Awlad al-Nas* brigade, which was made up of the sons of notables volunteering to defend Muslim holy sites. Behind them marched the naval force comprising soldiers and sailors, who were mostly Andalusian Moors led by the commander known as the Pasha* of the Moroccans. At the end of the procession, a unit of engineers, builders and carpenters marched in front of the sultan's tent.

Some 1,500 people had marched past the tent by the end of the parade. The audience now turned their eyes to the sea. A flotilla of new ships started moving in formations of galleys, fire ships and frigates, which were decorated with colourful flags including the yellow double-crescent ensign of the Mamluks.

For many, what they were seeing was nothing short of a miracle. The construction of this fleet was officially declaring that the Mamluk navy had returned to the seas after a long period of neglect and decline. The idea that these ships were going to deploy to India had galvanised Muslims, and cemented Ghawri's status as a protector and defender of Islam. The sultan needed to sell himself as such, as people had started talking about the trail of dead Mamluk amirs that led back to their opponent, the sultan. Ghawri had demonstrated that he was an impeccable master strategist; a year into his reign, he had eliminated all serious threats to his throne. The oath he made them take no longer had any value; in fact, it was his opponents who needed him to make that oath now.

The shore was filled with onlookers enthusiastically watching the flotilla; they had never seen an Egyptian or Muslim fleet before. The crowd ululated, cheered and launched cries of 'God is Great!' Some even danced. Behind them, a small market began to coalesce, redolent with the smell of pastries and sweets. For a short period of time, people forgot their worries.

The sultan was pleased with the preparations to fight the Portuguese. After the ceremony, he stood and shook hands with Hussein warmly. Those present felt a sense of – temporary – cohesion against an existential enemy. Hussein noticed the paternal look Ghawri gave him, the same look he had given him since he was young, and knew that his master still saw him as a son and that he was proud of what Hussein had accomplished.

'When will you set off, Hussein?'

'When you give us the order, Your Grace.'

'The information I have received indicates that the Portuguese have bombed some cities in East Africa, which they then tried to take. They have established an outpost on an island called Kamaran at the mouth of the Red Sea. But it is a barren island and they will not be able to stay there for long. They are trying to gain a foothold at the entrance of the Red Sea to control it.'

Ghawri turned his gaze back to the ships, which were now further away. 'The Portuguese have reached India, Hussein. If they manage to control it, they will disrupt the entire spice trade that we rely on. The Venetians want us to stop them by any means, and have even asked us to send delegations to the sultans of India warning them against dealing with the Portuguese. But the Portuguese pay many times more than what our merchants pay for their spices, and have coaxed the sultans of India into dealing with them directly. We are fighting a fierce, merciless enemy, Hussein. You must be merciless too, so do whatever it takes to prevent them from destroying our trade.'

'Your wish is my command, Your Grace. We have supplied our ships and we will sail to Jeddah tomorrow. Everyone is ready.'

The sultan raised his hand and pointed it at Hussein's chest, and said, 'The situation in Jeddah worries me. Most of the amirs who were sent there were corrupt, and ended up corrupting the merchants there. You will need to remedy this and put an end to the corruption. Start with those at the top because they are the source of the scourge. When you reach Jeddah, send back your predecessor. Do not let him remain for a single day after you arrive.'

Ghawri paused for a moment and then said, 'You will carry a letter from me appointing you the amir of Jeddah. You are my sword in the sea now.'

− 9 −

Al-Ahsa, Eastern Arabian Peninsula

As bin rahhal left the sultan's *majlis*, his mind was preoccupied with what needed to be done to ensure the success
of the campaign. If it failed, the Jabrid rule could collapse. It
was not an easy task, and the sultan's confidence in him meant
there was no room for error.

He rode his horse out of the main gate. People recognised
him and started crying out his name to get his attention. Some
wanted money and others wanted to sell him their products.
Bin Rahhal was used to all this and usually reacted with a large
smile; he ignored them completely only when something was
troubling him.

When he reached home, he started writing the letters Sultan
Muqrin had asked him to send. First, he wrote a letter to Emir
Zamel, the ruler of Salwa, asking him to prepare ships and men
for an important mission, noting that men with experience in
seafaring and fighting at sea were preferable, and so were any
large ships that could transport horses. He wrote another letter
to the emir of Julfar, containing the same requests. Bin Rahhal
did not specify an exact time and date, or a specific number of
soldiers, and left it to the two rulers to decide, each according
to his ability, though he asked them to give him their answer
as soon as possible.

After he finished writing the letters and sealed them, Bin Rahhal handed them to couriers to deliver them. He undressed and dipped himself in a small pond shaded by grapevines outside his house. He scooped up some water and splashed it over his head. He drew some water with his hands from where the stream flowed into the pond and drank it. He could have stayed there for hours, but he had to get some sleep before sunset.

Bin Rahhal was still a bachelor. After his father died, he lived with his mother for many years, looking after her. He was her only child. He had not thought about marriage and felt that he had to devote himself completely to her. Although many servants worked in the house, he would not let anyone care for her other than him. His mother had died nearly a year earlier, but Bin Rahhal kept her room, clothes, bed, jewellery and even her walking stick, and asked the servants to clean the room as though his mother were still there. He would visit the room from time to time, to catch a whiff of her scent and remember her. She was the world to him and he was determined to keep her memory with him for as long as he lived.

He wrapped the lower part of his body with a cloth and kept his chest bare; it was still very hot. He went to his deceased mother's room and opened the door, examining the belongings she had left behind. Bin Rahhal remembered the dagger the sultan had given him for safekeeping. He put it in a box that had belonged to his mother, and placed the ring the sultan had bought from the Banyan in the same box. They were both gifts meant for the caliph in Cairo – the blade from the Bahmani vizier and the ring from Sultan Muqrin. This was the safest place he could think of. He prayed God have mercy on his mother's soul, as he always did, closed the door and went to his room to rest.

Bin Rahhal could not fall asleep. He could not stop thinking about the campaign. He got out of bed and asked his servant to invite the Hormuzi messenger to his house for dinner. Perhaps he could obtain some information from him which would help him better plan the Jabrid expedition.

In the evening, the Hormuzi messenger arrived along with three other men. Bin Rahhal noticed that the messenger was particularly deferential toward one of the men, walking behind and giving way to him. The messenger even refused to eat the sweet grapes Bin Rahhal offered him before the other man ate first. The messenger waited for Bin Rahhal to finish welcoming and greeting his guests before he spoke.

'Master Bin Rahhal, allow me to introduce you to Shah Salghur.'

The messenger pointed to the man with great respect. Bin Rahhal's eyes widened in surprise.

Salghur spoke calmly, trying to move past the awkward moment. 'Yes, I am Salghur, king of Hormuz until my brother turned against me. I was able to escape in disguise and travel to your country. You might wonder why I came to Al-Ahsa and did not go to my father-in-law in Oman. Well, he let me down when I asked for his help, and I found nowhere else to go but here. I have kept my identity hidden to spare the sultan of the Jabrids any retribution from my treasonous brother who usurped the throne.'

Bin Rahhal was blindsided by the presence of the former king in his house. He could not let him go anywhere else, and would have to take him in as his guest until Sultan Muqrin made up his mind.

Bin Rahhal, while trying to hide his surprise, said, 'Your Majesty. Your presence here is a great honour to us. I believe

97

your messenger has kept you abreast of what was said at the court of Sultan Muqrin. The sultan takes the matter very seriously. But I must ask you to be my guest until I inform the sultan of your presence here. Consider this humble abode as your home.' He turned to his servant. 'Make sure the king has everything he needs. Do whatever he asks, he is my dear guest. Now prepare dinner.'

Later, the servants brought a roasted sheep garnished with raisins and nuts, and laid on flatbreads. Everyone started eating. The ice broke between them and soon the conversations moved beyond small talk. The former king narrated the whole story of what had happened with his brothers.

'My brother Shah Vays seized the throne with the help of a group of Persian mercenaries he had hired, under the pretext of strengthening our navy. I never imagined he harboured ill-will for me and my rule. I instructed my vizier, *Khawaja* Attar, to specify his powers in writing, but one night, a number of his mercenaries raided my castle and took me to the dungeons. I was kept there for several months until Attar was able to bribe some guards and help me escape.'

The king paused before he said, as though talking to himself, 'When a king must flee his kingdom, the world shrinks and becomes smaller than the eye of a needle!' Salghur continued in the same tone. 'Attar staged my escape with some of his confidants. We now live on a farm in Al-Ahsa not far from here. I hope Sultan Muqrin will agree to help me return to my throne and my people.'

The former king took a deep breath and then said sombrely, 'Exile for kings is a slow death sentence.'

Bin Rahhal asked the king about the fate of Attar should the current king find out what he had done.

'Do not fear for the vizier. He takes care of every detail. When he sets his mind on something, know that he would have studied it from all angles. He was my father's vizier, and after the king passed away, I retained him in the same post and so did my brothers, despite the hostility between us. *Khawaja* Attar remains my brother's vizier.'

He stopped as if he did not want to finish his sentence, then said with the same reluctant tone, 'I don't know whether I should call Vays my brother or my enemy! Anyway, Attar is his vizier now, although Vays withdrew many of his powers recently. Any king who sits on the throne of Hormuz has no choice but to appoint Attar as vizier; he is irreplaceable.'

Bin Rahhal took a bite of his food and started chewing it as he looked at the deposed shah and asked, 'Would you like to come with us on our campaign when the sultan orders it? Your presence could be necessary to reassure the people that their king had returned.'

The king was about to drink water but moved the glass away from his mouth when he heard Bin Rahhal. His hopes of returning home were boosted. 'Yes of course. I will be with you. We will then reorganise relations between our two kingdoms . . .'

Bin Rahhal interrupted the former king. He found this to be a good opportunity to get Salghur to agree to some concessions. 'What would we get for helping you, Your Majesty? You know how dangerous this whole affair is. Many of our soldiers could die. What's worse, the mission could fail and your brother might bar us from trading with India and Africa.'

The deposed king felt that negotiations for the mission had now begun in earnest. He asked to wash his hands and the servants brought ewers and pots, and poured water over his hands. His companions followed suit and washed their hands, then returned to their seats.

The king and his men spoke among themselves in quiet voices while Bin Rahhal was busy washing his hands. Sultan Muqrin's vizier knew the king was consulting them about the terms, and took his time washing his hands to give them the chance to talk.

When the king returned to his seat, he addressed Bin Rahhal. 'Vizier Bin Rahhal, you have honoured us greatly with your hospitality tonight. I hope to be able to return your hospitality in Hormuz. I know that the decision Sultan Muqrin will make will be momentous and could bring harm to the sultanate, and for this I will make you an excellent offer.'

He looked at his companions as though trying to get their approval for what he was going to say. 'The sultanate of the Jabrids pays annual tax to the kingdom of Hormuz. I will waive this tax if you help me return to the throne. I will also cede to you all royal possessions in Bahrain, except for the farmstead I inherited from my father there, if the sultan allows it.'

Bin Rahhal reclined into cushions piled on top of one another. He took a deep breath before he spoke. 'Your Majesty, as you know, it is not up to me to decide on such matters. But I will convey all your requests and wishes to the sultan, who will then decide. I shall meet him tomorrow and will report back to you. Now I will let you turn in and rest. You are my guests now and you should stay with me at my home. I will ask my servants to bring your luggage here.'

Salghur replied, embarrassed, 'We do not want to impose. We will remain on our farm and will visit you every evening.'

But Bin Rahhal insisted. 'I will not accept that. You are my guests now and you will not leave my home.'

The following morning Bin Rahhal went to the sultan's *majlis*. He obviously had not slept much. The sultan, teasing his vizier, as he liked to do, said, 'What kept you up all night, Bin Rahhal? I know you don't have a wife!'

'I wish it had been a wife, Your Grace. What has kept me up is much worse!' Bin Rahhal continued, 'After I left your *majlis* yesterday and went home, I tried to find out more about the situation in Hormuz. I invited the messenger to my house for dinner, but to my surprise, he brought with him three other men.' Bin Rahhal looked in the sultan's eyes, trying to prepare him for what was coming next. 'One of the men was none other than King Salghur. He is in my house right now.'

'What? The king is here in Al-Ahsa, and in your home?'

'Yes, Your Grace. He was with the messenger when their ship arrived in the port of Al-Uqair. To avoid an awkward situation, he sent you his messenger first to find out whether you are willing to help him retake the throne.' Bin Rahhal changed his tone slightly. 'He wants to make us an offer in return for our assistance.'

'What is this offer?'

'He offered to waive the annual taxes we pay to Hormuz and to cede all of Hormuz's possessions on the island of Bahrain, except for a farm he had inherited from his father.'

The servants walked in carrying plates of dates and fruits, which they placed in front of the sultan. Sultan Muqrin signalled to Bin Rahhal to eat before he said, 'We pay them around 10,000 dinars a year, which is a lot of money. Hormuz has many possessions in Bahrain but we also want a part of the ports in Oman. Having a port there would help our men in the Omani hinterland.'

Bin Rahhal chose a piece of fruit from the plate and toyed with it for a bit before he said, 'Clearly, he has no real control over the Omani coast. These ports pay taxes to Hormuz, but independent emirs rule them. He told us that he had asked his relative Suleiman al-Nabahani for help but that Nabahani ignored him. This suggests Hormuz is not in control in the way we think. In my opinion, Your Grace, we should accept having the tax abolished and the Hormuzi possessions in Bahrain, because we do not want the king to promise us something he cannot deliver.'

The sultan chased the flies away from the fruit plate. 'You may be right, Bin Rahhal. The kingdom has crumbled and I don't know yet whether this is in our interest or not. A strong Hormuz makes the entire Gulf safer and more stable even if we have to pay them a lot of taxes. Their absence could make controlling the sea a more difficult task. When kingdoms decline, people start fighting over power, and do not care how much they lose for its sake. May God protect us and preserve our country.'

Sultan Muqrin often spoke like a preacher. He was very devout, and almost fanatical about his Maliki doctrine, which his grandfather had embraced. The region had been rife with sectarian conflicts fuelled by political rivalries, but as soon as the Jabrids took Al-Ahsa and expanded their power to other regions, the strife subsided and people took up the doctrine of the ruling class.

Sultan Muqrin had used this as an opportunity to promote education and open religious schools to reduce the influence of the Shia sect rooted in some areas of his kingdom. The Jabrids did not take power easily. It cost them much blood and treasure as they fought against the remnants of the Qarmatian state in Hajr and the Bedouin tribes that had always coveted Al-Ahsa as a rich oasis in a sea of sands. Sultan Muqrin was therefore extremely sensitive about conflicts and tensions around him, and tended to put them down quickly before they festered and got out of control.

Bin Rahhal noticed that the sultan was not enjoying the food and their conversation as he usually did. He was preoccupied with the predicament that the Hormuzi messenger had carried with him. He tried to convince the sultan to make a decision. 'If you agree, Your Grace, let us write up a treaty for him to sign. We want to prepare for the campaign you have ordered as soon as possible.'

The sultan picked up a fan and started waving it in front of his face. 'Write it and show it to me before the king signs it. Keep him at your home and under your watch until I give the order.'

'I have already done that, Your Grace. I have ordered my servants to keep an eye on him because we want him to be with us as soon as we set off to Hormuz.'

'Well done. Have you written to Julfar and Salwa?'

'Yes, Your Grace. I expect them to answer within a month from now.'

'How long do you need to prepare for this campaign?'

'We will need about one year. We lack the ships we need. We shall import timber from India and shipwrights from Basra for the purpose. The emirs of Salwa and Julfar will send whatever material and men they can spare. We shall have our own fleet within a year from now, God willing.'

Sultan Muqrin raised his hands to the sky in prayer. 'With God's help, it may just be possible.'

10

Alexandria, Egypt

N EARLY A YEAR AFTER Covilhã first left Alexandria, the rabbi heard a knock on the door. It was very late at night. He did not dare open the door without first checking the identity of the person calling at this ungodly hour. He placed his ear on the door and called out, 'Who is it?'

A whispering voice came through the cracks in the wooden door. 'The Holy Sail.'

The rabbi answered back, clearly irked, 'Is it still heading east? I thought it had ruptured by now!'

He opened the door quietly and let Covilhã in, before he shut it tightly behind him.

The place was dark and Covilhã needed a few seconds to adjust to the light and see the rabbi's face. The rabbi stood still, scrutinising his unannounced guest. 'Is it you again, Covilhã? I was expecting you . . . but where is your friend Paiva?'

'We split up in Aden a year ago. He went to look for the kingdom of Prester John and I went to look for the source of spices in India. I thought he would have finished his mission and returned here before I did.'

'Don't bet on it, my friend. Things have become far more dangerous than they used to be. Let us pray he will make it safely in the end. Please sit down, sit down.' The rabbi moved some pillows that were thrown randomly on the chairs and pointed at one. 'Sit here. We have a lot to talk about.'

The rabbi continued, 'Do you believe the kingdom of Prester John really exists? It is the biggest lie in history, and only fools believe it. This kingdom and its king never existed. It is a myth that the Catholics are drawn to blindly, like sheep.'

Covilhã replied, 'I have also enquired about the kingdom. No one has heard of it. The captain of the ship that took me from Aden to Muscat told me there are Christians who live in the highlands of Abyssinia. But he said they were poor and live as hermits in their churches, isolated from people. From time to time, a priest visits them from Egypt to teach them the faith. What the captain described did not sound like a wealthy kingdom at all. He said their priests live in caves near the mountaintops and rarely mingle with people. They wear the same garments for years until they are completely worn out. Does that sound like wealth to you?'

The rabbi noticed something under Covilhã's arm. 'What are you carrying?'

Covilhã took out a large dossier from under his arm and laid it out for the rabbi. 'This is my report on the trip. I have written down in this guide all the information I gathered on the entrepôt, people, trade, wind patterns, ship technology, currencies used and so on. This is the fruit of a year's worth of perilous adventures. I sincerely hope the king will appreciate all this and treat us like he treats Catholics in his kingdom. This document has been a great burden during my journeys; I had to hide it often. It may save us one day from—'

The rabbi stood up abruptly, not wanting to hear the rest of it. He said to Covilhã, 'I will get you something to eat.' After he walked a few steps, his back still turned to his guest, and added, 'Don't be too optimistic, my friend.'

'What do you mean, Rabbi?'

The rabbi did not answer Covilhã. He disappeared into the dark corridors of his house, and came back carrying food and water.

'Go on, eat. It is delicious. I kept it from yesterday for my dinner tonight. Everything is so expensive now, even food. Can you believe it? No one expected food to become so costly, but this is what happens in times of chaos. Egypt is a right mess. When people want our money, they accuse us of being spies for the Christians, and when they want the Christians' money, they accuse them of being the corrupt sultans' money keepers. If they want the Muslim sultans' money, they accuse them of being apostates and on and on. We are all just sitting and waiting for our turn to become victims of someone or something.'

Covilhã repeated his question, as though he had heard none of the rabbi's rant. 'What do you mean, I shouldn't be too optimistic?'

The rabbi bit his lip and sighed loudly. 'During your absence, some Jews arrived in Alexandria after fleeing from Spain. They brought unpleasant news. When the Inquisition started persecuting Jews and Muslims in Andalusia, some of them escaped to Portugal thinking they would be beyond its reach. But the Portuguese handed them over to the Inquisition in Spain, which burned many of them alive. You wouldn't want to hear what they saw and suffered there.'

The rabbi shook his head in sorrow, before he continued, his eyes fixed on the ceiling. 'Many of those who survived the *auto-da-fés* boarded ships heading anywhere.

One survivor told me a French captain threw his Muslim and Jewish passengers overboard after he found out they had no money to pay him. But we made arrangements after that, and gave every fleeing Jew enough money to reach the shores of North Africa. Many of those who recently arrived in Alexandria told us this. The ports of Tunisia, Morocco and Algeria are now teeming with Muslim and Jewish refugees who have fled over the past several years. Every one of them has a story to tell. It is a great tragedy.'

The rabbi spoke with frustration, as though he had the weight of the world on his shoulders. He drank from the water jug, and then continued, 'King John II died and was succeeded by his son Afonso. But Afonso died shortly after when he fell from his horse. The king's brother-in-law Manuel the Fortunate now sits on the throne. He is the same person who sent you to India, my friend.'

Covilhã's heart pounded. He remembered their first meeting that cold night in Lisbon. Manuel was arrogant and vain even though he was not yet king. Covilhã could only imagine how much worse those traits would have become now that he wore a crown on his head.

'Did Manuel really become king?'

'Yes, yes. So don't expect the vindictive bigot to do anything benevolent towards us Jews.'

Covilhã pulled himself together. 'Couldn't it be good for us, though? He sent Paiva and myself here, so perhaps he will reward us if we bring him back all the information he asked for.'

The rabbi avoided encouraging Covilhã's optimism. He had seen and heard enough tragedies to rid him of any such hopes. He slapped his thigh in an attempt to rouse Covilhã from his ignorance. 'Hear me well, Covilhã. Before he became king, Prince Manuel promised you he would protect your family and Paiva's.' The rabbi paused, reluctant to say more. But then he made up his mind and said, 'Well, he hasn't kept his promise. Paiva's father was burned alive for heresy less than a year after you both left. Moses helped us smuggle out your family to Italy, and sent with them a box containing some of our scriptures including the Haggadah*!'

Covilhã's face turned red. He clenched his teeth until the muscles of his jaw could be seen clearly. 'Why? Do they not have a royal letter protecting them from the Inquisition?'

'Yes, but clearly the king felt that you had spent too much time on your mission, so he decided those letters had expired. He authorised the Inquisition to seize any person regardless of their trade, post or relation to the palace, save for a few of his cronies. Moses and the king's private physician, Dr Rodrigo, are the only Jews who have survived so far. By virtue of their professions, they can do a lot to smuggle people and preserve our scriptures.'

The rabbi was waiting for Covilhã to reach for the food and eat, but the succession of bad news had killed his appetite.

Covilhã lifted the dossier with both hands and said, 'What should I do with this now? Burn it?'

The rabbi reached for the file and took it quickly, fearing Covilhã would carry out his reckless threat. 'No, of course not. If you do, you would be putting Moses and Dr Rodrigo in grave danger. They were the ones who chose you for this mission. The dossier must reach the king, and who knows, this could help keep Moses and Rodrigo in their posts for some time. Remember, they would be presenting it to the king as a Jewish achievement.'

'And is my family all right?' Covilhã asked. 'Do you know whether they made it to Italy alive?'

'Your family is safe in Italy. They are the guests of the Grand Rabbi in Naples. But don't even think about going there right now. Conflict is raging between the Ottomans and pirates in Rhodes and we would not want you to be captured by either side.'

The rabbi started leafing through the pages of Covilhã's book. He then closed it and asked, 'What will you do about your friend Paiva now?'

'I will search for him. I cannot just leave him.'

'Where will you begin the search?'

'I think I will go from here to Zeila. From there I will travel inland. That was Paiva's itinerary. I will try to look for him there.' Covilhã added, 'I will write a letter that I hope you can deliver to my family in Naples. I will depart for Suez soon.'

The rabbi was dusting off the book. He said, 'For my part I will send this file to Moses so he can give it to the king. You have gone through a great deal to gather all this information.'

Covilhã finally showed some interest in the food in front of him, which made the rabbi feel a little reassured. After Covilhã put the first morsel in his mouth, he tried to change the subject. He felt it was not appropriate to talk about massacres and burnings at the stake while eating.

'Allow me to share with you some of my observations, Rabbi. I have seen many things in those countries, and even met with the Grand Rabbi in Aden. What caught my attention the most was how much tolerance they enjoyed, unlike in Portugal and Spain. The merchants there prefer to have partners from other faiths. The ports allow adherents of different religions to build their own places of worship. I also noticed that everyone had similar customs and traditions. Jewish women in Yemen wear the veil and Hindu women in the streets of Calicut wear headscarves just like Muslim women do. They resemble one another in almost everything. They trade in all known currencies and do not give a monopoly to a particular one. When they speak, they speak freely and without the fear we feel in Portugal. They are free, Rabbi. They don't have an Inquisition!'

He repeated the last phrase emphatically.

Covilhã continued, 'A Jewish boy pointed us in the direction of the synagogue in Aden. The rabbi there spoke freely as though the city was his own. Religion is hardly mentioned there except in the event of marriage or death. Otherwise, people are free to worship any way they want. When people are free they are naturally devout, and address God directly. They behave with the knowledge that He has created them and is looking after them, and they talk to Him about everything. When they sail on board a ship they raise their hands and whisper their prayers directly to God without an intermediary. Isn't that wonderful, Rabbi?

'I have met many Muslims. I have entered their homes and shared their food, and they never asked me about my religion. I felt they saw it as something strictly between me and God.'

Covilhã paused and looked at the floor with hollow eyes before he added, 'Sometimes, I wonder whether what I did was right. They showed me respect and gave me food and water, and yet I spied on them, knowing that King Manuel would send his ships to attack them!' The tone of his voice changed slightly. 'We are going to take their freedom away, Rabbi.'

The rabbi repeated Covilhã's last words in a sarcastic tone. 'Take their freedom away, huh?' He raised his voice; the word freedom had him all riled up. 'But this freedom is not something guaranteed. You have it and enjoy it until a sultan takes it away or the situation deteriorates. Then you will find your freedom hostage to a foolish rabble, as is happening now here in Egypt.'

The rabbi paused, before he added, 'Yes, there are two rival factions yet they both threaten freedom – the sultan and the rabble. Isn't it odd?'

Covilhã did not have anything else to discuss with the rabbi, who was clearly frustrated and disillusioned with everything. He decided to ask him the usual question any traveller asked a host. 'Tell me about life these days, Rabbi.'

'It's not so good. The unrest in Egypt makes us vulnerable to attacks by the mobs from time to time. We have to be very careful.' The rabbi lifted the jug of water and drank. 'Sultan al-Ghawri has launched his ships into the Red Sea. He had help from the Ottomans and Venetians. Travellers, meanwhile, have been bringing a lot of news about the Portuguese. Trade with India has been disrupted and goods no longer come from there. Merchants have lost their livelihoods, and if this continues, everyone will be in danger, everyone without exception.'

Covilhã, recalling what Attar had told him, interrupted the rabbi. 'How did they get to India? I thought they were waiting for our report. That's what they told us in Lisbon.'

The rabbi almost spat in outrage, but he pulled himself together. 'Do you believe that they were relying on your report to get to India? They sent others and told them the same thing. They are a bunch of self-serving killers.' He adjusted his seating position then added, 'They sent countless ships throughout the past years on scouting missions, to learn the strengths and weaknesses of their enemy. This time, however, the ships disobeyed orders and burned down the pilgrim ship *Maryam*, which people have been talking about for over a year.'

The rabbi put Covilhã's report in his lap. He struck it with his fist. 'Your report will bring their warships. You will have paved the way for invasion with all this information. They will come not with holy sails, but with sails stained with blood.'

11

The Red Sea

T HE MAMLUK FLEET SET off from the port of Suez. Its thirteen ships, comprising galleys, fire ships and frigates, were carrying 1,500 soldiers to Jeddah, led by Hussein al-Kurdi, now an admiral. Hussein stood on the deck of the flagship, contemplating the endless, deep blue sea. He heard the wind hitting the sails and the waves striking the sides of the ship. It was music to his ears, music that he had waited so long to hear. He had managed to build the fleet he was now commanding, and felt that he had the power to bring about the changes he so desired.

He looked at the back of the ship and saw Suez's dancing trees and palms bidding him farewell. He loved the city, which he had single-handedly turned into a shipbuilding hub. Hussein turned his head forward and breathed the sea air as though for the first time. He cast aside all thoughts of intrigue and conspiracy; he called all the shots in this fleet, and was his own master.

Hussein was leaving Sultan al-Ghawri alone to face many adversaries. Ghawri could have appointed someone else admiral, yet he had chosen Hussein for the mission because he was his closest and most loyal ally. At least, this was what Hussein told himself, trying to gather the strength to move forward with his mission.

He watched his soldiers and sailors. They were different in everything, in their clothes, their dialects and their aspirations. Hussein did not want his men to be idle during the long days ahead at sea, and had devised a strict daily routine for all of them: just after the dawn prayers, they had to climb and begin combat training, starting with melee weapons and then swords. After that, the men had to clean the ships. In the afternoon, the men were told to polish and sharpen their weapons, and to clean the cannons and cannonballs. Everything had to be shiny, from the heavy guns to the swords and daggers, and everyone had to work without interruption. Hussein was tense; he wanted the seamen, soldiers and peasants to become a disciplined fighting force, which required work, patience and training.

Days later, the fleet moored in Jeddah. The port was teeming with the city's residents, who came to take a look at this massive flotilla arriving to protect their city and the holy places from Portuguese attack. They had not forgotten how the Portuguese massacred pilgrims and disrupted trade with India. Dignitaries from the city in large turbans, including the sharif of Mecca, were among those standing on the wharf to welcome the fleet. The supervisors of Hajj convoys, wearing the traditional garments of their respective kingdoms, also attended the ceremony. They had the same rank as ambassadors and were treated accordingly. Everyone was waiting for the new ruler of Jeddah appointed by Sultan al-Ghawri.

Amir Hussein descended from the flagship into a small boat sent by the Sharif of Mecca to take him to port. The boat was festooned with decorations to welcome the new ruler. Even the oarsmen wore special brightly coloured costumes that reminded Hussein of the Prophet's birthday celebrations, when the noise of revelling mixed with the recitations and calls to prayers emanating from the mosques in Cairo's narrow alleyways. The oarsmen's costumes were not unlike the joyful garments worn by the Sufis in those celebrations.

Hussein loathed such extravagance, which he saw as a reflection of both fear and sycophancy, though he decided to keep these sentiments to himself for the time being.

He came down from the boat and shook hands with the dignitaries, and had to stand and listen to their poems of tribute and flattery. He then walked to the governor's palace overlooking the sea, away from the tent that had been erected in the port for the ceremony, to the annoyance of all those who had been quarrelling all day to get seats underneath it.

Hussein could not help but notice the extent of affluence in Jeddah. Pilgrims spent a lot of money here on their way to Mecca. The port collected hefty taxes from the merchants travelling from the four corners of the earth; it was a major port in the Red Sea, and all trade from India and China had to pass through en route to Egypt, the Mediterranean and Europe beyond it. The port had grown even more significant when the Gulf was closed off following the Safavid occupation of Baghdad, severing the trade route from Basra to Aleppo.

Merchants in Jeddah were happy about Hussein's appointment, or at least appeared to be. Politics did not interest them as much as business and the need to make the best of the circumstances that made their city an important corridor for trade. The merchants assumed that Hussein, like his predecessors appointed by Cairo to govern Jeddah, was a venal, incompetent agent of the sultan whose private interests he served first and foremost, in addition to his own. No matter what this new ruler was like, the merchants were prepared to bribe him to maintain their interests. All they had to do was to get to know him better to discover his weaknesses and deal with them accordingly.

Historically, the port of Jeddah was never too far from Cairo's authority and influence. It was located along the maritime route controlled by Egypt, extending from Aden to Suez via Jeddah. The city's people knew that the ruler appointed by the sultan of Egypt acted on behalf of the latter, and so accepted him, accustomed themselves to him and dealt with him as he was without resistance.

As soon as Hussein entered the palace, he sent for the treasurer, the commander of the city's guard and the harbourmaster. He asked the first to present him with a statement of the revenues available, their source and how they were disbursed. The treasurer looked annoyed with this request, but promised to prepare it as soon as possible.

Hussein did not wish to wait long. 'I want it tomorrow, Treasurer.'

'Admiral, I need to close the accounts and make calculations before I present them to you.'

Hussein squinted deliberately, intimating a veiled threat to the treasurer. He said, 'I want it tomorrow. There will be no further discussion.'

In an attempt to end the debate that the treasurer seemed to want to draw him into, he turned to the commander of the city's guard, who was standing ready to receive orders. The old officer wore a marvellous sword, though it was clear he had not used it for a long time. Hussein asked him, 'How many men do you have?'

'We do not have many, my lord. I have around 200 soldiers guarding the port and the road to Mecca. But we lack the

117

weapons we need to repel the Bedouins who attack the pilgrims' convoys from time to time.'

Hussein did not look at the man as he spoke. He said, 'Gather all the men you have. I want them in front of my palace within two days. Now go.'

'As for you, Harbourmaster, I want you to present me with a list of merchants, their assets, their ships, their turnover and the taxes they pay. I want all this ready within three days. I think you already have this information. Now go too.'

When celebrations across the city subsided several days later, people started feeling that there was something about Hussein that set him apart from his predecessors. The man did not come out to take part in the celebrations. He did not accept the invitations of the city's dignitaries, and had not left his palace since he set foot in Jeddah. He was of a different breed, and had firm and precise requests. He knew exactly what he wanted and did not share his plans with anyone.

There was much talk among the merchants in Jeddah's coffeehouses. Some staked their bets on his corruptibility, others on his brutality. But in the end, no one knew who exactly Hussein Pasha al-Kurdi was and what he wanted. The Jeddans were divided into those who believed the merchants in the city were strong enough to co-opt anyone, and those who felt this man was different. No two people meeting in a coffeehouse, street, shop or mosque failed to talk about him.

The early days passed quietly until the new governor circulated an order which couriers distributed among the neighbourhoods of Jeddah. The announcement read: *All men aged between fifteen and sixty must volunteer to build a wall around*

Jeddah, to protect it from Portuguese invasion. The treasury calls for donations to fund the works from private citizens.

The people of Jeddah did not take this seriously. They were still hoping that the Pasha, as they called Hussein, would not be able to resist the temptations of the merchants for too long. So it came as a shock to Hussein when his treasurer told him the Jeddans donated next to nothing, and that no more than fifty people had volunteered to build the wall – mostly poor people expecting to be paid for their work or, at least, to be fed.

Hussein issued another order compelling all men in the city to help in the construction of the wall. He confiscated some of the assets of the merchants and wealthy citizens to fund the works and fortify the city. Soldiers moved in the neighbourhoods to enforce this decision, which was seen as an extraordinarily bold one, though they finally understood how serious Hussein was when soldiers marshalled young people from the streets to register their names for the construction of the wall.

The people of the city grumbled and protested, but Hussein ordered the soldiers to flog anyone who failed to appear in the main square of the city. Hussein appointed whip-wielding supervisors to punish any slackers. A few days later, the residents of Jeddah realised Amir Hussein was a curse, and concluded that they just had to endure him until further notice, since the rulers of Jeddah never lasted very long.

Work on the wall took place from after the dawn prayer until sunset. Workers were divided into different groups: one quarrying stones from the mountain, another moving the stones to the coast, a third to cut the stones, and a fourth group to line them up. The heat was unbearable, and many died from sunstroke and dehydration. Hussein Pasha, however, did not tolerate any slacking or grumbling, and when some protested against the long working hours, the guard soon placed their severed heads on spikes near the wall for everyone to see.

When night fell and everyone went to sleep, Hussein stayed up thinking. He did not want to shed blood but there were many dangers threatening the realm. The sultan had shown great confidence in him personally, and this could be the only chance for him to prove to his master that he was worthy of the mission and the post. What else could he do when people stood in the way of achieving his objectives?

They were a group of traitors, Hussein thought, who were not even aware of the extent of their crime. How could they refuse to work on building a wall for Jeddah to protect the city from Portuguese assault? And how could they object to long working hours when others lost life and limb to defend the land and the faith? He had no answers.

Hussein spat on the floor in anger at the triviality and banality of those people, as he tried to find excuses for taking their lives and mutilating their bodies.

Days passed heavily for everyone. The wealthy felt this strange, stiff-necked man was too stubborn to be coaxed with money, and started smuggling assets that were easy to carry to other cities or even buried them in their gardens. When Hussein got wind of this, he summoned some of them to his palace and gave them a choice between the whip and handing over their money. More bodies were then hung on the walls, bloodied by the whips, to deter sluggards and those who were still thinking about smuggling their money out of the city.

Pressure on people in the coastal city increased. Many of its merchants went bankrupt. Some of the city's leaders decided to have a parley with Amir Hussein, and convince him to ease his approach. They agreed with one another to exaggerate their penury and not wear any expensive-looking garments as they usually did, and chose their most senior leader to address him on their behalf.

'Your Excellency Hussein Pasha. Your decrees have hurt us a great deal. Many of us have become poor after our possessions were taken, some of us even now beg in the streets and mosques. Our state must be no secret to you. Working on the construction of the wall is killing our livelihoods, so we implore you to exempt us from that work and return some of our confiscated money.'

Hussein squinted, which people now knew usually meant he was about to make a harsh decision. 'Is that why you're all here? To tell me you want your money, and that you don't want to work?' He started shouting, 'Is this what you want?' Hussein lowered his voice before continuing. 'Several days ago, people on the southern coast rescued a number of Yemeni merchants. The Portuguese had cut off their hands and noses and then tied them up in their boat, which they had looted. The boat and the victims on board were then pushed to the coast for everyone to see.'

Hussein began shouting again. 'Do you want the Portuguese to do the same thing to you? Do you want to see your women and children their slaves and prisoners? You do not understand the threat surrounding you. You are a bunch of greedy merchants who cannot see anything beyond your own pockets.'

He then turned to the commander of the guard who was standing near them looking alert, as though he already knew what he needed to do. Hussein said, 'Take them and flog them in front of everyone near the wall. Then let them work more hours to compensate for the time they have wasted in this frivolous conversation.'

The delegation started screaming and wailing. Not only had they lost their money and were being made to work as slave labour, but they were also to be humiliated and flogged in public, thanks to the scourge that was Hussein Pasha.

The wall started to take shape around the city. It was fitted with only two gates, one overlooking the sea and one in the direction of Mecca. The wall had six watchtowers, each tower having a perimeter of sixteen cubits. After arranging a guard unit and a plan for the defence of the city, Hussein appointed a deputy to govern in his stead and set sail to Aden.

From the top of one of the watchtowers, a soldier watched as Hussein's flotilla sailed south. He kept his gaze fixed on it to make sure it did not turn back. The soldier looked around quickly, and then spat in the direction of the flotilla.

– 12 –

Al-Ahsa, Eastern Arabian Peninsula

S ALGHUR GREW ACCUSTOMED TO life in Bin Rahhal's house. He enjoyed swimming in the pond from time to time and picking grapes from the vine that shaded it. In the evening, when temperatures cooled down, he would sit with Bin Rahhal and his close friends on a terrace outside the house, chatting and listening to the tales the guests and merchants had to tell. Bin Rahhal also brought many strange and wondrous stories from the sultan's *majlis*.

As time passed, the friendship between the two men grew stronger. Salghur was almost childlike in his spontaneity, while Bin Rahhal slowly took on an avuncular mentoring role. The newfound bond between them was like the bond between son and father, or little brother and older sibling. Bin Rahhal eventually took Salghur to see his mother's room, and told him how close they had been and how he had remained celibate to care for her in her old age. Salghur felt he had become part of Bin Rahhal's life, their friendship now indissoluble.

In the winter, the temperature dropped and cooled further with rainfall. Bin Rahhal decided to take Salghur and his company hunting. He prepared a party complete with servants and camping provisions, in addition to falcons and hounds.

The hunting party set off to Al-Ahsa's desert, which was teeming with gazelles, birds and hares. Salghur did not know much about falconry, but soon learned how to hunt game using the birds of prey. He was extremely pleased when his falcon caught a large bird and swooped down with it, before the servants came and retrieved the prey from its claws. Salghur was so happy with his feat that he displayed his hunt on his saddle for the rest of the day – like a small child refusing to let go of a new toy.

In the evening, the group sat around a fire to roast their hunt. Salghur sat watching the raptors. Their decorated hoods gave them an added look of beauty and pride. They were majestic birds that – as he saw them – were proud of their strength and looked dignified and gracious. These birds were made to live proudly and die proudly, he thought.

Carrying the falcon on his arm as he rode his horse was challenging. He could not keep his arm straight all the time, and failed to notice many times when the bird fluttered its wings to protest against the unsteadiness of his moving human nest.

After a year in Al-Ahsa, Salghur had learned that the world was much bigger than the small island his brother now ruled and that there were many experiences only those who left their homes, travelled the world and met and mingled with people could know about. However, he did not want to live in any place other than Hormuz. He had no other throne but the throne of Hormuz. Here, he was only Bin Rahhal's friend, nothing more, and that did not satisfy him. He wanted to be a venerated king ruling the people and the realm like his father and grandfather before him.

One evening, before he opened the door to his guests, Bin Rahhal gave Salghur a knowing smile. Salghur returned the smile and said, 'That smile hides many things behind it, my friend. I think there's something you want to tell me. Go on then, please, don't hide anything from me.'

Bin Rahhal's sly smile grew wider. He peeked at the fruit platter in front of them and took two large figs, offering one to Salghur. He said, 'These figs are miraculously tasty. I can never resist them. Don't eat them immediately. Use your fingers to split them in half, then take a good look at the shape and colour before you taste them. You have to enjoy what is in your hands before you put it in your mouth; always remember that.'

Salghur was too impatient for this banter. He tried to end Bin Rahhal's sleight of words and get straight to the point. 'Come. Tell me what's on your mind. I am at the end of my tether. I cry almost every day because of how frustrated I am and how much I miss home.'

'Be patient, my friend. You must always enjoy what you already have. The more you do so the more you will grow fond of it. Such is life. Try to remember the blessings around you; if you forget them, you have renounced them, and if you renounce them, you will no longer see the world as a beautiful place.' Bin Rahhal put half of the fig in his mouth and slowly savoured its taste, before he said casually, 'The sultan has agreed to prepare a campaign to restore you to the throne, God willing.'

Salghur stretched out his hand and grabbed Bin Rahhal's arm firmly, as though he was afraid he might lose him all of a sudden. 'Is this true?'

'Yes, it is true. We will leave soon for the Gulf of Salwa and from there to Julfar to rendezvous with our ships and men. After that, we will sail to your lost kingdom, my friend.'

Bin Rahhal offered the other half of his fig to his guest, who took it and kept it in his hand. Tears of joy prevented him from lifting it to his mouth. Up till now, he had lost almost all hope of ever returning home.

Salghur looked at the fig as though he had finally under-stood Bin Rahhal's lesson, and whispered, 'I think you have known about the sultan's decision for some time, Bin Rahhal, but you hid it from me, is it not so?'

'The sultan made the decision nearly a year ago, but I could not tell you before the sultan gave his explicit orders.'

'I will never forget your generosity for as long as I live, Master Vizier. I have found in you a brother that I do not have in those who are of my flesh and blood. Isn't it strange that my own brothers turned out to be my enemies, and a stranger like you has become a true friend and brother?'

Bin Rahhal replied quietly, 'It is all about money and power, Your Majesty. Almost all the blood that has ever been spilled has been spilled for their sake. Your relationship with your brothers was destroyed by this deadly twosome, which may well destroy your relationship with people you care about in the future. Never forget this. Money and power may bring you happiness if you handle them wisely, and misery if they get the better of you.'

Bin Rahhal chewed the rest of the fig before continuing. 'Also remember that you must enjoy what you already have. Treat everything you have like you treat this fig. Enjoy it with your eyes and nose before you put it in your mouth, because once you do, the pleasure you get from it goes away. Your relationship with those you love must follow the same idea; enjoy everyone around you with all your senses while they last.'

126

Bin Rahhal had not let the king leave his estate much during his stay; his movements had been strictly accounted for and tightly controlled lest people learn of his presence there. But the king felt bored from being restricted for many months, though he found solace in the idea that he would be returning to his kingdom soon, and consolation in his nightly meetings with Bin Rahhal that he eagerly awaited throughout the day.

Now that the sultan had overtly approved the campaign to Hormuz, there was no need to restrict his movements any more. People learned the former king of Hormuz was a guest at their vizier's estate, which tempered the secrecy imposed on the king's presence, whereabouts and movements.

In the remaining days leading up to the campaign, Bin Rahhal and his guest visited the large market in Al-Ahsa. Salghur was impressed by how well-organised everything was. There was a large shaded yard for tethering, feeding and watering animals. The shops nearby had a roof that was high enough to allow air to circulate. And goods like meats, vegetables and fruits all had tags with the prices written on them, something the former king had not seen in Hormuz. In one shop, Salghur noticed that the intact heads of slaughtered animals were displayed in front of their meats in an eye-catching way. When Salghur asked about this, Bin Rahhal told him it was so buyers could see what the animals whose meat they were buying looked like and examine their condition.

In a higher place of the bazaar sat the *muhtasib*. His job was to ensure the market was clean and in good order, and that no cheating was taking place. The *muhtasib* also had to resolve disputes between buyers and sellers. The market was divided into several sections, with a *muhtasib* supervising each part.

What bothered everyone, however, were the flies that hovered in large numbers over the market. Everything was covered with the insects. Bin Rahhal was used to this, but Salghur was appalled. When he asked about this, Bin Rahhal explained to him that Al-Ahsa was an oasis surrounded by desert, and with its many palms and fruit trees, it was an oasis for insects too. Bin Rahhal passed his hand over a heap of dates, sending a swarm of flies buzzing loudly which startled Salghur, as Bin Rahhal laughed.

Salghur saw many women and children selling produce from their farms along the roads. This was also new to him; Hormuz had no agriculture to speak of and people worked either in trade or in the army. Only rich people had some small plantations on the island, and there were not many other ways to make one's living. Al-Ahsa, by contrast, had everything, and all a person had to do was to take their merchandise to the market or the road to find buyers.

On the appointed day, camels laden with supplies and bags were made to kneel down outside Bin Rahhal's home. Rugged-looking armed cavalrymen escorted the camels, twenty camel cavalries and fifteen horsemen in total.

The convoy made its way through the narrow roads between Al-Ahsa's farms. The air was humid and heavy, and the sun was just about to come out. Palm trees on both sides of the road swayed, as though feeling for those passing underneath. The babble of the brooks mixed with the sounds of birds and insects, complementing the landscape that Salghur was unfamiliar with. Salghur knew he would miss the palms, fruit trees and running streams when he left the beautiful oasis.

The convoy travelled for several hours. Trees suddenly disappeared, giving way to majestic desert. Proud, daunting and eerily quiet, the desert was infinite. There were barely any signs of life, save for a passing lizard, a concealed snake, a bird flying away, or a gazelle hiding behind a hillock here and there. Salghur turned around to catch a final glimpse of the greenery before delving into the monochromatic desert, doing what many did when they left a place permanently: taking one last look back before looking forward, hopeful about what lay in store.

Salghur looked at Bin Rahhal. He was cleaning his teeth with a *miswak*, which one of his servants had given him. Salghur felt that he had to say something; covering the vast distance ahead would be much harder in silence. Talking to each other was going to be the only entertainment they would have to help them cut through the desert, so Salghur decided to break the wall of silence.

'How odd that all signs of life just vanish. From a lush green oasis, we're now in the middle of the desert. Have you not thought about digging canals to extend some of your streams to irrigate the desert? I've never seen water so clear and fresh as the water in Al-Ahsa. If we had water like this in Hormuz we would be one of the richest nations.'

Salghur caressed his horse's neck and continued. 'I planted palms around my palace to make it look more pleasing to the eye. My father made sure to farm the land around it too, but my brothers neglected it. I'm sure by now the palace's surroundings have become barren again.'

Bin Rahhal took the last small twig left of the *miswak* out of his mouth before he spoke. 'The oasis is enormous. Its bounty reaches all places, even your kingdom, Hormuz. We don't know where the water originates and where it goes. We see it pass under our homes and farms but we don't see it after that. Some say it goes into the ground, others claim it flows to the sea. Some of our brave men tried to dive in the waterways to find out where they ended, but they never returned. Legends say they go to the *jinn**, and that those who dive into the springs will be taken by the demons as slaves for the rest of their lives.'

Salghur pulled the reins of his horse to stay close to Bin Rahhal. 'I've heard these legends. I was told a gushing stream of water straddled my father's farm in Bahrain, but no one knew where it came from and where it went either. The *jinn* may have a role in it, but I don't know.'

The former king added, 'I had heard about Al-Ahsa before. My ancestors were interested in the oasis and bought farms and palaces there. A saying in Hormuz goes, "Hormuz dies when Hajr dies." I believe this is happening right now.'

Bin Rahhal smiled but did not reply.

After a three-day journey, the travellers caught the scent of the sea before they finally glimpsed it. Bin Rahhal judged it best for the convoy to set up camp near the shore before they arrived in Salwa; he loved the sea, its sound and its smell, and did not have many opportunities to see it.

They saw a three-foot-tall wall built with black stones in the shape of a horseshoe cutting through a large section of the shore. The semi-open enclosure started out from the coast, extended into the sea and curved back to the beach. Bin Rahhal, pointing at the structure, told Salghur, 'We call it a *masakir*. It traps fish when the tide is low and fishermen collect them afterwards. Let's go and get some. This is our chance to catch some fresh fish.'

Salghur looked around, expecting to see the structure's owners scrambling in anger after seeing his party there. But Bin Rahhal reassured him, saying, 'The owners of the fish traps do not come often to check them. Besides, travellers are allowed to use them provided that they only take as much as they need.'

The smell of barbecued fish soon filled the campsite. The *masakir* had trapped copious amounts of fish, but only a few men familiar with the sea dared swim to retrieve the catch. The rest preferred to remain on the shore and ate cured meat with dates and cheese, rather than try their luck in eating 'whales', as they called the fish.

That night after dinner, Salghur decided to take a stroll by himself. Bin Rahhal followed him with his eyes and saw him sit somewhere far along the beach. Salghur took off his turban and used it to wipe his face. Bin Rahhal understood that Salghur was tormented by the loss of his kingdom and that he pined for his home.

On the following day, the convoy reached an idyllic blue bay teeming with small boats. In the distance, red sand dunes towered over the silhouette of a docile-looking city along the coast, lined by palm and sidra trees; it looked like a paradise in the middle of a sea of sand. They saw a spacious tent that was pitched to welcome them. Standing outside it was Emir Zamel al-Jabri with a large group of the city's elders and notables.

Bin Rahhal turned to Salghur and asked him, 'How shall I introduce you, Your Majesty?'

'I think you are the only one who still addresses me by that title after my brother took the throne away from me!'

Bin Rahhal smiled. 'To me you are the king of Hormuz. Soon you will be its undisputed king. What shall I tell them?'

'Tell them I am a guest from Hormuz.'

Inside the visitors' tent, Bin Rahhal and his Hormuzi guest sat in the centre of the *majlis*. Within moments, large plates of food were brought in, each carried by four muscular men. Some of the plates held roasted lambs. On one enormous plate placed in front of the guests rested a roasted camel calf, fat seeping from its hump into the flatbreads underneath. Bowls of yogurt were also served.

Everyone started eating hungrily. One of the hosts held the head of a sheep, opened its jaw, grabbed its tongue and pulled it until it snapped off. He put it in front of Salghur and invited him to eat it. Salghur looked at the tongue in horror, and passed it to the person sitting next to him – who was pleased and started nibbling on it with appetite.

Bin Rahhal suppressed a laugh that almost escaped from his lungs. 'They offer the tongue to the guest to welcome him. You ought to have eaten it.'

Salghur looked at the person sitting near him. He was still cutting the tongue with his teeth. His anxious expression changed into an expression of relief; someone else had taken care of that great responsibility.

Crowds of people took turns eating from the dinnerware. As one group left another came, until they were all sated.

After lunch, Emir Zamel al-Jabri sat with Bin Rahhal and his Hormuzi guest in a secluded place, away from the rest of the crowd. The emir gave Bin Rahhal an update on the preparations.

'I have prepared what you requested, Master Vizier: fifty ships with eight banks of oars carrying 800 men, all experienced seafarers, along with five ships carrying horses and supplies. This is all I could get from the merchants I know.'

Bin Rahhal was astonished. He had not expected the emir to be able to amass this many ships and men. He knew the Gulf lacked in timber and skilled shipwrights to build large ships.

The vizier frowned and in a tone of surprise asked, 'How were you able to pull this off?'

'Ever since I received your letter, I sought people who could supply us with ships. I wrote to our allies in Basra and Zubarah, requesting men and ships, but I did not tell them why. They did not mind since I had promised to pay them in full.'

'Well done, Your Highness. Having this many men and ships will make our mission much simpler. We shall leave our camels, our horses, and some of our luggage with you and sail on the ships to Julfar. I hope its emir has also done his duty well.'

On the evening of the third day, with the high tide, the ships moved outside the bay and headed north, to circle around the Qatar Peninsula on the way to Julfar.

− 13 −

Tordesillas, Spain

THE GRAND PALACE WHERE the representatives of the kings of Spain and Portugal were meeting appeared quiet from the outside, after the commotion that accompanied the arriving delegates and their escorts. Only a few guards remained outside, carrying long pikes with steel axes at the end and wearing conical helmets. Some of the men guarded the internal and external gates, while others marched in synchronised steps around the courtyard.

The quiet outside the palace was misleading. Inside the great building, the main hall was abuzz with people conversing. The drone was suddenly interrupted by the sound of the chamberlain tapping the marble floor with his staff, announcing the arrival of the Pope's representative.

The cardinal entered carrying a long sceptre and wearing a mitre bearing a large cross in the middle. Two bishops followed in their distinctive cassocks. The mini-procession walked slowly in lockstep in the direction of a large table in the middle of the hall. A servant pulled up a chair at the head of the table for the cardinal to sit on. The cardinal remained standing until the servant finished, and then threw himself on the chair as though he had been waiting to rest his back and knees for a long while.

The cardinal took out a handkerchief from his pocket and wiped the sweat from his forehead and the sides of his face. He then set his eyes on the people in the hall and extended his hand in a subconscious way, expecting people to come and kiss it as was customary at every occasion he attended.

The delegates of the kingdoms of Spain and Portugal came forward and kissed his hand, and he gave them permission to sit. Then the escorts stepped in and placed rolls of paper and maps in front of each representative. One of the servants unrolled a map of the known world in front of the cardinal and placed paperweights at its corners. After the ritualistic preparations for the meeting were completed, an awkward silence descended on the hall. Everyone was waiting for the cardinal to inaugurate this historic meeting. The cardinal hemmed loudly before he said, 'Very well, gentlemen. This meeting has been a long time coming. We want to wrap it up as quickly as possible. It's hot today, and we don't want to spend the rest of the day in this room.'

The cardinal wiped his face again as he finished his sentence. The man was in his fifties but looked much older. He was fat and his laborious breathing sounded more like wheezing. Every move he made took exceptional effort that he did not want to make. His movements were excruciatingly slow and yet, somehow, they complemented his soft, effeminate voice.

The cardinal was notorious for his sloth, laggardness and corruption. He was in his post only because he was a nephew of Pope Alexander VI, who appointed his relatives to clerical positions to consolidate his power and influence the potentates of Europe. The Pope and his relatives had many enemies as a result, both in the Vatican and the royal courts of Christendom.

The cardinal was infamous for his love of money and women. He had fathered many bastards with his maids, concubines and even some noblewomen of Europe. He did not care much about concealing all this, since everyone needed his services, and he – naturally – collected a price in return, in any way he saw fit. Talk about the corruption of the clergy was a favourite topic for many, from the palaces of the rich all the way down to the taverns frequented by the commoners, who gossiped about the clerics when they became inebriated, and could no longer appreciate the seriousness of what they were saying.

The representative of Portugal spoke. 'I ask permission to speak first, Your Holiness.'

The cardinal nodded in approval.

'As you know, Your Holiness, the kingdom of Portugal has asked to discuss the previous agreement signed with the kingdom of Spain to divide the non-Christian world between us. We believe the previous treaty was unfair to Portugal, especially after *Senhor* Christopher Columbus discovered the New World, which Spain then laid claim to. These new lands are full of bounties that will make Spain a very rich nation. The New World is vast and almost limitless, and has many rivers, mountains and forests, and much gold. For Spain to have all that alone is a great injustice towards us. We must have our share of those treasures.'

The representative of Portugal fell silent. He had said everything he had to say and was now waiting for the cardinal to adjudicate on the dispute between the two kingdoms.

Like many others, the cardinal had heard of the New World, but like many others too, he was not aware of how big and rich it was. He knew that Spanish ships had brought back specimens of plants, animals and even humans but he was not quite sure how all of it would be divided.

The cardinal felt the discussion was going to drag on. He gave a long sigh, then took off his mitre and wiped his bald scalp with his handkerchief. He grabbed a pointing rod that was placed in front of him and aimed it at a number of small green islands to the west of Africa on the map. He said in his distinctive voice, 'I thought this meridian line passing through these islands demarcated the two kingdoms' lands, does it not?'

The Portuguese representative replied a little sharply, 'Keeping the demarcation line at that meridian would be unfair, Your Holiness. It is not right for the line to be kept there after Spain acquired so much new land to the west!'

The Spanish representative had tried to remain calm until this moment. 'You change your mind each time new lands are discovered. You have started harassing our ships headed west or returning from there. By what right do you search them and confiscate their cargoes?'

The Portuguese put his head on the headrest of his chair and then replied, 'We are exercising our rights in our ports. The riches Columbus stumbled upon in the New World will make you wealthy and powerful. It is not fair for us to be deprived of all that. If we wanted to stop him from leaving we could have. He sailed through our ports before he headed there, after all.'

The Spaniard could no longer tolerate the Portuguese representative's comments. Addressing the cardinal this time, he said, 'Your Holiness, we want to settle this matter once and for all. We no longer enjoy the freedom to trade and navigate the seas. The harassment of our ships by Portugal has gone too far.'

The cardinal tried to defuse the tension, but instead only made a fool of himself with his ignorance. 'I thought all these issues had been discussed before. I had the impression that I was only here to put the final touches on the agreement before it was signed. I want to know first, why did that madman – I forget his name – go there? Did he find the spices he was looking for? I have not seen any of those much-vaunted spices! All I saw was a bunch of filthy Indians and some strange beasts. If he had brought back a bag of spices it would have been much better than all of that.'

The cardinal's face flushed and he continued in a husky voice. 'I do not trust anyone who squanders money to sail into the unknown only to return with useless trinkets.' The papal representative raised his voice so that everyone could hear him. 'I don't understand how people go in those wooden boxes into the sea and call that discovery!' The cardinal let out a deep exhale after his diatribe. He then said, 'Let us return to the problem this man has created for us. What is his name?'

'Christopher Columbus, Your Holiness,' the Spaniard replied. 'No, he did not find the spices he went looking for. He thought there was another route to India that bypassed the Muslim lands, but he found another land instead of reaching India.'

'How long did it take him to get there?'

'Around thirty-six days. They were very difficult days for him.'

The cardinal gasped suddenly as if someone had punched him in his chest. 'What did you say? Thirty-six days at sea? This is madness! What did he find there besides trees, mountains and rivers?'

'He did not find anything of value, Your Holiness. He did not find spices or gold as he had expected.'

The Portuguese representative knew that his Spanish counterpart was trying to understate the riches Christopher Columbus had discovered and manipulate the cardinal into thinking the New World had no treasures to speak of.

The Portuguese representative rushed to correct the cardinal's information. 'Your Holiness, what the Spanish *senhor* is saying is simply not true. They have discovered gold in large quantities in those lands. It is even said that there are undiscovered cities there made entirely of gold. Their ships came loaded with all kinds of bounty such as furs, gold and silver.'

The Spanish representative took a deep breath before saying, 'Your Holiness, I have a mandate from the Catholic monarchs to end this dispute and make the decision that I deem to be in the best interest of the kingdom of Spain, but I want it to be a final and non-negotiable agreement.'

The cardinal turned to the Portuguese representative, and asked, 'Do you have the same kind of mandate?'

'Yes, Your Holiness. We also want to be done with this matter,' replied the Portuguese in a firm tone.

The cardinal leaned into his chair and waved the handkerchief in front of his face. 'Then tell us what your government wants.'

The Portuguese representative put his elbows on the table, looking directly at the cardinal. 'We want to move the meridian that passes through the Cape Verde islands by 370 leagues west.' The representative stood up, took the pointing rod in front of him, and traced an invisible line on the map. 'Here.'

The Spaniard turned his eyes to the map. He used a ruler to find the areas the new meridian passed through. Once he was

139

finished with his measurements, he turned to the cardinal and said, 'I do not understand the Portuguese request. The meridian passes through the open sea. I don't see anything worth discussing here. When the line is extended south, it comes out of the map we have in front of us. Is there something they know that they're not telling us?'

The cardinal began to feel dismayed. There was a lack of trust between the two sides, and clearly the matter was not going to be resolved as quickly as he had hoped. He said, with a tinge of weariness, 'Gentlemen, let's adjourn for an hour. Discuss with your advisers what you need to discuss, but let us settle it before nightfall for God's sake!'

The representatives dispersed. Each delegation went to a side hall to prepare for the next round. The air was full of anticipation. The treaty being discussed, according to pledges made by both the kings of Spain and Portugal, would be the last between the two sides. No modification or amendment would be possible in the future, and the successive kings would respect the treaty thereafter. The treaty would divide the entire world, with its riches, its people, its seas and resources, between the two great powers.

Everyone felt that the dispute between Spain and Portugal had far-reaching effects. The treaty would determine which power was the strongest, with strength being determined by the size of the wealth that would fall under the control of each side.

The Portuguese delegation entered its own private hall. One of the servants approached the head of the delegation and notified him that Afonso de Albuquerque wanted to meet him.

'When did he arrive?'

'A few minutes ago, *senhor*. He requested permission to enter.'

'Very well, you may go now.'

The head of the delegation turned to his closest aide and said, 'We must insist on our position, gentlemen. We shall not budge. We must not trust the cardinal. Though we have given him a lot of money to side with us during the negotiations, he also got money from the Spaniards, which is why he's trying to remain neutral. We also must not forget that the Pope is Spanish-born. He could side with them or give them information we don't know about. Who knows what happens behind closed doors? Lord knows how much I hate this sickening cardinal.'

Albuquerque entered the hall carrying a dossier in his hands. He walked to the representative and knelt in front of him in extreme reverence.

The representative extended his hand to shake Albuquerque's. 'Albuquerque, my friend, I have been eagerly awaiting you. When the king ordered me to handle negotiations with the Spaniards for this treaty I thought of you, but was told you were in North Africa fighting the Moors.'

Albuquerque bowed his head again. 'I am always in the service of the king and you, my lord. When I was told you were waiting for me in Tordesillas, I came here as quickly as I could.'

'Sit down, my friend,' the representative said, pointing to a chair nearby.

Albuquerque sat and placed the file on his lap but he did not let go of it, treating it like a precious treasure.

The representative spoke enthusiastically. 'As you know, we will redraw the areas we control in the world under the treaty we are discussing with the Spaniards. They control all the new territories Columbus discovered in the West. But for years now, we have been sending ships south to find a route to India around Africa. We are still spreading rumours that the distance to the far south of Africa is larger that anyone might think, and that it is impossible to reach the southernmost point of Africa. This rumour has circulated widely, and I think people believe it and in turn they have spread it further. The truth, of course, is different. We have succeeded in sending ships to the East secretly.'

Feeling a little warm, the representative took off his cloak. He continued, 'By acting this way, we want to achieve a number of things. We do not want others to learn that we succeeded in finding a route to India via Africa. We also want to acquire part of the territories Columbus discovered in the West. We also want to avoid war with Spain over the lands we discovered in western and southern Africa.'

Albuquerque was following everything the representative was saying very carefully. He felt that his future was to be part of this project of exploration and discovery. He looked straight into the representative's eyes – something that he had not dared to do before out of respect. Albuquerque had spent his entire life in the royal palace, but had always had a profound inferiority complex. He believed that he deserved to be treated like royalty; his father was an illegitimate son of a member of the royal family and had never been recognised. Albuquerque desperately wanted to be part of the king's inner circle, and he would never achieve that except by leading the expeditions personally sponsored by the king.

Albuquerque had a well-established reputation for being lowly, cruel and wicked. Beside his complexes, he had a face that did not inspire trust: he had a sharp nose between two bulgy eyes that were almost joined together, not unlike a somnolent crocodile's. He wore a heavy cloak over his shoulders to hide his emaciated body and his scrawny legs.

But Albuquerque had proven his loyalty to the palace, for whose sake he committed many atrocities in North Africa. Thanks to his knowledge, navigational experience and cruelty, he was the person chosen to lead the armada to India now that the first exploratory expeditions were completed.

Albuquerque pulled at his beard as he often did when he was nervous. He asked the representative, 'My lord, what is the purpose of moving the meridian at the Cape Verde islands to the west? I was told you requested this from the cardinal when I was waiting to be let in.'

The representative smiled before he said, 'There is a land to the south of the territories Columbus discovered. The meridian will cut through this land, which we want for ourselves. It is not reasonable that they take all those territories, and we come out with nothing.'

Albuquerque thought he had heard enough. He raised the document he was carrying and placed it in front of the representative, and said, 'My lord, this file contains very valuable information on the route to India. Our government sent spies to study the navigational routes and the regions our ships would have to pass through on the way there. One of our spies, whose name is Covilhã, was able to put it together after travelling across those areas for nearly a year. He delivered it to us through the rabbi of Alexandria. I believe we should set aside the dispute with Spain over the new lands and head east. It is richer than we thought. We have stumbled upon the source of spices. This is a treasure waiting for us to put our hands on!'

The delegate grabbed the guide and turned its pages one by one. He scanned the maps inside it and his face melted into an expression of glee.

Aden, Yemen

FROM ABOVE THE CITY wall, a soldier shouted at the top of his lungs, 'The Mamluk fleet is here! The Mamluk fleet is here!'

One of the people gathered behind the closed gate of the city shouted back, 'Are you certain? What flag are the ships flying?'

'I cannot make it out, sir. They are definitely not Frankish, there are no crosses on their sails!'

A person near the emir below put his hands to his mouth and shouted to the crowd, 'The emir orders you to wait. It may be a trick by the Portuguese. We will not open the gate until we verify the identity of the ships.'

The crowd waited for a long time behind the gate. Soon they grew restless and began to talk to one another loudly and grumble in a cacophonous whine. From time to time, they peeked at the front, where the emir was standing with his entourage. This made their wait a little more tolerable; the emir was also waiting, and though there was an umbrella over his head shielding him from the blazing sun, he was there with his people.

Emir Murjan al-Zaferi was mounted on a grizzled horse, surrounded by his viziers and advisers. Behind them stood a group of guards armed with pikes, swords and shields and with them, a group of unkempt soldiers of East African origin. They were bare-chested and barefoot, held short swords and wooden shields, and had hand-catapults wrapped around their heads. Behind them all stood the people of the city. Everyone was waiting for the soldier at the top of the wall to declare the identity of the ship so that the ceremony could begin.

As the sun rose higher in the sky, the remainder of the morning fog cleared. The soldier suddenly cried as loud as he could, 'They are Mamluk ships! I can see their flags. They are yellow and have crescents.'

The soldier had barely finished his sentence when people started cheering and shouting 'God is great!' The gate opened with a loud squeak. People hadn't seen it closed for many years, but they were wary of the Portuguese ships that had started to appear in these waters recently.

People surged out of the gate like water gushing from a small nozzle. They spread out across the port, carrying decorative palm fronds, flags and daggers, and waving coloured banners. They pranced as they walked in the direction of the city, which was now possessed by a rare festive atmosphere.

A boat was dropped from one of the ships, carrying a group of sailors. They rowed towards the shore where the emir was standing. The boat approached the wharf. One of the emir's bodyguards came and enquired about the commander of the fleet. Hussein identified himself and received an effusive welcome from the soldier, who then took him to Emir Murjan. The two men shook hands as if they were brothers who had been separated for years and were now finally reunited.

The people felt indescribably happy. The Mamluk fleet had come to support them and protect them from the Portuguese ships, which had started harassing these seas of late. People knew many horror stories about how the Portuguese tormented the unfortunate ships in their way and the souls travelling on them.

The situation with the Portuguese was still a mystery. Some saw Portuguese ships as ordinary commercial boats that paid handsomely for spices; others perceived them as aggressive entities that killed and maimed, and blocked trade routes. Those who believed the stories decided to barricade themselves behind city walls, including the people in Aden; other less-concerned cities welcomed the Portuguese as merchants. This continued for a long time even after the incident with the pilgrim ship *Maryam*, as more and more deadly encounters took place, affecting trade in the Red Sea and the Arabian Sea.

The air was filled with joy and happiness, and hopes that life would soon return to normal. The Mamluk ships were clearly carrying cannons and they almost matched the Portuguese ships in number. This would be enough to cast terror into the hearts of the Christian invaders and force them to depart from these waters, the people thought.

The convoy travelled in the direction of the emir's castle behind the wall. A group of men herding camels and sheep was waiting for them. As soon as the party dismounted in front of the castle, the men began to slaughter the animals at the guests' feet in a gesture of hospitality reserved for guests of high stature. The emir smiled when he saw the slaughtered animals' blood trickling through the sand. The soil beneath them, which otherwise swallowed everything in its path, seemed impervious to the blood that continued to flow in all directions, seeking out the path of least resistance, between the people's feet. When the sand refused to absorb it, it coagulated into a pool and changed colour, as though the blood had given up.

The emir ordered his vizier to distribute meat from the animals among poor and needy people, and then walked into his castle with his guests. Inside, they all sat on the floor, which was covered with rugs and pillows for their comfort. The windows of the hall were left open to let in the cool, fresh air from the sea. The servants brought fruits and refreshments. The commotion and excitement having now subsided, the emir struck up a conversation with Hussein.

'Our soldiers on the west coast alerted us of your arrival after you stopped in Mocha to re-supply. We have been waiting for you. Your presence is welcome news. The situation here has not been very good since the Portuguese appeared near our shores. Our trade has declined and we have become prisoners within the walls of Aden, behind a gate that we had almost never closed before.'

Hussein knew in detail what Yemen was going through. He knew about its crises, which had been made worse by the Portuguese arrival. Yemen was ruled by Sultan Amer al-Taheri, who was dealing with a rebellion led by Imam Sharaf al-Din Yahya. Recently, Sultan Amer was able to defeat his foe after he laid siege to Sana'a, and exiled the imam to Taiz where he placed him under house arrest.

The relentless civil war had drained Yemen's energy, claimed countless lives and created a rift in the sultanate. And the movement led by Imam Yahya advocating the doctrine of Zaidism* found many followers in northern Yemen, creating an undeclared dividing line between north and south.

148

Because of all these circumstances, Hussein did not expect much from Emir Murjan, the prince of Aden who owed his allegiance to Sultan Amer. But it was enough for the Mamluk fleet to feel it had a safe base at the mouth of the Red Sea to re-supply and repair its ships when needed.

Hussein replied to the emir's comment with a faint, diplomatic smile, and said, 'The pleasure is all mine, Your Highness. The trip from Jeddah was tiring. The entrance to the Red Sea as you must know is very dangerous. We had to re-supply in Mocha, and rested for a few days before we sailed south to Aden. Your generosity and hospitality have left us at a loss for words.'

Hussein was careful and did not want to divulge his precise plans. But the emir's questions forced him to disclose some information. Ultimately, Emir Murjan was a good ally and could be trusted and relied upon at this stage.

'What are your plans now, Hussein Pasha?'

Hussein reached for the glass of water in front of him and took a sip. The water was fragrant and sweet. Hussein did not know what had been added to it but he did not ask.

The emir noticed that the pasha liked the taste of the rose-water-flavoured drink, and ordered another to be brought for him. The pasha was pleased. 'Sultan al-Ghawri ordered me to fight and destroy the Portuguese fleet at sea. We're on our way to India. The sultans there have asked for our help to repel the Portuguese invasion of their country. We shall stay with you for a few days to rest and re-supply and then we will resume our journey.'

The pasha took another sip of water then continued. 'Your Highness, I want you to provide me with a guide who is familiar with the route to India. This is the first time our ships will be sailing to those parts. We are not very familiar with the route and its dangers.'

The emir raised both hands. 'Most certainly, Hussein Pasha. You are among your people now. We will give you everything you need to ensure your mission will be a success. As you can see, your presence here has brought joy and relief, rare sentiments these days. Consider all your wishes granted. You need only to ask.'

The emir, in an attempt to reassure Hussein further, added, 'Our ships travel often to India and China. We have skilled sailors and seasoned merchants who have settled in Java and the city of Zaitoun in China and other eastern cities. We have lost contact with them as the maritime routes have been cut off by the Portuguese. We live on trade in this city, Hussein Pasha, and if trade collapses, we collapse.'

Hussein Pasha did not understand what the emir meant. 'Where are those cities? Are they close to India?'

'No, they are very far east. You would need six months to get there. Zaitoun is almost at the far end of the world, and there is nothing beyond it except the magical land of Waq-Waq. What is strange is that Zaitoun, the city of olives, has no olives, and its people do not even know what olives are.'

'Then why is it called Zaitoun?' Hussein asked in astonishment.

'I think the Arab merchants gave it that name and it just stuck. The Chinese call it by another name, Guangzhou.'

The conversation between the two men went on for some time, branching into other matters, until food was served. Trays carrying meat and bread were distributed among the guests. The smell of barbecued food wafted through the hall. People gathered outside the castle and food was distributed among them too. No belly was left empty that day.

Suddenly, without warning, a Mamluk sailor cried, 'Long live Sultan al-Ghawri! May God grant him victory over his enemies!'

Anger flared among the Yemenis, who could not understand how the Mamluk sailor had the gall to pray for the Mamluk sultan when he was eating food provided by the sultan of Yemen. Some Yemeni soldiers tried to silence him, while others cried back, 'Long live the sultan of Yemen! It is he whom we must thank!'

Angry voices rose on both sides. It seemed that a crisis was about to break out, but Emir Murjan was able to contain it. He did not lose his smile throughout, though he could not hide his annoyance completely. Suddenly, Hussein Pasha cried vociferously in support of Sultan al-Ghawri, praying for victory for him against his enemies as well. Emir Murjan was taken aback by Hussein's behaviour. To him, it was not acceptable for anyone to eat his sultan's food and yet pray for another. Murjan wondered silently why Hussein had acted in this manner, and whether it was all a message meant for the emir.

Murjan decided not to speak his mind. He did not understand what had happened but seemed ready to accept any explanation that might be given to him.

After the food was cleared, a servant came carrying a large pot that gave off a strange, pleasant smell. He poured from the pot a black liquid in cups that he offered to all the guests present. The guests raised the cups to their noses and took a whiff of the drink, trying to identify it. For their part, the Yemenis sipped the drink slowly, enjoying its taste and smell, as they chatted with one another.

Hussein asked his host about the drink. Murjan replied, 'We call it coffee. Have you not tasted it before? Go on, try it.'

Hussein brought his cup close to his mouth and took a small nip. His face changed, his lips contracted and he frowned as though he had tasted something foul.

Emir Murjan laughed out loud. He then explained to his guest the characteristics of the drink, how its ingredients were extracted and how it was prepared. 'You will come to like it, Hussein Pasha. You just have to get used to it.'

In the evening, Hussein left his hosts and returned to his ship. He declined the emir's invitation to spend the night at his palace, preferring to be with his men. The small boats bringing supplies from the shore to the ships continued to shuttle back and forth throughout the night. The city's gates were open now, and celebrations in the port continued until the early hours of the morning.

The emir remained in his *majlis* that night too, celebrating with the people. Delegations of well-wishers came one after the other, until the receptions wound down and the *majlis* was finally empty. At that moment, one of those present approached the emir and asked to speak to him in private.

'What's the matter?' the emir asked. 'I noticed you were silent all day like you had something on your mind.'

'Yes, Your Highness. I have been waiting for everyone to leave to share my thoughts with you.'

After looking around to make sure no one else was listening, he continued, 'Your Highness, you have allowed the Mamluk fleet to dock at the port of Aden and celebrated its arrival. You have re-supplied it from the sultan's warehouses, and you will send with the Mamluk ships a guide to show them the route to India. However, allow me to remind you of what Hussein Pasha did in Jeddah. He enslaved its people and forced them to build its wall, and confiscated the possessions of the city's merchants.'

He paused for a moment to see what effect his revelations had on the emir, and then continued. 'I'm afraid he may try to control Aden and do the same things here.'

He felt that he now had the emir's full attention. 'My opinion, Your Highness, is that we should give their ships enough supplies to reach India but not make any other commitments. We must get rid of them as soon as possible, because if they overpower us, we will become their servants. They could take our money, or, at the very least, they could force us to pay tax to Sultan al-Ghawri!'

The emir recalled what Hussein had done at dinner. 'Why did you not alert me to this before they got here?'

'I had heard you give orders to honour them, show them hospitality and celebrate their arrival. I did not want to spoil that for you with my suspicions. But I believe it is not yet too late, and that you can still deal with the matter prudently. We just want them to leave as quickly as possible.'

'But what about the Portuguese?' the emir asked. 'What if they appear on our shores? Who will fight them if not the Mamluks?'

The man grinned, as though he had been anticipating this question. 'I heard what Hussein Pasha said, Your Highness. He said that he had orders to fight the Portuguese at sea, that he was going to India for this purpose.' He paused briefly. 'Let him do that, but not in our waters. Let him fight them there. The battles will weaken both sides, and our port, ships and money would be spared if neither Hussein Pasha occupies our land nor the Portuguese destroy our ships.'

After he uttered this sentence, he set his gaze on the emir, trying to divine what impact his words would have on him.

The emir remained silent. His eyes glistened and he started fiddling with the edge of the carpet. He finally said, 'I think you are right. Do not open the port for their ships if they return!'

– 15 –

The Arabian Gulf

T HE WIND WAS STILL, forcing the sailors to use oars to push their boats out of Salwa Bay and into the open sea, where the wind was more favourable. Once they detected an air stream, they lifted the oars. The ships proceeded north to circumnavigate the Qatar Peninsula en route to Julfar.

The Arabian flotilla did not remain anchored for long in Julfar. There were clear orders given to the men to stay on the ships. The ships were re-supplied quickly. Thirty more ships joined the fleet along with 600 men, and within two days the ships set off to Hormuz.

Salghur stood near the bow of the command ship, holding on to the mast and looking in the direction of the ship's sailing path. He filled his lungs with fresh sea air, which he had long missed. None of the sailors on the ship knew this man to whom Bin Rahhal showed great respect, why he was the first to be served with food and water, and why his companions made sure all his requests were granted. But the sailors were not the inquisitive type, and did not ask about or care to find out his identity, though they did gossip about him after dark when they knew no one was listening.

Two days later, Bin Rahhal felt they were about to reach the eastern coast of Jesm island. It was night time, and he decided to meet with Salghur. He lit a lamp and laid out a map of the Gulf containing the locations of the islands there and an approximate layout of the port of Hormuz.

Bin Rahhal laughed and said, 'Soon I won't be the only one to address you as "Your Majesty", because in a few hours, you will officially be king again.'

Salghur replied with a smile. 'I am very eager to hear that title again. I would have forgotten it had you not reminded me from time to time.' His face assumed a more serious expression, as he glanced at the map in front of him. 'Let me brief you on some things you need to know before we get to Hormuz. The port is guarded by about 2,000 guards, including 500 Persian archers. Their job is to protect the two ports day and night. Around forty oared galleys are stationed in the eastern port and can move even when the wind is calm. The western port is for smaller ships that sail within the Gulf or to Hormuz's possessions in Oman.'

Salghur lifted his gaze and looked in Bin Rahhal's eyes before continuing. 'There is a lighthouse at the northernmost point of the island. Soldiers light a fire at the top of the structure after sundown. The fire is not put out until sunrise the following morning. It illuminates a large area around the two ports and guides ships into harbour. We must be very careful not to be spotted by its light at night.

'There are around 3,000 fighters stationed around the island, some guarding the water reservoirs in the south, some guarding the king's palace, and others deployed along the coast opposite the Persian mainland near the lighthouse. These men are loyal to the king no matter who the king is. They will keep fighting until they feel the king is defeated, and then they will serve the new king. The element of surprise is our best weapon. We are greatly outnumbered, but they are far from the king's palace, which could give us an advantage.'

Salghur's face gleamed in the torchlight. There was tension in his voice and sweat glistened on his forehead. For him, these were crucial moments that could either put him back on the throne or sentence him to death after his eyes had been gouged out – the favourite punishment exacted by the kings of Hormuz against their rivals.

Bin Rahhal read it all in Salghur's face and tone. He summoned his commanders from the other ships, and moments later the ships converged and the commanders jumped into Bin Rahhal's boat. He was waiting for them while sipping the date juice he so loved.

They all gathered around the map laid on the deck floor. Bin Rahhal looked them in the eyes one by one to make sure he had their full attention before he spoke. 'Listen to my every word. The hours ahead will be decisive. We will make our landing at dawn tomorrow. Until then, I want our ships to stick together as closely as possible so we can make a quick, combined and synchronised landing. I don't want to see any fires lit after sunset tomorrow.

'The crescent will appear tomorrow night. When the moon is midway in the sky, we will go to the beach and break up into two parties. The ships that came from Salwa will go to the eastern port. Those that came from Julfar will go to the western port. As soon as the ships reach their targets, we will disembark and seize the ports. I will choose one hundred fighters whose mission it will be to storm the palace. We expect resistance from the palace guards, so this group will hold them off until reinforcements arrive from the ports.'

He looked at the faces of his commanders again to make sure they were listening, and then resumed, 'The group that will take the eastern port must put out the lighthouse beacon to prevent any other ships from docking, until we are fully in control of the island.' Bin Rahhal grabbed his sword to drive his point home. 'Kill anyone who resists you. You must be quick. We won't have much time. The element of surprise will be our only weapon, but without haste there will be no surprise.'

On the following day, ghostly shapes appeared on the horizon far from the island, approaching ominously. No one saw the ships, and no one was expecting them. Before dawn, they moved stealthily towards their targets until they reached the harbour.

One guard finally spotted them, appearing to him like beasts that had just surfaced from the depths of the sea. 'It's a raid! It's a raid! To arms!'

The ships rammed the wharf with great force. The soldiers jumped off shouting battle cries but resistance was not as fierce as they had expected. Everyone, including the guards, had been asleep. Those who did try to resist were soon silenced by piercing spears thrust at them from the darkness.

Bin Rahhal's men ran in all directions. They put out the fire at the lighthouse, plunging the two ports into pitch darkness. As the fighting moved into the main gate of the king's palace, people started to wake up as if from a dream; all Hormuzis felt something strange was afoot. Some came out into the streets in their sleeping clothes trying to find out what was going on. They heard sporadic screams from different directions in the city. When they noticed there was no fire lit at the lighthouse, they decided the problem must have something to do with the port; they lost interest and many returned to bed.

The fighting between the attackers and the defenders in front of the palace gate grew fiercer. Reinforcements came quickly for both sides as the battle intensified. People heard the fighting and saw the fires the attackers had started at the main gate of the palace. Rumours spread like wildfire: some thought the Safavids were invading the city, some thought the king's brothers were staging a coup against him. Many people decided on account of these rumours to barricade themselves and their families into their homes, take their swords out and sit waiting for the dust to settle.

By sunrise, everything was clear. The palace gate had been burned down and there was now a big gap in its place. Corpses sprawled in the front yard. The port was deserted, as merchants kept their distance from the shore fearing their ships would be burned or seized. As people started taking stock of what had happened in the latter hours of the night, life began to gradually return to the city. If the king was gone a new one would soon replace him; the Hormuzis did not care much for such events, which they were used to by now.

Inside the palace, Bin Rahhal sat in the grand *majlis*. He had a superficial knife wound on one of his arms and a physician was treating him with herbs and ointments; the two men were surrounded by a group of Bin Rahhal's soldiers and aides.

An exuberant Salghur was sitting on the throne which had been his father's throne before him, in the middle of the *majlis*. At the top of its headrest a beautifully inscribed Quranic verse read: *Authority belongs to none but God*. Each armrest of the throne was decorated with the face of a lion, with large agate stones placed in its open jaws. All of the late king's sons had sat on this throne, and now it was Salghur's turn to sit on it again.

While the king sat on the throne, Bin Rahhal began running the kingdom from where he was sitting, on the floor. Bin Rahhal did not stop issuing orders. The physician finished bandaging him, and lowered his arm slowly. He looked at the dressing and then asked Salghur, 'Where is Vays now?'

'I think he's hiding somewhere in the palace,' Salghur replied with feigned nonchalance. 'He has nowhere else to go. If he is not here then he could be with the Persian brigade he hired to protect him. Have you heard anything? He could cause us some trouble if we don't take care of him.'

Bin Rahhal was still examining his bandages. 'Our soldiers had the Persians surrounded. They surrendered and asked to be returned to the Persian mainland. They have been taken care of, but your brother was definitely not with them.' Bin Rahhal cried out to the guards, 'Look for Vays now, quickly. I think he is in the palace. I don't want him to escape.'

The vizier took his sword and joined the search.

The soldiers fanned out across the palace, moving furniture and looking for secret hiding places. They would put a few men to guard the entrance of a room or a hall, and proceed to search it, before they moved to the next place, each time tapping the floors and the walls with their swords, looking for a secret door.

They reached a staircase leading to an upper room that the king used as his *majlis* in the summer. They found Vays hiding there, behind a pile of discarded chairs, trembling in fear.

A few minutes later, Vays was brought before Bin Rahhal. Salghur watched from his throne, a vengeful smile crossing his face. Bin Rahhal did not want the charade to last too long, and, addressing Vays, said, 'We will not carry out the sentence usually given to treasonous Hormuzi kings. We will not gouge out your eyes and throw you in a dungeon until you rot and die. We shall exile you to India where you may take some of your servants. King Salghur will send you a monthly salary so you can live in dignity, providing that you pledge never to return here.'

The guards pulled Shah Vays by his arm to carry out the sentence. Bin Rahhal turned to Salghur, and in an attempt to pre-empt any protest by the restored king, said, 'I think you should have a grand ceremony for your coronation. Let people near and far know you have returned. You must take pledges of allegiance from those around you.' Bin Rahhal gave Salghur a smile that the new king understood very well. 'Though I think oaths of allegiance are now meaningless formalities.'

Salghur was not pleased with the quick sentence Bin Rahhal had handed to his brother. In his view, it was too lenient and not commensurate with his brother's betrayal. But he felt that Bin Rahhal was not going to let him dispute his decision.

Bin Rahhal removed his turban and wiped the sweat off his forehead. He then ordered his commanders to quickly fetch *Khawaja* Attar. Attar was going to be the actual ruler of the island, and he had to know what had happened and to whom the credit should go for restoring Salghur to his throne.

The servants in Attar's house heard knocking on the door. When they opened it they saw a group of palace guards accompanied by masked Arab soldiers. The servant who opened the door was uncertain of what had happened in the king's palace, but the news that came from the streets was that there had been a coup against Vays staged by one of his brothers, and that there was fierce fighting in the palace with the outcome not yet known.

The shaken servant went to Attar. His daughter, Halima, was sitting next to him. 'My lord, there are soldiers outside, from the king's guard I think. They have with them a group of foreign Arab soldiers that I have never seen before.'

The servant paused and gulped, reluctant to continue. 'They are asking for you, my lord.'

Lisbon, Portugal

THE WEATHER IN LISBON was misty and overcast. Rain droplets were suspended in the air, seemingly unsure of whether to fall or remain afloat, though sooner or later they made their way onto people's faces and bodies. Everything was damp: clothes, shoes and hats, and even the decorative flags were wet and heavy and flapped with great effort. Making matters worse, a north wind blew from time to time, carrying more drizzle and dankness. There were no dry spots; the wind carried the droplets everywhere, under the tents and between the clothes, as though deliberately chasing those trying to shelter themselves from the wetness.

A crowd gathered to bid farewell to Albuquerque's fleet, which was scheduled to set sail that day. Clammy malodorous bodies rubbed against one another as they tried to see the king, who was expected to come to the port for the send-off of his large armada bound for India.

It was the largest armada the king had ever sent to the East. The wealthiest people in Europe had helped build it, convinced the return on investment would be many times more than the capital they had pledged, when Portugal finally seized the source of spices and secured a monopoly over this precious commodity. The fleet's mission was to raise the king's banner on all territories made his possession under the Treaty of Tordesillas. The financing and the costly construction of the armada were done in secrecy, but that phase was now completed, and everyone was eager to get their share of the coveted treasures of the orient.

There were sixteen caravels* moored in the port. Their sides were bumping against the wharf, making a jarring noise. The caravels were like beasts in captivity waiting to be unleashed on their prey, but the thick mooring ropes kept them restrained for now. The seagulls hovering above could not tell the ships apart from the fishing boats. They screeched from the top of the masts and flew in circles around them, expecting food that would never come. Unlike the waves moving nervously underneath the ships, rocking them in a brisk and ungraceful fashion, the wind was mostly idle at that moment, blowing only in random gusts.

The caravels had proven their reliability and strength in the open sea. They had deeper hulls and structures that could accommodate a larger crew and more cargo and guns. Numerous modifications had been made to the new models, based on feedback from previous expeditions. The new caravels were nearly perfect, needing no additions or modifications. They were the pride of the Portuguese nation that made them, as Portuguese sailors boasted. The caravels were built from only the best timber. Their guns were mounted over wheeled frames to absorb recoil when firing. The new ships also had more room for water, gunpowder and cannonballs, making their size, strength and firepower second to none.

On the wharf, a special throne was brought for the king, and alongside it chairs for the princes, noblemen and commanders. Torches were lit around them, and the guards lined up in a ceremonial formation. Conjurers entertained the crowd before the king and his entourage arrived, but the heavy stench of dampness made worse by the wet climate continued to weigh on everybody's mood, and the incense burners failed to mask it.

After a long wait, the coaches carrying dignitaries began to enter the wharf area. People craned their necks to see them, the clothes they were wearing and how many servants had come with them; most folk in Lisbon lived in extreme poverty and anything that showed wealth and affluence attracted them like moths to a flame.

The guards started beating back the crowds with small whips to keep them away from the royal tent, as though they were disease-carrying pests. From time to time, people's heads turned in the direction of a commotion or a scream, but their curiosity soon died away. The sound of whips cracking and people screaming had become a familiar part of public events such as this one. People hardly expected any occasion to proceed without this, as they had become accustomed to humiliation, which they rarely questioned.

The king's wagon arrived, pulled by four white horses. When people spotted it coming from afar, they started cheering and chanting for the king. Whip strikes increased in frequency, as the crowds pushed against the soldiers. When the whips could no longer do the job, the soldiers carried their spears horizontally with both hands and used them to push the crowds back again.

Sweat mixed with the damp air, and the curses and insults on both sides with their shouts and screams, until trumpets blared announcing the arrival of the royal cavalcade.

The pandemonium stopped and both the soldiers and the crowds automatically turned to the king's coach. The king alighted and raised his right hand announcing his presence. A strange silence descended and everyone was suddenly calm as if by magic, save for a few murmurs; the stench still lingered. In the minds of the people, the king represented absolute authority, beginning with his sacred religious function and not ending with his ability to take people's lives without convincing or comprehensible reasons. He represented God's will on Earth, and he had to be accepted, despite the flaws, cruelty and bloodlust.

A military band started playing funerary music. A group of sailors emerged from the edge of the wharf. They wore a coarse, woollen habit-like garment that was nothing more than a rectangular cloth with a hole cut for the head and tied at the waist with a thick rope. Their legs and arms were bare. They were made to look deliberately pitiful to emphasise their dedication to their cause and mission. Each sailor carried a large candle with both hands. Albuquerque led them at the front. He wore a long beard that he had sworn never to trim until he killed all Mohammedans and controlled the spice trade.

The procession stopped before the king. They all kneeled like worshippers at an altar, and swore an oath of loyalty to him in a loud voice. After taking permission from the king, Albuquerque stood and made a speech.

'Your Majesty, these are your loyal soldiers. They have volunteered to go to the ends of the Earth to rid the world of the Mohammedan heretics. Our goal is to spread Christianity on the shores that we shall conquer. We will raise our crosses there and rule in your name. Before this expedition, ships were sent to explore, but we will go there to defend the Holy Cross. I ask you, Your Majesty, to allow your humble servants to set sail so that we may carry out the duties you have entrusted us with.'

Having finished his speech amid enthusiastic applause from the crowd, a tearful Albuquerque kneeled before the king and hugged, then kissed, his feet. A saintly atmosphere descended on the place, and people cried with Albuquerque, chanting religious slogans praising the king and the sacred mission he had personally organised. From that moment onwards, Portugal would enter an era of great conquests.

Albuquerque was keen to look like a figure from the Bible. He too wore austere robes that were filthy and covered in mud and his speech asking for permission to spread Christianity among the heretics emulated the way Christ's disciples asked Jesus to travel to the corners of the Earth to spread the faith. Albuquerque had designed this entire spectacle for only one purpose: to show that he had a sacred mission that the king and his subjects needed to support to the fullest extent.

The king looked pleased with Albuquerque and ordered him to stand. Albuquerque stood up and joined his hands to his chest; his tears, which now merged with the falling rain, wetting his beard.

The king tried to publicly show his gratitude for Albuquerque's efforts and for the campaign he was going to lead. He said in a loud, authoritative voice, 'I have given orders to the treasury to pay your wage and the wages of your officers and crewmen a year in advance. It will be ensured that you do not have any shortage of food on your journey. Each man shall have at sea the same meals he would have on shore. You have a difficult mission ahead: to spread Christianity across

God's Earth and join forces with Prester John to decimate every other religion!'

As the king finished his speech, Albuquerque collapsed dramatically on the floor, and hugged the king's feet again. He swore not to return until victory was achieved in the king's name in the East, vowing to gladly submit his neck to the king's sword should he fail.

Some of the noblemen there were disgusted by Albuquerque's theatrics before the king. They had never seen anyone behave this way before, and hoped this would not set a precedent for how they should show their loyalty to the king. They saw how pleased the king was with the contrived grovelling.

Horns blared from the ships announcing the official start of the military expedition. Albuquerque stood back up and gave a special signal to the ship's sailors. The mainsail of the flagship, the *São Gabriel*, dropped, revealing a large red cross. Just then, a sudden gust of wind hit the sail and thrust the ship forward, but the thick mooring rope prevented it from moving, which caused a violent jolt to push one of the sailors from the top of the mast onto the deck below. It was like a divine sign that the mission had been accepted and that this was its first victim.

Albuquerque felt that he had to take advantage of this incident. This was not a time for bad omens and death, he thought, must be seen as proof of the holiness of his armada. Pointing at the sailor's corpse, Albuquerque cried loudly, 'It is the Holy Sail, Your Majesty, the Holy Sail that will sail East when you give your order. Our men will die for their cross and their king. God has put us on Earth for this mission and he will take our souls for this mission. We offer our lives for the king and the cross and this fallen man is the first martyr of our noble undertaking!'

The king and his entourage crossed themselves simultaneously. The crowd saw this as a sign that they should start shouting, chanting and crying. People fell to their knees, took off their hats and scarves and recited prayers for the king and his sailors. The priests there took advantage of this sweeping religious sentiment to collect donations as they walked around carrying thuribles that burned incense to bless the crowd. Everyone felt they were the Lord's soldiers, sent to rid the world of evil and heresy.

After the commotion subsided, the king rose from his seat and walked to his coach. Albuquerque followed him and knelt one more time by its side in an exaggerated gesture of loyalty, as though he enjoyed humiliating himself.

After the king left, Albuquerque summoned his men and proceeded to carry out the final inspection.

An officer stepped forward and stood alert before Albuquerque, who looked almost comical in his strange garments, which were now soaking wet. His tousled hair covered parts of his face, and water was dripping from the pointed tip of his beard.

Albuquerque had been raised in the royal palace with his father. The king had chosen him to lead the armada thanks to certain traits he had discovered in him: Albuquerque was an odd man. He was utterly convinced of the existence of Prester John and believed he was expecting the Portuguese. The king shared this strange obsession with him.

Albuquerque was known for his fondness of the colour black. Everything he wore from head to toe was black, as though he was permanently in mourning until such time as the Earth was cleansed of heretics, and only his fellow Catholics were left alive. He wore a stiletto around his waist, and his beard was so long that it almost reached the handle of his dagger.

His deputy began reading a report he had prepared earlier. 'Captain, we have supplied the ships with enough food and water for three years. We have all the soldiers, equipment and munitions we need, and African guides and interpreters who are fluent in Arabic. We have also brought a group of convicted criminals whom we will use as scouts. The previous expeditions erected many crosses along the coasts they explored. Our men will never feel cut off, because the Lord will be with them at all times. They were selected very carefully. They are all experienced seafarers, have strong bodies and they can handle weapons very skilfully. They are the elite of our navy's soldiers.'

The officer looked at the sailors who were still dressed in their dirty clothes. Their appearance suggested they were fierce and violent men. Every man had scars on his face or head. They had beefy bodies and seemed like they were the kind of men who could kill with a smile.

The officer looked at the wet parchment in his hands and continued. 'The flagship carries twenty guns. They are enough to set alight every castle and put down any resistance. We only await your signal to set off, commander.'

Albuquerque looked behind him and saw his aide Miguel Ferreira carrying Covilhã's report. The file would guide the entire expedition. The conquistador felt reassured that the armada was ready, and that all that was left was for him to give the order. He signalled to his deputy to do so, and the officer bellowed, 'To your ships! Take your positions!'

The sails were unfurled slowly and cumbersomely. They were also wet, but the gusts that were still blowing helped drop them faster and fill them, pushing what water was left in them off and onto the sailors below. The sails then firmed up and arched, overwhelmed by the north wind.

The ships left the port of Lisbon pushed by heavy, moist winds. Flocks of sea birds followed them, still hoping to get fed.

Albuquerque entered his cabin to get changed. Minutes later, he emerged wearing his favourite black garments. Stroking his beard, he called out for his secretary Miguel, who came running, still clutching Covilhã's report.

Miguel was a short man. He had a broad jaw and his nose was deformed from an old battle wound. He had served with Albuquerque in North Africa and fought with him in many battles. He had been taken prisoner for many years, during which he was able to learn Arabic. After a prisoner swap, he returned to his country a poor and destitute man with a grudge against the king and the nobility. Miguel was greatly pleased when he learned that Albuquerque would be leading the new armada, and asked to accompany him. Albuquerque, in turn, was pleased to have such a person in his crew, because people like Miguel did not hesitate to do anything, no matter how base and wicked. Albuquerque liked that about him.

'Have you taken a look at the file, Miguel?'

'Not yet, my lord. I do nothing without your permission.'

Albuquerque's face remained as gloomy as always. He did not stop stroking his beard. 'You do everything without permission, Miguel. Go and read it because I want to hear your opinion when we get close to our destination.'

Miguel perused the file carefully for several days after that, trying to memorise every sentence and every line. By sunrise on the fourth day, he murmured to himself, 'I hope everything this Jew has written is true! If it is, blood will mix with spice, and Albuquerque will love nothing more than to taste the mixture!'

He laughed out loud, imagining Albuquerque savouring this gruesome combination.

– 17 –

The Arabian Sea

HUSSEIN SAILED WITH HIS fleet from Aden to the east. His Yemeni guide told him the journey would take a month. This was not particularly long for him and his crew, but Hussein prayed he would not encounter the Portuguese en route. There were no friendly ports where he could drop anchor and re-supply or repair his ships after Aden. He was not known in the ports along the way and they could well decline him entry, especially when they realised that his ships were not merchant vessels. Any problem along the way, Hussein thought, was going to seriously affect the fate of his campaign.

Hussein did not want to share his concerns with his officers and crew, and kept it all to himself. A few days after setting off, as he paced the main deck of his ship, he saw the Yemeni guide standing and looking in the direction of the north. He came and stood next to him.

The guide felt the pasha's presence. 'To the north of here is the Gulf, Hussein Pasha. We have received reports that the Ottomans have reached the area. It is rumoured that a contingent of musketeers has been dispatched by the sharif of Mecca to train the soldiers of his brother-in-law, the Jabrid ruler in Al-Ahsa. I would reckon the musketeers travelled there from Basra, as this would be easier than crossing the Arabian desert.

The *bunduqiya* muskets they carry are strange weapons, Pasha! They are faster and deadlier than the bow and arrow and have a longer range.'

He continued, and his voice took on a regretful tone. 'We have some muskets in Yemen brought by merchants, but they are extremely rare and very expensive. We also have some cannons that the sultan purchased from India with some cannonballs but they have started to rust. We don't know how to maintain them. Someone said we should coat them with fish oil from time to time, and I saw some soldiers doing that as we left the port. These cannons could be our last chance to defend Aden if the Portuguese were to stage a surprise invasion.'

The guide lifted his gaze to the sky, and said in the tone of someone predicting the weather, 'If I were a Portuguese commander, I would try to take three ports in particular at the mouths of the Gulf and the Red Sea.'

'Which ports do you mean?'

'Hormuz, Qalhat and Aden. Truth be told, Hussein Pasha, I put my hand on my heart each time I hear the Portuguese have appeared somewhere. They most certainly know what we know, and they will come at us with all their muskets and cannons.'

Hussein looked to the north. He could not see anything except an infinite blue horizon stretching all the way to where the sea met the sky.

The guide kept his eyes focused on the horizon as if he could see something Hussein could not.

'Tell me more,' Hussein said.

'When the wind is favourable, a sailing ship can cross the Gulf from south to north in four days or less, and from east to west in two days or less. It is really like a small lake, Hussein Pasha.'

Hussein checked the horizon again, as though he started to see something. He chose his words carefully, keen to get as much information out of this man as possible. He asked, 'And which are the most important ports in the Gulf?'

'There are many, of different sizes. The most important port is Hormuz on the eastern approach of the Gulf, followed by Siraf, and then Basra in the northernmost part of the Gulf. On the west coast, the key ports are Bahrain, Al-Uqair, then Oman, Sohar, Muscat and Qalhat along the western approaches.'

Hussein had grabbed a rope and latched on to it to relieve the pressure on his leg, which was starting to ache. He was still looking to the north. 'Who are the kings ruling those parts?'

'The strongest kingdom is Hormuz. It is a small island a few thousand cubits away from the Persian mainland, and about two days' journey from here. A powerful king ruled Hormuz but he died recently. His sons are still fighting over who should succeed him. This kingdom was able to conquer most ports on the western coast, whose sultans and emirs continue to pay tributes to Hormuz to this day.'

The guide spat into the sea before he continued. 'It is a rich, well-governed kingdom. The Hormuzis have many galleys of different classes, and do not rely on the wind alone to sail. They can quickly deploy a large number of soldiers in any port they want, and it is said that they have around 5,000 well-armed soldiers. They also have access to mercenaries from all nearby kingdoms. They have enough money to pay for anything they want to do, including war.'

The guide tapped on the ship's wood unconsciously. 'The emirs who rule the coasts of Oman mostly belong to the ruling family in Hormuz or those who are related to it by marriage. But over time, they started serving their own interests, though they still regularly pay their annual taxes to the king of Hormuz.'

Hussein pulled the tail of his turban from behind his neck and used it to dry the sweat from his face. 'You had mentioned something about a Jabrid sultan. Who is he?'

'He is the most powerful sultan in the western Gulf. He lives in Hajr, or as people call it today, Al-Ahsa. He sometimes sojourns in Bahrain. The sultan owns a vast swathe of land extending from the desert south of Basra all the way to Dhofar. His kingdom encompasses all of Najd, and he is married to the daughter of the sharif of Hejaz. We heard his army comprises 30,000 horsemen, camel cavaliers and infantrymen, but he has no navy to speak of. He is a wealthy sultan, or so I've heard. Some of his soldiers live in the Omani hinterland, and we have heard that he sends his soldiers to assist the emirs of the coast whenever they request it.'

The guide paused. 'It is rumoured that the Jabrid sultan wants to have a port of his own on the Omani coast, but he does not want to clash with the king of Hormuz.'

Hussein wanted to get additional information from someone who had first-hand knowledge of the area. 'Have you visited any of these ports?'

'Yes, Hussein Pasha. I have visited Hormuz, Oman, Bahrain and, of course, Sohar.' The guide paused again, then said, 'The ships that come from India and China must stop in Hormuz before continuing to any other destination. The ships coming from Zanzibar, Mombasa or even Sofala and other faraway ports must re-supply in Sohar. These ports are familiar to all sailors and travellers in this region. Most ships entering the Gulf are bound for Basra ultimately, where they can sell their cargoes at reasonable profits. From that entrepôt, goods are taken via the river to Baghdad, and from there, to Aleppo, where merchants can make even larger profits. However, this route has been cut off as the Safavids recently invaded Baghdad.'

Hussein's body stiffened, as though he had felt a sharp pain in his back. He pointed to the east and said, 'We will get to India within twenty days, as you said. Do you know which port we should call at there?'

The guide turned to the east too. He said, 'India is a very big place, its coast almost endless. Some local rulers are hostile to Muslims. We will drop anchor at Calicut. The Zamorin, a Hindu king who wants to open up his kingdom to trade, rules the city. In Calicut you will find many Arabs who live there permanently, and you will see Frankish and Chinese merchants. It is a wonderful kingdom. I truly love that country. Everything there is beautiful: the port, the mountains, the plants, the markets and, of course, the spices.'

The guide felt drops of sweat trickling from his forehead. He passed his thumb over his brows and flicked the sweat down onto the ship's deck. 'All the coastal cities from India to Sofala in East Africa depend on the spice trade, as you know. It is a source of livelihood for many people, and the force that drives ships on the seas. I think you rely on this trade in Egypt, too, correct?'

Hussein nodded. He remembered how the port of Alexandria once teemed with merchants and ships, and consignments of spices ready to be exported to Genoa. But he did not want to talk to the guide about the problems the sultanate of Egypt was facing and the conflicts between the Mamluk amirs. 'Indeed, honourable guide. We receive the best and the largest consignments of goods from India, which we then re-export.'

The wind remained favourable for the remaining days. Although the climate was hot and humid, the breeze did not subside and was generous enough to fill the ships' sails and drive them closer to their destination.

During that time, Hussein personally oversaw the training of his soldiers, to prepare them for every eventuality. He would rouse them unexpectedly, telling them Portuguese ships were attacking, only for them to discover it was a drill to test their readiness. They hated the surprise exercises and the harsh training. But they also knew that this was the price they had to pay if they wanted to achieve victory against the fierce enemy scouring the surrounding seas.

Days later, beautiful green mountains appeared on the horizon. The sea became extraordinarily quiet, though they spotted other ships around them now.

The humidity in the air was stifling. As the fleet approached the port, a small boat carrying a few men came out from the shore and reached the command ship. The men spoke with the guide for a few minutes, then left.

Hussein asked the guide who they were. 'They are from the king's guard, Pasha. It is a normal procedure for them to enquire about the ships that arrive, especially those that do not appear to be merchant vessels. I told them you are the admiral and the ruler of Jeddah, and that you were sent by the sultan of Egypt to meet the king. They asked us to drop anchor and wait until they return.'

Hussein had never met an Indian king before. To him, India was a mysterious place surrounded by myths, where fact often mixed with fiction. He did not know how to conduct himself in the king's presence, but he carried a letter and lavish gifts from Sultan al-Ghawri. He meant to ask him for help against the Portuguese.

Several hours later, a boat bedecked in gilded and colourful banners came, carrying someone who was clearly an important member of the royal court. As the boat stopped near the Egyptian flagship, one of its crew cried out in clear Arabic, 'Where is the messenger of the Great Sultan of Egypt?'

Hussein was surprised. He stuck his head out from the top deck and saw the boat. The man sitting in the middle caught his attention immediately. He wore gilded robes and a turban the likes of which Hussein had never seen before; it was flat in the front and rounded in the back.

Hussein replied, 'I am the messenger.'

The man responded in the same tone. 'The Zamorin is waiting for you. I have with me on the boat Qasimul Haq, the Zamorin's most senior adviser. We ask that you honour us and return with us. We shall escort you safely to the palace.'

A rope ladder dropped from the ship, and the sailors on the boat grabbed it and pulled it. Hussein climbed down the ladder to the boat. Qasimul Haq bowed down to him and invited him to sit on a silk cushion next to him. Hussein was dressed in his best Mamluk uniform and was accompanied by three of his lieutenants.

The boat began to move away from the flagship. Hussein turned to Qasimul Haq and asked, 'Do you speak Arabic then?'

'Yes, Pasha. I learned Arabic when I was young. I also lived in Mecca for a few years. I performed the Hajj then decided to stay to learn more about the faith and the Arabic language. Beautiful times.'

Hussein noticed that Qasimul Haq's accent was not the same accent he had heard from on board his ship. 'Who was it that spoke to us before?'

Qasimul Haq turned to one of the men sitting in the back, and then returned his gaze to Hussein. 'That was Si* al-Tayeb here. He came from Tunisia several years ago to trade, but he liked the country and decided to stay. He's an interpreter at the palace. He is fluent in Arabic and other languages, including Castilian and Persian.'

Hussein smiled at Si al-Tayeb, who wore Indian garments similar to those worn by Qasimul Haq, though his skin was fairer than the others. 'Have you come all the way from Tunisia to work here?'

'That is correct, Pasha. I went to Egypt for several months, enquiring about the spice trade, before I decided to have a go at it myself. My goal was to buy spices from Alexandria and then resell them, but the greedy Venetians had signed an agreement with the sultan to monopolise the purchase of all spices from Egyptian ports and sell them in Europe. I had no choice but to come here, to buy them from the source.'

Si al-Tayeb took his eyes off Hussein and adjusted his turban before he continued. 'My father is an Andalusian from Cordoba, and my mother is Spanish. My family was exiled to Tunisia, which is where I was born. My parents spoke Arabic and Castilian at home so I became fluent in both languages. When I came to this country as a young man, I decided to live in it, and married the daughter of Qasimul Haq and settled here.'

Hussein turned to Qasimul Haq, and found him wearing a weak smile he could not quite decipher.

The boat arrived at the port, where a large welcoming party escorted by a contingent of guards greeted it. As soon as they stepped foot on the shore, two young men came and placed a garland around Hussein's neck and did the same with the rest of the delegation. Then they offered them gilded pots containing fragrant water, which they drank. A woman painted a red vertical line on their foreheads as a sign of hospitality and respect.

Two groups of servants made their way between the crowd, carrying palanquins, each holding a small chair surrounded by silk curtains, and a roof above it protecting it from the sun.

Hussein sat on one and Qasimul Haq on the other. The procession then moved slowly towards the palace.

– 18 –

Hormuz

W HEN HALIMA SAW FEAR on her father's face, she said in a firm voice, 'I will come with you.'

Attar shook his head in opposition. 'No, you must not come with me. We don't know who these people are and what is happening in the palace!'

The Hormuzi vizier frowned and looked to the floor. He spoke loudly and almost mechanically. 'What if Vays learns of my collaboration with Salghur? Are those Arabs Jabrid soldiers or are they mercenaries? Hormuz has been overrun with the mercenaries that the rival princes hire. Last night was chaos. All we know is that people saw a large number of Arab soldiers on the island and corpses outside the palace gate.'

Halima interrupted him sharply. 'I will go with you, Father. You can't stop me. I want to be with you no matter what happens.'

She raised a scarf that was draped on her shoulder and covered her head with it, wrapping its edge around the bottom of her face like she always did when she went out. She was telling her father she was not going to take no for an answer.

Her father looked at Halima with affection. He saw that her tearful eyes still carried a look of defiance, and found himself compelled to lower his head as though surrendering to her resolve.

Attar walked slowly out of the house. Halima followed him, gesturing to her maid Farah to stay at home. Farah would not have allowed her mistress to leave without her, but Halima's stare was enough to convince her the decision was not subject to debate.

In front of the main gate of the house, she saw a group of armed soldiers escorted by Arab soldiers. One glance at their tough-looking faces convinced her that they were not going to answer any of her questions, so she decided to stay quiet. The servants brought a coach. She climbed in with her father and they set off quietly in the direction of the king's palace.

She watched her father out of the corner of her eye, and noticed a few teardrops that he struggled to conceal from his escorts; he looked as though he thought he was being taken to his death. Halima wondered whether this was the last time she would see her father. She had seen him saddened and crushed before, but she had never seen him cry. Men's tears were as precious as the things they lost.

Halima glanced once again at the soldiers escorting her and her father. Three of them were Hormuzi soldiers that she did not know, but whom she identified as members of the king's guard thanks to their distinctive uniforms. The rest were masked men armed with swords, daggers and spears. Some of their weapons had congealed blood at their tips, and Halima understood these men had just emerged from a fierce battle and had not yet had time to clean their blades.

The coach arrived at the palace. There were charred bodies outside the main entrance and traces of fire on the outside gate. Halima closed the curtain over the wagon window to avoid seeing any more carnage. But the vizier's daughter could not resist her curiosity and pulled back the curtain minutes later. The wagon travelled past the gardens and reached the palace entrance. They all alighted, and a guard led them to the royal court where Bin Rahhal was sitting.

Halima had not visited the king's palace before. The court was not as big as she had expected. A large and exquisite Persian rug extended from corner to corner. Cushions lined the walls for guests to sit on. In the centre stood the king's throne, the only chair in the room; guests were not supposed to sit on chairs in the presence of the king.

The windows were wide open. The sun had not yet risen all the way but its rays were falling directly through the windows, bathing the hall in light. The dust particles danced in the light, happy with the restored grandeur of the room.

Bin Rahhal sat away from the direct sunlight. When Halima entered the room, it seemed empty at first sight, but then she saw Salghur sitting on his throne in the centre of the court, and Bin Rahhal on the floor in a darker corner with one of his soldiers.

Bin Rahhal stood and shook hands warmly with Attar. He glanced at Halima, who was still putting on her veil, and was instantly mesmerised by her eyes, delicateness and beauty.

Halima was looking at the king. She wanted to greet him before she greeted anyone else. She saw her father approach him and sit on the ground in front of him. Attar kneeled and extended his right hand to touch the carpet on which the throne rested. He then kissed his own hand. Salghur stood up and embraced the Hormuzi vizier tightly.

Halima felt her father's spirit instantly lifted, his erstwhile paralysing fear dispelled, and knew that her father's plan had worked after all.

Bin Rahhal ordered the soldiers to leave. Only Attar, his daughter and Salghur – in addition to him – were left in the hall. Halima decided to remove her veil after she saw how Bin Rahhal greeted her father, and felt that all those present were friendly. As soon as she uncovered her face, Bin Rahhal's jaw dropped and his eyes widened. He was motionless for a few seconds before he returned to his senses and pulled himself together. Halima's beauty was breathtaking, and Bin Rahhal had never met anyone like her in his life. He felt his soul rejuvenated and his heart throbbing in a way that was new to him.

They all sat on the ground except the king, who remained on his throne; he did not want to leave it even for a second. Bin Rahhal started speaking, explaining the next steps and the decision he had made about Vays. Serious expressions appeared on the faces of those present, though Bin Rahhal peeked from time to time at Halima to catch a glimpse of her dazzling beauty. She sat behind her father, shielded by his shoulder.

Halima sensed Bin Rahhal's eyes seeking her out. She covered her face with the veil again and stuck closer to her father. She peeped at him when she saw he was looking away from her; she did not like the long braids that draped over his shoulders or the kohl he wore on his eyes. This was not customary in Hormuz, where people cared for their hair, dyed it and wore it loose. 'And kohl is for women,' Halima thought; she had never seen a man wear it. But none of this mattered: her father had succeeded in restoring Salghur to the throne, and everything would return to the way was before.

Bin Rahhal mentioned the punishment he had decided for the former king. Salghur took the opportunity to express his objections, now that Attar was here and could side with him. 'I do not approve of your verdict to exile my brother to India without gouging out his eyes. He betrayed my trust. It is the norm in Hormuz to take out a traitor's eyes. I insist on this, Bin Rahhal!'

Bin Rahhal was not the kind of man who backtracked on his decisions. But this was not the time for disputes. The Arab vizier tried to address the restored king with great tact. 'But I have already made the decision and pronounced the sentence, Your Majesty. Gouging out his eyes will not benefit you in any way!'

Salghur turned to Attar, seeking his support. 'Isn't this our custom with traitors, *Khawaja*? Would you explain this to Bin Rahhal? A king must be hard on his enemies so that they may serve as an example to others.' Salghur leaned back on the throne and continued. 'Gouging out his eyes would be a small price for his crimes. If it were up to me alone, I would have made an example out of him. I would have made losing his eyes the least of his worries.'

Halima felt her father had been placed in an awkward position and decided to intervene. She brought her mouth to her father's ears and whispered something to him.

Everyone fell silent for a few moments, waiting to find out what the young woman wanted from her father. After she finished, Attar smiled and said, 'You tell them. I can't remember all of that.'

They all looked at Halima in surprise. They did not expect her to be involved in something like this, but Bin Rahhal found this to be an opportunity to steer the conversation away from Salghur's dogged line of thought.

Halima spoke. 'Eyes are a window to the mind, and its most faithful interpreter. They are the most precious parts of the face. Shah Vays's eyes will remain a window to his mind, and losing them would not stop him from conspiring against the king if he sets his mind to it. However, if they are left intact in his face, they could shield him from shame and disgrace.'

She articulated her words as if she were singing. 'Bin Rahhal's sentence, cruel as it may be, will dignify King Salghur. People will see him as a compassionate, merciful king who accommodates people despite their mistakes and betrayals, as the king who did not sentence his brother to die alive but rather the king who sentenced him to live dead. His exile to India is a moral death that will also spare Hormuz from his wickedness.'

Halima fell silent, and no one spoke. They felt she had said something they had never heard before, in a style they were not accustomed to hearing.

Salghur and Bin Rahhal smiled. Attar beamed with pride at his daughter's eloquence. Afterwards, Salghur no longer disputed Bin Rahhal's decision.

Bin Rahhal was impressed by what Halima had said. A young woman had argued his own case in a way he could not articulate himself, saving her father from obvious embarrassment and calming the king's burning desire for revenge.

The foursome agreed to keep a Jabrid detachment in Hormuz until stability was restored, and for the king to retain Attar as his adviser.

Before the meeting was concluded, Bin Rahhal tried to remind all those present of the price Salghur had to pay in return for the Jabrids' assistance. He said candidly, 'We had an agreement with the king that Hormuz would waive the annual tribute we pay and cede all its possessions in the island of Bahrain with the exception of the farmstead the king owns there.'

Salghur nodded in agreement as Bin Rahhal spoke, confirming the validity of the arrangement in the presence of Attar. Bin Rahhal took out the document Salghur had signed in Al-Ahsa and showed it to the Hormuzi vizier to seal the deal, asking him to endorse it with his signature as adviser to the king. The meeting came to an end after the agreement was signed.

Bin Rahhal was captivated by Halima. Her image had engraved itself on his mind, dominating his thoughts and emotions.

That night when he put his head down to sleep, she appeared before him, without her veil. Never did he imagine this could happen to him; was it love? He barely slept that night. In addition to the pain in his arm, there was the throb in his heart and the niggle in his mind. Bin Rahhal turned over restlessly in his bed as if he had a raging fever. Halima visited him in his dreams, talking, smiling and then frowning. He chided himself for not taking a longer look at her when he had the chance. He regretted every moment he spent not admiring her beauty and contemplating the expressions on her face.

As the days passed, Bin Rahhal became preoccupied with helping Attar run the kingdom. Bin Rahhal's presence at the head of a military force gave Salghur and his vizier the impetus they needed to restore security to the island and reorganise its affairs.

At dawn one day, the call to prayer boomed in Bin Rahhal's ears. He had not slept all night again. He did not know why and did not care to know, but he felt that sleep escaped him when he needed it most. He thought of Halima. Her image had not left his mind for a moment, and she often appeared to him when he closed his eyes.

Bin Rahhal took a sudden decision. At sunrise, he summoned one of his guards and asked him to inform Attar that Bin Rahhal was coming to visit within a few hours to have breakfast with him. Bin Rahhal did not waste any time. He went to his private quarters, trimmed his beard and unbraided his hair, letting it flow over his shoulders; he had noticed that the Hormuzis did not wear their hair like he did. He put on the best robes he had with him, dabbed some perfume on himself and left the room.

On the way to Attar's *majlis*, Bin Rahhal was hoping Halima would be there, waiting for him. He could no longer bear being apart from her even for a few hours, now that she haunted him constantly. His life had become more joyful ever since she took off her veil that first day. All the bloodshed he had seen and the death he had brushed against since he set foot on Hormuz was now insignificant compared to the striking beauty of her eyes. Sometimes he even wondered whether she was a human or a fairy. Whatever the case, Bin Rahhal doubted he could now live away from the woman who had stolen his heart and enthralled his mind.

As Bin Rahhal sat at Attar's *majlis*, Halima entered bringing date juice and plates of dried fruits. She was not wearing the veil this time. Bin Rahhal took a good look at her to get his fill; this could well be the last time he saw her.

'I want to congratulate you on the return of King Salghur to the throne, Master Vizier. This would not have happened were it not for your careful planning and diligent work to smuggle him out of prison,' Bin Rahhal began.

Bin Rahhal was noticeably nervous. He had no idea whether Halima was married or betrothed to another. He was not sure whether Attar would agree for her to marry him. It was a gamble: he could either ask for her hand, or he could try to forget her for the rest of his life, and regret it.

Bin Rahhal did not listen to Attar, who was thanking him for his courage and leadership. When the Hormuzi vizier paused, Bin Rahhal made his move, unsure whether this was the opportune moment or not.

'Your Excellency, might I have the honour of asking for your daughter's hand in marriage?'

Attar had not expected such a request. He was pleased that Bin Rahhal was visiting his home, for this would increase his influence under the new king – influence that he sorely needed, having lost it with the previous monarch. Attar asked Bin Rahhal for some time to consult with Halima.

After Bin Rahhal left, Attar summoned his daughter. 'Bin Rahhal has asked for your hand in marriage. What do you think?'

Halima was shocked by the marriage proposal. She admired Bin Rahhal for his role in bringing things back to normal on the island. But she did not know how she should answer her father; she certainly had never considered Bin Rahhal as a husband. 'I have not thought about this, Father. I don't think I could leave you and the island. No, I don't want to marry him. I don't know him.'

Attar put his hand on Halima's shoulder, trying to calm her. He thought she had answered too hastily and he did not want that. 'Think about the matter carefully, Halima. Give yourself time to think. Do not rush your decisions.'

Attar would not have said this had he not known the marriage would help him manage Hormuz better. He knew

King Salghur was weak-willed and that it was he who had to govern. Attar's name had been associated with Hormuz since the time of Salghur's father. He also needed a military force by his side to protect the kingdom's possessions across the western shore of the Gulf, and an alliance by marriage with a leader like Bin Rahhal would bolster his status and help consolidate his power in Hormuz and beyond.

Attar stood, placing his hand on his daughter's head. 'Think about it, my child.'

He then departed, leaving Halima by herself.

Her maid Farah came, and sat in front of her examining her pale face. 'I heard what your father told you. Tell me about him, Halima. I know you better than anyone else in the world. Maybe I can help you make a decision.'

Halima gave a deep sigh. She had an almost glazed look in her eyes. 'I don't know, Farah. It would be hard for me to abandon my father, the island I love and the home where I have spent all my life, and leave it all behind to go to another place where I don't know anyone and where I don't belong!'

'That's not what I meant, Halima. Describe Bin Rahhal as you've seen him!'

'I've seen him with two different looks. Which one do you want?'

'I want the last one. That was the look he wanted you to see.'

'He's in his mid-thirties. He has a brownish complexion, a thick moustache and a beard that he trimmed recently. This time – thank God – he did not wear any kohl! He'd also unbraided his hair – I didn't like it when it was braided – and I felt he looked more attractive than the first time I saw him.'

'How did he address you and your father?'

'He didn't change the way he spoke to my father, either on the first or second time. He was polite and friendly, making eye contact with the people he was addressing and replying calmly as though he had thought carefully about what he said. He was not in a hurry to talk.'

'Listen to me, Halima. The decision to marry or not to marry Bin Rahhal is yours alone. All your father and I can do is give advice, so hear me well.' Farah continued, 'Bin Rahhal brought armed men to the island and restored King Salghur to the throne. He will be the actual ruler on the island as long as he stays here. And yet we never heard once that he was rude to the king or your father. Rather, he came to your house politely and asked for your hand. He could have made threats to get his way, but he didn't. Think about it, Halima.'

Farah was of average beauty and slightly taller than Halima. Farah knew no one who was as close to her as Halima. Attar had bought Farah, now in her thirties, from an Indian slaver when she was less than ten years old. He raised her at his home like a daughter. From childhood, she wished to marry a merchant and start a family with him, and to have her own house. Her memories about her birthplace and family were now like a distant dream, slowly fading from her recollection, but she was still able to reach back and retrieve them from complete oblivion from time to time.

Halima thought about the matter for several days, wavering between accepting and rejecting Bin Rahhal's marriage proposal. Her temptation to refuse came from her emotions, her love for her father and her concern he would be all alone if she left. And her temptation to accept was driven by her intellect and reason and her father's judgement.

Halima eventually made up her mind. She realised that if she continued to think she would be thinking to no end; the competition between her emotions and her reason would only be settled by making a decision.

She went to her father's favourite spot on the balcony over-looking the sea. Halima lifted his feet, put them on her lap and massaged them, while giving her father a loving, caring smile. Attar gave her a look of fatherly love that always warmed her heart. 'It's nice to see you smile, Halima. I have tried not to disturb you for a few days so that I didn't influence your decision. What's making you smile today?'

Feeling a little embarrassed, she lowered her eyes.

Attar laughed mischievously and continued. 'I thought you hated the Jabrids, being rough-cut Bedouins.'

Halima looked at her father's feet between her hands, trying to avoid his eyes. 'I was wrong. I will agree to the marriage if you judge it to be right. I think you will agree that we will not find a better man.'

Attar knew that it was Halima's mind, not her heart, which was speaking. He felt that her consent was for political and rational reasons that had more to do with him and Hormuz. Still, Attar had become well acquainted with Bin Rahhal over the past few days and he was certain Halima would learn to love him after she got to know him better.

He put his hand on her head and caressed her before he said in a sad and quiet tone, 'So you will abandon me and leave me alone to go with him. There will be a whole sea between us!'

Halima broke into tears. She pulled her hand off his feet to wipe a tear from her cheek. She said in a quavering voice, 'I wish Bin Rahhal could live with us in Hormuz, but I think that's impossible. The distance will still be short between us,

Father, won't it? It must be only a two-day journey. You can come and visit us or we can visit you. And if you want me to stay with you, I will, gladly.'

Attar held her chin, lifted her face up and saw her tearful eyes. 'If you are happy then I am happy, Halima. God bless you. I will tell Bin Rahhal that I have agreed to the marriage.'

Halima stood on her feet and hugged her father tightly, in a way that suggested to him that she was happy with the decision. She then ran out of the *majlis* to where Farah was waiting, and hugged her in turn.

Farah did not let go of her mistress until she made her promise she would take her wherever she went.

'Would I ever be able to be apart from you, even for a day, Farah? You're insane if you think I could live without you!'

Farah took her mistress's hand and kissed it, tears rolling down from her eyes onto Halima's hands, before she reluctantly let go.

The marriage celebrations were held in the royal palace and attended by the dignitaries and merchants of Hormuz. The streets were lit and decorated, and sheep were slaughtered for the guests. The marriage ceremony doubled as the coronation of the new King Salghur, who sat beside Bin Rahhal to receive congratulations and blessings.

The well-wishers queued in a long line that started from the palace's outer gates and ended at the court. People wore their best garments, and erupted into dance in the space between the city and the port. Bin Rahhal's soldiers celebrated by performing a sword dance traditional in Najd, and crowds gathered around them trying to see what the men who had toppled their previous king looked like. Near them, others performed a traditional Hormuzi dance.

With nightfall, the music died down and the crowds moved to the beach to sit in small circles, enjoying the breeze. Later in the night, an owl landed on the palace wall, and hooted several times before it flew off. Halima and Bin Rahhal were experiencing the sweetest moments of their lives, forgetting that the world never tired of coming up with new evils with each sunrise.

19

Mozambique

ALBUQUERQUE'S JOURNEY WAS NOT easy. His armada had to weather fierce storms and violent currents as he circled the southern tip of Africa. There were mutinies on some of the ships by sailors who were petrified by the prospect of being so far from home. They were not used to sailing this deep into the mysterious, terrifying sea. They had heard stories about monsters that emerged from the ocean to claim sailors and take them to unfathomable depths, never to return, and creatures that had tentacles with which they squeezed the life out of their unsuspecting victims. The uncharted sea, the distance from Portugal, and the uncertain future made the sailors edgy and prone to rebellion.

Nothing suggested Albuquerque would be dissuaded from pressing ahead, however. His life now depended on the success of this mission. He repressed the mutineers harshly. Albuquerque ordered the ringleaders to be beheaded, and bound the rest with iron chains on the ship's deck for days under the sun, until hunger and thirst got the better of them. Albuquerque instructed his men not to assist them, and even to spit on them and insult them whenever they passed near the mutineers. He did not allow them to be unchained until one of them succumbed and died, and the rest were on the cusp of dying. This was the only way Albuquerque could prevent future rebellions.

Albuquerque completed the turn around the southern tip of Africa. His armada was now sailing parallel to the east coast of the continent. The sea was calm and jungles started appearing again, and green mountains behind them. Albuquerque's crew expected to find ports nearby, but all they saw were long stretches of uninhabited beaches with no signs of life. Their eyes remained fixed on the spots where the greenery met the water, but for days on end the shores they passed had no traces of humans or animals.

A week later, they spotted a small dreamy settlement on an island close to the mainland. Wooden dhows* of various sizes and shapes were floating opposite the island. The sandy beach was quiet and serene. Fishermen were busy cleaning their fishing nets and drying their catch. Behind them was a market selling fruits and vegetables, just in front of the town's stone buildings. The town appeared neat and well organised; each house had a small garden planted with flowers and some fruit trees, all overlooking interconnected streets that sprawled onto the beach.

Albuquerque ordered his men to douse the ships' immense sails to reduce their speed. As soon as the ships came directly in front of the town, he shouted to the seamen to drop anchor, and asked his deputy Miguel to search for the settlement's name in Covilhã's guide.

The villagers began to gather on the beach to take a look at the huge Portuguese ships. Suddenly, everyone broke into dancing and singing, waving tree branches. Albuquerque and his crew did not understand what was happening. He ordered his men to prepare to fight and prime the cannons, and asked Miguel whether he had found out any information about the island yet.

'Nothing, sir. There's no mention of this town in the dreaded dossier!'

'Fine. Make a mark of its location on the map. We will enquire about its name later.'

Behind the crowds, a canvas umbrella appeared to be moving, surrounded by a group of guards. They made their way to the shore and then boarded a small boat. The party rowed in the direction of Albuquerque's flagship. Everyone followed the boat with their eyes until it reached the ship. Albuquerque's men then dropped a rope ladder, and minutes later, the sultan of the island and his entourage were face to face with the Portuguese.

Albuquerque summoned Miguel, who was fluent in Arabic, to interpret and mediate with the sultan.

The sultan wore a friendly smile and welcomed his guests. 'Peace, mercy and the blessings of God be upon you. Welcome to our country, the country of Musa bin Bek. I am one of his descendants and the sultan of this land.'

The sultan gave Albuquerque a long colourful string of prayer beads. 'This is my own *misbahah*. I give it as a gift to you. May it help you praise God after every prayer.'

Albuquerque took the *misbahah* and asked the sultan about the name of the town again. 'It is Musa bin Bek, commander. Musa bin Bek.' He enunciated the name slowly for Albuquerque to understand it.

Miguel said enthusiastically, 'I have written it down, my lord. *M-u-s-a, b-i-n, B-e-k*.'

The sultan gestured to a member of his entourage, who came forward carrying gifts of fruits, vegetables, china and jewellery, along with small prayer mats, fabrics and an assortment of spices. He offered the gifts to Albuquerque.

Albuquerque opened the bags containing spices. He sniffed them, then dipped his finger to taste them. 'Where do you get these?'

The sultan answered him with a smile that bordered on outright laughter. 'From India of course! It is the only source of spices that we know of!'

'Do you sail from here directly to India to import them?'

The sultan pointed at the ships anchored off the island-town and said, 'These ships cannot sail there directly, of course. They sail from here to Zanzibar, and from there, to Mogadishu, and then Aden. When they arrive in Aden, they have practically arrived in India, given how close it is.'

The sultan of Musa bin Bek noticed how curious Albuquerque was about the spices, and thought this was because he was fond of them. 'We have many of these spices, commander; I can give you as many spices as you want. Ships arrive from time to time loaded with them. We sell them to tribes in the African hinterland. They love the taste spices bring to their food, and give us gold, furs, herbs and precious stones in return for them. Sometimes they sell us prisoners they have captured from other tribes as slaves. I will gift you some of them as well if you like. You are our brothers and we shall help you as best as we can.'

Albuquerque realised there had been a mix-up. The sultan had mistaken them for Muslims, especially since they had furled the large sails displaying the Order of Christ Cross before they dropped anchor. Albuquerque decided to play along with the sultan. The confusion could prove to be advantageous, he thought, and they might just be able to exploit it to re-supply and repair the ships that had sustained damage from the storms and currents they had to sail through in the south. Albuquerque asked Miguel to only translate what he was saying without volunteering to elaborate anything to the sultan.

One of Albuquerque's officers brought gifts they had carried with them from Portugal, and the sultan was pleased. At Miguel's orders, the seamen lined up in two rows, in their full armour and weapons that they had polished and prepared for such occasions. The sultan, fascinated, inspected the men, especially the muskets they were carrying, which he was wholly unfamiliar with. To demonstrate how they worked, Albuquerque ordered one of his men to load his musket and fire it.

The sailor turned over the muzzle of his long musket and loaded it with a gunpowder charge. He rolled in a round ball of lead, and followed it with a cotton wad, and then using a ramrod, he rammed the wadding, bullet and powder down the barrel. The sailor aimed the musket at the sea. There was a bird perched on a boat nearby. He fired and a deafening boom followed, almost causing the sultan to fall to the ground. To the sultan's astonishment, the bird disappeared, leaving behind a few feathers floating about.

The sultan adjusted his green, gilded turban. He brushed his white robe and rearranged his embroidered waistcoat before he put his hands on his ears, which were now ringing.

A sardonic smile appeared on Albuquerque's face. He knew his message had been understood, but he wanted to continue the charade to the end with the poor sultan. 'We want to supply our ships with food and water for our journey to India.

We want you to send sailors with us to show us the way. We are not familiar with these seas.'

The sultan started regaining his balance, though the ringing in his ears did not stop. He stuck his finger in one and wiggled it around. 'Certainly. You will get everything you need. You are invited to stay at my palace as my guests. Tomorrow we shall perform the Friday prayer at the grand mosque, and then you can set off to your destination with Godspeed. But how did you come from that direction? I thought the caliph's soldiers came from the east, navigating parallel to the Nile down from Cairo.'

Albuquerque was the only person speaking in this strange conversation. Miguel did not smile and his face remained blank, like a skilled actor.

'The caliph sent us west to fight the infidels. We are on our way to India to trade and bring back spices. He is very fond of them, as you know.'

The sultan shook his head in surprise. 'I didn't know the caliph was so fond of spices. We would have sent him everything we had. We trade in them.'

Albuquerque suddenly asked, 'How long would it take to get to India from here?'

Taken aback by the question, the sultan turned to his companions. All sailors knew that travel times varied depending on the seasons, the winds, the size of the sails and the weight of the ship, but an appropriate answer had to be given to the caliph's soldiers. 'The travel time depends on many things that sailors are familiar with, Your Excellency.'

Albuquerque found this to be an opportunity to obtain a guide who would be familiar with these seas. 'We need a guide to help us get there. Is there someone you can send with us?'

'Of course, we are all in the service of the caliph and his soldiers. You will get what you want after the Friday prayers and lunch. We will now leave and expect you to honour us with your presence tomorrow.'

The sultan raised his hand and saluted them. 'Peace, mercy and blessings of God be upon you.'

None of the Portuguese returned his greeting. The sultan blinked several times in shock. Then he waved his hand and climbed back down to the boat, departing to his island. The sultan gave orders to his subjects not to inconvenience the guests and to give them whatever supplies they asked for.

Night descended on the dreamy island of Musa bin Bek. Fires were lit on the shore and the nearby ships. On the beach, the locals celebrated the arrival of the caliph's ships late into the night. They could not stop looking at them in awe, and were particularly curious about the ominous-looking gun ports whose function they did not understand. They were puzzled as to why the sailors had not come down to visit their town yet.

As the townspeople quieted down, the only noise that could be heard were the voices of people cheerfully talking about the formidable caliph of the Muslims, who had not forgotten his subjects even here, in the far south of Africa. They saw the arrival of the caliph's fleet as the beginning of a long-lasting relationship between Musa bin Bek and Cairo, the city they had heard so much about in legends and stories. Women even dressed their children in their best clothes, hoping the commander would take them with him to study in Al-Azhar and return them one day as accomplished scholars. That night, many women dreamed of seeing their sons wearing the iconic Al-Azhar turban.

Not far from the town, three boys decided to take advantage of the arrival of the caliph's ships to join their crew. They were not content with life on their small, remote island, where they could not aspire to become anything other than farmers or fishermen. The idea that they could become soldiers of the caliph tickled their fancy and revived in them a spirit of adventure.

Their small boat moved quietly in the dead of night, making its way from the shore to the Portuguese armada. They did not want the sultan or their parents to know about what they were doing. They rowed the boat so slowly and quietly that the boat was almost moving on its own. Before they got to the nearest ship, they stopped rowing and let the boat glide over the water using its momentum. As soon as the boat reached the ship, one of the boys jumped onto a rope hanging from above and climbed up. Once near the deck, he peeked over its edge and saw the sailors kneeling on the deck floor, before a priest holding a large metal cross. The priest was reading them the evening prayer.

The boy climbed back down to the boat very gently, where his friends were waiting. He silently signalled to them to return, and they rowed back to shore.

By the following morning, everyone in the island-town had learned the foreign men's real identity. The news reached the sultan, who ordered his people not to cooperate with the Portuguese and to wait until he clarified matters with them and convinced them to leave without causing any trouble.

On the same morning, Albuquerque's sailors noticed the shore had suddenly been evacuated. Even the market looked abandoned as though something had happened. Albuquerque did not understand what was going on, and ordered some of his men to land on the island and capture anyone they could find to interrogate them.

Several boats were released from the ships. They rowed to the far side of the port to avoid attention. Albuquerque's men walked through the woods in the direction of the town, meaning to flank it and surprise their victims.

With the sun halfway up in the sky, people were resting in their homes or in the shade. The Portuguese attacked and managed to capture five men, four women and four children of different ages, and took them back to their ships.

The sultan tried to negotiate with them. They demanded supplies of food and water before they released the prisoners, and the sultan complied. In the evening, the Portuguese allowed the women, children and elderly they had taken to go, sending them to the island in boats, but kept four men. When the sultan's delegate asked the commander to release all the prisoners as agreed, Albuquerque asked the sultan to assign him a guide to show him the route to India. The sultan told him that this would be difficult because sailors were now afraid to go with him. Albuquerque gave him until the morning to comply, and told him to listen to the 'music' that night.

The sultan did not understand what Albuquerque meant. After the evening prayer that Albuquerque attended, the manacled prisoners were brought to the ship's deck. Albuquerque ordered his men to tie one of the prisoners to the barrel of a cannon trained on the city. The others were tied in a crucifixion posture. One of the sailors started pouring boiling lard on their abdomens and genitals.

As the victims screamed in horrible pain, the sailors drank, sang and danced. The torture lasted all night. The following morning, people gathered on the shore to find out what was happening. When Albuquerque noticed the multitude of spectators, he ordered his men to fire the cannon that had one of the prisoners tied to its barrel. When the smoke cleared, people saw the victim's arms and legs hanging between the remnants of the ropes used to restrain him, but could not quite understand how the rest of his body had vanished.

Before dawn on the following day, a small boat navigated the short distance between the shore and the Portuguese flagship. A man climbed aboard and introduced himself to Albuquerque. 'I am Malima Kanakwa. The sultan asked me to guide you on the way to India.'

'I have no interest in your name or what people call you. Your only job here is to show us the way to India.'

The prisoners were taken down to the bottom of the ship. Albuquerque ordered his ships to fire at the town, and within minutes the dreamy island was turned into a pile of ashes, rubble and body parts. Cannon fire continued until Albuquerque was sure the town had been razed to the ground. He then gave his orders for the ships to head east.

The few people who survived started emerging from the rubble and the dust. Wailing shrieks were heard throughout the devastated town, echoing over the sound made by the indefatigable waves.

20

Calicut, India

T HE PROCESSION MARCHED TOWARDS the Zamorin's palace. Hussein saw how crowded the city was. He was able to make out Arabic amid a mixture of languages being spoken at the market, and lifted the curtain on his palanquin* slightly to be able to talk to Qasimul Haq.

'Do many people here speak Arabic?'

'We have many Arab merchants in the city. Some of us speak Arabic fluently, being the lingua franca of trade. You will hear it as long as you are in the market, and you may also hear it in the Zamorin's palace. The king's guards are mostly from Hadramout, from Aden to be precise; we call them the Hadramis. Many speak Arabic at the palace too, so you won't feel too far from home.'

Hussein was amazed by the variety of bright colours in people's clothing, accessories and homes, and by the blends of both familiar and exotic spices on offer in the markets. Everything here was colourful, even people's hair, beards and turbans. He spotted a man spitting a red fluid out of his mouth. A few yards later, he saw a number of men doing the same thing. He wondered whether this was due to some kind of medical condition.

When Hussein pulled the curtain of his palanquin again, Qasimul Haq gave him a big smile. 'I know what you're going to ask me. I saw what you saw. You want to know why people spit a lot here, isn't that right?'

'Yes! What's going on?'

Qasimul Haq leaned back, and with the demeanour of someone repeating something he had explained many times before, said, 'People here like to chew on *tanboul*, which is made from the leaves of betel plants mixed with some flavourings and colouring. Once their mouths are filled with that red liquid from the chewing, they spit it out. In your country, this may be an unacceptable practice, but it's quite normal here. Even brides and grooms do it on their wedding night!'

Hussein was still puzzled by the habit. 'Why do they chew it if they're going to spit it afterwards? Why not just swallow it?'

But Qasimul Haq was not close enough to hear him. The two palanquins had moved away from each other because of the crowd.

Hussein searched for the Hindu king's adviser. He felt that there were many things he had to learn and become familiar with. He was shocked when he saw a cow eating food from a shop without anyone stopping it, and another lying down on the road blocking traffic without anyone disturbing the animal. He did not want to ask questions again, and just pointed at the cows when he saw that Qasimul Haq's palanquin had drawn closer to him again, with the man now in sight.

Qasimul Haq was smiling as ever. 'It's a sacred cow. The Hindus revere them, and do not disturb them. Even we Muslims try to show respect for this animal and avoid offending the

Hindus.' Qasimul Haq continued, 'Many people outside India think Hindus worship cows, but I have never seen them do it. They revere them because they see them as the source of livelihood for the peasants and poor people, and treat the animals like they were members of the family that must be respected. I tried to read some Hindu books, and found that they call on people not to consume meat in order to have happiness in this life, but with time, it became a taboo.'

The Indian adviser looked again at the cows scattered in the market. 'Whatever cows produce is sacred to the Hindus, from their milk to their urine and dung. In fact, the red paint on the forehead is made from cow dung.' Qasimul Haq pointed at Hussein's forehead, reminding him of the mark that had been painted on it when he came to shore.

Hussein touched the dye on his forehead and then smelled his fingers.

Qasimul Haq watched Hussein while shaking with laughter. 'We don't use it on the Zamorin's guests. Don't worry!'

The convoy arrived at the palace. A group of soldiers carrying small sharp axes was guarding the outer gate. Some were carrying strange metal batons that Hussein had never seen before.

The convoy reached the stairs leading to the palace entrance. The escorts stopped and the two palanquins were lowered to the ground. Qasimul Haq and Hussein descended. The party then walked in corridors clad in white marble, interspersed with tall columns inscribed with gold-leaf ornaments of Hindu gods. The sunlight coming through the large windows was bouncing off small water ponds, which in turn reflected the light back to the ceiling, making the entire palace shine with bright white.

The delegation was now at a large golden door. Guards wearing armour and carrying swords stood outside. When they spotted Qasimul Haq, they opened the gate while greeting him in unison. 'Peace and God's mercy and blessings be upon you.'

The king's counsellor returned the greeting. He spoke in Arabic to one of the guards before he addressed Hussein. 'This officer is Hadrami. He is the commander of the Zamorin's guard. He also likes to chew betel leaves!'

The Hadrami laughed and opened his mouth, which was filled with the red paste, to show the counsellor, before he let the two men in.

The Zamorin sat on a gilded and silk-padded divan. He leaned on his right side, with his legs resting on the bed. The Hindu king wore a golden serpent-shaped bracelet that wrapped around his forearm. The serpent had a large green gemstone in its mouth. The Zamorin wore similar bracelets around his ankles and a bejewelled diadem around his head that was equally if not more spectacular.

He wore a white gilded silk *izar* from the waist down, and was bare-chested save for a white pearl necklace. The Zamorin was also chewing betel leaves. A tall, muscular guard carrying a broadsword and a gilded shield stood behind the king, looking alert and ready to carry out any order his master gave him at a moment's notice.

Hussein was awed by this strange sight. He decided to watch Qasimul Haq and then imitate what he did, telling himself that since Qasimul Haq was Muslim, he would not do anything that would anger God.

The counsellor drew close to the Zamorin, bowed in front of him, and then sat quietly on his knees. Hussein followed suit. The Zamorin gave them a cordial smile, then turned and spat a red paste into a pot decorated with emeralds and rubies that a servant was holding.

'Greetings, my friends from Egypt.'

Qasimul Haq translated the pasha's response. 'The honour is all ours, Your Majesty. You have received us well and showed us great hospitality. The sultan of Egypt wishes to extend a hand of friendship to you and offers his assistance to fight the Portuguese, who have started seizing parts of your territory.'

The Zamorin spat again in the pot. 'They have not seized any territories of ours, not yet at least. Several of their ships came here. The Portuguese made deals with some Indian kings to establish trading posts in their ports. They came as traders. Although their ships carried cannons, they did not use them against the Indians.'

The Hindu king paused, before he said, 'I have heard about the *Maryam*, and how they sank it with the pilgrims on board. However, I believe this was an isolated incident that will not happen again. Some Indian kings told me that the ship refused to stop for inspection, and that its passengers took up arms to fight.'

Hussein realised that focusing on the *Maryam* was not going to lead anywhere. The Zamorin was setting Hussein's word against that of the Portuguese, who now had common interests with some kings in India. The Mamluk admiral decided it would be more worthwhile to address the Portuguese threat in broader terms.

'Your Majesty, I have been sent by Sultan al-Ghawri, the sultan of Egypt and Syria, to fight the Portuguese. They have disrupted navigation between India and Arab lands. Our merchants can no longer buy spices from your ports. If things continue as they are, we all stand to lose.'

The Zamorin replied, 'We welcome all those who come to our country to buy spices. The Portuguese have forged alliances with some Indian kings along this coast. I cannot interfere in the decisions of other kings. If they find that their alliance with the Portuguese is in their interests, then there is nothing I can do. The Portuguese purchase spices in large quantities and ship them back to their country. So it seems to me the only party that loses because of this is you.'

Hussein noticed that the Zamorin was speaking more like a merchant than a king and statesman, and decided to emphasise the extent of the threat to everyone.

'Your Majesty, we have been acquainted with the Portuguese's thinking and their methods for a long time. They first come as merchants, to gather information about a nation and its weaknesses. They establish outposts that they claim are for trading, but soon send ships full of soldiers and armaments to occupy and hold those places.'

The Zamorin spat again, and everyone heard the spittle land in the pot. 'You are describing your own experience with them but not ours. We welcome all those who come to our lands to trade. We cannot see into the future.'

Qasimul Haq decided this was his chance to weigh in on the matter and warn the Zamorin. 'My son-in-law, *Si* al-Tayeb, lived with the Portuguese for many years and speaks their language. I implore Your Majesty to listen to what he has to say.'

Si al-Tayeb was sitting on his knees further behind. 'Your Majesty, I lived in their lands when I was a child. My father is an Arab Muslim and my mother is Spanish. Initially, we had agreements with them letting us practise our faith and traditions, and protecting our properties, when we still had our weapons. When we laid down our arms, everything changed; they prohibited us from praying in our mosques, confiscated our lands and prevented us from defending ourselves. After that, they took children from their parents to raise them as Catholics, and eventually drove us from our country to the north of Africa.'

Si al-Tayeb lowered his head, trying to cope with a flash of bitter memories. He continued, 'As you know, Your Majesty, the *Maryam* and its passengers were set alight, after they took young girls and boys. The Portuguese were drinking ale as they watched the people and the ship burn. People who do such things when they come claiming to be merchants will do even worse things in war. They will do the same to the rest of the kingdoms of India, one by one, until they take everything.'

Qasimul Haq and Hussein felt that they had managed to have an impact on the Zamorin. The Hindu king was silent in thought, save for spitting chewed betel leaves. After hesitating for a while, he said, 'Very well. You shall be my guests and you may re-supply your ships and purchase whatever quantities of spices you desire. After that, you will leave, like all other merchants. I don't want you to bring your wars to my kingdom.'

Hussein knew then that he would not be able to use Calicut as his base. Clearly, the Zamorin did not want to be a party to the conflict with the Portuguese.

After they left the royal hall, Qasimul Haq grabbed Hussein's hand. 'Listen, Pasha. You must leave for the city of Diu as soon as possible, after you re-supply your ships of course. You will find the assistance you seek there. King Malik Ayaz is an eager warrior who can be easily provoked and convinced of the Portuguese threat.' This time, a serious expression replaced Qasimul Haq's usual smile. 'He is the king of Diu and its environs. I will send my son-in-law with you to make the introduction. We go a long way back.'

Several days later, Hussein's fleet headed north.

– 21 –

The Arabian Gulf

O N THE DAY THE bride and groom were set to leave, the port of Hormuz was draped in spectacular festive decorations. Colourful flags fluttered in the wind as music from different parts of the island fused together. Water and sweets were distributed to the revellers, and conjurers performed their best tricks in front of the public. People almost forgot the casualties of the battle that had taken place a month earlier; it did not matter any more who had fallen and why, but only who the new king was.

In the distance, the booming sound of drums was heard slowly approaching. The steady rhythm was so strong that people felt their hearts jumping with each beat, and they realised the king's procession had arrived: a long convoy of camels festooned with gilded saddles and blankets, preceded by spear-carrying cavaliers in stunning formations.

The crowds parted into two lines, fashioning a road between their bodies to allow the procession through. The people craned to see Bin Rahhal and his new wife, Halima; Bin Rahhal was mounted on a decorated horse alongside Attar, both men riding a few metres behind the king. The crowds could not see Halima, who was with a group of women at the end of the column, hidden behind the curtains of a gorgeous *howdah*, a beautiful carriage on the back of a camel.

The procession arrived at the port. The camels were made to kneel while the king and Bin Rahhal dismounted from their horses. In the back, Halima and Farah emerged out of the *howdah*. The farewell ceremony began; women wailed in the back, and people who were parting embraced one another. There were so many tears shed that the crowds could not tell who was leaving and who was staying.

The ships sailed away from the port of Hormuz. Halima looked back for one last time at her island. As she focused on the crowds of people waving at her, she spotted her father. His gaze said a lot, though she could not interpret all the emotions it carried; she knew he was in pain from parting with her just as she was in pain from parting with him. She embraced Farah and started crying.

Halima's feelings were a strange combination of sadness and happiness. The tears flowing down her face came from both her sorrow for having to part with her home, and from her hopeful joy for the new life she was embarking on. She almost laughed and cried at the same time as she hugged her maid.

The newlywed couple arrived in Bahrain. Halima was very impressed by the abundance of trees and the springs flowing between them. The chirping of the birds made her feel she was in paradise. Everything grew here, unlike on the almost waterless, treeless island of Hormuz. Here she would never have enough of the water streams; she could gambol with her girlfriends around the springs, pick grapes hanging down from the vines, and eat the ripe fruits from the trees all around her. She would be able to do many things here that she had always dreamed of.

'My goodness, this farm is so beautiful, Bin Rahhal. I had never expected Bahrain to be this wonderful. It is truly a paradise in the middle of the sea!'

'I agree, it's very beautiful. King Salghur insisted that we spend some time here at the farm he inherited from his father. This is the estate he wanted to keep after he ceded all of Hormuz's possessions in Bahrain. I think you will be more comfortable here than if you came to live in Al-Ahsa.'

They went into the house. There were many gifts inside sent by Sultan Muqrin and his entourage, and the notables of Al-Ahsa and Bahrain. There was hardly a spot in the house that had not been used for presents, from antiques and jewellery to food.

As Halima looked at all the packages, she tried to guess what was inside them and who had sent them. There were beautifully ornamented boxes, large bags of spices and baskets of dried fruits and dates. There were silk fabrics, porcelain wares, precious jewellery and many other lavish gifts. Even the stable was filled with purebred steeds gifted to them by well-wishers.

Bin Rahhal held Halima's wrist and pulled her towards him. 'I have to travel in the next two days to greet the sultan and thank him for all these wonderful gifts. I have to brief him on what happened in Hormuz.'

Halima said with some eagerness, 'Do you want me to go with you?'

Bin Rahhal smiled. 'It doesn't work that way here, Halima. Women here do not sit with men as you do in Hormuz.'

She was puzzled by her husband's response. 'Why not?'

Bin Rahhal did not have a convincing answer, but he was not prepared to have a long debate with her. Halima had a tenacious character and strong opinions, and persuading her was not going to be a simple task. She was raised in a certain way that was not going to be easily changed.

Bin Rahhal tried to steer the conversation in a different direction. 'I have something in safekeeping at my home in Al-Ahsa that belongs to the sultan. I must take it to him too.'

Halima did not care much about what Bin Rahhal was saying. What she wanted most of all was for him to return quickly from his trip. She could not bear him to be away from her for too long. 'Those few days will seem very long, my dear husband!'

Bin Rahhal smiled and stared at her face, trying to get the most out of her beauty before leaving. 'I will not be long. You know how much I will miss you, but it has to be done.'

A few days later, Bin Rahhal entered Sultan Muqrin's *majlis* in his best robes. He was expecting the sultan to say something about his elegant attire and his marriage, and true to form, when the sultan saw him, he smiled mischievously and said loudly, 'Look at the groom! I thought I had sent you to help put your friend back on the throne. But you kidnapped their daughter and brought her here instead!'

Bin Rahhal came up to the sultan with a mischievous smile of his own. 'I did not kidnap her, Your Grace. She kidnapped me, so I decided not to return except with her.'

The sultan pointed to a cushion nearby. 'Sit, Bin Rahhal. I have missed you, my friend. But it's all right, now that you've succeeded in your mission – and returned with the spoils.'

Bin Rahhal kept a smile on his face. He wanted to see what effect it would have on the sultan. 'The spoils are mine alone, Your Grace. I do not intend to share them with anyone!'

The sultan laughed heartily. 'God bless your spoils. Now give me all the details.'

Bin Rahhal explained everything that had happened in Hormuz up until the final agreement was signed in the court of King Salghur, in the presence of Vizier *Khawaja* Attar and Halima. Bin Rahhal told the sultan that Attar also endorsed the document ceding Hormuz's possessions in Bahrain – with the exception of the king's private estate – and exempting the Jabrid sultan from having to pay annual tributes.

After Bin Rahhal finished recounting the events in Hormuz, he said, 'Salghur asked me to stay at his estate in Bahrain for some time. I want to ask your permission to stay there for a while before I return to Al-Ahsa. Living in Bahrain would be better for my wife than here as you can imagine.'

'I know, Bin Rahhal. That is fine with me. Many merchants come from various ports to Bahrain. She would not feel as cut off and alone there as she would here. Stay with her there for a while until she gets used to the situation and then bring her back here.'

The sultan leaned back on a cushion behind him. 'I was extremely worried before, but, praise be to God, I am relieved and happy now. I hope this king will rule his kingdom well, and avoid conflicts that would lead to nothing but the downfall of his realm.'

Bin Rahhal wanted to remind him of the dagger and the ring he had in safekeeping for his sultan. He felt they were a great burden that now had to be passed on. 'Your Grace, do you remember the dagger brought by the messenger of the

Bahmani kingdom in India and the ring you bought from the Banyan? You had asked me to keep them for you. I still have them in my home here, but since I am going to reside in Bahrain, it might be best if I return them to you. I cannot be certain they are safe when I am away from my home.'

'Yes, I remember them of course. I had intended to send them to the caliph in Cairo but I was preoccupied with other matters. I left them with you because of my many travels, and my palace is full of servants. Remind me of them again when the Hajj season comes. Then we shall give them to someone we trust to deliver them to the ruler of Jeddah, who would in turn deliver them to the caliph. The dagger has great signifi- cance for the Bahmani sultan and for us, and I made a promise that must be fulfilled at all costs, Bin Rahhal. The dagger will reach the caliph, God willing. Put the ring in the dagger's chest as well.'

The sultan waved his fan up and down. 'I will go in the next few days to discipline rebellious tribes in Al-Kharj. My cousin Nasser will be in charge of the sultanate while I'm gone. I have asked him to stay close to you in Bahrain until my return. You must help him, Bin Rahhal. He is a reckless young man. I am aware of his flaws, but you must guide him and coach him on the affairs of government. Perhaps he'll learn something from you.'

The expression on Bin Rahhal's face changed. He looked like he had a sudden pain in his side. He fell silent but tried hard to hide his emotions.

Several days later, Bin Rahhal returned to his home in Bahrain. Halima came to welcome him, expecting him to be cheerful as usual. But to her surprise, he looked sorrowful and crestfallen.

She had not seen him like this before. When she asked him what was wrong, he said, 'The sultan told me he was going to Al-Kharj to put down a rebellion there, during which time he would appoint Emir Nasser to rule in his stead. Nasser will be based here, in Bahrain.' He exhaled with force and added, 'I detest the man! I have tried to avoid him all my life, have tried to find excuses never to sit with him.'

Halima was taken aback by her husband's comment. He continued without looking at her. 'He's a despicable person. Absolutely lacking in chivalry. His comportment in public is different from his conduct in private. He pretends to be pious and courageous in the presence of the sultan, but in his absence behaves like a licentious drunkard, when the worst in the man comes to the surface. I really don't know how I'm going to put up with him in the absence of Sultan Muqrin!'

He took off his turban angrily and threw it on the ground. 'I heard many stories about women that he tempted only to threaten them and rape them. Like a snake, he does not bite until he makes sure his prey is at his mercy!'

Halima put her hand on her husband's shoulder to comfort him. 'If the sultan is going to be away, you have to put up with him until the sultan's return. Who knows what harm he can do? He represents the sultan now, and there is no one you can complain about him to. You have to endure the situation until we find a way out.'

Bin Rahhal replied angrily, 'Couldn't the sultan find anyone else? Did he have to choose this vile person of all people?'

She rubbed his shoulder, trying to give him some reassurance. 'He is the ruler now. You have no choice but to weather the storm until it passes.'

Bin Rahhal grabbed Halima's hand and kissed it. 'I don't know how I will do that, but I will try.'

From between his robes, he took out the box containing the dagger that Sultan Muqrin had given him, and put it between Halima's hands. He pressed her hands, as though suggesting she hold it tightly. 'This chest is more precious than everything else in the house.'

Halima opened the box and saw the masterpiece that was inside. She held it in her hands and turned it over a couple of times. She was beguiled by its intricate jewellery and crafts-manship. Halima returned the dagger to its slot. She took out the ring next and slipped it on her finger, examining its splen-dour before replacing it in the box.

Bin Rahhal said, 'This dagger is not a gift to me. It is a gift from one of the sultans of India to the caliph in Cairo. Sultan Muqrin gave it to me for safekeeping, so you must hide it in a very safe place that only you and I know of.'

Halima's expression turned serious. 'Where do you want me to hide it?'

Bin Rahhal pointed to the boxes scattered around the room. 'Put it one of those large boxes, and put the box in our room so that no one can reach it. Do you comprehend the signifi-cance of this dagger, Halima? It is very important to the sultan. He said it was a great responsibility entrusted to him, and now it is entrusted to me.'

She replied in a quiet voice, 'Don't worry. I will find a box and put the dagger inside it. I will put it in our room, which no one else will enter except us. But why did he give it to you rather than keep it himself?'

'He wants me to keep it until he returns from his campaign. He is always travelling, as you know.'

Bin Rahhal started visiting the *majlis* of Emir Nasser, who had arrived in Bahrain a few days earlier. He was compelled by his promise to the sultan to assist his cousin in carrying out his duties.

Initially, the relationship between the two men was not good. Soon, however, the emir started treating him with great respect, letting him sit with him at the centre of the *majlis* and consulting him in many matters. Bin Rahhal felt something had changed; it was not the habit of the emir to treat him or others like this, and Bin Rahhal was not quite sure what was behind it.

In the evening, after all guests and visitors had left the *majlis*, Emir Nasser would challenge Bin Rahhal to a game of chess in front of a selected number of people – who senselessly cheered every move the emir made. As time passed, a kind of bond grew between the emir and Bin Rahhal, who felt Emir Nasser had had some sort of change of heart. He was pleased with Nasser's new behaviour, and a strange friendship developed between the two men. And though Bin Rahhal could not comprehend it, he felt glad about it.

One day, after Bin Rahhal had left the *majlis* and the other guests had departed, one of the emir's slaves stayed behind. Nasser ordered him to fetch some ale. After a few sips, Nasser started to feel slightly inebriated. He looked at the slave with bulging eyes and said, 'Have you done anything yet, Jawhar? I'm still waiting for you to do your part.'

Jawhar was very close to the emir. His father had been the slave of the emir's father; he was raised to maintain blind loyalty to him. The emir trained him to do all his dirty work. He was a plotter and an assassin whenever called upon to become one. Jawhar's features did not conceal his role in life. With roots in Abyssinia, he was extremely tall, well built and muscular. He was almost handsome, were it not for his wicked-looking yellowish eyes. Jawhar had no respect for anyone save for his master. He was little more than a monster always ready to pounce on his – or his master's – prey.

'You have promised me a large reward if the plan succeeds, my lord. The prey has started to take the bait. You must be patient and wait a little.' Jawhar grabbed the cup of ale in front of him and drank its contents in one gulp. 'She is ineffably beautiful, my lord. She is worth the trouble and the wait, and the dreary courtesy you have to show to the man you so despise.'

Nasser sat up abruptly as though a scorpion had stung him. 'Did you really see her? Tell me everything! Describe her to me!'

Jawhar gave him a laboured smile, as though he were moving his facial muscles in this manner for the first time. 'No, I didn't see her. She leaves the house wearing a veil. But I saw her svelte body, her slender limbs and locks of her hair that had slipped from the bottom of her scarf. I tried hard to see more but I failed. I heard a lot about her beauty, and was told that when she lies on her back, you could roll an apple beneath her curves! She is not like any other woman, certainly not like the women you've had before. She is the unrivalled queen of her sex, my lord!'

Jawhar took a deep breath, his eyes fixed on a distant spot, imagining her. As he returned to his senses, he said, 'But I didn't stop there, my lord. My relationship with her maid Farah has improved. Before, she refused to talk to me. I told her I'm trying to buy my freedom from you, and that you were asking for a lot of money in return, so she has been giving me any money she can find at Bin Rahhal's house, thinking she is helping me raise the sum!'

Jawhar paused for a moment. His eyes turned red as was usual for him whenever he drank ale. 'I promised to marry her and take her to Hormuz or India, but I told her we won't be able to pull it off until we've gathered enough money.' The slave gave a loud, bizarre laugh that sounded like it had come out of his stomach. 'She has been showering me with money for our future! She's a stupid woman. I was able to fool her with a few words I learned from you.'

The emir almost jumped up and down in adolescent-like excitement. 'Tell me Jawhar, have you *had* the maid yet?'

'Not yet, Your Highness, not yet. But don't worry, it won't take much longer.'

The two laughed together as though they had heard a hysterical joke. Jawhar continued, 'She will soon fall between my hands like a wounded gazelle. When I devour Farah, know that Halima will be your next prey.'

Emir Nasser twirled his moustache and his eyes lost their focus. He said in a hiss, 'I will not be able to prey on her with her shepherd around. He must disappear to make her more vulnerable and sweet-tasting.'

– 22 –

Oman

ALBUQUERQUE'S EYES WERE FIXED on the rocky coast stretching northwards. He spotted a town lined by palm and fruit trees. In the middle stood a minaret, higher than all the trees, heralding the mosque's presence. To the north, there was a riverbed extending from the mountains, but the river was dry. Albuquerque saw no one on the coast and all the ships moored there were small. Everything seemed still.

The Portuguese commander summoned some of his officers to conduct a reconnaissance of the shore and try to determine what was going on. One officer pointed to four small cannons on top of the wall separating the town from the shore. They also noticed large rocks used to fortify the cob wall protecting the city. Albuquerque focused his sights on the wall and was able to spot groups of fighters carrying spears and bows holed up behind it; he realised the city had braced itself for his arrival and made preparations to fight him.

A boat was lowered from Albuquerque's ship carrying his lieutenant, Miguel, and made its way to the shore. Miguel disembarked and walked to the closed gate. The gate suddenly opened, revealing a man wearing a short *izar* that stopped at his knees. He was bare-chested and held a long spear and a small wooden shield. The two men stood staring at each other until Miguel finally spoke.

'I have been sent by my master, Albuquerque, who represents the king of Portugal. We ask you to surrender immediately, pay a tribute, receive the king's representative and swear allegiance to him. If you fail to comply we will destroy your city and kill all its inhabitants.'

The Omani soldier kept his eyes fixed on Miguel until he finished speaking. He then blinked several times before he turned back to where he came from. Just before he disappeared behind the gate, Miguel shouted out, asking him to tell him the name of the town. Without turning around, the man replied, 'Kuryat', then crossed the wall and closed the gate behind him.

The sailors on the Portuguese ships were watching closely the encounter on the shore. When Miguel returned, Albuquerque quizzed him about what had happened.

'Nothing much, my lord. He heard what I told him then returned to the town.'

'Damn! Is that all? He said nothing else?'

'I think they're prepared to defend the city. The Arab warrior did not come out to negotiate. I'm not sure whether he understood my message, but he told me the town is called Kuryat. News of our arrival must have reached these shores. I just hope the cities along the coast are not all waiting for us with cannons!'

Albuquerque fiddled with his beard, as was his habit when he was deep in thought. He continued to stroke it, until his eyes flickered with a look that was all too familiar to people around him – the look of a wolf who had just caught the scent of blood.

'Prepare to bombard the city. I shall lead the landing party myself!'

At his signal, the ships' guns began pounding the city with a barrage of cannonballs. The first shells landed a short distance from the cob wall, but those that followed were more precise. Parts of the wall were shattered along with bodies of the defenders; with each round, the Portuguese sailors cheered. Soon, they even began to place bets on hitting certain targets.

The rounds fired by the Omani cannons set up on the wall could not reach the Portuguese ships, falling in the water and making a splash dozens of cubits away. They were small and ineffective. Albuquerque's sailors felt triumphant seeing that their opponents were weak and that they were going to massacre them with great ease.

Albuquerque watched the town with his crocodile eyes as it was being levelled. When he noticed the residents were starting to flee towards the mountains behind their town, he ordered the landing party to lower the boats.

Each ship dropped two large boats. In seconds, dozens of soldiers wearing armour from head to toe jumped in. They carried muskets, which the defenders had never seen before, and long halberds.

The rowers raced to reach the shore. When the boats were almost at the beach, Albuquerque shouted his final orders. 'Kill all men, and spare the women, children and elderly, for I have something else in mind for them. Loot the town then burn it. And I don't want to see this mosque standing in its place afterwards!' Albuquerque then cried, 'Are you ready to defend your king?'

'We give our lives to the king! Long live the king!' they responded with one voice.

Albuquerque landed on the shore with his forces. The few defenders who were left thrust their spears and arrows at them, but they were useless against the attackers' armour.

Carnage ensued. The defenders' spears were no match for the muskets of Albuquerque's men. Only a few of the Omani warriors had swords, while the majority carried spears and arrows but little else.

Bodies piled up. Homes were looted then burned down. The mosque was set alight after being bombarded with several rounds of cannon fire from the sea.

The loot was carried in the small ships berthed at the harbour. The battle was uneven, and came to a quick end. When Albuquerque was about to return to his ship, the soldiers brought him a group of women, children and elderly who had not been able to flee from the battle. He ordered the women and children to be gored and then slaughtered, and forced the elderly men to watch the massacre. 'You have seen what I did to your city and your people. I will send you to Hormuz to tell them everything you saw today!'

He ordered his soldiers to cut off the noses and ears of the elderly men and put them on a boat to Hormuz, giving them only water. Albuquerque left Kuryat in ruins behind him. Plumes of smoke rose from the burning husk of the town and the ships in its harbour. There were no survivors.

Albuquerque continued sailing along the coast of Oman until he reached Muscat. The city immediately captivated him. He ordered his ships to drop anchor, as he wanted to analyse the best way to conquer it with minimal losses.

He studied the city, his eyes steady and unblinking, like a predator sizing up its prey, and at the same time, he nervously moved his fingers through his beard. Unexpectedly, he saw a boat approaching his ship carrying a few men. Albuquerque quickly ordered his men to load their muskets and aim them at the boat.

The boat stopped near the flagship. One of the men on board shouted up at Albuquerque. 'I have been sent by the ruler of Muscat. We heard about what happened in Kuryat. We do not want to repeat the carnage and are ready to listen to your demands!'

Albuquerque responded from deck. 'I want a letter signed by the ruler pledging obedience and allegiance to the king of Portugal. I must receive this letter by tomorrow morning with the ruler's seal. Is that clear?'

The messenger raised his hand, saluting Albuquerque and said, 'I will deliver your demands to the ruler.'

The boat returned quietly to shore.

Albuquerque felt that the massacre he had staged in Kuryat had paid off, and that the messages he wanted to send had been read and received well.

Albuquerque ordered Miguel to lead a scouting party and go to the coast to learn more about the fortifications and weaknesses in the city wall. At sundown, the party returned to the ship and Miguel reported back to Albuquerque.

'My lord, the city is surrounded by a twenty-cubit-high outer wall made from palm trunks, supported by boulders. Behind it there are other wooden defences that are ten cubits wide. The entrance to the harbour is a shallow creek that can only be accessed at night when the water level is high enough. It is also fortified by walls built between two hills, and the defenders of the city can seal it off with boulders if needed.'

As Miguel finished his report, Albuquerque muttered, 'Let us wait until tomorrow morning. I will not leave the city until

I make sure it swears allegiance to the king. Otherwise, I will raze it to the ground.'

The next morning, the envoy returned to inform Albuquerque that the ruler had agreed to write up the document he demanded and to make peace without preconditions. Albuquerque kept him while he consulted his officers, then came back with more demands.

'The city must pay tribute to the king of Portugal equivalent to the tribute paid to the king of Hormuz. The ruler must build a special port for the Portuguese fleet and supply it constantly with food and water. If these conditions are met, Muscat will be placed under the protection of the king of Portugal. Otherwise, we shall destroy the city and kill all its inhabitants.'

Albuquerque ordered his lieutenant to escort the messenger back to Muscat to deliver the demands straight to the ruler. In the evening, Miguel returned with several boats carrying food and water and told Albuquerque the documents would be signed on the following day.

In the morning, however, the city returned to silence. No boats arrived and not a living soul came past the closed main gate. Albuquerque was puzzled by the about-face, and decided to find out what had prompted the ruler to take this hostile action.

At night, a Portuguese sailor spotted a small boat trying to sneak out from the port. Albuquerque ordered one of his ships to pursue it and bring the people on board back to him. After they were tortured, they revealed that the city was gearing up for battle because the Jabrid's soldiers had arrived to help defend it.

Albuquerque asked Miguel to get more information from the prisoners about the Jabrid. After much torture and many mistranslations, Miguel was finally able to give his chief an update.

'They say the Jabrid is the sultan of the Gulf, Najd and Arabia. His name is Muqrin bin Zamel. The prisoners say the soldiers who came to help are based in the Omani hinterland and are loyal subjects of the sultan. They have convinced the ruler of Muscat not to hand over the city to us.'

Albuquerque replied quickly, 'Ask them how many Jabrid soldiers there are and what kind of armament they have.'

The prisoners started screaming as their torture continued. Miguel told Albuquerque, 'They say there are a few thousand Jabrid soldiers, armed with swords, spears and bows and that they will fight fiercely to defend Muscat.'

Albuquerque slapped his thigh in anger and ordered his men to prepare to destroy the city.

Later that night, Albuquerque sent a unit to infiltrate the coast and gather information on the enemy's preparations. But as soon as Albuquerque's men landed on the shore, salvos of spears and arrows descended from above, killing and injuring a number of them and forcing them to retreat back to their ships.

With the first signs of morning, the Portuguese ships rained down fire on the city for several hours. Bodies of the city defenders were scattered along the beach. The shelling opened several breaches in the city wall.

Landing boats were dropped and made their way to the points Albuquerque had specified. When they approached the coast, they were showered with arrows, stones and spears from every side. However, Albuquerque and his men were in full armour and carried very long pikes with sharp ends. They also had muskets that they fired from close range, with deadly effect.

The Omanis and Jabrids used everything they had to defend their positions, and threw rocks at the attackers from the rooftops. However, their primitive weapons were futile against the soldiers wearing armour and using modern weapons.

As time passed, the resistance gradually weakened. Portuguese soldiers started taking women and children prisoners from their homes. Albuquerque ordered all prisoners to be struck down with no survivors. Soldiers would hold the young ones in front of their mothers and impale them with their spears, or cut them down with their swords, sometimes splitting the children in two. The soldiers then moved on to the women and elderly, and the mutilated corpses piled up in the city's streets, rivers of blood flowing in the alleys.

Albuquerque ordered his men to pursue the locals fleeing the city, after erecting barricades to protect them against reprisals by the inhabitants. They saw many women and children trying to climb the mountains surrounding the city in search of safety. The soldiers chased them and tortured them too before killing them. Then they brought all the jewellery and food they could find to Albuquerque, who ordered them to search all homes and turn them upside down to find any gold buried in them.

The Portuguese razed the city after looting everything valuable from the markets and shops. They carried fresh water to their ships and did not leave the city until it was a wasteland, crows cawing over it.

Albuquerque returned to his ship and went inside his cabin. He took out a parchment and quill, which he dipped in an inkwell, and then wrote: *Muscat is a large and populous town, flanked on both sides with high mountains. There are orchards, gardens and palm groves with wells for watering them. The city is ruled by a governor appointed by Hormuz. The region that surrounds it inland is ruled by the Jabrids, whose power extends from Muscat to Dhofar, on the borders of the kingdom of Aden. The Jabrid rule extends to Bahrain and the coast of Qatif, where they rule on behalf of the kingdom of Hormuz.*

'I think that's enough,' he told himself. He snuffed out the candle and went to bed, happy with his victory.

On the following day, the armada navigated along the coast, which veered north, running parallel to a chain of black mountains. It reached a small bay surrounded by mountains in the shape of a horseshoe. The bay looked enticing; there were many fishing boats there, and the water was deep enough for Albuquerque's ships to navigate through it freely. The fleet came to a stop in front of a small village built from stone and cane.

The locals spotted the huge ships and left everything they were doing. They came to the coast to check them out more closely, but when they saw the red cross on their sails they ran away and vanished. A while later, horsemen and camel cavalries singing battle chants appeared, waving their weapons for the Portuguese to see them.

Albuquerque did not delay. He ordered his ships to open fire at the village, and within hours it was turned to rubble. Some of its inhabitants were able to escape to the mountains. At nightfall, Albuquerque ordered his soldiers to check the village and loot it, and sat on the shore waiting for his commanders to report back.

Miguel brought an elderly man as a prisoner. He carefully held a book wrapped in a rolled cloth. 'My lord, I found this old man at his home. He asked the soldiers to let him speak to you as they were about to kill him, saying he had a gift for you.'

Albuquerque looked at the elderly man in contempt, wondering what gift he might possibly have for him.

'This book is my most precious possession. I have decided to give it to you as a gift.'

Miguel took the book from the man and gave it to Albuquerque, who started leafing through it. He could not read it. 'What is this? Go on, ask him. What's the book?'

The old man replied quietly, 'It is a book about Alexander the Great. When I saw you, I saw that man in you. You are both great conquerors who invaded faraway countries.'

'What is your city called?'

'Its name is Khor Fakkan.' The man looked at his devastated city with horror, and corrected himself. 'Its name *was* Khor Fakkan!'

Albuquerque asked his lieutenant, 'Is he saying it is called *Gorfacan*?'

'Yes, my lord.'

'And is he really saying I am like Alexander the Great? Give him food and water and let him go!' Albuquerque took another look at the book. 'You must translate this for me immediately, Miguel!'

− 23 −

India

HUSSEIN'S SHIPS ARRIVED IN Diu. Located on a penin-
sular headland on the northwestern coast of India, the
port looked more like a military fort. The fortifications were
formidable. Soldiers patrolled the length of the wall running
alongside the port. Coloured signalling flags and pennants were
being waved in different patterns from the tops of the towers,
suggesting updates were being sent around the clock. Military
ships scoured the bays surrounding the port, inspecting incoming ships to prevent Portuguese spies from entering the city.

Hussein saw all this movement from the top of his ship. He
knew that he had finally arrived in a city that had declared war
on the Portuguese and was prepared for all contingencies. He
was pleased, because what he needed most was a military base
rather than a trading post.

Si al-Tayeb approached Hussein after he saw his sharp interest in the city. He wanted to brief him a little about the king
he was going to meet in Diu. They kept their eyes focused
on the city and its port as they spoke. *Si* al-Tayeb had many
insights about India that he had gained throughout the years,
and wanted to share them with Hussein.

'Malik Ayaz is one of the few kings who declared war
against the invaders and did not accept their presence in India.

He clashed with them several times when they were exploring the coast, but they left him alone once they were welcomed by other kings to the south of here, where the land is more fertile and trade is more profitable.'

Hussein's gaze remained fixed on the flags on the tower tops, as he tried to decipher what they meant. He was impressed by the skilled soldiers sending messages in this manner.

Si al-Tayeb continued speaking, while pointing at the flags. 'I think they are relaying the news of your arrival, Hussein Pasha. This is good news for Malik Ayaz and the people of this city. They feel they are alone against the Portuguese. Ever since they wrote to Sultan al-Ghawri in Egypt and the Jabrid sultan in East Arabia, they have been waiting for help to come. I have never been to this city, but Qasimul Haq has good relations with Malik Ayaz. This is why he asked you to visit Diu; he is confident the two of you will forge a formidable alliance that can ultimately repel the Portuguese invasion.'

Si al-Tayeb paused for a moment, carefully weighing his words. 'This land is as strange as its people. Nothing is what it seems. It's so enchanting that your mind will be charmed as well as your senses.'

Hussein asked *Si* al-Tayeb to elaborate on his cryptic remark.

'What I mean, Hussein Pasha, is that India is a vast country, where religion mixes with tradition, tribes with kings, and loyalty with hostility. It's difficult for strangers to decipher what's happening. Everything has two sides here and they think in a different way than we do. Their calculations are almost completely different from our calculations. Those who you see as friends could become your enemies in the blink

236

of an eye, and vice versa. Loyalty here is like water: its source doesn't matter as long as it quenches one's thirst.'

He knocked unconsciously on the wooden railing. 'Be wary of everything, Pasha!'

Hussein was still not quite sure what *Si* al-Tayeb's point was, except that he should be careful. But wasn't he always careful? What mattered most to him was that he had found a strong ally and a walled city – and well-armed soldiers ready to fight.

Hussein disembarked with *Si* al-Tayeb. They walked with a large delegation that was waiting for them on the shore towards the palace of Malik Ayaz. Located on a hill overlooking the harbour, the palace was clad in white marble and surrounded by trees, gardens and fresh water streams.

Hussein was fascinated by how beautifully designed the place was. The delegation continued its way inside the palace, where Hussein could not help but notice the sheer magnitude of the wealth Malik Ayaz and his city lived in. This did not please Hussein: affluence in his view was a liability in times of war. For one thing, Hussein thought, it meant people lived in comfort and made them averse to taking up arms and defending themselves. For another, wealth put rulers in the difficult position of not wanting to lose their fortunes, palaces and precious possessions. Hussein wondered whether things would be different with Malik Ayaz.

The delegation crossed several halls and corridors, until they reached a large gate guarded by soldiers wearing superb uniforms. The soldiers carried *urumis*, strange weapons that Hussein had never seen before; out of the weapons' handles, several whip-like curling blades protruded. The soldiers also had *bagh naksa*, weapons resembling predators' claws that they wore on their knuckles, and used to slash through the bodies or heads of enemy soldiers.

The gate opened quickly, revealing behind it a great marble hall. In the centre, Malik Ayaz sat surrounded by his viziers, commanders and officers. It was a spectacle of wealth and power.

Hussein could not hide his surprise when he saw Malik Ayaz. The man had white skin and a ruddy complexion, golden blond hair that reached his shoulders and eyes as blue as the sea.

Malik Ayaz stood up when he saw Hussein, hugged him and kissed him. No one had greeted Hussein in this manner since he had arrived in India; Indians did not kiss one another. Malik Ayaz's movements were commanding, even those expressing his respect and amiability. He was definitely not Indian, Hussein thought to himself.

Hussein sat down with Malik Ayaz for a long conversation. The two men discussed all matters of common concern, from the Ottomans, the Safavids and the Mamluks, to the Portuguese and the spice trade, and exchanged the information they had.

Later on, Hussein left for his wing in the palace. Wanting to know more, he grabbed *Si* al-Tayeb's hand and quizzed him about Malik Ayaz. He wanted to know how he was king over the Indians when he was so different in appearance and comportment from them.

'I don't know much about him, but Qasimul Haq told me he was a Russian slave captured in battle,' *Si* al-Tayeb said. 'He was sold and resold many times until he fell into the ownership of one of the powerful kings of India. As he showed strong loyalty to his master and courage on the battlefield, his master made him commander of the army. After the king died, Malik

Ayaz seized power and banished all his rivals, ruling the city independently.'

Hussein shook his head in surprise. He had not expected to find slave soldiers in India as well. He thought the phenomenon was purely Egyptian.

In the evening, Hussein returned to Malik Ayaz's hall. The ruler of Diu welcomed him warmly and introduced him to Muzaffar Shah, ruler of Gujarat, saying, 'Muzaffar Shah is an old friend and a new ally. We agreed to fight the Portuguese ever since they appeared near the coasts of India.'

Hussein enjoyed himself that night. He felt his cause was in good hands. Malik Ayaz and Muzaffar Shah had significant military capabilities. Hussein was reassured that his mission was not in as much danger as he had thought, and reckoned their combined forces would be able to defeat the Portuguese if they used the resources at their disposal well.

Later that night, as they sat in the hall after dinner, a guard entered and whispered something in Malik Ayaz's ear. The governor nodded and spoke with the guard for a few minutes before telling his guests, 'A messenger from the Zamorin has come. He wants to talk to me in private, but I have asked him to enter so you can hear what he has to say.'

Hussein's thoughts raced. He had been at the Zamorin's court a few days earlier, and the Hindu king had not agreed to help the Mamluk fleet, and even asked him to leave as soon as possible. What had changed? Did the Zamorin want to convince Malik Ayaz to expel him like he had?

The messenger, who was dressed in the manner of Banyan merchants, entered the hall. Hussein was perplexed. Messengers did not usually dress like this. He must have come disguised then, Hussein thought to himself; but for what purpose?

The messenger came to Malik Ayaz, looking at Hussein and Muzaffar Shah in a way that suggested he did not expect them to be there. Malik Ayaz said, 'They are my allies, messenger. Your secret will be safe with them. You may speak freely.'

After a short moment of hesitation, the messenger spoke. 'Your Grace, you are aware that my master the Zamorin loathes the Portuguese. But he is in a difficult position. His kingdom relies on trade and he cannot close his borders to anyone. If he decides to fight them, he would be alone amid the Indian kingdoms allied to Portugal. He knows that the future of his kingdom depends on free trade. And he is aware that, though the Portuguese have not yet used violence, they will use it in the future. They are invaders, and invaders know only how to act like invaders!'

The messenger continued, 'My master will take part in the battle with you but he will keep his distance. The Portuguese will not know of it. He will send you men, money and supplies, but his only request is that you should keep this secret. He will deny having any links with you if something goes wrong.'

The men exchanged surprised looks before Malik Ayaz replied. 'We thank the Zamorin for his wisdom and his support. We will be grateful. I hope you will convey our best regards and wishes to your king.'

The messenger knelt, his palms joined together, and then stood and left. Before he exited from the hall, he stopped and turned to those seated. 'Qasimul Haq asked me to tell you that the Portuguese viceroy in India has learned of Hussein Pasha's arrival in Diu. He asked his son Lourenço de Almeida to lead the Portuguese fleet to meet Hussein in battle. I believe the Portuguese are on their way. It is advisable for you to begin preparations.'

'When do you think their fleet will be here?' Malik Ayaz asked.

'You will see their ships over the horizon within three days, I would reckon.'

It suddenly dawned on Hussein why Qasimul Haq had advised him to come to Diu. The city had declared war on the Portuguese, unlike other cities which were still reluctant or had even forged alliances with Portugal. His presence in Diu, he thought, would give him the moral and material support he needed in his war with the invaders. Qasimul Haq back at the Zamorin's court served as his early warning against any imminent Portuguese military action.

The leaders present at the court agreed to choose Hussein Pasha as the commander of the fleet that would confront the incoming Portuguese force. Hussein was asked to develop a battle plan.

Before the Portuguese were set to arrive, Hussein sent most of his fleet out to sea to conceal it. He kept two galleys flying the Mamluk flag at the entrance of the port, in addition to other Indian ships he asked to fly the Mamluk flag and remain near his two ships. He ordered the garrison manning the towers to place piles of firewood on their tops and to wait for his signal.

Three days later, exactly as the messenger had predicted, the Portuguese reached Diu. As their flotilla approached the port, they opened fire at the ships anchored at its entrance, believing them to be the entire Mamluk fleet. Hit by Portuguese cannonballs, the ships caught fire and some even exploded, sending shrapnel and debris in all directions. As soon as the Portuguese came closer and moved into the bay of Diu, however, Hussein gave orders to set the firewood on top of the

241

towers alight. The Mamluk ships he had sent out to sea spotted the beacons, and sailed stealthily towards the port, laying siege to the Portuguese fleet and blocking its path outside the bay.

Lourenço knew that he was trapped. He ordered two of his ships to break the siege by any means. The two ships scurried towards the Mamluk fleet, but the Mamluk sailors resisted fiercely. They were able to board the Portuguese ships, and melee combat ensued at close quarters, with swords and daggers. At the same time, the small Indian ships that were hiding behind the Mamluk galleys joined the battle. When Lourenço saw this, he decided to raid the port and try to take it at any cost, having now lost all hope of getting out.

Hussein's ship followed Lourenço's caravel and forced it into shallow waters. The Portuguese commander's ship ran aground and keeled sharply on its side, losing its ability to move. Mamluk and Indian ships surrounded it and opened cannon fire. A shell hit Lourenço's leg, and as he was screaming in agony, another shell hit him and tore him to pieces. The Mamluks and their Indian comrades boarded the Portuguese ships and put their sailors to the sword. Only nineteen men survived. They threw themselves into the sea before the other ships rescued them.

After the Muslims learned of Lourenço's demise, they allowed the remainder of the Portuguese ships to leave the port safely. As the battle ended, the Muslims thought this would be the end of the Portuguese presence in the sea. All regions of India that supported the resistance celebrated. News of this resounding victory spread across all ports, and Hussein Pasha was seen as their saviour. People raised Mamluk flags throughout the land to honour the heroes who had managed to deal with the threat.

The Portuguese despaired of their defeat. They barricaded themselves in their *feitorias*, waiting for a miracle. They had been routed far from home, and now had only a few ships left. They started seriously considering the prospect of leaving, if orders from Portugal came for them to retreat.

– 24 –

Bahrain

JAWHAR STOOD OUTSIDE THE farmstead where Bin Rahhal and Halima lived. He spoke to the guard and then put something in his hand, and the guard let him in. He walked through the dimness of the night towards the house, which sat in a quiet corner of the estate. Only a torch in front of the main door of the house provided light in its immediate surrounding, but beyond that everything was cloaked in pitch-black darkness. All Jawhar could hear were the frogs croaking and crickets singing. He was not used to the noises, and felt there was a deliberate attempt to unsettle him that night. He came close to the house and headed to the left side, walking along the fence for a few steps before stopping.

A silhouette appeared from behind the house and moved in his direction. He heard a small whistle that caught his attention, and looked around to make sure no one was following. He then walked in the direction of the whistle; Farah was there, waiting for him.

'Did you bring anything with you?' Jawhar asked in a hissing voice.

'Yes.' She lifted a small pouch and waved it in his face. 'This is the most precious thing I could find.'

'Is it the dagger you told me about?'

Farah nodded. 'It's the most valuable item in the whole house. But you must go now.'

The maid saw Jawhar's teeth flicker in the darkness. He was grinning. 'I'm not going anywhere. I'm coming with you to your room.'

'Are you crazy?' Farah gasped.

'Listen to me, Farah. You have given me everything of value that you could find. I will soon be free and we will marry. Why can't I come to your room? I cannot bear being apart from you any more.'

'You're insane! Nothing is going to happen until you're free and we're married!'

He grabbed her hand and pushed her roughly back through the door she had emerged from. She could not scream as he closed the door behind them.

The insects outside did not stop singing. Moths and all kinds of flying insects continued to dance around the torch, making a whispering-like noise, oblivious to the scorched bug carcasses scattered underneath.

On the following morning, as Emir Nasser entered his palace, he was surprised to see how few merchants were there. Usually, many more would be present in his *majlis*. Spotting Jawhar, he asked him, 'Where are all the guests? Why did they stop coming?'

Jawhar called out to an Indian merchant sitting not far from them, and asked him to explain the small number of Indians at the emir's court.

The Banyan came and bowed slightly. 'Things have changed, Your Highness. The sea routes have become too dangerous. The Portuguese have shown their fangs. Before we leave India, we must now go to their trading posts to get the *cartaz*, the permits, and pay duties on the goods we want to bring with us. Having these trade licences protected us from Portuguese ships, which intercept us from time to time. Recently, they started demanding bribes even after we show them the passes and proof of tax payments. It's just better not to trade because the taxes and bribes we pay to Portugal are more than any profit we can earn. Things are different now, Your Highness. The trade route between us is no longer passable.'

'Why does India not fight them and get rid of them?'

'There are great rivalries among Indian kings. They all want to woo the Portuguese, believing they are strong and that they would protect their trade. But this has not happened. In the end, only a few of our kings dared stand up to Portugal, and refused to have Portuguese trading posts in their territories. One such king is Malik Ayaz, who is now at war with the Portuguese.'

After a brief pause, the Banyan continued. 'A fearsome Egyptian fleet led by Hussein Pasha has arrived in India. I heard that the fleet dropped anchor in Diu before I came here. God knows what happened after that. Things are getting worse with every passing day. The Portuguese traders are mutating into warriors, and the disputes between our kings are sharper than ever before.'

The emir made nervous gestures with his finger. The few guests there understood he wanted them to leave. The *majlis* now empty, Nasser instructed Jawhar to send an urgent message to Sultan Muqrin, asking permission to send a fleet to fight the Portuguese, who had disrupted trade with India. Emir Nasser cautioned that if the situation were to remain unaddressed, then the entire trade of the Jabrid sultanate would be in danger.

Jawhar did not understand the purpose of this message; Emir Nasser was not the kind of man to be concerned by such matters. Jawhar stopped writing, looking at his master and trying to fathom his intentions.

'Don't stop, Jawhar. This crisis is our only chance to send the shepherd away from the herd!'

The emir let out a jarringly loud laugh. After he calmed down, he resumed dictating to Jawhar. 'As you know, Great Sultan, I suffer chronic pain in my back that prevents me from travelling and riding my horse. I shall therefore send Bin Rahhal to lead the fleet in my stead. He is the best man for the job.'

After Jawhar finished writing the sentence, he looked mischievously at his master. He finally understood Emir Nasser's motives, and shook his head in surprise at his cunningness.

The emir saw Jawhar looking at him and returned his wicked smile. 'Did you expect me to leave for India when I am so close to ensnaring her? Come then, seal the letter and send it to the sultan at once!'

Twenty days later, a message came from Sultan Muqrin to Emir Nasser, agreeing to his proposal to send Bin Rahhal to join the Mamluk fleet fighting the Portuguese. The sultan instructed his cousin to give Bin Rahhal all the money, men and military supplies he had access to without delay.

One day, Bin Rahhal sat playing chess with Emir Nasser. The emir's pawns fell one after the other to those of Bin Rahhal, who seemed immersed in the game, deeply thinking and calculating every move, unlike the emir, who seemed preoccupied with something else.

The emir stroked his moustache. 'You have already won, Bin Rahhal. I'm not in check yet, but you have taken most of my pawns. Anyway, listen, I've got news for you.'

Nasser reached for a parchment by his side and gave Bin Rahhal the sultan's letter. Bin Rahhal read it and immediately concluded that it was Emir Nasser who had suggested that he lead the campaign to India. No one else could have gone to the sultan with a matter like that.

When Bin Rahhal read Sultan Muqrin's orders to Halima, she could no longer stand. She burst into uncontrollable sobbing, her tears soaking Bin Rahhal's shoulder. Bin Rahhal did not tell her that it was Emir Nasser who had nominated him to go to India, and kept it for himself for the time being.

'Halima, I want you to go back to your father's house in Hormuz as soon as I set off. Don't stay here for too long after I leave. I won't feel comfortable with you here by yourself.'

Halima replied with a quavering voice. 'But I'm happy here. I can wait for your return—'

'No, you will not stay here! You will leave straight after me, understood?' he interrupted her.

'All right, all right, don't be angry. I promise, I will leave straight after you do. But I don't understand the reason for this insistence and urgency.'

'I will explain everything to you later. But now, you must prepare yourself to leave.'

Her dream of having a quiet, happy life with the husband she loved was shattered. As the days went by, she came to terms with the idea that she would soon be separated from him. She gave Farah money to distribute to the poor, instructing her to ask them to pray for her husband's safe return. But Farah gave the money to Jawhar, in the hope of collecting enough money to elope with him.

On the day Bin Rahhal was set to depart for India, the port filled with crowds of people, including women, children and the elderly, for their warriors' send-off. Bin Rahhal's ships did not have cannons like the Portuguese ships. They were smaller and were rigged with only two sails. Sultan Muqrin sent with him 200 Ottoman musketeers seconded to him by the sharif of Mecca to help him in his war effort.

Halima and Farah put on their veils and went to bid Bin Rahhal farewell, even if only from a distance. Halima could not bear staying at home and not seeing her beloved husband as he departed. The two women blended in with the others, trying to remain anonymous; Bin Rahhal never would have consented to their presence at the port.

Bin Rahhal was busy ensuring the fleet was well stocked with food, water and armaments. The port was teeming with people who came for various purposes, well-wishers and tearful folk saddened by the departure of their loved ones. Bin Rahhal appeared from time to time amid the crowds. Halima's eyes tirelessly scoured the sea of faces around her looking for him; whenever he emerged she smiled and wiped the tears from her eyes to see him better, and when he disappeared again she let loose the tears she was with-holding. Farah was by her side and went through the same emotions as her mistress, helping her find Bin Rahhal each time he vanished.

Ships started departing the port one after the other, until they were all gone. No one was left except the sons, wives, relatives and friends who chose to stay a while longer to catch a last glimpse, scent or wave from their loved ones.

Halima and Farah sat under a palm tree not far from the scene. Emir Nasser also stayed behind, waving his hand in exaggerated grief, with Jawhar by his side; the slave was scanning every direction, looking for the women.

Finally, Jawhar spotted Farah under the palm tree not far from the port. He knew that the woman standing next to her was none other than Halima. 'The shepherd has left and the herd is here,' he whispered in Emir Nasser's ear, pointing at the two women. 'I also have a surprise for you, Your Highness. I will show it to you when we are alone in the *majlis*.'

'What surprise? Come on, tell me!'

'I will tell you, Your Highness, don't worry. But I expect a gift in return!'

The emir fell silent. Jawhar's request for a reward convinced him to drop the subject; the slave had been talking excessively of freedom and money, Nasser thought to himself.

Halima kept her eyes fixed on Bin Rahhal's flotilla as it disappeared into the distant horizon. Her heart ached at his parting. She was all alone in a land where she knew no one. Her tears flowed down her face and she unconsciously reached for Farah's hand; Farah was crying too. The two women embraced tightly and comforted one another, as though making an unspoken oath never to leave each other. They both had an odd feeling, a feeling of isolation, weakness, defeat and fragility all at once. They felt like life had turned its back on them, had declared war on them, turning their lives upside down. The whole world and its colours had turned a dreary grey; the dreadful darkness left no room for goodness, and hope was removed from its roots.

Emir Nasser, from afar, could not see that the two women were shaking and weeping. His obsession with Halima blinded him from empathising with her pain and with what people felt in general when separated from their loved ones. Nasser did not shift his eyes from Halima. 'Jawhar, go to her and tell her I will visit her tonight. Tell her anything, but I must see her tonight.'

Jawhar looked at his master in surprise. He was not sure Nasser understood his own words. 'But she will never agree, master. She is sad for the departure of her husband. You must be a little patient until her sadness abates—'

Nasser interrupted him angrily. 'Damn you! How long should I wait? I want her as soon as possible. I'm in a hurry. You know when I want a woman I usually get her, and Halima will not be the exception. Do you hear?'

Jawhar knew that his freedom and his future depended on satisfying his master by any means possible. Halima might be the last woman he would bring for his master, because after he got his freedom and the money he was promised, he would leave him and depart for another country. 'Give me some time, Your Highness. I will do what I can to help you get her. My surprise will help you get what you want quietly and without a fuss. You just need to be patient.'

He looked at his master out of the corner of his eyes. 'But don't forget what you promised me, Your Highness. Freedom ... and money.'

Emir Nasser scanned the horizon to make sure Bin Rahhal's ships were gone. Nasser turned his eyes back to the place where Halima was. She was still there, sitting on a small rock; she felt so weak from sorrow that her knees and legs were no longer able to support her. Farah stood by her side. 'Let us go and speak to her. She is at her most vulnerable now,' he told Jawhar.

Farah saw Emir Nasser approach them. She shook her mistress's shoulder. Halima looked at the place Farah pointed at with her eyes.

Halima dried her tears with the tip of her scarf, which she then lifted to cover her whole face. Only a simple contour of it was now visible. Emir Nasser and Jawhar came up to the two women. Halima tried to stand up but could not, and Farah pressed on her shoulder suggesting she should remain seated; this was no time for meaningless courtesy, Farah thought.

Farah kept her sight fixed on the two men. Halima's breathing quickened to the point that it was almost audible to her maid.

The emir greeted them. 'Peace, mercy and blessings of God be upon you.'

Farah forced herself to return his greeting. Halima's lips moved to do the same, but only a murmur came out.

Emir Nasser could easily and quickly switch between two contradicting personas. He was the kind of man who could change his personality at will to deceive others. Nasser spoke in a tone different from his usual one, with the demeanour to match it. 'Don't be sad, Halima. Bin Rahhal left us to defend Islam and fight the Portuguese. He will return to us safe and victorious, God willing.'

Halima remembered what her husband had told her about Nasser. She squirmed in discomfort. It occurred to her that he might have had something to do with sending her husband to India, but there was little she could do about it now. Halima wanted him to leave her to weep for her husband alone, but this man's arrival in her life was not unlike the sudden onset of disease. She had to deal with him because he was in charge in the absence of Sultan Muqrin, and she had no idea what he was capable of while her husband was away.

Nasser's eyes scanned Halima's body frantically, looking for a gap in her clothing through which they could sneak in. Halima took on an uninviting posture, hiding what she could of her figure, feeling the sting of his lustful ogling.

The emir stood for some time in front of the two women without speaking. He was afraid to say anything that could spoil Jawhar's plan. 'I pray God return your husband safely. He is the only one capable of leading a great fleet like this.' He paused for a moment, wanting to remind her of his position, stature and power. 'I must return to the palace to tend to some important matters there. No one can lift a finger without me.'

Halima did not hear what he said, however. She was looking at the distant horizon beyond which her husband had vanished. She felt rage against the horizon now – the place past which eyesight breaks down and loved ones disappear – and wished she could fling the emir beyond it, into oblivion.

Nasser left and Jawhar followed him. Halima felt the overbearing weight of his presence lift from her shoulders. She drew a deep breath and then let it back out gently, as though she had been holding her breath for all the time he was near her.

Farah offered Halima her hand to help her stand up. Halima had not been sitting for too long, but she felt her knees were stiff and her thighs ached. Her mouth was also dry. She held on to Farah's arm for some time before she said, 'Let us go back home. I'm very tired. We must leave for Hormuz tomorrow, and it will be a long and arduous journey.'

Halima entered her bedroom. She took a look at the chest housing Sultan Muqrin's dagger and some of her and her husband's valuables and clothes. She decided to pack it for her trip. She was not going to let the chest leave her sight. After a few seconds of hesitation, she reopened the chest and took a robe belonging to her husband and smelled it. She took it with her to bed, trying to catch Bin Rahhal's scent while tears sprang into her eyes.

Suddenly, Halima remembered that she had not seen the dagger in the chest. 'Where could it have disappeared?' she asked herself. It must be under the piles of clothes, she thought, dismissively.

She wrapped herself with the bedcovers and drifted off to sleep. Halima had a strange dream: she was walking aimlessly on a path, apparently lost. On her arm was perched a beautiful colourful bird that sang continuously. As she contemplated its features, the bird started morphing into a raptor, with frightening eyes and a long, sharp beak. The bird grew in size so much that her arm could no longer support its weight. When the raptor spread its wings, Halima, oddly, spat on it, and suddenly the bird returned to its original size and shape, beautiful and colourful, and resumed its singing. As she tried to shift it with her other hand, it flew away and vanished into the sky.

Halima woke up and found herself drenched in sweat. She called out for Farah who ran back to her. Halima told her maid about the dream. 'Can you explain it to me, Farah?'

'It sounds strange, my lady. Probably jumbled dreams with no meaning.'

'No, Farah. I remember every detail vividly as though I could still see it. Even the bird's eyes spoke to me in a way that I almost comprehended. Everything about it seemed familiar. There is something about this dream, Farah.'

Farah gave her a strong embrace. 'You're going through a difficult time. You have not taken Bin Rahhal's absence well. But everything will be fine, my lady.' Farah pushed Halima's shoulders away from her to be able to see her face. 'Listen to me, my lady. You have to be strong. You are not a young girl any more. Don't let sorrow get the better of you. I can't bear seeing you miserable. We must help ourselves to be able to cope with the remainder of our days alone. Neither one of us will make it on her own. I implore you, my lady!'

Farah took the tip of the blanket and brought it to Halima's face to wipe her tears. 'Come now, let's move. We have a long trip to Hormuz.'

Halima got out of bed. Farah followed her, holding her arm. Before she left the room, Halima pointed at the chest where Bin Rahhal had placed his most valuable possessions and clothes. 'I have opened the chest but I didn't see the dagger that Bin Rahhal gave me for safekeeping. I need to make sure it's there under the clothes to be reassured.'

Blood rushed to Farah's face. She gulped several times quickly. 'Why are you thinking about the dagger? Don't worry yourself about it now!'

'It's very important. It belongs to Sultan Muqrin.'

Farah replied with a stutter, 'Where would it go? It must be in the chest, but you didn't look for it well. Forget about it now. We'll look for it later.'

Farah felt like she wanted the earth to open up and swallow her. The magnitude of what she had done both to her mistress and herself was beginning to dawn on her.

Suddenly, a loud voice boomed from outside. 'Keep your luggage in its place. Sailors have spotted Portuguese ships scouring the Gulf. They refuse to sail with them around. We won't be able to make the journey to Hormuz for now!'

– 25 –

Hormuz

THE AIR BLOWING ACROSS Hormuz's beach was cool and refreshing. In September the weather usually turned mild, and the humidity subsided. Hormuzis went for strolls at the beach or at the market.

That morning, a mist hung in the air, though it added a tinge of charm to the brittle glass-like sea. As the sun inched higher in the sky, temperatures rose. The fog lifted and the sky cleared. Hormuzis at the market opened their umbrellas to shield themselves from the blazing sun as they shopped for food and groceries to stockpile.

Conversations exchanged during the buying and selling were subdued. Merchants hiked their prices and people bought whatever they could with whatever money they had. Their faces looked crushed and dejected. No one at the market spoke of new merchandise, wind patterns, ships' movements or trade activity any more. Instead, the only topic was the Portuguese raids on the coast of Oman.

Ships carrying dismembered and mutilated bodies had come to shore, and people could not forget the small boat that came from Oman, whose passengers gave horrific accounts of Portuguese massacres there. The survivors had been terribly maimed: their ears and noses cut off, so starved and emaciated that their bones almost perforated their skin. Many of them had bled to death. The Hormuzis were not going to forget that ugly sight for as long as they lived. Hormuz was facing a harsh reality and a ruthless butcher who had sent them an unequivocal message about what he intended to do to those who dared resist him.

The port looked deserted. Visiting ships did not stay long any more. They would offload their goods, re-supply and leave as fast as possible. All the talk about the looming Portuguese threat made the merchants edgy and fearful, and the deserted port in turn signalled to other merchants that things were not right, prompting them to take their money out of the island. The flight of business and trade meant the island too would bleed to death if things did not change.

Without warning, a horn blared from the direction of the king's palace walls. People turned to the source of the noise, and heard a man nearby pointing at the horizon and crying, 'They have arrived! They are here!'

The Portuguese armada towered over the horizon like primeval monsters. No one had seen anything like this before: huge masts rising over the sea so high they were almost flying, propelled by grandiose square-shaped sails displaying an intimidatingly large red cross.

Hormuz was ill-prepared to deal with these death-bearers. The islanders were not even sure what they were seeing: were these floating fortresses? Or was it their terror that made them see the invaders as more awesome than they really were? Either way, they had no choice but to defend their city in every way possible.

The cry was a wake-up call to those who could bear arms. All capable men brought all the weapons they could to the

257

coast. In the previous days, Hormuzis had seen many boats carrying women and children from the island to the Persian mainland, to escape impending death. The exodus took place furtively, because the wealthy people of the kingdom did not want Hormuzis to say they were smuggling their families and treasures off the island. The rich were often the first to benefit from good fortune, and the first to flee from adversity.

After the war horn sounded, the flight from the island was no longer a concealed affair. Many families were seen dashing to the shore where smugglers waited to carry them in their boats to any destination, charging them large sums of money. The north coast of the island was crowded with fleeing people carrying their portable valuables. It was a tragic scene that the island had never experienced before: the screaming of women and children intermingled with the voices of the boatmen who now demanded impossible fees for their services.

The men came out with their shields and weapons, and lined up randomly in front of the port. Behind stood cavalrymen in gorgeous uniforms, and camel cavalries carrying long spears. Sailors rushed into their small ships, and within hours everyone was ready to fight; or so they thought.

The palace gate opened and the king emerged riding on a horse shorn of its usual caparison. He advanced towards the harbour. Attar and the commander of the army accompanied him.

The king and his men joined the troops at the harbour. Attar saw the Portuguese ships and was awestruck by their sheer size and the number of cannons sticking out of their gun ports. He took one look at his army and realised he would be fighting a losing battle.

The Hormuzi army looked weak and undisciplined. Ever since the conflict began between the brothers several years ago, it had been neglected and little training or equipment had been supplied. It was too late to do anything about it now.

People were transfixed by the beasts and their holy sails charging in their direction. Everyone looked alert and angry about what they had heard and seen with the mutilated victims arriving on their shore. They did not want to be another entry in the long list of the people tormented by the Portuguese.

The ships drew very close to the harbour and dropped their anchors. Albuquerque had gathered extensive intelligence from the prisoners and sailors about Hormuz's military capabilities and wealth. He was eager to capture and control it at any cost.

What Covilhã had written about the island's wealth and charm was the real motive for Albuquerque's arrival on its shores. Throughout their journey, Miguel had never tired of reminding his boss of what Covilhã had written in his report about Hormuz. The descriptions stoked his thirst for blood and love of money, and Albuquerque decided to conquer it before going to India as he had initially planned.

A Portuguese ship lowered a small boat carrying Albuquerque's personal delegate, Miguel Ferreira. It made its way between the military ships scattered in the port, and reached the wharf. When he debarked, a Hormuzi officer took him to the king and his vizier, Attar. Miguel proceeded to read a letter from Albuquerque demanding the king of Hormuz surrender and pay tribute, or face the destruction of the city and the obliteration of its people.

The king asked him, 'What do you want from us? Why do you not leave us alone?'

Miguel replied in a tone that suited his cruel, sunburnt face. 'We are the messengers of the king of Portugal. All these lands, cities and people belong to our great king pursuant to the papal bull and the Treaty of Tordesillas. We are here to raise our flag and cross, spread Christianity and save humanity from heresy. You must therefore submit.'

When Miguel finished, the king said, 'We ask Albuquerque to give us time to consult with the leaders of the city. We shall give you our answer tomorrow morning.'

Albuquerque interpreted the king's response as a challenge to him, and decided to raid the island the next day, before the answer was supposed to come. At night, he ordered his ships to get as close to shore as possible without being noticed.

In the morning, people were roused by the sounds of explosions, which caused noises they had never heard in their lives. They went up to the roofs to find out what was happening and were stricken by terror when they saw the Portuguese caravels raining down hell on them. Fires were raging throughout the city and blood-curdling screams were coming from all directions.

The kingdom never expected to be invaded and bombarded with cannonballs, and many felt trapped in a terrible nightmare. The flying death shooting out of the caravels blockading the entrance of their city had them wrapped in its wings now.

It was deadly mayhem. People scrambled through the city's alleyways and streets, not knowing where to go and where to take shelter from the shells, as women wailed and children screeched. Not far away, the king's palace came under a heavy barrage of cannonballs, turning many parts of it into rubble.

260

The Hormuzi dhows and galleys started leaving the harbour to attack the Portuguese ships. But the caravels gave them no chance and destroyed them, ship by ship, as soon as they retracted their anchors. The Portuguese dropped their landing boats carrying soldiers, who proceeded to finish off the wounded and drowning Hormuzi sailors, stabbing them with short spears or swords. Afterwards, they used grappling hooks to pull the dead bodies close and loot their armour, weapons and valuables. The port's entrance was flooded with floating corpses and limbs and many of the ships anchored there had caught fire.

The Hormuzi army was scattered. Its casualties were too many to cope with, and neither horsemen nor camel-mounted knights were able to repel the seaborne death. In a matter of seconds, the army was in disarray. There were no leaders, formations or orders left.

In the distance, white flags were slowly hoisted above the king's palace. Others followed suit and raised the banners of surrender, in the hope the Portuguese would see them and cease their bombardment.

Albuquerque's reptilian eyes watched this unfold from the deck of his ship. Miguel was behind him, clutching Covilhã's precious report; he needed to open the file from time to time to respond to Albuquerque's incessant queries about the island, its fortunes, and its strengths and weaknesses. Miguel kissed the manuscript as if it were his lover.

At sundown, Albuquerque ordered his ships to cease fire. The once-beautiful kingdom of Hormuz was now in ruins.

After the last cannonball shot by the invaders, people needed a few minutes to ensure the white flags had worked. The noises of war gave way to screaming from under the rubble and the survivors on the roads, some of whom were burned or dismembered. Corpses began to wash up on the shore joining ghastly-looking piles, as some bodies were animated by the waves in a sickening sight. Attar felt that Judgement Day had come, and that Hormuz would never be the same.

Albuquerque smiled contentedly at the sight of the white banners fluttering over the city's skyline. Addressing his officers, he said, 'Now we can negotiate with the defeated.'

The people of Hormuz did not know what they should mourn most: their devastated city, the souls that had been stolen by the Portuguese cannons, or the ill fortune that brought these ships to their shores. The kingdom of Hormuz was burning, homes were levelled and roads turned inside out; dead bodies filled up alleys and passageways and soldiers' corpses were cast back to shore by the waves. Everything that had taken them and their ancestors centuries to build had been obliterated by Albuquerque in a matter of hours.

The call to prayer came from the minaret of the grand mosque. The muezzin sang with a sobbing voice, and could not continue the *azan*. Some people tried to finish the call to prayer on his behalf, also while sobbing, but Albuquerque ordered one of his officers to fire at the minaret and silence it once and for all. The shell did not hit the tower directly, but exploded nearby, causing a strong aftershock that destroyed part of the minaret's foundation. It leaned slightly to one side, prompting the muezzin to flee quickly. The minaret fell silent, and the *azan* would never be heard again from this mosque.

The kingdom of Hormuz slept that night to the cries of the wounded and the bereaved. The screams came from every neighbourhood, alleyway and district of the city. The wounded were gathered at specific points on the roads while people rushed to find someone to treat them and care for them.

Cries of horror and grief echoed whenever a soul departed its body. Gravediggers worked non-stop to cope with the number of corpses, until they tired and started throwing the dead into shallow pits, covering them with a thin layer of dirt. With food for both humans and animals now in short supply, starving dogs came later at night and dug some of the bodies out.

The next morning, the Hormuzis watched nervously the floating fortresses besieging their shore, afraid that the ships would decide to fire again and snuff out whatever life was left in their kingdom. Then they saw a boat dropping from one of the vessels, making its way to the harbour; they knew that Albuquerque's messenger had returned.

Those who had some strength left in them gathered around the king's palace, waiting to see the outcome of the messenger's visit. They were afraid to meet the same fate as the people of the Omani coast.

Inside the palace, King Salghur was stricken by panic and grief, and was not in a state that allowed him to meet the messenger. Attar came instead.

As usual with Albuquerque's messengers, Miguel did not come to discuss terms but to dictate them. Miguel was armed and armoured to the teeth. Standing impertinently in front of Attar, he unrolled a scroll and began to read it:

I, on behalf of Governor and Captain-General Afonso de Albuquerque, order you to surrender and accept the following terms:

- *Hormuz shall pay an annual tribute to the king of Portugal to be determined by Governor and Captain-General Albuquerque.*

- *Hormuz shall open its port to Portuguese trade.*
- *All tax revenues shall be paid to the king of Portugal.*
- *The Portuguese flag shall fly over the royal palace.*
- *All Hormuz's possessions and settlements shall become the possessions of the king of Portugal.*
- *A Portuguese adviser shall be appointed to rule the island on behalf of Governor and Captain-General Albuquerque.*

When Albuquerque's messenger emerged from the palace, people were still unsure of the outcome. Miguel boarded the boat and left. Attar then came out, walking with heavy steps and looking down. He addressed the small crowd. 'The kingdom of Hormuz has surrendered to Portugal!'

The people's reaction was a combination of relief and sadness. Relief because they felt that the immediate ordeal of war and death had lifted, and sadness because they knew they had lost their king, their kingdom and their centuries-old way of life forever, their future now in the hands of a merciless invader. Many of them broke into tears, as the shocking realisation hit them.

In the afternoon that day, the Portuguese paraded their forces on the main road outside the port, carrying a cross in brazen provocation. Hormuzis spotted another flag bearing the cross fluttering over the king's palace, and knew that the worst was yet to come.

– *26* –

India

NEWS OF THE MAMLUK victory spread across the western coast of India. Fact mixed with legend as was usual for the tales told by sailors in their gatherings. Amir Hussein who came from Egypt became a symbol of resistance. Many who did not have the chance to see him tried to imagine what he looked like. Some were fanciful and concocted different images for him in their heads. There were stories that he rode on a magic carpet above the water, and that he fought with two swords, one made from fire and one from lightning. Mothers told their children stories about Hussein to comfort them and alleviate the terror they felt at the accounts they heard about the Portuguese. Hussein became the hope of the terrorised people of the coast, and a legend for young people inspired by his resistance.

Apart from the many myths woven around him across the regions of western India, Hussein's victory drew different reactions. In devastated Hormuz, the news of the Mamluk fleet's victory over the Portuguese was a glimmer of light dispelling some of the darkness of their own defeat. Hope started to replace despair, and bands of partisans began to operate, hunting down drunken Portuguese sailors, burning their food stores and looting Portuguese tax collection offices at the port.

Albuquerque was particularly incensed over the Mamluk victory. The Portuguese conquistador ordered Miguel to find the best spot on the island to build a fort to protect the Portuguese from partisan attacks, and from which he could rule and keep all his treasures in safety.

Miguel's search did not take long. The sound of the call to prayer had alerted him to the grand mosque in the city centre. Enormous and easily modifiable, it was perfect, and it would not take too much time to get ready.

Attar learned of Albuquerque's intentions. He called on him at his residence, pleading with him to change his mind. A decision like this would enrage the populace, the Hormuzi vizier argued, and would kindle a spirit of resistance on the island. The vizier told Albuquerque the Safavids could use this as a pretext to intervene as well.

After a few meetings between the Portuguese conquistador and King Salghur and Attar, it was agreed to build a fort on the cape north of the island, not far from the Persian mainland, to protect Hormuz against any possible Safavid assault. Though the tax collection office was in the port, the two sides agreed the money would be moved every day to the fort guarded by Hormuzi and Portuguese soldiers. Until the fort was completed, however, the Portuguese would use the grand mosque in the city as their garrison and treasury.

Albuquerque stood after the meeting without looking at the king or Attar. He pointed at the promontory at the far north of the island and said, 'We shall build a large fort there, and call it the Fort of Our Lady of Victory.'

Attar glanced at King Salghur, who was now only interested in surviving on the throne, having forfeited everything else. The Hormuzi vizier knew the poor king had lost his sense of place and time, and had thus become a burden on the island and the throne.

Miguel replied in a spiteful tone, 'It's a beautiful name, my lord. Our Lady of Victory.'

Attar clenched his fists, trying to suppress his outrage. He turned to Miguel, who was sitting next to Albuquerque. Their eyes met and Miguel stared back in defiance as he said, 'Yes, my lord, a very nice name indeed, Our Lady of Victory. The whole world will remember this name for centuries to come. Victory over these heretics is the work of Our Blessed Lady.'

Miguel gave Attar a wicked smile, as his words cut into him like a razor-sharp blade.

In Diu, celebrations continued for several days until news of Albuquerque's victory in Hormuz finally came. The dispatches said the Portuguese commander was building a mighty fort that would become his base to launch attacks and conquer the rest of the ports in western India.

Bin Rahhal reached Diu in this climate. His arrival was a huge event; people felt that Muslim forces had started mobilising in earnest to defeat the Portuguese, and a spirit of *jihad* and resistance spread among the populace like wildfire.

In the royal court, Malik Ayaz seemed at the peak of his activity, vitality and euphoria. He had triumphed over the Portuguese, becoming a name to be reckoned with. The victory reinforced his legitimacy, and this former Russian slave was now a master to be obeyed and a holy warrior.

Ayaz sat himself in the manner of Indian rajas, lying on a gilded divan padded with silk and chewing betel leaves. A visibly cheerful Hussein sat beside him, trying to chew the leaves Ayaz offered him. It was not as easy as it had seemed to him initially; chewing something and trying not to swallow the resulting paste was difficult and required practice.

Ayaz spat in a gilded bowl on a table nearby, then wiped his mouth with the back of his hand. 'A dear guest has arrived from Arabia, Hussein Pasha. We are very pleased to have him with us. He brought with him many ships and seasoned warriors that we desperately need. I have ordered my people to make sure he is received well, but I also want you to meet him.'

Hussein replied, trying to speak clearly in spite of the betel leaves in his mouth, 'This is good news, indeed, Your Grace. We don't know how strong Albuquerque's armada in Hormuz is. It might be more formidable than the fleet we defeated. We must be prepared for Albuquerque too. The Portuguese cannons have proven effective in battle as you know.'

Bin Rahhal was dressed in his best robes and wore kohl and perfume. He wore on his shoulder a cloak with gilded embroidery, and selected his best turban to wear on his head. He wore a gilded dagger in a cummerbund around his waist. And yet his attire, like that of all Arabs, was not flamboyant, but rather simple and modest when compared to the attire of the Indian nobility.

The Arabian vizier entered the royal hall where Ayaz and Hussein were sitting. He was awestruck by its grandeur, craftsmanship and the affluence of its master. Malik Ayaz received him in exaggerated cordiality, embracing him tightly. He invited him to sit near Hussein.

Bin Rahhal felt relieved when he heard Hussein address him in Arabic. 'So you are the infamous Hussein! Your reputation has travelled across the sea. Sailors sing your praises, and have described you as a superhuman.'

Hussein guffawed. 'I'm afraid I'm too human, and most certainly do not wield lightning and thunder.' Hussein's tone then changed. 'What news do you have?'

Bin Rahhal tried to banish the phantom of Halima forming in front of him. He said, 'As we approached Debal, we heard that a Portuguese conquistador called Albuquerque had raided and destroyed several ports along the Omani coast. This Albuquerque attacked and ransacked the kingdom of Hormuz as well. It's my belief that he's en route to India, intending to seize the routes used in the spice trade between India and Arab lands. His home-land is in dire need of controlling this lucrative trade.'

Bin Rahhal had never met a Portuguese before. He did not know what they looked like or how big their galleys were, or anything other than what sailors had told him. He knew that sailors' yarns were infused with myths, and did not want to convey news to Hussein that was not credible. 'Sultan Muqrin ordered me to come here and join the war effort against the Portuguese. I shall have the honour of taking part in the *jihad* alongside you. We have heard so many things about you since you came to India from Egypt.'

Hussein smiled at Bin Rahhal's flattery. 'We are delighted with your presence, brother. Having you with us will help in our battle and make us more confident in ourselves.'

The bond between Bin Rahhal and Hussein grew gradually stronger. They became good friends who easily opened up to one another. Being so far from home was a catalyst for friendships, as it made them a more urgent need and source for safety and reassurance. They would meet at the end of the day on one of their ships or at the palace, to share their hopes and concerns.

One night, as the two men sat together, Bin Rahhal suddenly asked his friend, 'Do you know what love is, Hussein?'

'I know love, but I have not experienced it.'

Bin Rahhal slapped the front of his turban and then adjusted his seating position. 'You should experience it, but don't go looking for it. Like fate, it will come to you without you planning it.'

'Clearly you speak from experience?'

'Yes, I do. It happened to me in Hormuz, the kingdom that now lies devastated.'

'In Hormuz?' Hussein asked in surprise.

'Yes. I had just come out of a battle there when I first saw her. I couldn't take my eyes off her. Everything about her face and body captivated me – her eyes, her nose, her lips, even her eyebrows. I couldn't sleep that night, a night that felt as though the sun had decided not to rise the next morning. Days passed slowly afterwards, until I decided to ask her father for her hand in marriage, having despaired of the prospect of ever forgetting her.'

'That quickly, huh, Bin Rahhal? Couldn't you have waited a little?' Hussein teased.

'You can imagine what it was like as I sat waiting for what her father would say after I told him I wanted to marry her. I felt he wasn't too fond of the idea. Oh, Hussein, I could barely believe that she was finally mine when the order came for me to leave Bahrain. My heart was broken. She was standing on the pier of the harbour crying bitterly, while I pretended not to see her to avoid being embarrassed by my affection for her. She came to bid me farewell. I didn't want her to be there but she insisted on coming, without my permission. I know her too well. She is stubborn, and her heart is so full

270

of pure love that it can almost accommodate everyone in the entire world!'

Hussein thought it best to change the subject. 'What have you heard about Albuquerque, Bin Rahhal?'

'I was told he likes to drink ale from the skulls of dead children. Terror travels ahead of his ships, and ruin and destruction accompany him wherever he goes. I heard that he is a bloodthirsty person who enjoys tormenting others. He is not a normal person. A person who dismembers people and cuts children in half in front of their mothers can't be human. There is a monster under his human skin.'

Hussein knew what the Portuguese were like. He knew that they had no mercy in their hearts, and saw other people as heretics who must be expunged from the Earth. Albuquerque was not going to be any better than his predecessors, and was possibly much worse.

The Mamluk admiral was once again given to his thoughts. He also wanted to include Bin Rahhal in his next plan. 'We must be ready, Bin Rahhal. A lot has been said about this man. What I think we have on our hands is a cunning and brutal enemy. He has not yet arrived and he is not familiar with the plan we used with Lourenço de Almeida in our first battle. We might be able to implement the plan to the letter against him again. However, your ships are not fit to take on the Portuguese fleet. They are small and carry no guns, though we might be able to use them as bait when he arrives.'

Bin Rahhal was surprised. 'What do you mean, bait? I'm going to need those ships for my return journey!'

Hussein laughed. 'If we are defeated, your ships will be no good to you either. Your men are not used to dealing with cannons, Bin Rahhal. They may be good with daggers and swords but guns are something else completely.'

Bin Rahhal responded with resolve. 'True, but you must train us on how to confront and deal with them.'

The two men soon became like brothers. Bin Rahhal had no qualms about sharing his most intimate concerns with Hussein, whenever he had the chance. One day, Hussein asked him about the reason for the sadness on his face.

'Being apart from Halima is killing me. And I know nothing about what has happened to her since I left. I asked her to leave for Hormuz as soon as I set sail, but the Portuguese have conquered the island. I don't know whether she is there or whether she is still in Bahrain, but either way I'm fearful for her safety.'

Hussein tried to comfort him, but Bin Rahhal continued, 'She's completely cut off from me. I don't know where she is. After what happened in Hormuz, mail stopped travelling between ports. I truly despise those Portuguese for managing to ruin everything beautiful about the sea.'

Bin Rahhal lifted his head and looked at Hussein. 'What do you intend to do about Albuquerque?'

'We must be prepared for him. We don't know his combat tactics, though we have been told he uses artillery to level cities and kill civilians, and then lands with his forces to finish everyone off. He doesn't take prisoners, as his ships have no room for them, being already crowded with soldiers. If he takes prisoners, it is to use them to send warning messages after he dismembers them and sends them to the cities he intends to attack – to tell his enemies: "If you don't surrender, this is what I'm going to do to you."'

Over the next days, Bin Rahhal and Hussein became preoccupied with training troops, building fortifications, and upgrading and supplying their ships. They relied on Qasimul Haq to provide them with intelligence on the Portuguese movements. The Portuguese now had a trading post in Calicut, and it was from there that news about their activities was leaking.

– 27 –

Bahrain

J AWHAR MADE HIS WAY to the palace of Emir Nasser before
sunrise, holding a package in his hand protectively. He sat
with the servants who were sipping coffee in a yard outside
the palace. He detested the bitter black beverage that a Yemeni
merchant had brought a while back. Jawhar had heard him tell
the emir coffee was a magical drink that banished sleep and
reinvigorated the body. But the drink did nothing for Jawhar,
save for leaving an unpleasant bitter taste in his mouth.

He poured his cup on the floor and watched the ground
quickly absorb it. Jawhar grabbed the package and felt its
contents to make sure the dagger was still inside. He had
managed to sleep with Farah, but he had not told his master
yet, and preferred to wait until he got his reward when he
delivered the dagger.

Emir Nasser entered his *majlis* a short while after sunrise.
Jawhar approached him wearing a knowing smile that Nasser
recognised well. The two men, who went a long way back,
had by now developed their own unwritten and unspoken
language. 'What do you have for me, Jawhar? That smile tells
me you've done what you were asked!'

Jawhar sat down quickly and set the package before his
master in the manner of someone laying down the hunted

carcass of a rare animal. 'I have devoured the small bird. Now all that is left to do is for you to devour the big one, Your Highness!'

Nasser was astonished. He sat up quickly as was his wont whenever a woman was mentioned. 'What are you saying? Tell me everything, quickly!'

Jawhar smiled, revealing his teeth. 'As you know, I've been courting her maid Farah for months. I told her you wanted a hefty sum in return for my freedom. She gave me any valuables and jewellery she stumbled upon so that I could buy back my freedom.' He pointed at the package in front of him. 'This is the surprise I told you about, master!'

He paused for a brief moment before he took the package and opened it slowly, savouring his master's tense anticipation. Jawhar took out the dagger and brought it to Nasser, who let out a strong exhale before he said, 'What the devil is this? I've never seen anything so beautiful!' Nasser turned the dagger over, scrutinising each jewel embedded in it and relishing its workmanship. 'It's glorious, Jawhar. Did she tell you how much it's worth? It must be worth a fortune!'

As the emir spoke to his slave, his eyes were transfixed by the bladed artefact. Deciding he had seen enough, he put it in his cummerbund. He was pleased to have it there, complementing his waist.

Jawhar, concerned that his master had decided the dagger's best use was ornamental, shed his smile. 'Allow me to explain the importance of this blade, master. This dagger comes from a raja of India, who had it made from jewels belonging to his mother and wife, as a gift to the caliph in Cairo. The raja's messenger brought it to Sultan Muqrin to deliver it to Egypt, and the sultan left it with Bin Rahhal for safekeeping when he had to put down the rebellion in Najd. I expect the sultan to ask Bin Rahhal for the dagger at any time.'

Jawhar paused and then continued, 'Bin Rahhal feared more for this dagger than for his own life. Halima hid it in a chest containing his clothes and private effects, and hid the chest in her room. Bin Rahhal did not want the dagger to leave his sight, not even for a second, but Farah knew about it, being Halima's trusted maid, and was able to steal it and give it to me. She asked me not to tell anyone about it, expecting the dagger to go a long way towards buying back my freedom.'

The emir did not take his eyes off the masterpiece at his waist. 'You are a demon, Jawhar!'

The slave laughed. He loved it when his master flattered him. Then, in a half-whispering voice, he said, 'The dagger's presence in your possession means that you've been in Halima's bedchamber. You can blackmail her with this. People, even her husband, will not believe any story other than that she gave it to you herself. You can use the dagger to get her. You have no better leverage. But you must do it quietly and without a fuss, master. It might take a bit of time before she falls into your trap.'

The emir laughed out loud. His demeanour became brisk and his face reddened with euphoria, as though he had just won a battle. 'If you weren't my slave, I would kiss you. I have a great prize for you, Jawhar, if I manage to have Halima.'

Jawhar's smile disappeared again. 'Will you not give me anything in return for this dagger, master?' he asked in disbelief.

'You will not get anything until I get Halima. Do you understand?' Nasser stressed every syllable of the sentence; Jawhar took it as a veiled threat and did not persist.

After a moment of silence, Emir Nasser spoke again, in an impatient tone. 'You must go to Halima now and tell her I want her. Tell her I have the dagger and, if she resists, then I will declare that she is my lover and that she has gifted me the dagger her husband kept in her bedroom. Say this clearly, and make her understand that everyone will know about it if she hesitates.'

Jawhar was shocked, not out of compassion but because he knew that such a scandal would cause nothing short of an earthquake in the city, and that heads would roll as a result. Bin Rahhal was Sultan Muqrin's trusted vizier, and Halima was the daughter of *Khawaja* Attar, the famed vizier of the kingdom of Hormuz. In his mind, Jawhar had imagined that the whole affair would be conducted inconspicuously. True, Emir Nasser could blackmail Halima with the dagger now, but Jawhar thought the matter needed the sort of subtlety that this fool was so lacking in.

Dismayed by the prospect of a full-blown scandal that would be the result of his own actions, Jawhar held his head in his hands. He wanted to explain to his master the disaster that awaited them if Halima rejected him, but it was clear that Emir Nasser was determined to go down this road.

'Listen, Jawhar. I cannot bear to wait any longer. You shall go to Halima and tell her I have the dagger and tell her that I want her. Tell her if she doesn't submit, then I will tell everyone that she gave me the dagger her husband hid in his private chest in his bedroom as a gift, after she fell in love with me. Everyone will believe me and doubt her; I am the emir. Tell her so.'

Jawhar tried to explain his point of view. 'Your Highness, you have the dagger now. You can use it as leverage to get to Halima in a different way. You can get close to her, then talk to her about the dagger quietly. She will understand that she is at your mercy without you having to declare it. But to threaten her like this exposes us to a big scandal that could be our undoing!'

The emir's expression hardened. 'Curse you, you lowly slave. You will never change no matter what I do for you. Go and do as I command, and never dare second-guess me again!' Jawhar was about to move when the emir said, 'Have you heard about how the Portuguese ransacked Hormuz recently? After that crushing defeat, her father is no longer the vizier. He may have even died in the battle. She has no one now. She is all alone and at my mercy. Tell her she will not be able to resist me and that she must submit. Now go. Come on, go.'

Jawhar left reluctantly to Bin Rahhal and Halima's farm-stead to meet with Farah. She alone could convey Emir Nasser's demands to Halima, and she alone could convince her to surrender to the prince's lust.

Jawhar stood coolly in front of Farah. 'Yes, Farah, he wants her. And if he doesn't get her, he will slander her. He will tell everyone that he slept with her and that she gave him the dagger as a gift.'

Farah's eyes rolled and she began to shake. Her face flushed as though she was looking at a terrifying beast. 'What? What are you saying, Jawhar? How did the dagger end up with Emir Nasser? Didn't I give it to you to sell in order to buy your freedom?'

She sat on the floor and slapped her head mournfully, as though she had lost a close relative.

Jawhar made up excuses for his actions. 'I was bargaining with Emir Nasser over the dagger, Farah. I expected him to agree to give me my freedom in return for it.'

Farah did not hear what this fiend was saying. She seemed to be in a catatonic-like state now. Her hands moved in a mechanical way as she slapped herself on the head. She began to sob and begged Jawhar to convince the emir to desist. Still kneeling on the ground, she grabbed him by the hem of his robes. Tears rolled heavily down her cheeks. 'Bin Rahhal could be dead and then she would be free to marry him. Halima does not deserve all these calamities. She is all alone in a strange country. She knows nothing about her husband. You have to give her time to mourn Bin Rahhal. What you're doing to her is not fair, do you hear me, you horrid man?'

Jawhar pulled his robes away from Farah's hands. 'There's nothing I can do. You have to convince her to surrender to the emir. There's no other way. And you're the only one who can do it.'

He glanced at Farah again. She was still kneeling, tears streaming down to the ground beneath her. 'Think about it, Farah. What would happen if the emir shows the dagger to people and tells them he slept with Halima, and that she gave him Sultan Muqrin's dagger as a gift? Who would dare doubt him and who would believe her? Even Sultan Muqrin will accept what Emir Nasser says as true. There's no other solution, Farah, so let us be done with this as soon as possible.'

Jawhar paused, as though preparing Farah for what he was going to say next. 'She is not the only woman to succumb to the emir. There are hundreds of them, and everyone knows it. Tell her she isn't the first and she won't be the last. Perhaps that will make it easier for her.'

Farah lifted her head and looked at Jawhar with angry tearful eyes, and clenched her jaw. 'You're a despicable human being. You used me to get her, you scoundrel. Your master is as despicable as you are. You are nothing but a pair of marauding, ravening wolves interested in nothing more than satisfying their instincts by blackmailing women and desecrating their honour!'

Farah tilted her head backwards and then spat with force in the direction of Jawhar. The slave's malicious smile returned to his lips. 'Well, I have delivered the message now, and you must take it to Halima. I will give you a week and not a minute more, Farah. Otherwise, scandal awaits the daughter of the vizier of Hormuz and the wife of Vizier Bin Rahhal.'

Before he left, he delivered a final blow. 'I forgot to tell you, the Portuguese have raided Hormuz and annihilated everything and everyone there. God alone knows where her father is. She has to understand she is all alone now. Tell her that.'

Then he looked at her askance and left the place. Farah stayed behind, cursing the bad luck that had brought upon her this disastrous situation.

Farah could not see how she would ever be able to take the matter up with Halima. With each passing minute, she felt like flesh was tearing off her body, that years were being shaved off her life. She knew she had to act quickly before Emir Nasser carried out his threat, but her heart made her reluctant: Halima was her best friend, and she did not know how she would approach her with something like this. She did not know if there would ever be a right time to do it: when Halima looked miserable, she did not want to make her feel worse, and when Halima looked happy, she did not want to ruin it for her.

The whole matter now felt like a gangrenous mass under her skin, or like a painful decaying tooth that had to be removed.

*

One day, Farah finally approached her mistress, moving towards her with hesitant steps.

'Mistress Halima, I need to talk to you about certain things that you should know.'

Halima smiled. She assumed Farah's problems had to do with the usual servant quarrels, or involved the farmers who looked at her inappropriately whenever she left the home, or perhaps it was about some of the guests who sometimes overstayed their welcome. But then she noticed that Farah's face was different this time and carried a terrifying expression. This was not the face Halima was used to; Farah's appearance had changed markedly, and she was plainly afraid of what she was intending to say. Halima started feeling concerned.

Farah's tears beat her tongue, but she was finally able to speak. 'In the last few months, Jawhar has spared no occasion to court me. He brought me jewels and gifts until we became close. I don't know how to describe our relationship, but it was beautiful then. We could talk about everything: our dreams, our future and our ambitions. He told me that when his master set him free, he would marry me, and then we would go and live in Hormuz or India. There, he said, he would trade in spices and I would get my own house with my own servants . . . and we would have children.'

Halima was listening carefully to every word coming out of Farah's mouth, expecting the worst to follow soon.

'After several months of showering me with gifts, he came to me one day and told me that Emir Nasser wanted a large sum of money in return for his freedom. It was my turn to give him money. First, he took back all the gifts he had given me, and after that, I started giving him my own money. When I ran out of cash, I started looking everywhere for anything of value to help him.'

Farah looked down to the floor for a few seconds, before she gazed back up at Halima. 'I gave him the dagger in a moment of weakness, the dagger that was in the chest. I gave him Master Bin Rahhal's dagger!'

Blood rushed to Halima's face. She felt the first of many things she did not understand were starting to be revealed. 'Go on, Farah!'

'Stealing Sultan Muqrin's dagger was the biggest mistake of my life. Jawhar has taken it to Emir Nasser.'

'What? Why the dagger, Farah? You could have taken anything else! It belongs to Sultan Muqrin who gave it to Bin Rahhal for safekeeping and you know it!'

Farah started crying bitterly. 'I wanted to have a different life. I'm sick and tired of being a maid. I wanted to be the mistress of my own household, with my own palace and servants. Jawhar told me the dagger alone was enough to buy his freedom. I also thought everyone had forgotten about the dagger by now.'

Farah stood up and threw herself at her mistress's feet. 'I beg you, forgive me. I have made a terrible mistake. I have placed you at the emir's mercy!'

'Why is that?'

'Because if you don't submit to him and his desires, he's going to say you gave him the dagger after you fell for him and pursued him during Bin Rahhal's absence!'

The whole world suddenly stopped for Halima. The air, her breathing, the conversation, the tears; everything stood still. Halima's eyes froze and she stared into the emptiness. Her face wore an arrested expression, and nothing moved except her twitching eyes and lips. She then overcame her trance-like state and stood up, taking a few steps before her legs failed her, forcing her to sit back down, this time sobbing.

Farah stood up to help her. Suddenly, Halima's face transformed into an angry expression. 'What are you saying, you wicked woman?'

Halima pulled her maid by the hair violently, removing locks of it with her bare hands. She then slapped her face several times until Farah started bleeding from her nose and mouth. 'Get out of my sight, you harlot. How could you do this to me? Get out of my house! I don't want to see your face any more!'

Farah was still on the floor, begging. 'Please forgive me, Mistress Halima. I have betrayed you, I know, but please forgive my error!'

Halima did not hear her. Every word of Farah's fuelled her anger. Halima said hysterically, 'Get out of my face, you traitor. I don't want to see you ever again!' Then she broke down in a fit of uncontrollable weeping.

Days passed in which no stove was lit, no food was ordered, and no laughter or conversation was heard in Halima's house. The sad, dark days and nights passed emptily. Everyone else was gone, and nothing was left except the memory of the people who once lived there. Few sounds were heard in the house of mourning, save for crying and sobbing. It was as if a great calamity had visited the place and refused to leave.

One day, Farah mustered enough bravery to enter Halima's room. She approached her bed, where her mistress was sleeping quietly, and kissed her forehead.

Halima felt it and screamed, 'Get out of my face, harlot. I don't want to see you!'

'My lady, we are in a difficult position. I want to atone for my sin!'

'And how would you do that? He's asking me to sell my honour in return for the dagger. Is that what you want me to do? Tell me!'

Farah spoke very quietly, trying to calm Halima down so she could hear what she had to say. 'My lady, I will pay a hefty price to fix my mistake. Let me explain and then you can say whatever you want.'

Halima turned on her side, revealing her tear-battered face. Dark circles surrounded her eyes. This was not the Halima that Farah had known all these years.

Farah sat on the ground in shame and disgrace. She tried to explain her plan without looking at her mistress. Her tears, the tone of her voice, and the signs of slapping on her face were enough to make the conversation extremely serious.

'I will summon him to the house, my lady.'

'Are you insane?'

'I'm asking your permission to invite him here. Then I will take it from there. All I want you to do is agree to my plan and then leave the house. Do not return until the following morning.'

Halima was appalled by Farah's words. She sat up abruptly. 'I still feel betrayed by your actions, Farah. But I can never accept for you to give him your honour—'

Farah interrupted her forcefully. 'We don't have time, my lady. It's going to have to be either your honour or mine. I am your servant. No one knows me and I have no family except you. My honour is worth nothing to anyone but me. I gave it to Jawhar in return for empty dreams. I don't mind giving it away for you and for this ordeal to end. It is eating me from the inside and killing me slowly.'

Halima was in a state of near-collapse. 'You can't. I will not allow it Farah. There must be another way.'

Farah sprang up, looking away from Halima. 'There is no other way. You have to listen to me this one time. I have lived my entire life listening to you.'

Halima stood up in turn, as though wanting to confront her. She said in an angry voice, 'I will not let you, Farah. This is madness!'

Farah pulled Halima by her shoulders and embraced her, wanting to regain the bond between them. 'I have caused you great harm, Halima. I must pay the price. Please, just listen to me.'

Halima and Farah embraced for a long time, like two long-lost friends. Halima felt her body relax and she started to feel the sense of reassurance she had been missing. This was how she felt before in Farah's warm embrace.

Halima remembered her dream that she had spoken about to Farah some time ago. Was Farah the bird from her vision? What did it mean when the bird flew away? Halima was not quite sure whether what she was going through now was the interpretation of that dream.

– 28 –

Hormuz

ALBUQUERQUE WAS ATTEMPTING TO bolster his authority in Hormuz. Every day he oversaw the construction of the Fort of Our Lady of Victory. He monitored trade transactions at the port and levied taxes on the ships arriving and departing.

His biggest problem was rebelling soldiers and officers. The heat, coupled with the unbearable humidity in Hormuz, prompted many to abscond from the island and flee to more hospitable places. One of Albuquerque's ships, captained by one of his officers, had even deserted to India. Albuquerque's most pressing goal now was to find more money for the Portuguese garrison on the island to avoid waking up one day with all of its soldiers gone. But the coffers were empty and Albuquerque knew he had to restore trade to normal so that tax revenues would once again flow.

Albuquerque appropriated the wing of the royal palace in Hormuz where Salghur once received his guests and delegations. The king was left with a few private rooms and a large hall that he turned into a *majlis* for his dwindling guests.

Albuquerque ordered his men to summon Attar. He was the only person whose opinion Albuquerque held in high regard, even if his loyalty was still to King Salghur and Hormuz.

Albuquerque wished the man would switch loyalties and become his personal adviser. Either way, Attar would present his arguments and views to Albuquerque, who had the final say over whether to accept or reject the vizier's advice, as he had many times before.

Attar entered the hall out of which Albuquerque now operated. The conquistador sat on a wooden chair behind a large desk piled with official documents, including slips given to shipmasters as proof they had paid their customs duties. Albuquerque no longer allowed anyone else to sign these documents, after he learned that the Portuguese harbourmaster he had appointed was collecting duties from the merchants without recording them in the books. Albuquerque knew that his officers were trying to hoard the kind of money they had no access to in Portugal, and were bent on returning home with their own fortunes.

Attar did not use the traditional local greeting with Albuquerque, because he never responded appropriately and also because Attar knew Albuquerque was averse to everything Arab and Muslim. Instead, he used the greeting Albuquerque preferred to hear.

'Greetings, Governor.'

'Sit down, Vizier. I want to consult you on an important matter.'

Attar sat down. He did not look thrilled to be there. The relationship between the two men was not good, and they were only cordial when mutual interests were at stake. Albuquerque needed Attar's opinion on many matters and decisions concerning the kingdom. In turn, Attar wanted to maintain a minimal relationship with Albuquerque, because he wanted people to know that Albuquerque needed him, yet he did not want people to think it was anything more. It was after all a relationship between a soldier and a prisoner. The two men were in agreement over the need to maintain stability in Hormuz and for things there to return to normal, although each had his own vision for how to achieve this.

Attar knew that Albuquerque was keen to keep things in Hormuz safe for him and his sailors. He was also desperate for trade to quickly recover, because his fleet was financed through taxes collected from merchants. If trade ground to a halt, his fleet would be under-funded, and this was something he would not be able to weather after the recent wave of mutinies.

'I need money, Vizier. I want to raise taxes on trade.'

Attar frowned and shook his head in disapproval. 'As you know, Governor, trade in Hormuz depends on the services we provide to the merchants. They come here because we are a safe kingdom and have warehouses where they store their goods, and offer many services that other ports do not have. This is why they come here to trade, and so far, they have paid their taxes gladly.' Attar tried to restrain himself. He was boiling inside because he felt that Albuquerque's decisions were irrational, his only logic being to hoard the money that he so worshipped. 'Imposing more taxes in the absence of security will drive away the merchants. The city and the port will suffer and people will leave.'

Attar pointed at the sea, and addressed Albuquerque like a lazy pupil. 'The harbourmaster you appointed was collecting money from merchants as tax, but did not note the sums in the records. The merchants were paying them willingly, and yet many of them had their goods confiscated after they left the port because they did not have the official receipts. The

288

corruption blighting us comes from your officers, Governor. They love money more than they love their mothers.'

Attar stood up and went to the window, trying to see the harbour. 'Have you seen the port recently, Governor? The number of ships at the port is hardly more than a quarter of the number we used to have at this time of the year. The ships have been driven away. Do you not see this?'

Albuquerque approached Attar and said in a threatening tone, 'Listen to me, Vizier. I need money and I need it now. My men are fleeing this cursed island because I don't have enough cash to entice them to stay. Do you hear me?'

Attar toned down his voice, trying to appeal to Albuquerque's reason. 'I am only an adviser, but I am telling you with the utmost sincerity that your decision to raise taxes is in neither the kingdom's interests nor your own. Do you plan to raid all the cities along the coast for money? All these places depend on trade too. If the merchants become wary, they will go somewhere else. I have seen with my own eyes the demise of trade in our ports. It's not like it was before. Many merchants now prefer to stay home because the income is not worth the risk.'

Albuquerque kept his eyes fixed on Attar but did not say anything. An awkward silence ensued, and lasted for a few moments until movement outside Albuquerque's office interrupted it.

Miguel knocked on the door gently, trying to get Albuquerque's attention. 'A messenger from Shah Ismail is on the island. He requests your audience, my lord.'

Albuquerque did not take his eyes off Attar. 'When did he arrive?'

'A few hours ago, my lord. He has come from the Persian mainland.'

'Very well, let him enter. We need someone like the shah to be on our side. I've heard a lot about his wealth and power. He's the only king who can stand up to the Ottomans. If we can make a deal with him, he could open up for us the trade route from Basra to Baghdad, and from there the route to Syria. We would be able to cut the distances very short. Let him in.

'You may go, I don't need you now,' Albuquerque told the vizier.

Attar left in a hurry, running away from a discussion he felt was futile. A few moments later, the Persian messenger entered followed by his dragoman and servants carrying large chests.

The messenger wore luxurious Persian garments and rings on his fingers adorned with large gemstones. He knelt before the Portuguese conquistador in an exaggerated fashion, then read out a written text extolling Shah Ismail, his dynasty and his heroic deeds, followed by praise for the king of Portugal and his conquests. When he finished, he folded the paper and gave it to one of his servants, then ordered them to open the chests and showcase their contents to Albuquerque.

The chests were stacked with expensive silk, pottery, precious stones and gilded swords and daggers.

Albuquerque was very pleased and asked the messenger to sit.

The messenger adjusted his seating position and took out a handkerchief. He used it to wipe his neck and face, complaining to Albuquerque about the heat. The Persian envoy then put his hand in his belt and said, 'Master Albuquerque, there has been much correspondence between Shah Ismail and the king of Portugal to coordinate an attack on the Ottoman Empire, a bane for both of our great kings. The rapprochement has achieved ample results. Great King Manuel was even able to convince the Pope in the past few months of the need to attack the Ottomans from the west, while we attack them simultaneously from the east.'

The messenger paused to wipe his face again, then continued. 'The plan could have worked, but it hit many snags. The European kings did not agree on what form this alliance should take. Some were hesitant because of problems at home. Another problem was that we could not find allies in the region to help us with the plan, by bringing us intelligence from inside the Ottoman Empire and exposing its weaknesses. Shah Ismail subsequently decided to send an emissary to Qansouh al-Ghawri, sultan of Egypt, to convince him to join the alliance against the Ottomans. Sultan al-Ghawri's armies in Syria continue to engage in skirmishes with the Ottoman forces there. The emissary is en route, and if successful Ghawri would be a formidable ally. Our alliance would comprise three powers: you, Ghawri and us, and the Ottomans would stand no chance.'

The messenger paused again, this time wiping the sweat off his head after removing his turban. 'Shah Ismail is willing to cooperate with you as the representative of the king of Portugal, to defeat the Ottoman Empire. I do not hide from you the fact that Shah Ismail is planning to subjugate Mecca and Medina, to gain the religious legitimacy derived from protecting holy places and become the caliph of the Muslims. If this happens, the king of Portugal would gain many territories and concessions in this region and would have a share of its incredible riches in perpetuity.'

Albuquerque stood up and paced the hall back and forth, pondering what the Persian messenger had told him. He realised now that there were communications between Persia and Portugal, and that news of his activities would henceforth be conveyed to King Manuel through the Persian court, without Albuquerque being able to influence or even learn the content of the reports. Before this day, he had been the only source of information of the kind received from the region, but now, it seemed, there was another.

There was no time to think the matter over. In the end he decided to reply courteously, as Albuquerque appreciated the importance of the relationship between the two sides. 'Master messenger, I doubt this alliance would work. I heard that Sultan al-Ghawri was enraged by our move to seize the spice trade. His country is suffering greatly, and spice caravans no longer come to Tripoli and Alexandria. Everything is stagnant, and the Egyptians now have a shortage of gold that they used to get from their Venetian partners.'

Albuquerque stopped and waited for the interpreter to finish relaying what he said, before he continued. 'Sultan al-Ghawri has sent threats to the Pope saying that if the Portuguese do not take their hands off the spice trade, he would destroy the Church of the Holy Sepulchre.'

The Persian messenger addressed the interpreter, who then asked Albuquerque, 'My master is asking, what is the Church of the Holy Sepulchre?'

Albuquerque's crocodile gaze returned. 'It is a church in Palestine that is sacred to us Catholics. But that doesn't matter now. What matters is that I told King Manuel that I have a plan that will put an end to the sultanate of Egypt, after we bring Sultan al-Ghawri to his knees and stop him in his tracks.'

'May I know more about this plan, Your Grace?' the messenger pleaded.

'I'm busy these days planning to go to India to reverse the disgraceful defeat of the Portuguese armada and destroy the Mamluk fleet there. After that, I shall sail to the Red Sea and the port of Yanbu. We will make our landing there and proceed to Medina where their prophet is buried, open his grave and take his body with us. We will use it as leverage with the Mamluk sultan in exchange for the Church of the Holy Sepulchre. And we won't stop there. We will bring many Christians to the kingdom of Prester John, and with their help, we will dig a canal from the Nile to the Red Sea. We will divert the Nile away from Egypt until everyone there dies of thirst and hunger. Then we will resettle it in the name of the king of Portugal.' Albuquerque paused and fiddled with his beard. 'This plan is still secret. I know you will share it with Shah Ismail, but I don't mind. We are allies now.'

Shah Ismail's messenger rubbed his hands together. 'The delegation we sent to Sultan al-Ghawri is on its way there. We won't be able to catch up with it before it arrives. I don't know whether our plan to bring him into the alliance contradicts your plan.'

Albuquerque was still stroking his beard. He looked outside the window and replied, 'No, let your emissaries go. Both plans work to our advantage. If Ghawri is not cajoled by the shah's offer, our plan will then come into play.' Albuquerque smiled as though remembering a joke. 'I serve Great King Manuel. I will do everything he asks me to do. Let us exchange ambassadors; I will send a consul to the shah's court, and I hope the shah will send a consul to Hormuz as well.'

Albuquerque stood up and walked to the window overlooking the sea. 'I'll move to India within days to strike Ghawri's fleet. It's clear that all communication between the Mamluk fleet and the sultan of Egypt has broken down because of the sheer distance between them. I won't wait to see whether Ghawri decides to join the alliance or not; his fleet has decimated a Portuguese armada and I must avenge Portugal to preserve her prestige and might.' He paused. 'If we want to control maritime trade, we must eliminate all resistance against us in these seas.'

The messenger replied reverentially, 'Master Albuquerque, our ambassador to the Zamorin has told us of the reason the Portuguese fleet was defeated. Do you care to hear it? It might spare you a similar defeat if you are bent on fighting them there.'

'Of course, messenger. What would that reason be?'

The Persian messenger told Albuquerque the details of Hussein's plan to defeat the Portuguese armada in Diu. He cautioned him not to be lured into Hussein's trap again, and to think more resourcefully if he wanted to defeat the Mamluks. Then he added, 'I am at your disposal, Your Grace. Shah Ismail asked me to be in your service. We shall give you all the support you request, but if I may, sir, my lord the shah has another request.'

The messenger did not wait for permission to continue. 'We ask that your fleet assist us in moving our forces from the east coast of the Gulf to the west coast. We need to maintain a permanent presence there, but we don't have the necessary ships and the experience to build them.'

'Why does the shah want to put his forces there?'

The messenger replied coolly, 'Not far from here lies Bahrain, a luscious island with fertile soil and abundant water. We wish to annex it to our kingdom. With your help, this may just be possible. Also, by being there we would be close to the holy sites. Our army could move on them if the shah orders it.'

Albuquerque had heard of Bahrain before, and had been planning to raid it. But he had other priorities now; eliminating the troublesome Mamluk fleet in India had to be done quickly and without delay, before any other undertaking. Albuquerque wondered whether the Persian request was a warning to him that the Safavid shah considered Bahrain his property and that he therefore had to back off the island.

Albuquerque now wanted to end the meeting quickly. 'I will think about it, messenger. I am busy with planning the assault on India. I will consider your request as soon as I return.'

Diu, India

T HE PORTUGUESE ARMADA LED by Albuquerque moved on the city of Diu. Following a signal from the flagship, several caravels split from the flotilla and headed to the open sea, while the rest continued their way to the bay. Albuquerque heeded the advice of Shah Ismail's messenger when he visited him in Hormuz; he did not want to repeat the previous fleet's error.

Hussein and Bin Rahhal came in their flagship to meet Albuquerque in battle, and the two sides opened fire. Hussein gave a signal to his men to ignite the flames over the towers. Mamluk ships hiding at sea came and joined the battle, trying to flank the Portuguese fleet. Suddenly, the Portuguese ships that had split from the armada appeared and engaged the Mamluk ships. Two battles ensued, one at the entrance of the bay and one further out at sea.

Hussein ordered his crew to intercept both flotillas of the Portuguese armada, as his plan to encircle the attackers had failed. The defending ships emerged out of the bay of Diu followed by Bin Rahhal's smaller ships, which carried fighters but no cannons. Malik Ayaz remained in the city to defend it in the event of a Portuguese surprise landing.

The battle between the warring ships raged throughout the day. With the sun beginning to set, Albuquerque noticed that the Mamluk fleet was not putting up the same kind of resistance as earlier, and ordered his captains to pursue the retreating ships and seize the opportunity to sink them. After sundown, the Mamluk sailors jumped ship. Bin Rahhal's boats tried to rescue as many as they could, while avoiding the non-stop barrage of Portuguese cannonballs.

Bin Rahhal realised that it was only a matter of time before the entire Mamluk fleet was destroyed. In the distance, he saw some of the ships trying to approach the Portuguese caravels to engage them in direct combat, but the Portuguese ships soon turned their guns and fired on them. The boats sank quickly with everyone aboard.

He turned to Hussein and tried to convince him to end the battle and cut his losses. The plan had failed. The Portuguese ships clearly moved faster and had out-manoeuvred them, and had more powerful cannons with a longer range.

Without warning, a Portuguese cannonball hit a spot on the ship's deck near them. Shrapnel flew in all directions, and a shard of wood pierced Hussein's side. Hussein fell to the ground, groaning in pain. Bin Rahhal ordered the crew to sail at full speed back to the port to get him help.

Bin Rahhal stood watching the Portuguese ships taking his burning ships one by one. Portuguese soldiers would jump onto a ship, take the flags of Sultan al-Ghawri and Hussein Pasha, and then leave the ships to burn down. When everyone saw the Portuguese desecrating the sultan of Egypt's flag, their morale collapsed and the defeats rolled in.

As night fell, the bay in Diu was overrun with shipwrecks, floating corpses and wounded survivors screaming in agony as they made their way to shore. There, the survivors were stretched out around fires lit by volunteers. Mamluk officers wrote down the names of the dead and ox-drawn wagons took the corpses away to their final resting place.

The Portuguese ships imposed a tight siege on the harbour to remind people who had triumphed. The Portuguese also wanted to let the people of Diu know this was just the beginning.

Malik Ayaz appeared on his steed. The horse moved warily around the port, as though it had caught scent of the blood. Its hooves touched the ground cautiously, trying to avoid stepping on an injured person or a dead body. Malik Ayaz moved between the bodies and fires. He was visibly in shock.

Everyone saw a floating flame coming from the sea towards the port. They concluded it must be a small boat that had lit a fire along its mast, probably carrying a messenger sent by Albuquerque to dictate the terms of surrender. When the boat finally reached the shore, they saw a man armoured from head to toe debark. He then asked to meet Malik Ayaz in person.

The messenger was taken to the ruler of the city, who had a look of absolute despair on his face. Ayaz had lost everything, and his city was on the cusp of being destroyed by Portuguese cannons.

The messenger approached him. Without greeting Ayaz, he handed him a letter, looking directly in his eyes to deliberately insult him.

Ayaz broke the seal and read the letter.

To the Great King Malik Ayaz of Diu,
I represent King Manuel of Portugal, and govern on his behalf all the lands he possesses with the blessing of the Pope under the Treaty of Tordesillas. I therefore warn you not to antagonise the

298

*king or myself, because our wrath will be violent and great, and
will destroy your kingdom and every living soul in it.*

*There is no personal animosity between us, and there is nothing
to prevent an agreement between us. I order you, however, to expel
the commanders of the Mamluk and Arabian fleets from your city
by sunrise. You must expel all combatants from your kingdom
within three days to whence they came.*

*Consider this an ultimatum, and heed it and obey. My messen-
ger must return to my ship with your answer.*

*Afonso de Albuquerque
Representative of His Majesty the King of Portugal*

Malik Ayaz folded the letter and kept it in his hand for a few
seconds, while looking at the messenger. He said in a faint voice
unusual for him, 'I surrender the city to Albuquerque. I will do
what he asks, and expel those people from Diu before sunrise.'

The messenger left quickly back to the boat he had come
in. The Portuguese ships remained stationed at the mouth of
the bay, waiting for Malik Ayaz to fulfil the agreement.

Before dawn, three horsemen emerged from the back gate of
Malik Ayaz's palace, before they galloped their horses off toward
the north. The men were Bin Rahhal and Hussein, who could
barely sit up straight on his horse, along with *Si* al-Tayeb.

Hussein and Bin Rahhal had no idea where to go now that
their fleets were destroyed. Malik Ayaz had asked them to leave
his territories quickly, and all the areas along the western coast
of India were now either under direct Portuguese occupation
or did not want to antagonise Albuquerque. The two men felt
they were stranded in an ocean of adversaries, and had to be
very vigilant.

Bin Rahhal, Hussein and *Si* al-Tayeb did not know the area. They headed towards a small village a day away to the north of Diu. There, they stayed in a small, filthy inn for a few days, during which time *Si* al-Tayeb wrote to his father-in-law, Qasimul Haq, asking advice and assistance.

Qasimul Haq wrote back saying that the situation had become very dangerous, and advised them to keep a low profile until the crisis blew over. Albuquerque was emboldened by his victory in Diu. Everyone was apprehensive about the next steps in his destructive plan. They were told they had to reach the port of Debal further north, where it would be easier for Hussein and Bin Rahhal to travel to Hormuz or Aden in disguise. Qasimul Haq sent them clothes and money with the messenger who brought his letter, to help them get by without drawing much attention to themselves.

Si al-Tayeb decided to travel with them to Debal, where he would remain in hiding for some time until he found his way back to Calicut. Hussein and Bin Rahhal decided to take a ship from Debal to Hormuz because it was the closest destination, especially since Bin Rahhal could contact his father-in-law, *Khawaja* Attar, who would help them return home.

They walked for several days through hot farmlands infested with mosquitoes and cobra snakes – a single bite from which would be enough to kill a horse in minutes. Their feet sank into rice fields flooded by farmers for irrigation. Travelling across the area was troublesome, difficult and stressful, and there was nothing to shelter them from the sun except some straw and leaf huts. Starved and exhausted, the three men stumbled and staggered in the heat for days, until they reached a small village called Nawanagar. They tethered their horses near a miserable-looking eatery along the coast. They weren't hungry, and ordered a herbal drink *Si* al-Tayeb recommended. The men then started making queries about the best way to cross the sea into the north.

The villagers in the area were dark-skinned and emaciated, and wore turbans that were disproportionately big for their bodies and ornamented in a way that contrasted oddly with their destitution.

The fishermen there told them the best way was to wait for the ferries that operated at daytime between the coast and Mandra, a village further north. The ferries did not operate at night, as the winds were not strong enough to propel the crafts. With sunrise, however, a breeze blew and the ships used it to cross the sea.

Back on the road, Hussein suddenly fell off his horse. All that time, he had been suppressing his pain to avoid hindering the others. But now he could go no further.

Bin Rahhal lifted Hussein's shirt and saw blood covering the area between his waist and legs. The reeking wound had festered and was oozing pus. Bin Rahhal estimated that Hussein would survive his injury only if treated quickly.

The following morning, the three rode to Mandra. It was a poor, remote village consisting of straw huts inhabited by a small number of villagers who earned their livelihoods from drying small fish they caught from the coast nearby. The stench of sun-dried fish was overpowering and clung to everything: the water, the air, the food and even the people there.

From Mandra, they continued onwards to Debal, a town located in marshland that ran along the coast. The three men had to find safe routes to avoid falling into the quicksand pools concealed by wild plants, ready to swallow their next victim.

The town was inhospitable. It was very hot. The water was brackish and tended to be yellow, and the locals who drank complained of bloated bellies. Hussein did not understand why anyone would live in such a dirty swamp, until someone explained to him that this was the only place they could hide from powerful northern tribes that rustled their cattle, kidnapped their children and stole their crops.

They asked for a healer who could treat a deep festering wound. The villagers pointed them in the direction of a mud hut where they said an old man might be of help.

By the time they brought him Hussein, his wound had become much worse. The old healer pulled up Hussein's tunic, revealing the festering infection, and put his hand on his nose. He looked at Bin Rahhal and *Si* al-Tayeb in a way that suggested he blamed them for the delay in his treatment. Bin Rahhal handed the man several silver coins and one golden one, which the healer shook in his palm before putting them in his pocket. He instructed them to move Hussein to a wooden bedstead in the corner of the room.

The old healer stood up and brought a heavy-looking bag. He sat near Hussein, untied the bag, and looked inside. The Indian instructed Bin Rahhal and *Si* al-Tayeb to restrain Hussein using fibrous ropes made from coconut coir. They did as he asked, and gave him a look that suggested they now expected him to do his part.

The healer reached inside the bag and took out a heap of small black leeches, and laid them out on Hussein's wound. The leeches seemed starved. They latched themselves on to the wound and the congealed blood around it.

Suddenly, Hussein started to laugh. 'They're tickling me! They're tickling me!'

Everyone laughed with him. After some time, the tickling turned into itching, and Hussein cried, 'Untie me! I want to scratch the wound!'

The healer signalled to Bin Rahhal and *Si* al-Tayeb not to move.

'Untie my hand. I need to scratch the wound. The leeches are killing me!'

No one reacted. A short time later, Hussein started screaming in pain and the healer spoke. 'Go and get some sleep. He's going to be like this until sunrise.'

Bin Rahhal and *Si* al-Tayeb did not understand anything and they seemed reluctant to leave their suffering friend in the hands of a stranger.

Hussein's screams shattered the quiet of the night, even though the old healer put a cloth in his mouth to bite on.

Bin Rahhal and *Si* al-Tayeb could not sleep that night, and decided to stay up near the fire they lit outside the hut, waiting for the sun to rise. When they entered the hut at dawn, they saw Hussein was perspiring profusely. He had dark circles under his eyes.

The healer removed the cloth from Hussein's mouth and examined the wound, where the leeches were now frantically pushing against one another. He started removing them one by one and replacing them in the sack, revealing a pinkish, clean wound. The old man dried it with a clean cloth. He then placed some herbs and ointments on the site, before he wrapped it with a large cloth and left Hussein to sleep for the rest of the day.

Si al-Tayeb asked the old healer about his strange treatment. The healer explained that the leeches ate dead flesh and congealed blood, so when he put them over the wound and the leeches started moving, Hussein had a tickling sensation. Then when the leeches latched on to the dead flesh, he felt itching, and when the leeches started nibbling away at the rotten flesh, Hussein started feeling pain. The Indian healer said it took the leeches several hours to eat off the infection.

'His wound is clean now. You can take him with you, but he has to be careful to avoid re-infection. He should wash the wound with clean sea water twice a day to keep it clean,' the old man urged.

Si al-Tayeb decided to remain in the village for a few months until it was safe to return to Calicut. Bin Rahhal and Hussein decided to continue their journey once Hussein was recuperated.

They waited for a few days until they could find a ship bound for Hormuz. Not many ships were sailing these days. The two men had to show they had money to finally convince the captain to take them on board.

'Hormuz has been conquered by the Portuguese. The Arabian Sea is now under their control,' the captain told them, explaining that he would be travelling by night parallel to the coast to avoid Portuguese ships. The Portuguese often intercepted ships and seized their cargoes, before burning them and killing or capturing their passengers, the captain said.

The ship moved in the dead of night without any light, emerging out of the tall grass that hid the village in the direction of the sea. Sailing in water this shallow was not easy. A man had to stand near the bow of the boat to guide the captain.

The only source of light was the moon that illuminated the swamps, which were teeming with exotic life and sounds. Before dawn, the ship reached the sea, though it travelled extremely close to the shore. By midday, the captain hid the ship between the rocks and grass lining the coast or in small, uncharted bays.

Before they arrived in Hormuz, the captain told them he would cross the gap between the Persian mainland and the island at night, and enter the port at dawn when everyone would be asleep. He instructed them to get off the ship as quickly as they could, after which he would sail back to the mainland, all before sunrise.

Hussein and Bin Rahhal disembarked in Hormuz disguised as merchants. They did not exchange more than a few words with anyone there, as the two men knew their lives depended on keeping their lips tight at all times. The dreary, near-empty port met them there.

The Mamluk admiral and the Arabian vizier jumped on the pier, letting the captain deal with the tax collector. They breathed a sigh of relief as the sun finally rose, and they were able to blend with people in the market without being noticed.

Hussein walked behind Bin Rahhal, who knew the way to Attar's home.

They knocked on the door. A servant opened it but did not recognise them.

'Is Attar here?'

'Yes, he is, but who are you?'

'Tell him he has two guests from Bahrain who want to meet him urgently.'

'Wait here.'

The guard closed the door behind him, and did not let Bin Rahhal and Hussein in. He came back a few minutes later, and asked them to follow him. The servant took them to the same hall where Bin Rahhal had asked Attar for his daughter's hand in marriage. Nothing in the house had changed.

Bin Rahhal drew in a deep breath. Halima had sat on that chair when he visited their home for the first time. Could Halima be here? he asked himself, wishfully.

A few minutes later, Attar entered. He took a quick look at the guests then, scrutinising Bin Rahhal's face, smiled. 'Bin Rahhal? Is that you?'

The two men embraced warmly. Attar reminded Bin Rahhal of his wife, and Bin Rahhal reminded Attar of his daughter.

'You're the last person I expected to see, Bin Rahhal. When the servant told me there were guests from Bahrain, I thought Halima had sent me a messenger. She wrote to me several months ago, telling me you had gone to India to fight the Portuguese.' He almost whispered the last two words, fearing someone might hear him. 'Who's with you?'

'This is my friend Hussein Pasha, Egyptian admiral and ruler of Jeddah.'

Attar stood up and greeted Hussein, using both hands to shake his. 'Welcome to my home. Your presence here honours us, Pasha.'

Bin Rahhal did not want to put his father-in-law in harm's way should they be discovered. The situation in Hormuz was not reassuring due to the heavy Portuguese presence. They were enemies of Albuquerque, Hormuz's new ruler, and if they were found to be hiding at Attar's home, then Albuquerque would make sure they all died a slow, agonising death that he would personally inflict and enjoy.

Almost unmindful of what Attar said about Halima's letter, Bin Rahhal asked the Hormuzi vizier in a plaintive voice, 'Is Halima here?'

Attar was bemused. 'No, she is not. Did you expect to find her here?'

Bin Rahhal's tone turned sorrowful. 'Yes, I did. I had asked her to come here as soon as I left Bahrain. I don't know what happened!'

Attar sat back down. He could no longer stand for long periods of time. 'She told me in her letter that she was planning to come, but that the Portuguese presence prevented her. After that, everything broke down. The letters don't arrive as before.'

Bin Rahhal sat, and Hussein followed suit. 'We don't want to compromise you with our presence, *Khawaja*. We are in a hurry to go back home. I especially want to return to Halima. I left her all alone, and now only this sea stands between us, and I intend to cross it as quickly as possible. We ask for your help to return to our homes. Hussein would then go to Al-Ahsa from Bahrain, and from there, to Jeddah with the caravans that travel to the Red Sea. We also ask you to give us some money and clothes, as we have exhausted everything we had during our arduous journey.'

Attar smiled, bringing much-needed reassurance to his guests. They did not know much about the exact situation in Hormuz, and whether the vizier still held sway there or was struggling to keep his head above water himself. His smile restored some of their hopes that he still controlled some strings which he could move whenever he wanted. 'You will get everything you need, gentlemen. Just stay here and do not leave until I tell you.'

Bin Rahhal asked what had happened in the region after he left for India.

Attar exhaled audibly, as if he had been holding his breath for a long time. 'The situation is extremely bad. Albuquerque is the actual ruler of all these ports except the ones still held by the Jabrids. He's hesitant to move on them because he doesn't

307

have sufficient numbers of soldiers. I think he's trying to raise more money to hire mercenaries. If he pulls this off, he would be able to seize Bahrain and even Al-Ahsa.

'A messenger sent by Safavid Shah Ismail recently visited Albuquerque. They agreed on a number of things, including offering Portuguese help to move Shah Ismail's forces across the sea to seize Bahrain. These forces would be ready to march on Hejaz whenever the shah orders it. The shah is waiting for the Ottomans to be defeated to declare himself caliph of the Muslims, and this is something he wouldn't be able to do unless he has the holy sites in his hands.'

Attar fell silent when some servants brought food and drinks for the guests. After they left, he continued. 'I cosied up to Shah Ismail's messenger, who then shared with me everything that took place between him and Albuquerque. I think the plot goes way beyond Albuquerque seizing the ports of the Gulf and India, as the messenger also told me there were secret contacts between Shah Ismail and Sultan al-Ghawri.'

When Attar mentioned the sultan, he looked at Hussein to gauge what effect it had on him, then he decided to press the matter anyway, whether Hussein accepted it or not, given how serious it was. 'They want Sultan al-Ghawri to join an alliance that comprises Shah Ismail and a number of European kingdoms to strike the Ottomans and end their state. The shah sent an emissary to Sultan al-Ghawri with this offer a few weeks ago.'

Bin Rahhal looked at Hussein, expecting him to respond. They all realised how grave the matter at hand was and knew they needed to act.

For Bin Rahhal, a Persian invasion of Bahrain would end the Jabrid state, and the sharifate in Hejaz if Shah Ismail decided to invade it too.

For his part, Hussein's view was that Sultan al-Ghawri could be lured to join an alliance that would not be in his favour. The Portuguese and Safavids would be collaborating with one another and using the sultan only until they achieved their goals, after which they would discard him. Ghawri would emerge a loser whether the alliance prevailed or failed.

After the three men discussed all issues they needed to talk about, Bin Rahhal found there was an opportunity to ask about his wife. 'When did you get the last letter from Halima?' he asked Attar.

'A few months ago. She was bemoaning your absence, but other than that she said everything was all right. But to be honest with you, Bin Rahhal, I know my daughter. She doesn't like to upset me in any way, and even if she were suffering, she would still say everything was fine. I don't know why, but I wasn't reassured by what she said. My heart tells me she is not well.'

A few days later, on a pitch-black night, Hussein and Bin Rahhal boarded a ship far from the main port. Lights were deliberately put out on the boat. They bade farewell to Attar and set sail for Bahrain.

− 30 −

Bahrain

T HE FARMSTEAD WHERE HALIMA lived was quiet as usual. No one entered or left except a small number of workers or servants. Sometimes, a vendor would knock on the door, selling wares that he carried in a large bundle on his back. In the evening, the gates of the farm were closed and a torch was lit at the home's entrance. Hardly any sound was heard in the night other than the croaking frogs and singing insects.

In the same dark corner where they usually met, Jawhar was waiting for Farah. She had asked him to come urgently, telling him there was something important to inform him of.

'Halima has agreed to receive Emir Nasser at home,' Farah said without introduction when the two met up.

Jawhar was overjoyed by the news. 'Are you sure? I hope Halima will not upset my master. He has been waiting for this moment for a long time.' Jawhar's voice grew more ecstatic. 'Do you know what this means Farah? I will be free! When I gave the emir the dagger, he was thrilled, but it wasn't enough. He said he would only give me my freedom after he spends the night with Halima. I can almost smell my freedom. We will leave this place soon, you and I, and go to India. There I will become a merchant, and you shall have your own house and servants. We will have children together.'

Farah was melancholic, and was not pleased to hear Jawhar's promises this time. It was too dark for Jawhar to notice the bruising on her face – and he was too caught up in himself to notice the bruising of her soul.

The emir's slave continued to speak, but Farah was not listening. Her mind was somewhere else, until he tried to kiss her. She pushed him away violently. She was furious with him from the last time they met. 'What are you trying to do, you loathsome man? You raped me once, but I won't let you do it again. Go and tell your master Halima will be ready for him tomorrow night. He must bring the dagger with him, do you hear? Otherwise, nothing will happen!'

Farah pulled Jawhar by his clothes to get his attention. 'Hear me well, Jawhar. My mistress is a dignified woman. She has never done anything like this before. Your master must come alone and in disguise an hour after sunset when it's already dark. We don't want anyone to see him and she doesn't want anyone to see her either. Then he must leave before the dawn prayer. Did you get all this? Tell your master!'

Content with the plan, Jawhar replied, 'I will tell him Farah. Don't worry.' Leaving, he cried out, 'Tomorrow I will be free!'

On the following morning, Farah had a good idea about what she was going to do. There was only one thing left to organise.

Farah went to Halima. 'You must sleep tonight on the roof of the house. Do not return until sunrise.'

Halima scowled at her. 'We have known each other for a long time, Farah. Tell me what you're up to. You know I don't like to be kept in the dark about what's going on around me.'

'We're going to carry out the plan. We just have to set things in motion. All I'm asking you to do is to be on the roof today before dark.'

Halima raised her voice and said in a threatening tone, 'Farah, you have to explain to me exactly what you intend to do!'

Farah replied quietly, trying to avoid causing further tension. 'I have asked Emir Nasser to come here tonight.'

'What? Are you mad?'

'I'm not mad. We need to retrieve the dagger from him. Otherwise he will continue to blackmail us with it and make our lives a living hell.' Farah came closer to comfort Halima. 'I asked him to come at night to trick him into thinking I am you. I will distract him and then lull him into a false sense of security until I get the dagger from him. Nothing else will happen, so don't worry.'

Halima was horrified. 'Farah, he wants me. He wants to do with me what a man does with his wife. He doesn't just want to mess about. He wants to take my honour in return for the dagger! I told you before, I won't allow you to sacrifice your honour for mine.'

Farah spoke quietly, trying to assure her mistress. 'Nothing like that will happen. I know what men are like. I will take the dagger from him with some promises. Men are weak when it comes to women. I'll take advantage of this, so please trust me just this once!'

Halima was beside herself. Farah did not manage to reassure her, but what other option was there? If the dagger stayed with the emir, she would remain in a vulnerable position. She would be at the mercy of any rumour he could fabricate about her, so there was no other way but to trust Farah and her plan, even if it did not feel right to her.

The sun went down. Farah pressed her mistress to go to the roof, asking her not to return until sunrise. Farah then sat in the dark, waiting.

As the minutes passed, Farah played the plan in her head over and over again. She was afraid she might have forgotten something. How was she going to deal with the emir? How would she address him, and what was she going to tell him?

Farah did not know the man, but she had seen him at the harbour in Al-Uqair when she was with Halima secretly taking part in Bin Rahhal's send-off. She remembered that she did not like his comportment or his tone.

The only fuzzy detail in the plan was what she would do between the moment he entered the house and the moment she retrieved the dagger from him. Farah knew she had to rely on her resourcefulness and fortitude, but she felt these could be unpredictable and ineffectual against someone so base and villainous.

There was a knock on the door. It was Emir Nasser. Farah lifted her eyes to the sky as if in prayer, then walked towards the door, holding a lantern in her hands. The flame danced with her movements. Her hands were shaking and her trembling knees could barely support her.

Farah put her ear to the door. 'Who's there?'

A whispering voice answered back, 'It is I, Emir Nasser.'

Farah blew out the lantern and opened the door very slowly. It was pitch black outside, and the emir could barely see her silhouette. She asked him to follow her inside.

He walked behind her trying to find his way in the dark, until they reached a room not far from the entrance. Nasser knew this was not Halima's bedroom, but he thought to himself that it would nonetheless do the trick. Nasser was optimistic this would be the start of a long affair.

313

He felt his way until he found the bed, and sat down on it. 'Who are you? Are you her maid Farah? Go fetch your mistress fast!'

The stench of alcohol and the emir's obvious inebriation helped Farah gather some courage, which she sorely needed. 'Fine, my mistress will come in a few minutes. But she too has conditions.'

The emir retorted loudly, 'What conditions does she have this time? I've never seen anyone coyer than this mistress of yours!'

'She asks you not to speak with her at all. Then you must leave before dawn.'

The emir caressed the bed with both hands to check how soft and comfortable it was. 'Aha! Now I know why we are sitting in the dark. But that's all right, it'll change once we get to know each other better.'

Farah stretched out her hand in front of him. 'Did you bring the dagger with you?'

The emir reached inside his garments and took out the dagger. He stuck out his left hand trying to find hers, then grabbed her right hand and placed the dagger in her palm. 'Give it to your mistress this time. I hope you don't have a lover other than Jawhar to give it to. Try not to lose it again.'

The emir let out a howl of amusement that made her shudder. She felt a strong urge to pull her hand away from his. Farah did not feel safe having her wrist being held like this, since Jawhar had done the same thing. She realised Jawhar was little more than his master's faithful dog, who told him everything – including what he had done to her.

Farah's heart was broken. She almost grabbed the dagger and stabbed the emir but she did not have the courage. She thanked her lucky stars Nasser was not able to see the expression on her face.

'So your mistress doesn't want me to talk to her! Fine. She will want to talk to me soon enough. Women are all the same. Now go and get her.'

Farah left the room, trying not to say anything else. She felt her heart was about to jump out of her chest. She closed the door behind her, leaned against it and began to weep.

A few minutes later, Farah trudged back to the room. She was shaking, and tried as best as she could to steady her limbs. She closed the door with a click that the emir heard. He was lying on the bed.

'At last, Halima! You've resisted me for too long. Come to your new lover!'

Moths swarmed around the lantern outside, undeterred as ever by the sight of the dead insects on the ground beneath, burned by the flame. The frogs seemed to croak louder, as though purposely trying to cover up the misdeeds of the night. A young tortoise moved slowly towards a nearby stream. It fell in and made a splash, causing the insects to stop singing, if only for a few moments.

Shortly before dawn, when it was still dark outside, Farah tried to rouse the emir. She shook him repeatedly but he would only mutter unintelligibly and then return to snoring. Farah kept trying until he opened his eyes and sobered up; he knew that he had to leave. Farah did not let down her guard until she saw the door close behind him, and heard the sound of the horse's hooves fade away.

The sun rose, and bathed Halima's face as she slept on the roof of the house. Initially she had been unable to fall

315

asleep. She could not stop thinking about Farah, and she was tormented with guilt. But she had finally drifted off late in the night.

A swarm of flies buzzed over her face and woke her up. She sat up abruptly, as though awaking from a disturbing nightmare. Halima tried to organise her thoughts: what had happened the night before?

Halima darted to Farah's room. The maid was still in bed, under the covers. Farah shivered from the cold. Her skin had turned pale blue, and she had black bags around her eyes.

Halima pulled back the cover. She saw a pool of blood covering half of Farah's body. She had slit her wrists with the same dagger that the emir had returned to her. The blood-stained dagger was by her side. Halima grabbed the dagger, quickly examined its blade, and then threw it away.

'No! What have you done, Farah?'

Halima shook Farah, trying to revive her. She heard her slur something.

She put her ear closer to Farah's mouth and heard her falter, 'W-w-we finally got the dagger, H-H-Halima. Please forgive me! I didn't want to put you in that position. That bastard J-J-Jawhar betrayed me. I tried to defend your honour with mine.'

Farah licked her lips and asked for a drink of water. Before Halima stood up to fetch water, Farah grabbed her hand as though pleading with her to stay.

Farah quivered and let out one last exhale. Her body froze, her wide-open eyes staring at the ceiling.

All the servants in the house heard Halima's ear-piercing scream, as she began to cry inconsolably. 'Don't leave me by myself, Farah! Don't leave me! They have killed you . . . Damn them, I swear to God I will avenge you!'

The servants did not understand whom she meant. Wailing in front of the dead never meant much anyway, they thought.

The sun beat down on the farmstead. The frogs and insects fell silent. Halima's loud sobs could be heard sporadically.

The mood was different at Emir Nasser's *majlis*. Nasser and Jawhar, who was eager to get his reward, were celebrating.

'How was your night, my lord?'

'Not great, but not too bad. Next time will definitely be better. She cried all night, and didn't want to talk to me. Things will change once she gets used to me.'

Jawhar's expression turned into a sinister smile. 'Where is the gift you promised me? I want my freedom, Your Highness. Haven't I served you faithfully all these years?'

'You will get what you want, Jawhar, don't rush it. But first, there is something else I need you to do.'

'What do you want me to do, my lord?'

'I want you to spread word that I slept with Halima last night. I want everyone in Bahrain to know. I want her to come begging me to marry her and save her reputation. Now go!'

– 31 –

Yemen

A T THE FOOT OF a mountain east of Aden, a shepherd hurled stones at several sheep that had started to stray. He repeated this a few times, but the stubborn sheep paid him no attention and stayed away from the herd. In the distance, the sea stretched out to infinity. He noticed a few dark silhouettes moving on the horizon. He focused his gaze, trying to make out their shapes, and realised it was an armada sailing from the east. The shepherd held his hand over his eyes to shield them from the glaring sun. He was able to see red dots on their sails, which a few minutes later crystallised into clear red crosses.

The shepherd left his herd and dashed to the village. He explained what he had seen to an elderly man there, who ran back with him to a spot where the entire sea was visible. The man circled his eyes with his hands and looked out to sea. His face changed. He then hurried back to the village, and a few minutes later, a group of men were on their way to the shore. There, they took a small oared boat and set off to warn Emir Murjan in Aden.

The coxswains knew they were in a race against the Portuguese fleet and had to reach the city before the Portuguese did. If they managed to alert Aden in time, it might just be able to prepare for this floating death before it arrived. The posse took the shepherd with them; being young, he would be able to run and reach the emir's palace the quickest.

The men rowed as fast as they could, their elder urging them to go quicker and not to stop. Beads of sweat formed on the exposed parts of their bodies, and the elder was now chanting battle songs while the others joined in chorus. The cityscape began to emerge in the distance.

The villagers finally reached the coast. The young man jumped off the boat and sprinted towards the palace of Emir Murjan near the city wall. All but one of the guards failed to notice him. The guard hit him with a thin cane on his back, trying to stop him from barging in on the emir and his guests, but he failed. The shepherd writhed in pain but kept going.

The young man entered the emir's *majlis*, gasping for air. He reached behind his back and rubbed the place where the cane had hit him. The guard appeared behind him carrying a long stick, making a whipping motion in a last-ditch attempt to stop the young man who had not complied with his orders.

'Your Highness! Your Highness!'

'What do you want, boy? What happened?'

The shepherd, still panting, said, 'The Portuguese armada is coming. You have only a few hours to prepare. We spotted the ships from our village and came to warn you as fast as we could.'

Emir Murjan had been expecting the Portuguese. It was now a frequent occurrence for mutilated corpses and burnt ships to wash up on their shore. The tales of torture and suffering inflicted by the Portuguese that the survivors carried with them made people in Aden wary and apprehensive. In the past few months, the Adenis put piles of firewood on the mountaintops surrounding the port and along the coast, to serve as warning beacons.

After the Battle of Diu, Albuquerque knew that he would not be able to maintain the upper hand unless he prevented Mamluk ships from reaching India. To achieve this, he had to take Aden, whatever the cost. The city was at the entrance to the Red Sea, and conquering it would ensure his control over the maritime route from Suez to India, and stop Mamluk galleys from participating in any future battles in the Arabian Sea.

The Portuguese conquistador prepared the largest armada in the history of the Portuguese navy. Albuquerque assembled 1,700 sailors and soldiers, and 800 Malabars whom he crammed into twenty vessels of various sorts and sizes. He told his men that the goal was to occupy Aden, but withheld further details of his plan to maintain secrecy. He told his officers that the plan would change the course of history.

When Albuquerque's fleet reached the coast in the evening, the Yemeni defenders were ready for him. They lit a series of fires on the hilltops to illuminate the coast, almost turning the night into day, and preventing the attackers from slipping in under cover of darkness.

Preachers in the city's mosques urged people to be patient and to help fortify and defend the city. A warlike spirit of *jihad* was kindled quickly among the populace, as the imams and scholars took up arms and were seen sermonising to people while leaning on their swords and spears.

On the following day, as Albuquerque was about to order one of his ships to sail close to the shore to scout the area and test the city's defences, a Yemeni bunder boat* carrying gifts paddled towards the flagship. One of the men on board requested an audience with Albuquerque.

The deckhands on board the *São Gabriel* dropped ropes, which the men on the boat used to tie the gifts for the sailors to pull up. They repeated the process several times until everything on the small boat had been transferred to the Portuguese ship. The Yemeni messenger then climbed up and found Albuquerque waiting for him, standing in front of the pile of gifts randomly thrown about on the deck. Albuquerque ignored the messenger's greeting.

The messenger greeted him again, only to be ignored a second time. Albuquerque's reptilian eyes were fixated on the messenger, who now felt nervous.

Albuquerque broke his silence. 'Hear me well, messenger. I want you to take your gifts back where you came from. I will not accept any tributes from your leader until all my demands are met.'

The Yemeni did not move, waiting for Albuquerque to lay out his terms. 'Your emir must open the city gates, sign the terms of surrender and submit to the king of Portugal. Our forces shall then parade in the city streets and our flag shall fly over the emir's palace.' Albuquerque gave him a rare smile before he continued. 'If he refuses, then we will obliterate the city and extinguish every living soul inside.'

The messenger returned to Emir Murjan with Albuquerque's demands. The emir realised that war was inevitable, but he wanted to buy himself more time to finish preparing the battlements and fortifications, and to mobilise his men. He asked Albuquerque for more time to consult the city elders and leaders, but the conquistador refused and gave the emir just a few hours to comply.

Albuquerque gave instructions for all sambuks and dhows moored in the harbour to be commandeered and brought close to the armada, meaning to use them to transport soldiers to the coast when needed.

After the ultimatum expired, Albuquerque sent three columns that attacked along three axes, but the small ships he had seized from the port to carry his soldiers were forced to stop short of the coast as the sea had receded. The soldiers had to disembark with their armour, weapons and gear, and swim the distance to the beach, while water leaked into their gunpowder sacks.

The first column made it to the main gate and engaged the defenders there. They could not breach the gate, however, as the Yemenis had built a solid wall behind it. The Portuguese climbed the siege ladders they had brought with them, using their harquebuses to strike anyone in their way. They ascended to the top of the wall and hoisted the Portuguese flag there, and shouted cries of victory to let the other soldiers know they had succeeded in their mission.

The second column led by Albuquerque marched to the right of the main gate. This detachment comprised Albuquerque's elite soldiers. As they tried to scale the wall together at the same time, the siege ladders broke under the weight of their bodies, armour and weapons. Some soldiers tried to bring more ladders from the first column, but they also broke as the attackers climbed them.

The third column was supposed to use the ladders left behind by the first two once they were successfully over the walls, but there were none left. In the end, they remained at the bottom of the wall, unable to take part in the fighting at the top and on the other side.

The first column began to climb down the other side of the wall, but the Yemeni defenders put up a fierce resistance, forcing the attackers to climb back up. The officer leading the column ordered his retreating soldiers to attack again, raising a cross that was in his hand to encourage them and boost their morale. The soldiers made one battle cry and charged down, pushing the Yemenis back. The Portuguese were able to seize a few homes near the wall, sending terror into the hearts of the Yemenis, some of whom fled away from the wall.

The emir saw the large number of defenders deserting the battle. He wanted to order them to retreat, as he felt the weapons they had were no match for those of the attackers. There were many casualties in the ranks of his army and morale had collapsed, with the city on the verge of falling to Albuquerque. One of the sheikhs by his side urged him to ride his horse and lead the counter-attack, warning him that certain defeat was the only alternative.

The other Portuguese columns had breached parts of the wall and slipped in, and were now supporting the first column. It seemed that the battle was going in their favour until Emir Murjan appeared in the ranks of the defenders on the back of a grey horse. The emir raised his sword, pressing his soldiers to follow his lead to defend their city and their honour.

A fierce battle ensued between the two sides, in which all sorts of weapons were used. The attackers and the defenders fought tooth and nail at close quarters, until the Portuguese were pushed back to the wall, trapped between the Yemenis and the battlement. Some of them were able to climb and jump off, but many Portuguese soldiers died that way or fractured their limbs. The Yemenis climbed the wall behind them, carrying bundles of firewood that they set on fire and threw on the Portuguese, many of whom were immolated.

When Albuquerque saw that his forces were routed and were too exhausted to attack again, he ordered them to retreat. The survivors who could walk used the dhows in the port to return to the armada, but many wounded Portuguese soldiers were left behind to die.

Portuguese cannons shelled Aden for two consecutive days, destroying large parts of the city. Then Albuquerque ordered them to sail away, leaving the defiant city almost razed to the ground.

When the shelling stopped, Emir Murjan began surveying the damage and counting the dead. He found the body of his counsellor who had ordered him not to open Aden's gates to the Egyptian fleet. His head had been hewn by an axe. The emir was told the man had been trying to flee, carrying some of his precious possessions; the emir could not pause and mourn him, as there were too many dead to grieve for them all.

Albuquerque's fleet circled the southwestern tip of Yemen and headed north, bypassing the city of Hudaydah and anchoring at Kamaran Island. He told his officers to take a census of the troops and count the casualties after the battle at Aden.

It soon emerged that half of the attacking soldiers had perished during the battle. Albuquerque felt the weight and impact of his rout. A defeatist mindset spread among his soldiers and officers, and morale among his forces hit rock bottom. Albuquerque wanted to restore their dignity and infuse in them faith in themselves, and gave them two days to rest and recuperate on this remote island.

★

On the day he decided to address his soldiers, Albuquerque made sure copious amounts of food and ale were distributed among them. When evening came and temperatures dropped a little, he ordered his aides-de-camp to set up a platform near a large cross that the fleet's masons were able to fashion out of trees found on the island. Albuquerque wanted his soldiers to forget what had happened to them at the walls of Aden, and he saw no better way to achieve that than with food and wine.

After he let them eat, drink and revel for some time, Albuquerque ascended the platform. He looked at his soldiers for a few moments without saying anything. Then he declaimed, 'O soldiers of Great King Manuel, we have a sacred mission ahead of us, a mission that will change the course of history. Any sacrifice we offer pales in comparison to our noble goal, to raise the Holy Cross high and purge the Earth of all heretics.' The soldiers roared after each sentence Albuquerque uttered, especially upon mention of the cross, the heretics and the king – words that brought out the worst kinds of frenzied fervour in them.

'In the past few months, the sultan of Egypt wrote to the Pope threatening to burn the Church of the Holy Sepulchre if Portugal did not stop sending fleets to spread Christianity in these parts. This heretic sultan does not know that all these lands and the people on them belong to the king of Portugal and his descendants under the Treaty of Tordesillas, which the Pope has blessed until the Day of Resurrection.'

The soldiers clamoured and cheered for the king and Christianity. Priests made passes around them waving their thuribles and crosses to create an atmosphere of divinity during the conquistador's speech. The moment for Albuquerque to divulge his plan had arrived.

'We have two objectives: declare the Red Sea a Christian lake and then conquer the port of Yanbu, and proceed from there to Medina where the prophet of the Mohammedans is buried. We will open the tomb and exchange its contents for the Church of the Holy Sepulchre that Sultan al-Ghawri controls.

'We will not allow anyone to threaten our holy realm. We shall bring one million Christians to these parts, to work under Prester John. They will divert the Nile to the sea, bringing famine and drought to Egypt. After we destroy the sultanate and its people, we will restore the Nile to its original course, for the land with all its bounty shall be ours!'

The troops cheered Albuquerque's diabolical plan hysterically. They knelt in front of him when he raised a cross to remind them what they were fighting for. The priests sprinkled holy water on the soldiers to cleanse them of their sins, turning the secluded island into a giant, outdoor church. The warrior-worshippers then took turns blessing the cross in whose name they had slain scores and destroyed entire cities.

Several days later, the weather began to turn. Dark clouds gathered over the island and a northerly gale tossed everything in its path. The Portuguese armada was paralysed. Sails were ripped and some ships were forced south. The sea became dangerously choppy, and some ships that ran aground crashed against the rocks.

The Portuguese were stranded on the island. Soon, food and water supplies ran low. Some sailors saw this as a sign from God telling them not to move forward with their plan.

Dysentery spread among the sailors. Some of the food had rotted from being stored in bad conditions for too long or because it had been damaged by leaks caused by the rough weather. Albuquerque ordered his few remaining healthy soldiers to erect a large wooden cross on the island and bury whomever died during the storm underneath.

When the storm abated, the ships were able to sail again, heading south this time. The sailors kept their eyes fixed on the large cross they left behind on the island, towering above many of their fallen comrades. Albuquerque thought about trying to conquer Aden again, but his troops resisted. They had lost hope, and saw the raging storm that had hit them as a divine warning, a sign of the wrath of the god of the Mohammedans. The battered armada sailed past Aden on its way back to Hormuz. The city was in ruins, but it was ready to defend itself once again if needed.

– 32 –

Bahrain

O VER THE NEXT FEW days, Halima visited Farah's tomb often. The grave was dug under the shade of a sidra tree on the left side of her home. It was a simple grave, marked by two small tombstones, one of which Halima wrapped with a green cover. Halima laid palm fronds over the tomb that she replaced whenever they dried and faded.

She would leave the house each morning and sit on a rock by the grave. She often cried until her tears no longer came, and then returned home.

Halima spoke to no one, and isolated herself from people. She learned from her servants that people were gossiping about her, saying she had sold her honour to Emir Nasser. Halima felt that she hated everyone and everything, and she no longer trusted anyone. Her life became bleak. She had become a prisoner in her claustrophobic home, and she could no longer feel alive. Oddly, Farah's grave became more welcoming than anywhere else, and it was the only place she could air some of her emotions, grief and fears.

Halima could no longer distinguish friend from foe, and felt everyone was against her. She was being slandered behind her back, and everyone seemed to her to enjoy gnawing her flesh, without anyone bothering to hear her side. Had people become used to believing all the lies and banality they heard? What had happened to people to make them enjoy smearing her reputation?

It had occurred to her to tell people the truth about what had happened. She thought she should let them keep talking until they got bored, but then they never seemed to get bored. It showed in their eyes and their demeanour when people saw her, exchanging whispers, winks and sinister smiles.

Emir Nasser had succeeded in ruining her reputation and destroying her honour. He caused the death of the person closest to her. Halima often wished for death, and entreated Farah in her grave to come take her to the underworld. Halima felt she would now welcome death with open arms.

A ship from Hormuz arrived in Bahrain. Bin Rahhal and Hussein, still disguised as merchants, disembarked; no one in the port recognised them. The two men chartered horses and rode at speed to Bin Rahhal's farmstead. The guard stopped them at the gate. When Bin Rahhal identified himself, the man tried to run to the house to give Halima the good news in the hope that he would be rewarded, but Bin Rahhal stopped him.

Halima was on her bed when she heard the hoof beats outside, coming in the direction of the house. The sound suddenly stopped, and she heard the main door open. She darted out of her bed and locked her bedroom door; she was afraid Emir Nasser had decided to visit her unannounced.

Bin Rahhal knocked on the door. 'Halima, are you there?'

Halima recognised her beloved husband's voice immediately and raced to the door to unlock it. Her heart fluttered in excitement, and her trembling hands could barely hold the key to open the door. Her body was resisting her: her hands, feet and lungs. She wanted to embrace him, to smell him and to throw her emaciated body over his.

Halima opened the door and saw him, before she fainted without saying a single word.

Bin Rahhal scanned her face. She was gaunt and pale. Her eyes bulged as though protesting the state of neglect they were in. This was not the Halima he had left when he went to India.

A few minutes later, Halima opened her eyes. She found Bin Rahhal sitting in front of her. He had laid a damp cloth on her forehead. Halima stretched out her arms and hugged him tightly. He felt the warmth of her body and its frailness and brittleness. He embraced her back, trying to comfort her.

Bin Rahhal gave her a cup of water. She took a sip and gave him a look that suggested she was not yet sure whether he was really there. She had suppressed much suffering in her heart, but this had obviously taken its toll on her body. When it could no longer bear it, it rebelled in the form of illness.

'Sleep now, my love. You must be very ill. You have a fever!'

'No, I'm not ill. I'm just very happy to see you back. You have brought me back to life, Bin Rahhal. I couldn't even stand eating without you. I've been through so much. You must know what happened!'

'You will tell me everything, my dear. But you must sleep now. We can talk later.'

In the days that followed, Halima's grief turned to joy. Her vitality and her legendary beauty returned. She told Bin Rahhal the whole story about what had happened from when the dagger disappeared from their room until it fell into the hands of Emir Nasser. Then she told him how Farah had tried to redress her mistake by inviting the emir to their house and tricking him into thinking he had slept with Halima.

Halima trembled again as she finished telling her husband about the ordeal, especially as she told him how Farah had cut her wrists with the same dagger, how she had apologised on her deathbed, and how Farah's departure had brought death to everything beautiful in the place.

Halima told her husband that the hardest part of the experience was not knowing whether Bin Rahhal was alive or dead. Letters from him had stopped coming after his fleet was defeated in Diu. At the same time, she had not wanted to leave her house and try to reach her father's home in Hormuz, fearing this would lend credence to the rumours that she had betrayed her husband and fled. Nor had she wanted her father to be in a position where he had to defend his daughter's honour.

Life returned to the couple, and once again Halima was able to enjoy things around her. Even the sunrise had a different meaning, the birdsong had a sweeter melody, and the sounds the insects made at night seemed softer and more relaxing.

Hussein was introduced to Halima, who showed him great hospitality and made him feel like he was at home and among his family. He and her husband were close friends and kindred spirits. Hussein told them stories from Jeddah, Cairo, Alexandria and India. Hussein opened her eyes to the many worlds that existed outside Hormuz and Bahrain.

But Hussein could not stay for too long far from Sultan al-Ghawri. Attar's revelations about secret communications between Shah Ismail and Sultan al-Ghawri were worrisome, and the sultan had to be warned about the intrigue. After two weeks in the hospitality of Bin Rahhal and his wife, he decided to travel to Al-Ahsa, and then from there to Jeddah. He left without alerting anyone to his identity. He departed as he had come: silently.

Not far from Bin Rahhal's farmstead, Jawhar entered Emir Nasser's *majlis*. He was early, as was his habit whenever he wanted to speak to his master in private. Jawhar sat near Nasser.

Jawhar still had high hopes that his master would grant him his freedom. He was sick of being a slave, sick of being merely an instrument in the hands of another and sick of Emir Nasser's unfulfilled promises. He had seen freedom within his reach after he satisfied his master's desire to get Halima. What was stopping Nasser from making him a free man?

Emir Nasser, in turn, was trying to find an excuse to delay giving Jawhar what he wanted. He was never short of excuses, but he had become annoyed by his slave's incessant nagging. Before Jawhar had the chance to speak and repeat his request, the emir tried to control the conversation. 'I think you are aware Bin Rahhal is here in Bahrain, Jawhar. He's like a demon who can't be killed!'

Jawhar fingered the dagger adorning his waist. 'If you want him dead, my lord, my dagger can slay even demons. You just have to say the word.'

Emir Nasser stretched out his legs, then grabbed a cushion that he put behind his back. 'Not yet, Jawhar. Not yet.' With a malicious smile on his face, he added, 'Anyway, I thought you were going to retire from the killing business after your sweetheart Farah died!'

'She was a beautiful girl, my lord, but it was perhaps best for her to die along with my promises.'

Emir Nasser's smile remained on his face. 'You didn't tell me how she died.'

'The guard at the farm told me she had slit her wrists and bled to death. Her mistress buried her near the house. I think she killed herself out of guilt after stealing the dagger and then finding out it was used to blackmail her mistress. The guard

332

told me she did it to atone for her sin, but I still don't know why Halima has not killed herself too! She was the one who sold you her honour in return for the dagger!' Jawhar rolled his eyes, as though trying to think of an answer. 'It seems your plan has become more complicated with Bin Rahhal's return, my lord. The man has not left his house for days. The couple seems clearly happier. The guard at the farmstead has not even opened the gates since Bin Rahhal entered. So what's happening? Does the man not know what his wife did with you in his absence?'

Emir Nasser twirled his moustache, deep in thought. 'Are you sure you have spread news of our affair properly?'

'I assure you, my lord, there is no one in Bahrain who does not know about it. Your story with Halima has become the talk of the town.'

'I don't understand, Jawhar. We might need to get Bin Rahhal out of the way too. Whatever is happening behind those gates, it's a mystery to us.'

Emir Nasser took a date from the plate in front of him and put it in his mouth. Jawhar was distracted. The emir took the seed from his mouth and flicked it at the slave to get his attention. The seed hit Jawhar's face and he turned angrily towards his master, but quickly controlled himself.

'When I speak to you, you look at me, slave!' Nasser then softened his tone. 'Did you find out who the guest was that stayed at Bin Rahhal's estate for a few days?'

Jawhar wiped the place where the seed had hit him and gave his master a grudging look. 'No, I didn't. Bin Rahhal has not spoken to anyone about him. Maybe he's a Hormuzi friend he met after he ran away from India. Anyway, isn't he supposed to present himself to you on his return to Bahrain?'

Emir Nasser was still twirling his moustache. 'He wrote to me to tell me his wife was unwell and that he had to be with her. He said he would come as soon as she recovers. But let's wait a little and see what Halima is going to tell him, and if he will act as if he has not yet heard about the affair. Her reputation is dirt! We expected him to divorce her after he heard the stories about her, but he hasn't yet. Isn't that odd?'

Emir Nasser found no other solution to his predicament than to send a clear message to Bin Rahhal, telling him he had slept with his wife. Bin Rahhal would then divorce her and she would be his, Nasser thought.

For his part, Bin Rahhal was now plotting his revenge against Emir Nasser. The best way to do it would be to go through Jawhar, Bin Rahhal realised, because the slave was the only one who could confess to stealing the dagger before Sultan Muqrin. And the best way to get to Jawhar was to bond with Emir Nasser again. Jawhar was a poor slave who needed money to buy his freedom, and Bin Rahhal could take advantage of this to achieve his aims.

Bin Rahhal turned things over in his head: people were still saying Emir Nasser had copulated with Halima, and they were waiting to see his reaction when he supposedly learned about it. But what if he did nothing? How would people react if his relationship with the emir grew stronger, and what would they say?

Any other reaction and Bin Rahhal would be confirming the rumours, so he decided to act in a way that went contrary to what people would expect. Bin Rahhal did not have a single way to silence all the allegations, but at least he could make people doubt their conclusions.

Bin Rahhal started visiting Emir Nasser once again. Soon enough, they resumed playing chess as though nothing had happened. Then, as he had expected, many question marks were raised over his unexpected behaviour. People asked: If Halima had cheated on him with the emir, then why was he still with her, and why was he frequenting the emir's *majlis*?

Bin Rahhal decided to let everyone know what had truly happened, and started circulating the story of how Emir Nasser had slept with Halima's maid rather than with Halima herself, who had successfully tricked him to avoid his treachery.

People did little more than spread rumours and counter-rumours. Almost every conversation on the island centred on Halima, her maid, Bin Rahhal and Emir Nasser, and the plots they hatched against one another. As people generally disliked Emir Nasser, they started believing that Halima had indeed tricked him into sleeping with her maid.

Bin Rahhal met with a smile all the rumours he heard by way of his servants and confidantes whom he sent forth to get the pulse of the street. He knew his battle could be long and painful, but he felt his plan was moving in the right direction. The Arabian vizier let things run their natural course, like leaves in a stream whose path and fate were determined by time and the flow of water.

One night, Jawhar went to see the emir. The slave was feeling discontent; his plans to gain his freedom had been thrown down the drain when he heard a rumour that the emir had slept with Farah rather than Halima. This meant that the vizier's wife had tricked the emir, who would have more reasons not to set him free once he found out.

'What's going on in your head, slave?' asked the emir.

'Nothing, my lord. Nothing!'

335

The emir became enraged and raised his voice. 'Nothing? There are many things. Did you hear the rumour that it was Halima's maid who slept with me that night? I, Emir Nasser, slept with a maid? Is it possible that I went to bed with a maid that you, a slave, had also had? If this is true then it would be a black mark that will haunt me forever!'

The emir fell silent for a few moments, but his agitated breathing was audible. Then he spoke again. 'There is one way to find out the truth, only one way.'

At Bin Rahhal's home, Halima took out some clean clothes for her husband. He was going to pay Emir Nasser a visit again. This night in particular, however, he put a big bundle of money in his pocket. What Jawhar knew was priceless, and he had to find a way to talk to the slave privately and give him the money to buy his loyalty.

Bin Rahhal mounted his horse and set off to the emir's *majlis*. The emir welcomed him cordially as though nothing had happened, and as though the battle of rumours between them in Bahrain were not still raging outside.

During a chess game, just as Bin Rahhal was about to end the game in his favour with a swift move, Emir Nasser leaned to one side, twirled his moustache and said,

At night the wolf prowled
Devoured your herd
And ate until he was satisfied
If you want him slain
The chum you keep company
Then don't go about it
With sycophancy.

Bin Rahhal did not respond immediately. He moved his chess piece and took out the emir's king, ending the game. Then he leaned back in turn on a large cushion and said,

The wolf set out to hunt
A most dangerous game
But the wolf got the runt
And nothing to his name
A tale all people know
Despite his claim.

Emir Nasser's expression changed suddenly and blood rushed to his face. He understood what Bin Rahhal was alluding to, and realised that the disgrace of having slept with the maid was real and that it would remain with him for the rest of his life. He could not bear it and cried out for Jawhar, who came running.

'Kill him, Jawhar! Rid me of him!'

Bin Rahhal turned around quickly but Jawhar was quicker. He wrapped his arm around his neck, drew his dagger and stabbed him in his heart with great force. Bin Rahhal fell to the ground covered in his own blood. He automatically put his hand on his wound trying to stop the bleeding, before he grabbed the robes of his killer. Bin Rahhal arched violently, then his grip loosened gradually until his body became completely still. He was dead.

Emir Nasser spat on Bin Rahhal's corpse. 'Damn you and your wife. You made me sleep with a maid and brought me scandal! I will take revenge against your wife soon too!'

He turned to Jawhar. 'You have done well. You must take his body and dump it in a canal near the road, so people think bandits have robbed him and killed him.'

Jawhar reached into Bin Rahhal's pockets, looking for anything of value. 'Let us search him first. He may have some money on him.'

The slave searched the slain vizier's clothes thoroughly, until he found the purse that Bin Rahhal had brought to bribe him. He jiggled it and then put it in his pocket. He took the body and threw it into a remote, isolated canal.

When Bin Rahhal did not return home that night from Emir Nasser's *majlis*, Halima went to the farmstead guard and asked him to go and look for her husband. She sat nervously waiting for the guard's return.

The guard returned a few hours later. His face did not suggest there was a happy ending to his mission.

Halima was standing near the gate of the estate. 'Did you find him?'

The guard did not respond. His face was grim and he seemed to be in shock. Halima approached him and grabbed him by his clothes.

'Tell me! Did you find him? Did you?'

The guard shook his head, looking away from her. 'They found him dead. I think highwaymen tried to rob him and he resisted.'

Halima opened her mouth to speak but no words came out. She tried again but her voice betrayed her. She loosened her grip on the guard's clothes. She stared at him in disbelief and then she fell to the ground unconscious.

When she woke up a few hours later, her house was filled with women she did not recognise. She looked shocked, confused and lost, her eyes wandering aimlessly. Halima tried to figure out what had happened and who those women were, and was not sure whether Bin Rahhal had really died or whether it was all a bad dream.

She looked at them, and heard wails, sobs and groans. She could make out the words 'Emir Nasser' . . . 'Farah' . . . 'slept with' . . . 'scandal' . . .

She did not recognise their faces and she suddenly screamed, 'Who are you? Get out of my house! Get out now! I don't want to see you here! It was Emir Nasser who killed Bin Rahhal. Who else other than this murderer would dare do it?'

The women lumbered out of the house muttering to one another. Mentioning Emir Nasser in this way could bring them dire consequences.

Halima was still in shock. She felt her soul had been ripped from her body. She thought about getting a knife and cutting her wrists like Farah had done. There was nothing to live for any more.

She got out of bed and started looking for anything with a sharp blade, meaning to end her suffering and her misery. Death felt once again like an attractive prospect, an oasis to a thirsty traveller lost in the desert.

Halima then fainted again. This time, no one came to help her. The maids were afraid of her and had locked themselves in their rooms to avoid her wrath. The sun went down, never tiring of rising and setting on people's misfortunes. The night insects and frogs came out; the sounds they made outside the desolate-looking house suggested it would be a long night.

Halima woke suddenly from the slumber that had allowed her to forget for a few fleeting hours her terrible loss. She heard the crickets singing outside and remembered Bin Rahhal's death. She started wailing again, and pulled a lock of her hair so strongly that she managed to rip it out. Halima wanted to wake up from this terrible nightmare, and struck the ground with her hands repeatedly until they went numb. Suddenly, she stopped and wiped her face with the palms of her hands.

She went to her bedroom and put all her jewellery and money in a small box. She broke the lock on Bin Rahhal's chest and took out some of his clothes and valuables, including the wretched dagger. Her box was heavy with the relics left behind by her beloved Bin Rahhal. Halima then packed clothes randomly in another box, and spent the night looking for whatever valuable effects she could fit in the boxes. She was intent on travelling to Al-Ahsa to meet Sultan Muqrin and ask him to punish Emir Nasser, her husband's killer.

– 33 –

Jeddah, Arabian Peninsula

H USSEIN ARRIVED IN JEDDAH. People in the city were not happy to see him again; everyone had hoped he had been killed after his defeat in Diu. But the devil, as they called him, had now returned.

The city had not changed much during Hussein's absence. It was peaceful without his harsh decisions and punishments, but people feared Sultan al-Ghawri might send someone even worse than Hussein al-Kurdi. As time went by with Hussein in India and the sultan not sending anyone in his stead, people felt as if they were in limbo, or a purgatory of sorts. But Hussein had returned – by land this time – and entered the city using the gate they had never expected to see him pass through.

Hussein entered the palace. He knew there were many things he had to catch up with, and asked for his unread mail to be brought to him. The letters he had missed contained much news waiting to be read.

The *dawadar* brought him a set of scrolls that had arrived during his time away, at the top of which was a letter from Sultan al-Ghawri. Hussein picked it up quickly. 'When did this letter arrive?'

'A few days after you set sail to India, my lord. The date is noted on it. I have collected all the letters that arrived from the day you left until your return. The last letter came a few months ago.'

The *dawadar* paused and then said, 'Everyone here and in Cairo thought you had been killed in the fleet's defeat in the Battle of Diu, but we received a letter from Sultan al-Ghawri asking us to go ahead with the measures you had begun before you left, to be overseen by your deputy until your return. You have been gone too long from us, Pasha.'

The *dawadar* smiled as though bearing good tidings. 'But don't worry, my lord. Everything here is fine. The soldiers are still stationed on the wall you ordered built. Things have returned to the way they were before you left, except that merchants are now complaining again – as is their wont – about everything. Also, the sultan sent some money to restore the dome of the Prophet's Mosque. It is in much better shape now, and has been painted a bright green colour. The dome is visible from a great distance. The architect brought the money and left after he finished the job. You have to see what the dome looks like now.'

The *dawadar's* memory was faulty. He remembered things intermittently and pronounced whatever came to his mind first. He was over sixty years old, but he was loyal to Hussein and discreet, qualities that made Hussein trust him. 'Ah, something else. We brought carrier pigeons from Egypt because we need to have a faster way to send and receive mail from Cairo. The situation there remains volatile, my lord, and we cannot wait the many days it takes mail to arrive by sea.'

Hussein felt the *dawadar* had said everything he had to say. 'Write a letter to Sultan al-Ghawri informing him that I have returned safely to Jeddah and that I am ready to carry out any task he requires of me.'

342

'Very well, my lord. I shall send it via carrier pigeons. We have yet to put the birds to use.'

Hussein opened the scroll in his hand and began to read. It was a long letter that the sultan had personally dictated to his *dawadar*. Ghawri wanted to keep Hussein abreast of the deteriorating situation in the region. He told Hussein that Sultan Selim, after murdering all his brothers who were contending for the throne, had decided to fight the Safavids. For this purpose, the Ottoman sultan had put together an army of 140,000 soldiers, and was at the time of writing on his way to eastern Anatolia to meet Shah Ismail in battle. Sultan al-Ghawri expressed his concerns about both powers, writing that whoever won would pose a threat to Egypt, particularly if Sultan Selim was the victor, given how close he was to the borders of the Egyptian sultanate.

The last paragraph in the letter described how the sultan had sent gifts to Sultan Selim to placate him, and that he had ordered his commanders on the northern fronts to avoid skirmishing with the Ottoman army. At the end of the letter, Ghawri wrote that delegations had been sent by Shah Ismail asking him to join an alliance against Sultan Selim and the Ottomans.

Sultan al-Ghawri's letter ended abruptly on that note. Hussein summoned back the *dawadar* and asked, 'Has there been a battle between Sultan Selim and Shah Ismail?'

'Oh yes, my lord, the Battle of Chaldiran. The Ottoman sultan won a great victory but I heard the victory was not complete. The sultan withdrew back to Turkey quickly, giving Shah Ismail the chance to recover from his defeat and regroup his forces.' The *dawadar* lifted his hands to the sky as if in prayer. 'God have mercy on us, much blood was spilled in that battle! People are still talking about it.'

Hussein signalled for the *dawadar* to leave. He then took to reading the other letters, trying to bring himself up to speed on the many events he had missed during his long absence.

A few days later, the *dawadar* entered Hussein's office with quick steps that were uncharacteristic for him. He was carrying a piece of paper no bigger than two inches long, folded in a special way to appear much smaller than its true size.

'This message arrived from Cairo today, my lord. These birds are incredibly fast!'

Hussein took the thin piece of paper. It was from Sultan al-Ghawri and was written in small print.

Glad you are back safe and sound. I will send you ships and men to put your fleet back together. We must defeat the Portuguese. They have left our trade in ruins.

Hussein flipped the paper over. There was another message written on its back.

Sultan Selim has learned of our contacts with the Safavids, and sent us threats.

Hussein did not know what he was supposed to do. Sultan Selim was clearly enraged by Sultan al-Ghawri contacting his Safavid enemies. The Battle of Chaldiran was a pyrrhic victory in which the sultan had lost many soldiers. The Ottoman sultan would need a long time to regroup his forces and address the shortages in men and material, but he had no tolerance for betrayal. Hussein wondered what the wounded sultan's next move would be, and whether he was planning to invade Egypt.

Hussein's old fears returned to him, haunting his thoughts. He summoned the treasurer and the quartermaster, ordering them to prepare reports on the state of finances and armaments in Jeddah, and to prepare for the arrival of the fleet from Suez.

The Hajj season came, bringing with it a flurry of news from all around the world. The Safavids had wreaked havoc in Iraq, where much blood had been shed, and massacres took place on an almost daily basis. The Safavids had turned the Imam Abu Hanifa Mosque into a stable for their horses, and slaughtered a great number of Sunni scholars. They also brought large numbers of Shias from India and Sindh to resettle them in Iraq.

But one report in particular greatly vexed Hussein and made him extremely concerned about the future. Emir al-Mahmal of Egypt, who was in charge of the ceremonial Hajj palanquin, told him that the Ottomans had intercepted an emissary sent by Shah Ismail to Sultan al-Ghawri. They found with him a letter asking the Mamluk sultan to join an alliance with the Portuguese to fight the Ottomans.

'Sultan Selim swore an oath to take revenge against Ghawri for his betrayal!' Emir al-Mahmal said.

Hussein remembered the conversation that had taken place at the home of *Khawaja* Attar in the presence of Bin Rahhal. Attar was right when he said that the Safavids were in contact with Ghawri to lure him into an alliance with them and the Portuguese. Hussein wondered whether it was possible for the letter to be a fake, meant to drive a wedge between the Ottoman sultan and Sultan al-Ghawri. Hussein had trouble reconciling Ghawri's desire to fight the Portuguese in the sea and forge an alliance with them and the Safavids on land, and felt deeply anxious about all these contradictory messages.

Hussein asked the *dawadar* to send a letter to Cairo asking the sultan to tell him the truth about the Safavid emissary who had been apprehended by the Ottomans in Syria.

Many days passed and no response came from Cairo. Hussein knew this was not normal. After Hussein insisted on sending

345

another letter, a response finally came from Cairo. The sultan had left for Syria to meet the Ottoman army marching south in battle.

Hussein knew that war between the two sides was inevitable. There was nothing he could do now. The swords had already been drawn, and would not be sheathed again until they had been satisfied with the blood of their victims. Hussein knew too well that wars started with mutual threats and ended with rivers of blood.

Only three ships made it to Jeddah from Suez; delivery of the others was impossible. Nothing came from there, the *dawadar* told Hussein; everything was paralysed.

Hussein learned afterwards that the skirmishes between the Ottoman and Mamluk armies had escalated dramatically, and that the two sides were gearing up for a pitched battle outside the city of Aleppo.

The days that followed passed like months, weighed down by anxiety and uncertainty. Carrier pigeons stopped coming, and all other means of communication were disrupted. There was nothing to be done but wait for the dust to settle.

Hussein did not know what he should or could do. He had no fleet that could sail to fight the Portuguese. He could not leave Jeddah for Cairo because of the military situation. Rebellious tribes in Hejaz were emboldened, attacking the Mamluk garrisons from time to time. The road from Jeddah to Mecca was no longer safe, and the few hundred untrained and ill-equipped Mamluk guards could do little to repel these attacks. Only Jeddah's city wall held.

34

Al-Ahsa, Eastern Arabian Peninsula

ACCOMPANIED BY A HANDFUL of servants, Halima took a ship from Bahrain to Al-Uqair and then to Al-Ahsa, where she would stay at Bin Rahhal's home in the desert oasis.

The house was exactly as its owner had left it, a shrine to Bin Rahhal just like his late mother's room was a shrine to her. The servants received her warmly, trying their best to console her after her husband's death.

Everything in the place reminded her of him: his clothes, his bedroom, his books, his papers piled up on the desk, and his weapons hanging on the wall. Even the pond where he liked to bathe in the summer was a memento of Bin Rahhal.

The servants did not withhold any information from her, and were very forthcoming when she asked about the house and its late owner's routine there.

Halima asked for directions to Sultan Muqrin's estate. When she got there, she was told he had not yet arrived, but that he was expected back in Al-Ahsa in the next few days. She did not manage to get an exact date, and she was not told for how many days she would have to wait. No one knew, and she had to live with her unbearable regret, pain, anger and sorrow for an indefinite period of time until his return.

The world turned dark. The sultan could be away for months, she told herself, and the palace were only telling her he was going to be back soon to avoid upsetting her. She returned to her late husband's house and decided to visit his mother's room.

Everything in the room appeared to be frozen in time: her bed, her walking stick, her prayer mat and gown and her prayer beads. Halima entered cautiously and searched every corner in the chamber. She moved some sheets that were used to cover a large old wooden chest. It had beautiful but faded engravings of animals grazing near a stream. She made two passes over the chest with her hands, wiping the dust from the engravings. Halima then took a cloth and dusted off the chest, revealing marvellous hidden drawings.

She opened the chest gently, and saw inside many head-scarves belonging to Bin Rahhal's mother, and a tied sack that contained a large piece of ambergris. She re-tied the sack and replaced it where she had found it. Halima reached to the bottom of the chest, where she found a metal box. She opened it and found a pile of gold chains, bracelets, anklets and pearl necklaces.

She stood up and searched the room more thoroughly, and found another box containing a large quantity of pearls. She laid all the treasures on a large sheet. She left the room and returned with her own jewels she had brought from Bahrain, adding them to the pile on the sheet. She wrapped it and tied it tightly into a heavy bundle of jewels, gold and pearls.

On the following morning, she asked one of the servants to point her in the direction of the best jeweller in Al-Ahsa. She took the bundle and went to his workshop, accompanied by a maid and a bodyguard. When she got to the jeweller's, she asked the guard to remain outside and stop anyone from entering behind her.

She unpacked the wrapped sheet in front of the jeweller, handing him the items one by one. He weighed each item and noted it down on a piece of paper. When all the items had exchanged hands, she said, 'Put your seal on this paper to prove you have received them from me.'

The jeweller took out a small seal from his pocket and stamped the paper, which she took and put in her pocket. 'I want you to make me a golden palm tree using all the gold before you. The fruits must be made from the stones, and the base from the pearl beads. I want it to be a masterpiece the likes of which no one has ever seen before. Use all the jewels I gave you, because I am going to count every stone and every pearl to ensure you have done as I say. If you finish the job to my satisfaction, a very precious prize will be yours.'

The jeweller knew he had to make a masterpiece fit for a king. He was determined to create the best work a jeweller had ever made in Al-Ahsa, hoping it would immortalise his name and open the doors of kings' palaces before him.

The jeweller finished within a few weeks. He placed the piece inside an airtight box of sandalwood, on which he installed a lock. He gave the key and the box to Halima, asking her not to open it until she was in a safe place and telling her that his creation was something for which kings would go to war.

Back at Bin Rahhal's home, Halima closed the door behind her. She opened the box and saw a majestic master-piece that she had not imagined even in her dreams: a palm, a cubit long from top to bottom, with fronds crafted from melted gold. The date-shaped parts were made from colourful gemstones, threaded together in a breathtaking manner. The golden stem had the same intricate protrusions of real palm fronds. And the whole tree was planted in a small meadow of black and white pearls of all shapes, the largest ones placed near the stem and decreasing in size as the pearls stretched outwards.

Halima examined each jewel, pearl and engraving with her hands, fascinated by the object in front of her. This tree contained her and her murdered husband's entire fortune. She had turned their fortune into bait that no one could resist, and that could undermine any principle or value in the blink of an eye. Halima understood the power and influence of money, and wanted to use it to avenge Bin Rahhal.

She took out a sheet of paper and wrote a letter to her father.

Dear Father,

I was pleased to hear from the herald that you had survived the Portuguese invasion. I hope and pray to God that you will remain safe.

I have tried in the past months to hide from you the truth about my circumstances, but I can't bear to conceal it any longer.

Before Sultan Muqrin left to fight in Najd, he appointed his cousin Emir Nasser to rule in his stead. He is a foul person and a licentious drunkard. His reputation among women is akin to the reputation of a wolf among sheep.

The emir sent my husband away to India to partake in the fight against Portugal, hoping he would perish there so he could have me for himself. My husband must have known this, as he ordered me to sail to Hormuz straight after his departure. But the Portuguese lurked in the sea, and by then had occupied Hormuz, cutting us off from each other. I decided to remain in Bahrain hoping for Bin Rahhal to return.

Emir Nasser's slave Jawhar tricked Farah into thinking he would marry her if he could buy his freedom from the prince. Farah blindly gave him a precious dagger that Sultan Muqrin had given my husband for safekeeping. Jawhar gave the dagger to the emir, who started using it to blackmail me. But Farah sacrificed her honour for my sake and was able to retrieve the blade, before she killed herself.

The emir murdered Bin Rahhal upon his return from India. I am now all alone in this world, and I have no family but you. I want to avenge my husband and Farah and punish this murderer.

I have travelled to Al-Ahsa to meet Sultan Muqrin and tell him the whole story, but he has yet to return from his expedition.

I can no longer bear it. I have waited for too long. I am sending with this letter a gift. I am hoping you may deliver it to King Salghur, and remind him of the hefty price he paid to return to the throne. You must tell him that whoever rules Hormuz and Bahrain will rule the Gulf. This gift might induce him to retake Bahrain and kill Emir Nasser, because there is no room for both of us in this world.

I will not be able to return to Hormuz before meeting Sultan Muqrin and explaining to him what has happened. This gift has consumed all my fortune. Spare no effort to use it as the price of Emir Nasser's life.

Your daughter,
Halima

Several days later, the box containing the jewelled palm reached Attar. The Hormuzi vizier was pleased to see his daughter's letter enclosed with the parcel, and started reading it without opening the box. As he took stock of her revelations, he became gradually incensed, while at the same time feeling bereaved for the death of Farah, whom he had treated as a second daughter. Attar decided to act.

He entered the king's palace escorted by two of his servants carrying the box. Attar ordered them to place it in front of the king in his *majlis*, then told them to leave the hall.

He opened the box gently and took out the palm, which he kept by his side. Attar watched the king to gauge his reaction.

'What do you think, Your Majesty?'

Salghur left his throne and approached the palm. He caressed it with his hands as though touching soft silk. 'Is it . . . is it real?'

'Everything you see in front of you is real. Everything that glitters is made of gold, everything that is white is made from pearls, and everything that is coloured is a precious stone. This is a priceless masterpiece, Your Majesty!'

'Who is it from? Who sent it?'

'My daughter Halima has sent it from Bahrain. She is trying to tell you that this island is so rich that its palms almost produce pearls like the seas that surround Bahrain, and that its land is pure gold. We have paid a heavy price for the Jabrid intervention, but we can retake the island once more.'

Salghur sat back on the throne, but he could not keep his eyes off the masterpiece. 'We have signed an agreement with the Jabrids, ceding our possessions in Bahrain and waiving the taxes they used to pay us—'

Attar interrupted him. 'Indeed, we have agreed with them on all these things, but the situation has changed. We are in dire need of Bahrain now. We don't have sufficient funds to run Hormuz since the Portuguese arrived. Trade has ground to a halt, and without Bahrain and its fortunes, we won't last for very long.'

Salghur stood up from his throne again and walked to the window overlooking the sea. 'Master Vizier, as you know, we no longer have an army. We don't control our own affairs. Albuquerque does!'

Attar returned the palm to its case, fearing someone might suddenly enter. Albuquerque and his officers could enter any room in the palace without asking permission.

'Listen to me, Your Majesty. I know there is nothing we can do on our own. We are Albuquerque's prisoners and we are alive because he permits it. But what I'm saying is that we can change all that if we want to!'

King Salghur returned to his throne. 'What are you trying to say exactly, Attar?'

'I propose the following, Your Majesty: we show this master-piece to Albuquerque. It will entice him to conquer Bahrain. We will be with him because he needs us. He does not know the island as well as we do. If the campaign succeeds, he will also need us to run the island, and we would be able to do with it as we please. You must understand, he who controls Hormuz and Bahrain controls the Gulf.'

On the same day, Attar and the king went to the hall that Albuquerque sat in, with two servants carrying the box.

'Gentlemen, what is this?'

'A present for you, Governor, from my daughter Halima who lives in Bahrain.'

'You never told me you had a daughter there!'

'She is married to the Jabrid sultan's vizier. He died recently. She sent you this gift to let you know how wealthy Bahrain is.'

Attar opened the box, took out the palm and placed it in front of the conquistador.

Albuquerque raised his eyebrows. His reptilian gaze disappeared for a few seconds before it returned. He approached the piece and touched it in several places, scrutinising the jewels decorating it.

'I had asked you about Bahrain before but you said nothing about its fortunes. I suspected you might have been hiding something from me, so I sent a scout ship to sail around its coasts. The captain told me he saw a luscious green island with plentiful fruits and fresh water. He said the sea around it is abundant in pearls that the Jabrid sultan profits greatly from. I've been waiting for reinforcements from Portugal to send an expedition to take the island.'

Albuquerque approached the vizier until their chests almost touched. 'Hear me, Attar. You must know that there is nothing you can hide from me. Never do it again. Now tell me, if this island is so rich, why did you relinquish it?'

Salghur hesitated but then decided to answer instead of Attar. 'This was the price for helping me retake the throne, Governor. We signed an agreement with them waiving the tribute they paid and ceding Hormuz's possessions in Bahrain.'

A harsh look returned to Albuquerque's eyes. 'To hell with the treaties you signed with them! We will take the island. We need the money.'

Albuquerque gave Attar an angry look. 'Prepare as many ships and as many men as you can. I will send them an officer who never lost a battle in his life. I will send them António Correia.'

35

Al-Ahsa, Eastern Arabian Peninsula

HALIMA FELT SHE HAD stayed for too long in Al-Ahsa. Her main activity was to enquire from time to time about Sultan Muqrin, who had not yet returned from Najd. People knew Halima was staying at her deceased husband's home. Some women tried to make her acquaintance, and the short visits they paid her were her only leisure. The days were monotonous, and people were concerned with the same things as the Bahrainis, except that they did not gossip about her and the intrigue with Emir Nasser.

Halima was reluctant to return to Bahrain. In the house in Al-Ahsa mementos of her husband, his childhood, and even of his mother, whose memory he had kept alive, were all around her. Bin Rahhal's phantom was with her everywhere in Al-Ahsa, and though they had memories in Bahrain, in Al-Ahsa his presence was gentler. She had also made a new life for herself here and new friends, and in Bahrain she would be returning to the painful memory of her husband's death and the rumour mill that Emir Nasser continued to feed.

She expected her father to avail himself of the gift she had sent him, and use it as leverage with King Salghur to convince him to retake Bahrain. Most of all, she wanted to avenge her husband and slay Emir Nasser. She was aching to see Emir Nasser dead, as her bitter thirst for vengeance could only be quenched by blood.

Halima got her servants to load her luggage in a small convoy and headed to Al-Uqair. When she reached the harbour, she saw it was unusually crowded. Horses and camels were being led into large boats that were lined haphazardly along the wharf. There was much shouting and quarrelling and chaos, and Halima did not quite understand what was going on. She ordered her convoy to stop not far from the place, and asked one of her servants to investigate and report back.

Her servant came back running to her *howdah*, pointing in the direction of a dust storm from the direction of the desert.

She looked to where he was pointing, and saw thick dust filling the horizon. 'What's happening?'

'It's Sultan Muqrin's army, my lady. He has just arrived from Najd and is on his way to Bahrain. The bedlam you see at the port is the vanguard of the army, which will carry rations to Bahrain. I don't think we will be able to sail today or even tomorrow. The shipmasters are refusing to even talk to us, as they have chartered their boats to carry the army and its gear.'

'For what reason?'

'They are saying a fleet of Portuguese and Hormuzi ships have lain siege to Bahrain meaning to occupy it. Sultan Muqrin is going there to defend the island.'

She descended from her *howdah*, wearing her Hormuzi burka. She stood by the side of her convoy, waiting for Sultan Muqrin to spot her. Halima kept her eyes fixed on the dust

356

storm approaching. She was not sure what she would tell him. Should she expose Emir Nasser to him in these circumstances, or should she tell him it was she who invited the Portuguese and Hormuzi fleets to Bahrain? She had not wanted Sultan Muqrin to go there to fight. She just wanted Emir Nasser to be slain, but clearly things were now out of her control.

Sultan Muqrin's army approached the harbour. The crowd grew into a sea of swarming people. The dust cloud followed the army, bringing sudden darkness to the place. People used their clothes to shield their mouths and noses, a layer of dust covering their faces.

Halima was not going to give up. She had to meet the sultan. She saw him appear then disappear in the haze. Halima ran to him and approached his horse, but the guards stopped her before she could draw his attention.

'Great Sultan! Your Grace!' she yelled at the top of her lungs.

The sultan glanced at her and squinted.

She shouted again. 'I am Halima, wife of Bin Rahhal.'

The sultan stared at her for a few seconds and then turned to a sheikh who was riding behind him. He exchanged a few words with him while pointing at Halima. The sultan then waved at her before he disappeared in the stubborn dust cloud hanging over the harbour.

The sheikh approached Halima and dismounted from his horse. He was a venerable old man with a long white beard. He wore a turban that was wrapped around a red felt hat with a tassel attached to the top. Halima had not seen anything like it before.

The man introduced himself. 'I am Jamal al-Din Tazi. The sultan has asked me to take care of you.'

Halima gave him a quick look before turning her gaze back to where the sultan had gone, trying to find him again, but he had vanished. Halima turned back to the sheikh with tearful eyes. 'I have many things to tell the sultan, Sheikh Tazi!'

'Don't worry, child. You can tell him everything you want after he returns. Now come with me.'

Tazi took Halima back to her convoy. The haze began to subside, and the rabble of people moved off with the sultan towards the sea. Halima and the sheikh waited for the noise to die down before they could speak. They did not have to wait for long; the ships were now ready to move the army, and as they left, the chaos in the harbour eased.

The sheikh looked at Halima with dusty but compassionate eyes. He introduced himself again. 'I am Sheikh Jamal al-Din Tazi from Morocco. I met the sultan during the Hajj and he asked me to come here with him to teach people the Maliki creed. He has now asked me to look after you until he returns from his campaign.'

The sheikh took out a handkerchief from his pocket and wiped the accumulated dust on his face before continuing. 'The sultan told me about your husband's death. He wept when he heard Bin Rahhal had been killed. The sultan was performing the pilgrimage to Mecca. He was determined to find his killer, but when we drew close to Al-Ahsa, news came to him of the Portuguese blockade of Bahrain. Don't worry; I left my wife who had come with me in Al-Ahsa for the sultan's send-off. We will return to Al-Ahsa together where you will meet her. She will take good care of you until the sultan returns.'

Halima returned in her small convoy to Al-Ahsa. She was thinking about what she should do: should she tell Sheikh Tazi what she had done, or should she say nothing about that? All the bloodletting that was about to take place was her fault. Had she made a mistake?

358

Halima stayed with the sheikh and his wife, and the three became inseparable. She started learning more about her religion, which she never cared much about during her formative years in Hormuz. She was born Muslim, but Islam for her was a formality, a series of rituals and a part of her identity much like her dialect, clothes and family; she had not given it much thought beyond that.

However, the sheikh and his wife approached faith in a very different way. It was the centre of their lives and not merely a ritual. It was real and tangible, and they found joy in it. They talked about it often and would stay up during the night praying. Halima even saw them crying in worship, and then smiling shortly after, and could not understand why.

She started learning many things she had not known about before. She asked about things that had never occurred to her. 'If God created us and God is merciful, then why does so much misfortune befall us? Do we worship Him to avoid His wrath? What's going to happen to people who were not born Muslim, are they going to hell? Why did God create bad people if He was going to torment them in the afterlife? Why did the sheikh cry when he prayed to God?'

Halima would ask the sheikh's wife all these questions, but the old woman did not have answers and told her to save her questions for the sheikh. The sheikh would listen to her queries patiently and oblige her by answering her questions, because he thought she had a right to ask anything she liked. He told his wife, 'She is at the threshold of the house, and she wants to know what's inside before she comes in.'

★

When Sultan Muqrin arrived in Bahrain, he found preparations were in full swing to repel the Portuguese invasion.

Before the sultan arrived, Emir Nasser had built defences from palm fronds and cobs along the coastline surrounding the city, leaving only two openings overlooking the sea.

The sultan took over command of the soldiers and proceeded to give the defenders their assignments. He divided them into three brigades and put each one under the command of one of his most trusted men. Sultan Muqrin had a formidable force at his disposal, comprising 300 horsemen, 400 archers and a large number of infantrymen, though he had no cannons or muskets.

On the Portuguese side, António Correia ordered Attar to lead the Hormuzi fleet and remain at sea, to prevent the Jabrid ships from carrying out a pincer movement and flanking them from behind, but told him to prepare to support Portuguese foot soldiers if needed.

The weather was hot and humid. It was summer, and at this time of the year, temperatures in the region rose dangerously high, especially at midday. The blistering sun, the stifling humidity and the boiling water, sand and air were merciless.

Correia landed with a force of 170 fighters, followed by one of his commanders with fifty men. Before dawn, they snuck up the coast. A number of Portuguese soldiers were able to climb over the parapet after quickly dispatching the defenders. As the sun began to rise, everyone saw the Portuguese flag flying over one of the towers there. The other Portuguese regiment advanced towards the wall, climbed over it and crossed to the other side after all the Arab defenders had withdrawn.

The muskets the Portuguese soldiers deployed dominated the battle, and many of the defenders were unfamiliar with them. The shots they fired dropped cavalrymen from a long range, and repelled their counter-attacks very effectively. All the tactics the Arabians knew were useless against this weapon.

Suddenly and without warning, Sultan Muqrin's soldiers charged from all directions, trapping the attackers between themselves and the battlements. A large battle followed in which many were slaughtered on both sides. The battle lasted until noon, when temperatures peaked and the fighters started collapsing from dehydration and the unforgiving sun. The two armies retreated back from their positions, pulling with them as many dead and injured from their side as they could.

The Portuguese soldiers decided to remove their armour. By now, these panoplies were the equivalent of ovens, though taking them off exposed them to the defending archers.

Attar had an idea to end the battle swiftly. He disembarked from his ship and went to the coast to find Correia, who by now had realised that the real enemy was the heat and that the battle had to be settled now or abandoned.

Attar's advice was for the skilled archers to train their arrows on the commanders of Sultan Muqrin's army. The vizier explained that the Arabian troops were large in number and distributed all along the fortifications, which meant that commanding officers were the only way to keep those forces organised and disciplined. If they were to be taken out, however, the Arabian army would fall into disarray.

Attar chose 200 of his best archers, and positioned them behind the infantrymen, between the attackers and the sea. Their mission was to pick off the Arabian officers.

As the sun went down, preparations were also being made on the other side. Oddly, however, the Jabrid commanders did not think much of the men who came down from the ships carrying bows, and thought they were part of the attackers' formations that had to be dealt with on the battlefield.

As the fighting resumed, volley after volley of Hormuzi arrows came down on the defenders, killing many of their commanders. Chaos ensued in their ranks, and the Arabian army could not cope without them.

The sultan was on his horse fighting alongside his men. When he saw the mayhem spreading in the flanks of his army, he rode quickly to investigate. The sultan was suddenly hit with a bullet, which ripped through the upper part of his thigh. Muqrin fell from his horse bleeding profusely. Soldiers took him to a nearby mosque which had been converted into a makeshift hospital. As the sultan disappeared from the battle along with the slain officers, signs of defeat of the Arabian army began to emerge.

Emir Nasser, learning of Sultan Muqrin's injury, raised the white flag and asked for a parley with the Portuguese.

The remaining commanders decided to move Sultan Muqrin across the sea to Al-Uqair, fearing he would fall into the hands of the attackers. They had not expected Emir Nasser to raise the flag of surrender so quickly. The wounded sultan was placed on a stretcher and rushed to a boat not far from the battlefield, which the sultan had left behind for contingencies.

Emir Nasser initiated negotiations with the Portuguese. The Portuguese demands were for the Arabians to surrender the island, accept raising the cross atop its fort, and accept the governor that the Portuguese would appoint. Emir Nasser wanted to be the governor they appointed.

The sultan's men felt Emir Nasser had decided to surrender without having a mandate to do so and that he was now looking after his own interests and no one else's. Muqrin's loyal men opted to escape the island fearing retribution from the Portuguese, given their notorious reputation for tormenting and mutilating their enemies.

Small boats began to carry off soldiers and families from Bahrain and to Al-Uqair. When Attar learned about this, he ordered his flotilla to circle Bahrain from the south and head off the fugitives.

Attar was enraged and held a deep grudge. He wanted to avenge his daughter's husband and her maid. When he saw a boat trying to escape, he ordered his ships to pursue it and apprehend everyone on board.

The Hormuzi ships circled the Bahraini vessel. It was none other than the boat carrying the wounded sultan. Clashes ensued between the two sides, in which all of the sultan's defenders were killed. Only the boat's three crewmen survived.

Attar stood over the injured sultan. 'Who are you?'

'I am Sultan Muqrin bin Zamel of the House of Jabrid.'

Attar frowned in surprise. 'The sultan of the Jabrids? I did not expect to see you in captivity.'

The sultan was groaning in pain. He was pressing on his thigh, which was bleeding heavily.

Attar looked at the wound. 'Where is Emir Nasser then?'

'Aaahh . . . I don't know—'

'I have a vendetta against him, Sultan Muqrin. He tried to tarnish my daughter's honour!'

The sultan was writhing and moaning after each sentence he uttered. 'Who is your daughter?'

'Halima, wife of your vizier, Bin Rahhal. I am *Khawaja* Attar, vizier of the kingdom of Hormuz.'

The sultan recalled Bin Rahhal's victorious return from his mission in Hormuz, and the banter they had exchanged about marrying the vizier's daughter. He was awoken from his memories by a sharp pain that shot down his thigh. The sultan screeched. When the pain abated, he whimpered, 'Yes, Bin Rahhal was deeply in love with your daughter.'

In a different life, Attar and the sultan could have been good friends. But circumstances put them now in a position where they were enemies. Attar also had something against the sultan, whom he saw as a cause of his daughter's plight.

'Yes, Sultan Muqrin. He loved her immensely but the horrid man you appointed as emir of Bahrain and as your viceroy murdered him.'

The sultan was not aware of what had happened in Bahrain during his absence. 'Emir Nasser killed Bin Rahhal?'

'Correct. My daughter told me.'

The sultan now understood why Halima had tried to talk to him at the port in Al-Uqair, and why she had been so desperate to meet him.

'This man you appointed has initiated negotiations for his surrender in return for being appointed the governor of Bahrain. He betrayed you in your absence, and has betrayed you again while you lie covered in your own blood.' Attar began to scream in anger, as though he blamed the sultan for all the tragedies that had befallen Halima, Bin Rahhal and Farah. 'You did not choose your deputy well. You cared only that he was loyal, even if he was a murderer like Emir Nasser. You ignored his insolence and wickedness because all you wanted was someone to protect your throne. You monarchs are all the same. You do not think of your subjects, but only of your interests and your interests alone. Because of you, my

364

daughter lost Farah, and you lost Bin Rahhal, your throne and your kingdom!'

The sultan's eyes froze and he stopped breathing. 'He is dead, my lord,' a soldier said.

Attar glared at the Hormuzi soldier, then returned his gaze to the sultan, now a lifeless corpse. The deck of the boat was covered in the blood that had gushed from the sultan's wound.

Attar ordered his men to return to Bahrain. The Hormuzi ships approached the coast tugging a small boat behind them. Correia knew that Attar had caught something valuable, and went into the water trying to see who was on the boat. He managed to glimpse a body lying on the deck and spotted Attar.

'It's Sultan Muqrin, Officer Correia. He was trying to flee to Al-Ahsa,' Attar said.

The Portuguese commander ordered his men to decapitate the body and send the head to Hormuz to be shown to Albuquerque.

The Hormuzi and Portuguese fleets loitered near the Bahraini coast. There was systematic looting on the island, and the soldiers and sailors wreaked havoc in Bahrain.

Days later, a ship from Hormuz came bringing a letter to Correia. It was from Albuquerque, congratulating him on his victory and asking him to change his name to António Correia Da Bahrain, so that his triumph would forever be associated with his family. Albuquerque even suggested that Correia devise a new coat of arms for his family, showing an arm carrying the head of Sultan Muqrin.

Attar knew that it was Emir Nasser who was the cause of Farah's death, and knew it was he who had murdered Bin Rahhal too. There was not much he could do about it, however, as the man was under Correia's protection now.

Attar decided to visit his daughter's home and collect any belongings she may have left behind. He also wanted to visit Farah's grave. He chose a group of bodyguards and rode to the farmstead. He knew exactly where it was; it belonged to the father of King Salghur, who had excluded it from the agreement with the Jabrids.

Attar found the gate to the estate had been pried open, and the place abandoned. Everyone had fled when the invaders overran the island. He dismounted his horse and walked inside, leading the animal behind him by its reins.

The Hormuzi vizier walked between two rows of palm trees towards the house. He gave his horse to one of his men and walked to the grave. Attar read a verse from the Quran over the tomb. He then cleaned it and replaced the wreaths Halima had placed over it before she left for Al-Ahsa.

Attar remembered Farah when she was a little girl. When he bought her from the slaver and brought her home, Halima was overjoyed. The two girls played together and grew up together like sisters. He could not imagine Halima without her. They were like twins, and Attar treated them with almost equal love and affection, though he kept a bit of distance from Farah. After all, she was not of his flesh and blood.

Attar felt a warm tear roll down his cheek. He wiped it gently and then placed the same hand on the grave, as though trying to convey his grief to Farah.

Suddenly, he heard a noise coming from inside the house.

36

Jeddah, Arabian Peninsula

C ARRIER PIGEONS WERE OF little use for conveying detailed information. Hussein learned of the Mamluk defeat in the Battle of Marj Dabiq, but did not know exactly what had happened. And he had no idea what would happen when the Ottoman Sultan Selim entered Cairo.

A torrent of thoughts rushed into Hussein's head. The conflict he felt brought back his insomnia and affected his judgement and behaviour. Everything in his life had become muddled and unclear.

One morning, the *dawadar* entered his quarters to inform him that a merchant who had returned recently from Egypt bore news for him.

'Let him in without delay.'

The Battle of Marj Dabiq was a historic turning point in the region. Sultan Selim was at the head of the young Ottoman Empire, which was perpetually pushing its borders in an attempt to expand its territory as far as possible. Many were of the view that the Ottoman sultanate was the only Sunni Muslim force able to stand up to the Safavid Empire, which in turn was constantly trying to expand. The flurry of reports about Safavid massacres in Iraq prompted people to look for a new power that could protect them from the

Safavids. This meant that the Ottoman victory in Marj Dabiq came as good news for many, even in Egypt. The decisive battle closed the book on the long reign of the Mamluks that many would not miss. People rarely recalled what was good and right at the beginning of the Mamluk power, but remembered very well the misdeeds of the Mamluks near the end of their reign.

The merchant sat in front of Hussein. He understood immediately that the Mamluk pasha had no patience for flattery, and that he was anxious to hear the news he carried. The man cut straight to the point.

'I think you are aware, Hussein Pasha, of the animosity between Sultan Selim and Sultan al-Ghawri. Ottoman troops apprehended a Safavid emissary from Shah Ismail. When they searched him they found a letter to Sultan al-Ghawri asking him to join a Portuguese–Safavid alliance against the Ottomans ...'

Hussein did not want to sit and listen to what he already knew, and to what he suspected was a story fabricated by Sultan Selim to justify an invasion of Egypt. He interrupted the merchant vehemently. 'Forget these tall tales and tell us about the battle!'

The man organised his thoughts. 'The Ottoman sultan marched with around half a million soldiers and 350 cannons. When Sultan al-Ghawri learned of this, he wrote to the Mamluk governor in Syria to rally as many men as he could to his banner and meet him in Marj Dabiq. The governor mobilised a large number of fighters from Syria and Mount Lebanon, bringing the total number of soldiers in the Mamluk army to 450,000, armed with eighty cannons. The two armies then met on the battlefield.

'Shortly after the battle began, the Mamluks flanked the Ottoman army and dealt it a heavy blow that threw it into disarray and forced it to initially retreat. The Mamluk fought valiantly in that battle, Hussein Pasha.'

Hussein's thoughts took him back to when he was a boy in the Mamluk barracks with his friend Suleiman. They would cry because of the harsh training and would eat under the bedcovers to avoid being spotted by their warden. Those who had been trained in combat from an early age would no doubt show great courage in battle, he thought.

Hussein returned to the present, listening to the merchant's report.

'As the Ottoman army was on the verge of fully retreating, the Mamluk governor in Damascus went over to the enemy along with a large number of fighters, joining Sultan Selim's forces. Sultan al-Ghawri, who was fighting alongside his men, saw this with his officers and soldiers. As morale in the ranks of the Mamluks collapsed, Ghawri made a great battle cry to rally his fighters, urging them to hold their ground. But his voice was lost in the heat of the battle.'

The merchant paused before he spoke again. 'All of a sudden, Ghawri's voice betrayed him. His eyes protruded and his body became limp. The sultan dropped his sword and clutched at his chest, before he fell off his horse. When the soldiers saw this they knew his heart had stopped beating, and they collapsed before the Ottomans. After that, Sultan Selim was met with little resistance and he eventually entered Cairo.'

Hussein put his head between his hands and shook it as though trying to wake up from a bad dream. Ghawri's defeat in Marj Dabiq was even harsher than his own defeat at the hands of the Portuguese in Diu. Egypt had fallen to the Ottomans, the very same people he was raised to despise for many years.

The Mamluk pasha wondered what the Ottomans were now up to in Egypt. He had nothing but the city wall he had built to protect Jeddah from Ottoman raids. He also knew he was on his own, with no supporters to defend him. It was a catastrophe.

News of the Mamluk defeat spread like wildfire among the Jeddans. It dawned on them that Hussein Pasha was cut off from Egypt and had no one to rely on for support. He had also lost his legitimacy as the governor of Jeddah. Many in the city started plotting to overthrow him.

The rebels started attacking the military outposts that were far from the city wall. At night, they burned the storerooms near the gates and dumped huge amounts of sand and salt in the water reservoirs that fed the palace and the barracks. Next, the rebels cut off the road to Mecca.

Each morning, the commander of the guard brought new reports of casualties among his soldiers, or sabotage of his posts. Hussein's authority was being weakened by an organised insurgency. The Mamluk governor did not know why people were doing all this. After all, wasn't he here to protect them from the Portuguese, who could attack the city at any moment and ransack it? Did these people not understand his responsibility and what he was doing for their sake?

Hussein was like a cat pushed into a corner. He knew the people of Jeddah hated him and did not want him here. But he also knew that no one would take him in should he flee. He had nowhere to go. All he could do was to hole up inside the area of the city where he could still impose his authority, including the palace and its immediate vicinity.

In the following months, Hussein barely removed his shoes, clothes and weapons, which he often slept embracing. Each day, he felt death coming closer and closer, especially when he heard Bedouin battle cries just outside the wall, or learned of an attack close to the palace.

One morning when he was inspecting the guards on the side of the wall overlooking the sea, he heard a soldier shouting. The soldier was pointing at black shapes ominously approaching from the northwest over the sea.

The identity of the ships was not clear. Anxious speculation over the owners of the floating fortresses ensued in the ranks of the soldiers – some saying they were Portuguese and others insisting they were Mamluk vessels.

When they got closer, one of the veteran guards was able to make out the emblem on their banners. They were red with green spots in the middle. 'They are Ottoman ships, my lord!'

Hussein ordered his men to shut the gates, fortify them and prepare for battle. Sultan Selim's army had reached the gates of Jeddah, as he had feared.

The fully armed guards climbed up to the top of the wall at the orders of their commanding officers. They opened the gun ports and began to load the cannons. Behind each cannon stood a soldier carrying a linstock, awaiting orders to light the cannon.

An eerie silence descended. All eyes were focused on the five ships creeping towards them. The ships came as close as they could without running aground, then dropped their anchors. Their gun ports were not open, and the ships did not look like they were primed for battle. They were close enough that Hussein Pasha could have ordered them destroyed if he wanted to. The Ottomans were behaving oddly, he thought.

The ships remained immobile for several hours. Then they dropped a small boat carrying a Janissary officer and a group of sailors, who paddled until the boat reached the Jeddan coast.

Hussein came down from the top of the wall and went to the gate, ordering his men to open it. It took the Mamluk guards a while to get the gate open, as they had barricaded it with large wooden panels. After a few strong soldiers moved the heavy panels away, the gate was opened and Hussein found himself face to face with the Ottoman officer waiting on the other side.

'Are you Hussein al-Kurdi?' the Janissary asked.

'I am.'

'This is for you, my lord,' the Ottoman said, handing him over a long tube. Hussein opened one side and pulled out a folded letter. He unfurled it and began to read.

> *To my brother, Hussein al-Kurdi,*
>
> *It has been many years since we parted ways. Our last meeting was under a fig tree, when we shared a meal at the inn where our friend Jaafar worked. Do you remember?*
>
> *Let me tell you what has happened to me in these intervening years. I set off with the amir to fight pirates in Rhodes. I was captured after suffering a grave injury. I remained for several years on the island with a group of Ottoman prisoners of war. They were very difficult years. They forced us to work building fortifications around the city, until Sultan Selim secured our release, setting free a number of Frankish prisoners his navy had captured in return for our freedom.*
>
> *I am now an officer in the Ottoman navy. I am the commander of the ships you see in front of you. I have not changed much, and I hope you haven't either.*

Know, Pasha, that with the victory God has graced upon Sultan Selim the Grim, he has been declared the new caliph. The last Abbasid caliph, Al-Mutawakkil III, abdicated in his favour. In this capacity, loyalty and obedience must be to him.

You are alone now, with no one to support you in Muslim lands, which have all accepted Sultan Selim as their caliph. The sultan of Yemen has recently pledged his allegiance to Sultan Selim. All Muslim ports and realms will close their doors to you. Your only option is to surrender.

Accordingly, I call on you to open the gates of Jeddah and hand over its keys. Under the orders of Sultan Selim, I will be the new governor.

Peace,
Suleiman Pasha the Ottoman

Hussein began to tremble and his limbs became numb. His best friend was now on the side of his enemies, and was even asking him to surrender. Had Suleiman forgotten their laughter, their crying, their sweat and their conversations? How could the cheerful man who never worried about anything have become a senior commander leading five ships? Could people really change that much?

Hussein had no answers any more. The Janissary stood in front of him waiting for his reply, but Hussein felt unfocused and unsteady. He did not want the Ottoman to see him like this and learn his weaknesses, so he told him he would send back his reply soon and dismissed him.

He returned to his palace feeling defeated and as if he had lost a major part of his life. Hussein's entourage wondered what the letter he read contained, and whether it was a threat to destroy Jeddah or kill the pasha.

Hussein isolated himself in his palace as rumours about the Ottoman letter spread among the populace, who took to speculating about its contents. Whatever message it carried, they all agreed that the Ottoman arrival meant Hussein was finished, his grip over the city irreversibly loosened. Jeddans felt they had to do something to take advantage of the situation and the presence of the Ottoman ships anchored just outside the harbour. If they failed to act and the ships left for any reason, they thought, Hussein Pasha could return to his old ways, dealing with them heavy-handedly and confiscating their money.

Mobs of people gathered in several quarters of Jeddah. They agreed to instigate a rebellion against Hussein. There was a favourable opportunity to topple him as long as the Ottoman ships were there.

Hussein spent the night thinking about how he should reply to Suleiman. Should he resist handing over the city? What would happen if he agreed to his terms? Did he have enough men to resist the ships and their cannons that could come out of their ports at any moment?

Many conflicting ideas were raging in Hussein's head. Suleiman was not by his side to give him counsel and reassure him; it was Suleiman himself who was the source of the problem this time. Hussein cursed the way events had played out.

On the following day, the *dawadar* folded Hussein's reply into a metal tube, closed it, and gave it to the chief guard to deliver to Suleiman Pasha.

– 37 –

Jeddah, Arabian Peninsula

O N THE DECK OF the Ottoman flagship, Suleiman Pasha opened the letter from Hussein. Before he read it, he looked toward Jeddah. He could not see it very well. The sun that was now behind it was too bright. The city appeared tranquil and surrendered to the morning sun, and had he not been here with the letter in his hand, it would have been just like any other morning.

He read:

My dear friend Suleiman Pasha,

I had not expected to see you in the sea off Jeddah of all places. I have waited many years to see you again. For so long I shared my worries with you, and you were a good listener despite my many complaints. But here we are now, standing on two opposing sides, each serving a different sultan, though yours has ended the life of mine.

I never wanted to meet in circumstances like these. When we met we were boys in the Mamluk barracks, and now, we – hair greying – meet at sea. This is God's will, and I know not what God has ordained for us. I do not know how this story will end. I do not think I want to know.

Sultan al-Ghawri, God have mercy on him, appointed me governor of Jeddah. I see no reason to hand the city over to you without

defending it until the last drop of my blood has drained from me.
But let us agree on one thing if we both get out of this alive: we will
share a meal under the fig tree at Jaafar's inn. Agreed?

I do not know if I should wish you luck or wish it upon myself,
and I see little difference either way.

Admiral Hussein Pasha al-Kurdi
Amir of Jeddah

Suleiman tried to control his emotions and held back a tear that had formed in the corner of his eye. Hussein's words struck him like a whip but Suleiman would not forget their long history of friendship, loyalty, sadness and joy.

He sat thinking about his next step. If he decided to bombard the city using cannons, he could obliterate it but would certainly lose Hussein forever. Many civilians could lose their lives. If he did nothing, the siege could last a very long time. The best way was for Jeddah to fall from within, with its people rebelling against Hussein and then handing him over to Suleiman.

Suleiman's ships did not make any move in the days that followed. The guards watching them from the top of the city wall did not notice any suspicious movement on them either. People were now used to the ships and returned to their normal lives, unaware of the history between the two commanders.

Also unbeknownst to the people was that, at night, secret contacts were taking place between the rebel leaders and the commanders of the Ottoman ships. When it was dark, rebels would take a small boat and paddle to the Ottoman ship or, vice versa, Ottoman spies would go to shore to meet with them. The two sides had agreed to carry out a coordinated, well-choreographed uprising against Hussein with Ottoman help – which Suleiman conditioned upon the rebel leaders handing Hussein over to Suleiman alive after they stormed the palace.

One night, a mob of Jeddans armed with swords and daggers attacked a guard post at the edge of the wall. A few hours later, another mob attacked a guard post on the other side of the wall, killing many soldiers that Hussein was counting on to control the outskirts of the city. At the same time, there was a fire in the market, and people rushed to put it out.

Suddenly, the gate overlooking the desert was opened by a large number of armed Bedouin warriors. Pandemonium ensued throughout the city. People locked themselves in. Many families took refuge under the same roof in search of safety. People were heard screaming in the streets, and no one knew what was going on in their neighbourhoods.

Many enthusiastic youths joined the rebellion to rid themselves of Hussein Pasha al-Kurdi, who had taken their money and humiliated them. Opportunistic thieves also came out that night to loot shops and homes, taking advantage of the mayhem.

Jeddah's defence collapsed as soldiers fled from their positions. Even the granaries were looted. Some people exploited the unrest to carry out vendettas against their foes. As bodies piled up in the streets, vigilante groups formed to protect their homes and neighbourhoods, armed with canes and whatever melee weapons they could find. A toxic atmosphere permeated the city, which seemed to have caught fire that night.

Suleiman was watching the bedlam unfold from the deck of his ship. He prayed to God to protect Hussein from the uncontrollable chaos. Revolutions, he believed, were like bushfires: hard to predict and hard to contain.

The Mamluk guards loyal to Hussein decided to assemble at the palace to protect their pasha. The Mamluk cohort knew they would not be able to survive if they remained scattered, and formed a single line standing shoulder to shoulder in front of the main gate. The Mamluk guards decided to try to hold their position until morning, after which they would be able to find out what was happening. They were edgy and alert, as death might come from any direction and any angle.

Hussein was in the palace the whole time. He ultimately resolved to take up arms and join his men. The soldiers felt a sense of reassurance when they saw their pasha carrying his sword behind them. There was only this palace left to protect.

Hussein thought of Suleiman. He wished he could peer through the distance separating them and see what his friend was doing as Jeddah burned. Many questions troubled Hussein. Why did people change? Did the soul itself mutate or become tainted? Or was it self-interest that remoulded people and their worldviews, in which case their souls had no choice but to follow suit?

His grip on his sword slackened as he became distracted by his thoughts. A sudden commotion broke out in an alleyway to his right, followed by another to his left a few seconds later. Hussein and his guards closed rank, unsheathed their swords and stood waiting.

Mobs armed with swords, knives, sticks and makeshift weapons appeared, with more angry rabble joining them from the alleyways that terminated in front of the palace.

The mobs hesitated when they saw the Mamluk guards with their swords drawn, and exchanged a few stares, the spectre of death hanging heavy over the hall. But the mob's thirst for revenge was unquenchable. Their eyes became bloodshot, their hearts pumped bile and they decided to charge.

The two sides merged into a brawling mass of monsters digging their teeth into their victims. Blood spattered and heads flew, and the injured were trampled and asphyxiated by the stampeding hordes. The fighting continued until the Mamluks' resistance faltered. As the wounded groaned and the disarmed survivors begged for their lives, a voice cried among the raging crowd, 'Take no prisoners! Kill them all!'

All kinds of weapons were used in striking the necks of the captives and wounded. The entrance to the governor's palace turned into a bloodbath, but Hussein and a small number of his guards were able to escape further inside the palace, and barricaded themselves in a hall. They were panting and shaking in terror.

The gate that separated the angry mob from Hussein and his group began to give way, quickly breaking wide open under the weight of the crowd of attackers. It was a terrifying sight: the weapons and bodies of the attackers were covered in blood. Some carried decapitated heads dripping blood.

Hussein ordered his soldiers to drop their weapons. Resistance was futile. The angry mob was behaving like a horde of mindless sleepwalkers who were ready to do anything they were ordered to do, without questions.

Hussein was their captive. One of the crowd bellowed, 'Let's take him to Suleiman Pasha! He's waiting for us on his ship!'

The crowds marshalled a bloodied Hussein and his guards in front of them. They were stripped of their clothes save for their undergarments. They had been beaten until their faces were swollen. The mob and the humiliated prisoners reached the port.

On the Ottoman flagship, a sailor rushed to get Suleiman Pasha to the deck to see what was happening. Suleiman came quickly and saw the angry crowds, but he could not quite see what was going on.

'What's happening? What do they want?'

The officer standing near him replied, 'It's the rebels, Suleiman Pasha. They have Hussein, if you can see him from this distance, the naked man standing on the edge of the wharf. We don't know what they want. I think they're trying to hand him over to us.'

Blood rushed to Suleiman's head. 'I agreed with the ring-leaders to hand him over unharmed! Why would they do this to him? Where are they now?'

'We could not get in touch with any of them, sir. The city is in complete disarray,' the officer bumbled.

Suleiman kept his eyes trained on the mobs, then ordered his men to rush to the shore and rescue Hussein from their clutches.

A small boat was dropped slowly from the flagship. When it hit the water, the officer and four armed escorts jumped in.

On the coast, the mindless hordes were now in a state of blind, frenzied rage. As they clamoured and quarrelled, a voice at the back yelled, 'What are you waiting for! Kill them! No one seems to want them!'

As the crowds drew their swords to carve up and behead the captives, another voice screamed, 'Throw him off the wall that he tormented us with. Tie him to stones from it and drop him in the sea and let's be done with him!'

Hurriedly, people broke off the mob to get large rocks that had fallen off the wall during the turmoil. They placed them at the feet of the doomed captives and tied them to the rocks tightly. The captives' hands were bound behind their backs.

Hussein and his men began to say their last prayers. Their limbs were paralysed but they did not weep.

The boat carrying the Ottoman soldiers was moving closer to shore. The officer urged the rowers to hurry up before it was too late. Back on the ship, Suleiman Pasha could no longer shout, and was paralysed as he watched the slow execution unfold.

The officer on the boat stood up and shouted to the sailors to row harder. 'Faster! Faster! Come on!'

On the coast, the stones were pushed into the water, dragging the victims swiftly behind them. A few moments later, bubbles emerged from the depths of the sea. It was done.

Silence fell on the angry crowd, as if the murder had drained their energy and exhausted them. They dropped their blood-spattered swords, daggers and clubs and dispersed.

The officer on the boat sat down helplessly after he saw what had happened. On the Ottoman flagship, Suleiman first screamed in agony, and then was hit with a wave of nausea and sobbing. He had lost a friend whose blood, he felt, was on his hands.

38

Bahrain

A TTAR HEARD A SOUND from inside the house. He ordered his men to identify and surround the source quietly. A few moments later, Jawhar came out skulking, carrying a huge bag on his back. The soldiers caught him and brought him back to Attar, who was still standing near Farah's grave.

One of the guards snatched the bag from Jawhar and opened it, revealing many valuables. He laid them out at Attar's feet. The Hormuzi vizier glared at Jawhar and snarled, 'Who are you?'

Jawhar answered in a proud tone, 'My name is Jawhar. I am Emir Nasser's slave.'

Attar recognised Jawhar's name from the letter his daughter had sent him, informing him of Farah and Bin Rahhal's deaths and explaining Emir Nasser and his slave's involvement in their demise. The man kneeling before him was the cause of Farah's death and Halima's ordeal and a part of the plot she had told him about.

Attar gestured with his foot toward the stolen items. 'What are these?'

Jawhar's boastful tone disappeared. 'The house seemed to be abandoned. As you know, Your Excellency, the war has displaced many people. The Portuguese have been looting homes in the city, so I decided to take what I could from the house before anyone else came.' Jawhar tried to come up with further excuses. 'If I hadn't taken them from the house someone else would have. As you know, my lord—'

Attar did not let him finish his sentence. 'Where is your master Nasser?'

'I don't know. The last time I saw him, he was near the wall before he surrendered. I have not seen him since.'

'Do you know who is buried in this grave?' Attar asked, pointing at Farah's tomb.

Jawhar gulped in fear and surprise. 'It belongs to a maid who worked in this house. I don't know how she died, my lord.'

Attar signalled his men to restrain Jawhar before he spoke again. 'Let me tell you about this maid, Jawhar.'

He approached the grave and wiped the tombstone. 'This is the grave of *my daughter* Farah. I raised her as if she was my own, alongside my real daughter Halima. This is the grave of the woman you lied to and forced to steal the dagger from her mistress to give to you, and which you then gave to your master Nasser to blackmail my daughter! You have caused Farah's death by making her sacrifice her honour to protect Halima from your master!'

Jawhar tried to wriggle out of his restraints to escape. The man standing in front of him was Halima's father, who knew everything about the house, the dagger and the plots. The words coming out of his mouth suggested he had a score to settle with him. Jawhar was struggling to undo his ties to no avail. When he realised he wasn't going to escape, he fell on his knees and tried to appeal to Attar to show him mercy.

'My lord, all I know is that Farah killed herself after she gave me the dagger out of guilt and regret, for having betrayed Halima. I had nothing to do with what happened after!'

Attar returned to Farah's grave, removing the dry twigs and leaves and wiping the dust off the tombstone meticulously. It was as though he thought the tombstone was a portal to Farah's soul, and he wanted her to listen to what was being said. Attar turned back to Jawhar.

'The dagger you gave to your master was used to black-mail Halima, but Farah was able to trick him and rescue her mistress from disgrace. Farah cut her wrists because she could not cope with the shame of what she had done!'

Attar paused. He seemed pensive, like he was carefully weighing the situation. Attar then looked straight into Jawhar's eyes.

'Your blood must be spilled on Farah's grave so she can find peace in her final resting place. She died sad and angry, and her soul will not rest until she knows that she has been avenged. In Hormuz, we have a traditional way of exacting revenge. Do you know what it is, Jawhar?'

Jawhar knew he was dead if he did nothing. He tried to make a run for it but the guard grabbed him violently by his arm.

Attar did not want the charade to last much longer. He gave the signal to his guards, who shoved Jawhar to a spot near the grave and forced him to kneel.

Jawhar started squealing and wriggling again. One of the guards took out a dagger and sliced his Achilles tendon to prevent him from standing up and moving. Jawhar's hysterical screaming was silenced abruptly when a sword sliced off his head, which rolled away from the grave. His lifeless body slumped to the ground near the tombstone. Silence fell save for the sound of blood squirting out of his severed arteries onto the dry sand.

Attar waited for several minutes until the corpse stopped twitching and the blood stopped gushing onto the ground around the grave. Attar ordered his men to place the severed head in the bag along with the loot, and to bury the body away from Farah's grave.

The posse rode back toward the coast, to where the battle had taken place a few days earlier. The area had been turned into the headquarters of the invading force, and now received supply ships from Hormuz on a daily basis. The soldiers were resting and enjoying themselves on the sands there, having finished burying the dead.

António Correia sat with Emir Nasser under the ruins of the mosque that the Jabrid had used as a field hospital during the battle. It was clear the two men had reached an agreement, and that all that was left for the emir to do was to demonstrate a little more loyalty before he was chosen to rule the island on behalf of the Portuguese.

Attar and his men approached the mosque. Attar asked them to get Jawhar's head out and show it to Emir Nasser, whose face suddenly assumed an expression of shock and horror.

Attar addressed António. 'This is the head of a slave belonging to Emir Nasser, who sent him to loot King Salghur's home. We caught him in the act. These are the stolen items that were in his possession.'

One of the guards tossed the sack containing the loot found with Jawhar at António's feet. The sack hit the ground, and precious stones, large pieces of amber, daggers with ivory handles, kohl containers and other valuable items spilled out.

António glared at the emir and asked him to explain.

'This is a baseless accusation, Admiral Correia. He was acting alone. Would I dare rob King Salghur's home? Absolutely not!'

António ordered his men to take the stolen goods to his ship. Emir Nasser did not want the incident to spoil his relationship with the Portuguese, and continued his protests. 'As you must be aware, Admiral Correia, there was widespread looting after your victory and Sultan Muqrin's death. It would be impossible for me to control what all my servants and slaves were doing!'

Nasser turned his eyes to Attar, who was still standing in front of them. 'What I think is that Attar has an interest in tarnishing my reputation in front of you. His daughter is the widow of Bin Rahhal, Sultan Muqrin's vizier. She is still in Al-Ahsa as far as I know.'

The look in Emir Nasser's eyes turned more sinister. 'His daughter has a bad reputation. He stands to gain if he gets rid of me because I know many things about him and his daughter. Ask him, Admiral Correia, why did he go to the king's farmstead to begin with, if his daughter no longer lives there?'

Blood rushed to Attar's face, which turned bright red. He was about to do something he might regret, as this was the first time in his life that he had been insulted in this way. António was waiting for him to explain, but Attar was still thinking about the caustic words that came out of the Arabian emir about his daughter and her honour.

Attar stuttered a little before saying, 'I went to visit the grave of my adoptive daughter Farah, who is buried there!'

Emir Nasser was waiting for those exact words to come out of Attar's mouth, and retorted, 'Your Excellency, ask him how she died. I know that she did not die a natural death.'

António was enjoying this quarrel between the two men, which he felt he had to feed and exacerbate. He knew that if these two leaders worked together, the Portuguese ships, if not the entire Portuguese presence in the Gulf, would be in grave danger; sowing the seeds of mistrust among the occupied prevented them from ever joining forces against the invaders.

Attar understood, from one look at António's face, that he was enjoying this feud that revolved around his family's honour. He wanted to put an end to the subject that Emir Nasser was trying to drag him into.

'She committed suicide, Admiral Correia, because she could no longer bear living in a corrupt and rotten world!'

Emir Nasser roared with an obnoxious laughter that everyone around heard, before he suddenly fell silent. 'Are you sure about that? You have slain my slave Jawhar because he knew the whole story. Farah sold herself to him in return for cheap promises, and your daughter sold herself to me because she was jealous of her maid and did not want to be left out! They were both cheap women!' Nasser turned to António, who was smiling, and added, 'But very beautiful ones.'

With his eyes still on the Portuguese commander, he pointed at Attar and said, 'This man has a grudge against me and you, commander. He is a danger to us both. He will not hesitate to stab you in the back if he can.'

Listening to the squabble, António became certain that there was no threat of these men ever agreeing on anything. He made a decree appointing Emir Nasser governor of Bahrain and representative of the kingdom of Portugal, and left for Hormuz with Attar. Attar felt weak and had a profound pain in his chest, having been insulted in a way that his body and soul could not cope with.

39

Al-Ahsa, Eastern Arabian Peninsula

A S NEWS OF SULTAN Muqrin's death spread, a painful sense of bereavement pervaded Al-Ahsa. Halima in particular was stricken with both grief and guilt, as she felt she was the cause of his death.

The Portuguese were now a stone's throw away from Al-Ahsa, and everyone felt it was only a matter of time before their legions appeared on the horizon. Sultan Muqrin and his army were now history, the realm had disintegrated and even the Bedouin tribes were now mounting daring attacks on the edges of the city, which had descended into lawlessness. People were barricading themselves in their homes and inside the forts scattered around the area.

Halima became panic-stricken after the sultan's death. She blamed herself for his and his men's demise, and for the fall and sacking of Bahrain at the hands of the Portuguese, and she hated the world and herself for it.

Halima wandered around aimlessly, recalling her life as a pampered princess with her father in Hormuz, her marriage to Bin Rahhal who treated her like a queen, and then his murder, leading up to the wretchedness and misery she was now living. She often had bouts of rage and sobbing, with feelings of utter loss and despair, throwing sand on her head and shrieking in terror and distress. These bouts would last for a few minutes until she fell unconscious. Sometimes, when children saw her in this state, they summoned the sheikh's wife, who would rush to Halima with wet cloths to wipe her face and rouse her. The older woman would escort her back home and help her clean herself, and waited with her until the sheikh returned and consoled her with some verses from the Quran.

People thought *jinn* had possessed Halima. But what she was going through, dreadful as it was, was not the result of some supernatural entity. She felt that she had lost every reason to live, that there was nothing beautiful left in the world to endure for. She felt her soul had been shattered into a million pieces, and that everything she had taken for granted had been violently overturned. Death seemed to her to be the salvation, and spells of madness a way out of her painful reality.

There was little Halima could enjoy in life now, and happiness was to her like a deeply buried memory. All food tasted bitter to the forlorn woman, who neglected her body. Halima felt a trace of cheerfulness near graves and envied the dead for their departure. She was on the brink of insanity, rebounding between the dismal reality and the long lost, blissful past.

The days passed like weeks, and weeks passed like months, but by now Halima's shock had started to wear off, and her misery had begun to fade. Her emotional state improved, and the bouts of mad grief were not as frequent as before.

She had no one left but her father now, but she was too ashamed to return to him. How could she return having lost her husband and her fortune, and having caused Sultan Muqrin's death and the occupation of Bahrain? Halima did not know what she wanted in life, or what life wanted from her, and she wished her soul would depart her weary body.

Sheikh Jamal al-Din Tazi decided to return to his home in Morocco. Life in Al-Ahsa had become difficult and unpredictable. Since Halima did not want to remain by herself in a city where she had no one else, she decided to travel with them as far as Mecca, the Holy Land.

Halima remembered that she still had the Bahmani dagger in her possession when she was packing. Sultan Muqrin, she recalled, had promised the Indian king who gave it to him to deliver it to the caliph. Halima realised that this promise had to be fulfilled, even after Muqrin's death.

She turned the dagger over in her hand, then took it out of its sheath. She had cleaned Farah's blood from the blade. No one else could fulfil Sultan Muqrin's wishes but her now. Halima set her mind on delivering it to the caliph by any means. She packed it with her luggage without having a clear plan of how she was going to do it, and placed it in the same box as the ring the sultan had bought from the Banyan merchant, also as a gift to the caliph. She had managed to keep both precious items safe, but it was now time to pass them on.

Sheikh Tazi's wife was helping her pack and sort out her belongings when she suddenly asked, 'And just where do you intend to go after Mecca, Halima?'

'I don't yet know. I may remain in Medina until I die. Al-Ahsa does not want me any more, nor do I want it.'

'Why don't you go back to your father in Hormuz?'

Halima sighed. Any mention of her father still rattled her and made her pine for her childhood. 'I have no one else in the world but him. I sent him a letter telling him I am going to the

390

Hajj but he did not approve. May God forgive me! I will not return to Hormuz before I perform the pilgrimage and visit the tomb of the Prophet.This is a once-in-a-lifetime opportunity and I will not find in the whole world a better company than yours. I will stay in Medina for some time, and fulfil Sultan Muqrin's wishes to deliver his dagger to the caliph.'

'Who will you stay with there, Halima? I fear for you staying alone after we leave!'

'Do not worry yourself. Calamities have befallen every land around us. Even my country has become inhospitable after the Portuguese took it. The things my father has told me in his letters are heartbreaking. If I go there, I will be happy to see him for a few hours but then I will have to live in a crucible of fear and pain like him. No, I will carry out my religious duty and then let God guide my path from there on. I don't care whether I live or die afterwards.'

She looked at the dagger before she spoke again. 'I loved my husband with every fibre of my being. My husband had the utmost love and respect for Sultan Muqrin in turn. I will do right by them and take the dagger to the caliph. Perhaps that will expiate my sins and misdeeds.'

The elderly woman frowned. 'Sins and misdeeds? What are you talking about, child? Nothing bad could ever come from you!'

Halima smiled and tried to avoid having this conversation. What she had done, inviting the Portuguese to Bahrain, still caused her insurmountable guilt and heartache. 'It doesn't matter. What matters is that the dagger should reach the caliph's hands.'

'Which caliph, Halima? My husband and I spent time in Cairo on our way to Mecca the first time. The caliph was known to be weak, easily manipulated by the Mamluk amirs and commanding obedience from none but his harem!' She paused and then quipped, 'And I'm not so sure he even controls his harem!'

Halima replied absentmindedly, 'Whatever the case, I have to fulfil the late sultan's wishes.'

The sheikh's convoy headed west with a group of pilgrims and a larger group of people simply fleeing from Al-Ahsa. The caravan was large and well guarded. The roads were no longer safe with the Arab tribes further inland rebelling and in the absence of a powerful central authority that could rein them in.

The travellers lifted their hands to the sky and prayed for a smooth and safe journey. The caravan's departure was a bleak sight, amid the tearful goodbyes of the travellers and their loved ones. The cameleers began singing a sad tune that reminded the travellers of the forbidding, lonely road ahead and the loved ones they were leaving behind for a long time.

The caravan reached Mecca shortly before the pilgrimage season. Halima saw droves of people of all nationalities and complexions, who had come from all around the world speaking in different tongues – trading, eating and drinking, and conversing. She had hoped to spot pilgrims from Hormuz, whom she would be able to recognise from their clothes and appearance, but none were there to be seen. She was told the sea route to Jeddah was now perilous and few ships dared traverse it. She felt annoyed; it had never been this bad before the ships bearing the large red cross came.

The Hajj was a unique experience for Halima. She had left her small island only when she got married. Now, she was seeing and experiencing the world and its diversity. She drank putrid water, experienced hunger, ate foul-tasting cured meat, and tasted dirt in her mouth and felt it inside her eyes.

Halima rubbed her head in the sand and prayed humbly to the Creator. She experienced things she would never have encountered in the palace of her father the vizier. And she saw how big the world was, much bigger than the world she had lived in at the palace or even the estate of her slain husband. The eye-opening, multilayered and multicoloured discoveries she made distracted her from thinking about her ordeal.

At the Hajj, Halima learned that the Abbasid caliph had surrendered his title to the Ottoman Sultan Selim, who was now the official caliph of the Muslims. She could not understand how the caliph could be a non-Arab.

Halima asked Sheikh Tazi to whom she should give the dagger and the ring now, the deposed caliph or Sultan Selim, and in the event she were to give the gifts to the latter, then how would she be able to reach him.

Sheikh Tazi's advice was that she should deliver them to the Ottoman sultan, since he was the current caliph of the Muslims. But since the sultan was too far from her, he said, she should go instead to the highest Ottoman authority in Hejaz, namely, Suleiman Pasha, commander of the Ottoman Red Sea fleet and ruler of Jeddah. The sheikh told her she had to wait until the Hajj season was over, however, as Suleiman Pasha would be busy receiving the delegations from around the Muslim world.

The Hajj season was soon finished. The pilgrims started leaving the Holy Land. Long caravans carrying luggage headed in all directions, and others made for the port of Jeddah where the pilgrims took ships back to their homes in the lands of Zanj, India and China. Mecca gradually shed its crowds and life returned to normal until the next Hajj season.

Sheikh Tazi and Halima's caravan set out for Jeddah, the city where Suleiman Pasha, the new Ottoman ruler who could deliver the dagger to Sultan Selim, was based. Suleiman was popular among the Jeddans, in contrast to Hussein Pasha al-Kurdi. In Jeddah, Halima and the sheikh and his wife would go their separate ways; they were going back to Morocco via Egypt, but she did not yet have a specific destination in mind after her mission was completed.

The sheikh's small caravan crossed the gate of Jeddah, which was now wide open. The guards did not ask them where they were going and what their purpose in the city was. Jeddah was now much safer, and life had returned to the normality that existed before the devil, as the people called their previous ruler, had come. The pilgrims stayed at a small inn, immediately adjacent to the wall.

The sheikh was able to find someone to vouch for him at the palace, and get a hearing with the governor. Tazi asked Halima to come with him. 'You must come with me to the palace, Halima. Then you can deliver the dagger and the ring to Suleiman Pasha yourself.'

Halima was not too keen, and was nervous about going there. 'I will give them to you, uncle. I don't want to go to a place where there are too many men I don't know.'

The sheikh persisted. 'I will be with you the entire time. You must give him the gifts yourself, Halima. This is not the time to back down. You have come all the way from Al-Ahsa for this and you must get it done.'

Sheikh Tazi, accompanied by Halima, entered the governor's palace. Tazi asked her to wait in a small hall outside the pasha's private *diwan*, and entered by himself. The hall was brimming with guests. The sheikh sat and waited for his turn to meet the governor. Eventually the governor received him, asking him what the purpose of his visit was.

'My name is Jamal al-Din Tazi. I come from Morocco. I went to Al-Ahsa last year with Sultan Muqrin al-Jabri, but he was killed in a battle with the Portuguese defending Bahrain. The situation there has become dangerous, so I decided to come for the Hajj and then return to Morocco.'

The pasha seemed interested in what the sheikh was saying. 'One of the people who frequent my court told me two days ago that you were coming to meet me. He said you were carrying news from East Arabia, and that you had an important matter to discuss with me.'

'Indeed, Pasha. I will brief you on developments in East Arabia so you can do what needs to be done. I also have another matter I want to discuss with you.'

The pasha gave him a broad smile. 'Very well, let us begin with the news, Sheikh Tazi. I am very interested in what you have to say about Sultan Muqrin and the Portuguese.'

The sheikh began his report. 'As you know, Your Excellency, the Portuguese have seized the trade routes between India and Arabia. For this reason, trade has never returned to normal. More importantly, the Portuguese spread terror and death everywhere their ships have visited, levelling cities and massacring people. Only a handful of cities have been spared their muskets and cannonballs.'

The sheikh did not want to prolong the conversation. He knew the pasha must have met many people already and

395

probably did not want to hear any more unpleasant news, so he tried to be brief. 'Sultan Muqrin sent his fleet to India to assist the Mamluk fleet led by Hussein Pasha al-Kurdi, but both fleets were defeated in the Battle of Diu. The Portuguese have commanded the seas since that day, and there has been nothing to stop them from raiding our lands. They have conquered and sacked Bahrain, and killed the sultan who died defending it. The Portuguese beheaded him and sent his decapitated head to Hormuz!'

While he spoke, the sheikh watched the pasha's eye to determine the impact of the events he was describing on the Ottoman governor. He continued, 'After subduing Bahrain, they will most definitely move on to Al-Ahsa. If they take it, then they will occupy all of East Arabia. As you know, Pasha, the Portuguese have an alliance with the Safavids, who have occupied Iraq and sacked Baghdad, and even turned the shrine of Imam Abu Hanifa into a stable for their horses.'

The sheikh paused when a servant came and brought him water. 'The situation is very dangerous, Your Excellency. If Sultan Selim, the caliph of the Muslims and protector of Muslim lands, does not act, then they might mount a surprise attack from the south.'

Suleiman followed everything the sheikh said up until he mentioned the Mamluk fleet and the Battle of Diu. Suleiman stopped listening after that, and remembered his friend Hussein and his eagerness to repel the Portuguese. A stream of memories passed through his head, and the pasha could not conceal his emotions. He said, 'Hussein Pasha al-Kurdi was my friend. We grew up in the Mamluk barracks together, and for many years were inseparable. But such is God's will!'

The sheikh, remembering Halima, said, 'I have someone with me who knew him well, Pasha, someone who wants to meet you too.'

'Who may that be?'

'Her name is Halima, the daughter of the Hormuzi vizier *Khawaja* Attar and widow of Bin Rahhal, Sultan Muqrin's vizier. She has something she wants to give to you.'

The pasha rose unconsciously. 'Where is she now?'

'She is in the small hall, waiting to be let in, Pasha.'

Suleiman went with the sheikh to the place where Halima was sitting, away from the men in the palace. She wore a traditional Hormuzi veil through which only her beautiful eyes were visible. When she saw Suleiman Pasha she stood up in reverence, but did not extend her hand to shake his, and then sat back down.

Suleiman glimpsed a lock of her hair creeping out of her headscarf and touching her eyelashes. Her eyes radiated both charm and sorrow.

She spoke to him about the Portuguese threat in the Gulf and told him how her husband, Bin Rahhal, had gone to India to assist Hussein Pasha al-Kurdi until their defeat in Diu. Halima told Suleiman about their escape to Bahrain via Hormuz, disguised as merchants, and Hussein's subsequent departure for Jeddah. Suleiman was impressed by Halima's intelligence, logic and soberness.

Suleiman's eyes welled with tears as he listened to Hussein's ordeals, which had stayed with him until his horrific death not far from the palace where they now stood. Halima noticed the tears in the pasha's eyes and asked him why he was tearful.

'He was once my best friend. We knew each other for many years until time sent us on separate paths. It is also a long story.'

397

Halima took out the dagger from between the folds of her clothes and removed the silk cloth she had used to cover it, before handing the dagger over to Suleiman. He took it from her and examined it carefully. He immediately realised how valuable and unique an artefact it was. Halima also gave him the ring, but Suleiman was not interested in it, and was still fascinated by the dagger. He then asked her about the story behind it.

'I will tell you the story as I heard it from my slain husband. A messenger from Vizier Imad al-Din Mahmoud of the Bahmani kingdom in India brought it to Sultan Muqrin, asking him to deliver it to the caliph in Cairo. The dagger was made from gold and jewellery that once belonged to the vizier's mother and wife. The Indian vizier had great confidence in the sultan, who was a fair and just ruler known far and wide. Sheikh Tazi could tell you more about him.

'Sultan Muqrin gave the dagger to my husband, Vizier Bin Rahhal, for safekeeping as he was leaving Al-Ahsa to put down a tribal rebellion in Najd. The sultan did not want to leave the dagger in his palace during his absence. Before my husband set off to India to fight the Portuguese alongside Hussein Pasha, he asked me to keep an eye on it until his return, and told me that, in the event of his death, I was to deliver it to the caliph by any means in fulfilment of Sultan Muqrin's wishes.

'Upon his return from India, my husband was killed treacherously. When Sultan Muqrin returned from his campaign, he did not stop in Al-Ahsa and I did not have the chance to meet him. He went straight to Bahrain to fight the Portuguese, who had mobilised their fleets to invade the island. Sultan Muqrin never returned; he was killed in the battle.'

Halima started to weep. Suleiman saw her tears drop on her veil below her eyes. He looked away to avoid seeing her in her moment of weakness and sorrow. He only turned back to her when she spoke again.

'I didn't know how and to whom I was to deliver the dagger. That is, until God sent me Sheikh Jamal al-Din Tazi, who did not mind me joining his caravan to Hejaz. After we arrived here, we learned that the Abbasid caliph had abdicated in favour of Sultan Selim. As Sheikh Tazi told me, the dagger now had to be delivered to Sultan Selim. There is no one else I can trust to do this but you, so I ask you to deliver it to the caliph to fulfil the wishes of the late Sultan Muqrin and my husband as well.'

Suleiman looked at the dagger again. Silence reigned over them, until Suleiman spoke. 'I shall deliver it, God willing.'

He then glanced at her furtively and said, 'Tell me about you, madam. I detect a strange accent in your speech.'

She looked away from Suleiman and set her eyes on the floor of the *diwan*, as though trying to hold a painful memory at bay. 'I am Halima, daughter of *Khawaja* Attar, the famed vizier of Hormuz. I met Bin Rahhal when he came to our island to help restore King Salghur to the throne, which had been usurped by his brother. He asked for my hand in marriage a few days after the battle.'

Halima's look changed again. Now she was smiling, recalling good memories. Suleiman saw this, and felt she was remembering a happy chapter in her life. He felt pity combined with admiration for this woman. She was the daughter of an important citizen of Hormuz who went on to live in a strange land. She had lost loved ones and yet she was here all the way in Hejaz, delivering a valuable artefact that had been entrusted not to her, but to her husband, though she could have lived a decent life if she had sold it.

'Do you intend to return to Hormuz after the Hajj?' Suleiman asked.

'No, Your Excellency, not yet. I intend to remain in Medina for a while. I don't know what God will decide for me. The Portuguese have occupied Hormuz where my father is, and Bahrain where my husband is buried. They might have taken Al-Ahsa by now too. I don't want to return to any land occupied by those criminals!'

Sheikh Tazi suddenly spoke and asked for a drink. The guard brought him a glass of water, which the sheikh held up to his eyes and asked, 'Is this holy water from Mecca?'

'Yes, Sheikh. We only drink *zamzam* water in this palace. It is brought here each day straight from Mecca,' the guard replied, and then turned back and left.

The sheikh drank and then poured some of the water over his hand and wiped it on his face. He said, 'Have you heard of the *hadith* "If you drink *zamzam* water then let your faces have a share of it"?'

Suleiman said perplexedly, 'I have never heard of this *hadith*, Sheikh Tazi.'

Halima was also confused. 'I was with you in Mecca for several days and heard you speak about the virtues of *zamzam* water when we drank it, but you never mentioned it, uncle!'

The sheikh removed his turban and used the cloth to wipe his face. 'I forgot to tell you about it, Halima. But it is a *hadith* and we must respect it. Give me your hands.'

Suleiman extended his hands, which he had joined together to allow the sheikh to sprinkle them with *zamzam* water, and then wiped his face as the sheikh had done. Tazi waited for Suleiman to dry his face and then asked Halima to follow suit.

Halima hesitated for a moment. She did not know what she was supposed to do with her veil and whether she should reveal her face to the pasha.

The sheikh seemed to have read her mind. 'Uncover your face, Halima. The *zamzam* water takes precedence and we must follow the *hadith*!'

Halima obeyed, revealing her face and her breathtaking beauty. Suleiman was riveted by her. He did not want to take his eyes off her, as though he knew this opportunity might not be repeated.

The sheikh poured water on the palms of her hands, which she then lifted to wipe her face quickly, before putting the veil back on.

Suleiman needed a few moments to move his eyes away from Halima. He said, 'You will be my guests until the dagger reaches Sultan Selim. I will not let you travel until then. The sultan may enquire about you after he receives it, and if you leave, what would I tell him then?'

The sheikh began to pray for Suleiman. He said, 'I am here with my wife. We intend to go back home with the convoy that will return to Morocco soon. We must leave, Pasha, but if you find a suitable accommodation for Halima in the city, I would be very grateful. She was the one who brought the sultan's dagger and she is the one who wants to stay in the Holy Land. She is like a daughter to me and I want to make sure she has been taken care of before I depart.'

– 40 –

Hormuz

ATTAR COLLAPSED IN HIS favourite chair on the balcony overlooking the sea. He had grown used to being alone since Halima left. But he wished she were with him now, massaging his tired feet while he touched her head in affection like they used to do years ago.

Attar now had no life to speak of. His daughter and only child had gone to perform the Hajj and he had no idea when or if she would return. He had tried his best to convince her to come and live with him, having now lost almost everything. His house was ramshackle and it felt lonely, and the whole of Hormuz was no longer the same as it had been. The house was covered in dust, as the servants no longer did their jobs properly; everything around him was filthy, even his chair. His meals tasted off, and his appearance was a shadow of its former elegance and refinement, with no one to look after him and no one to look after. Attar felt he would die a lonely, broken man.

He rose from his chair and walked over to the parapet, near which he liked to stand when the weather was nice. He felt Halima's spectre by his side. Attar turned towards where she used to stand, hoping to see her face, but all he got was emptiness. She was not there and this was something he had to accept, he told himself.

Attar looked at the horizon beyond the sea. He saw a few small ships cruising the calm water and others anchored in the harbour. This was not the Hormuz he once knew. He spotted three Portuguese ships moored nearby. Their gun ports were open, as though ready at a moment's notice to level the city if Albuquerque ordered it. Attar felt intense hatred for the Portuguese who had destroyed everything beautiful on his island.

He suddenly heard shouting coming from the street outside his home. The king often passed through there, causing a great nuisance to the residents. The street had become filthy, just like his chair and his home, and everything else around him.

The yelling was now louder. Street vendors outside his home were brawling.

Hormuz never had this many poor and homeless people and beggars before. It used to be a wealthy city, legendary for its affluence throughout the world. The street outside Attar's home saw many executions of people he did not know – thieves, mutineers and merchants. Some were burned alive, some were killed by cannon, and others were killed in ways he did not want to remember. The crowds that witnessed those executions were also damaged psychologically. Anyone who saw the horrific deaths soon understood that the Portuguese did not know or understand justice, but were nothing more than sadistic killers who enjoyed torturing their victims. Many people, having witnessed those killings, returned home to pack their belongings and leave the island forever. A country where people were often detained without charge and killed without justification was no place to live.

Attar returned to his chair. What had happened to his city? The Portuguese had attacked and destroyed it, and then hijacked its trade. Corruption and bribery followed shortly thereafter.

This was new to the Hormuzis. Previously, the law exacted harsh punishment on the corrupt, but the venal Portuguese officers brought it with them. Now, everyone had to bribe everyone for the smallest matter, and bribery became the oil that made life possible in Hormuz. People sold their ships, their homes and their valuables to bribe an official here or an official there to be allowed to trade or even leave. Life in Hormuz had become hell, and even escape from it came with a price.

Was this really his Hormuz? Was this the city that was once the pearl of the world, where guests enjoyed everything without paying a dirham, because everyone was generously provided for?

Attar was agitated and could no longer remain seated. He rose and walked back to the balcony, looking for a breath of fresh air that the Portuguese had not yet managed to spoil. He could not bear it any more, and was now determined to do something, anything, to change this insufferable reality.

'Where are you now, Halima? I miss you immensely. I hope that I won't die without seeing you again. What could you be doing now, all alone in Hejaz?' Attar muttered to himself.

Attar returned to his chair briefly, then stood up and went to a shelf where he kept a stack of papers and inkwells beside them. He pulled out a few papers and set out to write some letters, and did not finish until well into the night.

The letters were addressed to the rulers of Al-Ahsa, Khor Fakkan, Sohar, Kuryat and Muscat. Attar resolved to lead a rebellion against the Portuguese in the Gulf. He set a date for an uprising that would take place in many cities at the same time. Everyone had to take up arms on the fateful day and kill all the Portuguese on their lands. The occupiers, Attar reckoned, would not be able to deploy to all those spots at once, and their efforts would be scattered. The rebellion would also burn down their ships, trading posts and forts. If successful, the rebellion would restore things back to the way they were, but people had to sacrifice blood and treasure to regain their freedom, and purge the Portuguese flag from their shores and their holy sails from their seas.

Attar set a date for the rebellion. He asked all the participants to burn Portuguese ships, trading posts, forts, churches and anything and everything that the Portuguese had brought with them. The Portuguese had to return to where they had come from, or go to hell.

After he wrote the letters, he sealed them with his signet and sent them to the emirs and rulers of those parts.

Attar invited some of his trusted associates to his house and told them about the plan. Everyone agreed with the plot, but they protested because he had sent the letters to the rulers of the ports in the Gulf without first consulting them. Attar's reply was that he wanted to present them with a *fait accompli*, because there was no backing down; they could either decide to live with dignity or die with dignity.

The men meeting at the vizier's home devised a plan to take over Hormuz and agreed that *Khawaja* Attar should be the one to lead it.

The letters arrived with the rulers of the ports one by one, and they set out to make preparations for the rebellion. A new spirit of defiance spread among them after years of oppression and persecution, and people waited anxiously for the day set for the insurrection.

But when Attar's letter reached the ruler of Muscat, he had a different reaction. He read it and reread it carefully. He then decided that an alliance with the Portuguese was better than participating in a rebellion with an uncertain outcome. The ruler of Muscat folded the letter and sent it to Albuquerque after adding a short briefing in the margins.

Albuquerque received the Omani ruler's letter a few days before the rebellion was scheduled to begin. He had to act quickly to snuff out the rebellion.

Attar was arrested at his home and taken to a dungeon. Albuquerque proceeded to request reinforcements from the Portuguese garrisons and trading posts in India, and wherever Portuguese ships were located.

The conquistador ordered his soldiers to secure the entrances to the city and the port and tighten security around all important installations. At the designated hour, a large group of men armed with melee weapons came out chanting battle cries, but were met with a volley of bullets and cannonballs, destroying entire quarters near the epicentre of the rebellion. Albuquerque's harsh, bloodstained message to all rebels was that he could destroy them and destroy their whole cities if he wished.

The other cities rose up as well. The rebels killed many Portuguese soldiers and sailors, but Portuguese reinforcements soon arrived and massacred all those who bore arms and their families. Many cities were razed and chaos spread.

The Portuguese ships anchored in the waters opposite these cities, terrorising the locals, and most rebellions died down in a matter of days. The ringleaders were executed in the most terrible ways. The Portuguese actions turned the survivors into walking dead men and women, fearful of deviating from total submission, and all thoughts of rising up against the occupiers were lost or abandoned.

Albuquerque decided to get rid of Attar once and for all. He finally realised there was no way to buy his loyalty or placate him. The Portuguese governor ordered his men to bring him the golden palm tree and then to drag Attar from his dungeon without removing his manacles.

Attar was shackled with a chain between his ankles and another between his wrists. He was bare headed, his long white hair hanging over his ears on both sides of his head. When they saw Attar dragged in this way, the Hormuzi guards, who had never seen him bare headed before, knew that the goal was to break him and humiliate him.

As Attar walked, his iron chains made a jarring clanking noise. Albuquerque ordered him to sit on a chair in front of him. The golden palm was placed between them.

'Do you remember this palm, Vizier?'

Attar ignored the artefact. 'Yes, I do, Governor. What of it?'

'I just wanted to remind you of the palm that your daughter had made after Emir Nasser killed her husband. She used all her jewels to make it, correct?'

Attar did not respond. He realised where Albuquerque was going with this.

Albuquerque continued. 'I think she put in it everything she owned, her entire fortune. Your daughter fell into poverty afterwards. She is now destitute and has nothing to her name.'

As the conquistador spoke, his reptilian eyes stared at Attar. 'How can she survive in those strange lands where she knows no one?' Albuquerque asked, trying to goad Attar.

The Portuguese was trying to torment him and manipulate his emotions, but Attar focused his mind on the ornamental palm tree, trying to imagine his daughter and ignore Albuquerque's provocations.

After a few caustic remarks, Attar was no longer able to put up with Albuquerque's taunts. He did not want him to enjoy torturing him by mentioning the person closest to his heart. 'What are you trying to get at, Governor?'

Albuquerque's insidious smile grew wider. He knew he had succeeded in disquieting his victim. 'All I'm saying is that a beautiful woman like your daughter will not run out of ways to eke out a living.'

Blood rushed to Attar's angry face. But before he could say anything, Albuquerque quickly changed the subject. 'Do you know why you're here?'

Attar lifted his head in defiance. He peered out the window overlooking the port. This was the same place where he had met with Bin Rahhal, Halima and Salghur following the Jabrid intervention to restore the king to the throne. He breathed deeply, as though trying to catch his daughter's scent in the room. 'Since you came to our home, we have lived in perpetual misery. You have ruined our lives, destroyed our kingdoms and robbed us of our wealth. Hormuz is in ruins when it once was the centre of the world. You destroyed morality among people after you ruined their lives. You are monsters sent by the devil. We have seen the face of death in the sails that brought you to our shores!'

'Do you mean the sails of the Holy Cross?' retorted Albuquerque maliciously.

Attar was past his breaking point. His face swelled with an old wrath that had been buried for too long. 'There is nothing holy about it! It carries death and destruction! You worship death and serve the devil, ignoring all of God's commandments! You have brought us the Inquisition to peer into the hearts and minds of men, and torture them until they say what you want, before you kill them to satisfy your sick souls!'

Attar stopped and started breathing heavily. His health could no longer cope with this much rage. He started feeling numbness and sluggishness spreading to his limbs, almost paralysing him, and opted to remain silent.

Albuquerque realised that Attar was not going to live much longer, and resolved to bring about his death by humiliating him. He wanted him to die a slow, miserable and undignified death.

'You have shown your true colours, Vizier Attar. You have a grudge against us and you want to see our downfall. That is why you sent your letters to our dominions in the Gulf urging them to rebel. You are behind all of it, the death of our soldiers and sailors, and the loss of our treasures!'

Albuquerque pointed at the golden palm, saying, 'I intend to send this to the king of Portugal. You should rejoice because the jewels of your daughter and her husband will be in our king's hands. What an honour that will be!'

Albuquerque paused then continued, 'I will seize all that you own. You will have nothing left except the clothes on your back. You have become poor and penniless, Attar. All your possessions now belong to the king of Portugal, to compensate for some of the damage you have caused. If I could take your daughter too, I would make her a petty servant on one of my ships.'

A shiver went down Attar's spine. He felt his limbs grow numb again and understood this was the end. The only thing that made him hopeful was the knowledge that his daughter had decided not to return to Hormuz, and that she was alive and free away from this monster.

'Do as you please, Albuquerque. I don't care any more. I will curse you until my last breath!'

'This may well be the last thing you do while you're still alive, Attar. But it doesn't matter, I will enjoy tormenting you,' Albuquerque retorted, laughing rowdily.

He suddenly fell silent, and his gaze was now irate. 'I shall send you in shackles to Lisbon, where you will rot in a cold, damp cell. I will write to the king to show you hospitality in the Portuguese way. Now let me wish you a pleasant journey there.'

The world faded to black for Attar. He had wished to see his daughter for one last time before he was sent to the unknown. He did not expect to end up an impoverished, alienated prisoner exiled into a prison in Portugal.

'May I have one final request, commander Albuquerque? Might there be in some part of your heart an iota of mercy?' Attar asked. He then turned his eyes to the sky outside, as though pleading with heaven to have mercy and assist him in his request. 'My daughter is in faraway lands and I know nothing about her. All I ask before you send me to Portugal is to let me write her a letter informing her of my fate!'

Albuquerque looked straight into Attar's eyes and said in a tone meant to rip his heart from his chest, 'No, you will send no such letter. No one will know anything about you. Your request is denied.'

He then signalled to the guards to take Attar away.

– *41* –

Istanbul, Turkey

Years Later

I n front of an elegant home in an upscale neighbour-hood of Istanbul stood a scruffy man in shabby clothes. His appearance contrasted starkly with the neatness and beauty of the street. Rows of pine and apple trees were planted on both sides of the road, and the air was redolent with the fragrance of roses and fruit trees that had bloomed after a long winter.

The grubby-looking man grabbed the poles of the outer fence and peeked through the gaps at the house's tidy garden. He scanned the premises looking for something or someone. The miserly dervish* would not have drawn much attention, as he resembled many men who like him roamed the streets of Istanbul to solicit donations through Sufi dances and prayers. But what made this man stand apart from other dervishes was the size of his paunch, his noticeably slanted shoulder and the jolliness in his face.

A guard emerged from a booth attached to the garden, and shooed him unkindly. 'Go away, dervish. Get out of here!'

The man let go of the fence cautiously, and then approached the guard, who now looked alert. 'What do you want? I said get out of here, before I make you!'

The man's features suggested he was kind and docile, especially when a hopeful smile tugged at the corners of his mouth. 'Please, kind sir, forgive my intrusion. I am only a poor dervish who means no harm.' When he felt the guard was reassured somehow by his demeanour, he asked, 'Is this the home of Suleiman Pasha?'

'Yes, it is. But you must go before he comes and punishes the both of us.'

The dervish ignored what the guard said and continued, 'He knows me well. I'm an old friend of his. I fell into destitution, true, but I'm his friend nonetheless. I have not changed much since we went our separate ways, well, save for the grey hairs on my head, the wrinkles on my face and the bigger belly. But it's still me, his old friend.'

The miser rubbed his face, his belly and his robes as if trying to ensure he had indeed not changed.

The guard was uninterested in the dervish's tales and ordered him to leave again. 'Come on, just go! You are starting to annoy me!'

The dervish was unfazed by the guard. 'He knows me. I'm his old friend. Just tell him I'm here.'

The guard lost his temper and started threatening him. A woman emerged suddenly from between the newly trimmed trees, carrying a small flower plant. The trees had been concealing her as she planted flowers in the garden and the dervish had not seen her. She addressed the guard in a quiet voice. 'What's going on? Why all the shouting?'

The guard pointed at the potbellied men. 'This dervish doesn't want to leave, my lady. There are too many beggars in this neighbourhood. I know you have instructed me not

413

to dismiss anyone but this man in particular was just too insolent!'

'My lady, I am Jaafar from Egypt. I am a friend of Suleiman Pasha. He knows me, please tell him I'm here!'

Jaafar clutched the iron poles as though his life depended on it.

The woman looked at him with suspicion. How could the pasha know someone as miserable looking as this man? She said cautiously, 'Fine. I will send you some food and money but you must go after that.'

Jaafar gripped the fence even tighter, fearing he would miss his chance. 'My lady, I have come from distant lands in search of the pasha. Please don't send me away. The pasha knows me well. I am Jaafar from Egypt. Please, just tell him that!'

The woman scrutinised the dervish's features. She was saddened by his pathetic persistence and the humiliation on his face. She ordered the guard to open the gate and let the man into the garden. She then ordered her servants to bring some food and money for him.

The servants laid out the food on the grass and urged the man to eat and then leave.

The man sobbed and did not eat. 'Tell the pasha who I am, he knows me!'

The woman could not bear seeing the man cry. She took out some money and gave it to him. He took it reluctantly then he sobbed again, repeating his request to see the pasha.

The woman was perplexed. She sat near him and asked, 'How do you know the pasha?'

The man wiped his tears with the edge of his filthy green turban and in a quavering voice replied, 'I am Jaafar from Egypt. I used to be a soldier in the Mamluk army before I was injured in battle and discharged. I worked as a waiter at an inn on the coast of Alexandria. The pasha used to eat there with his friend Hussein al-Kurdi when they still lived in the city. After Suleiman left for Rhodes to fight off pirates, I did not hear anything about him.'

Jaafar looked at the food again but decided against eating. He continued, 'After the Portuguese came to dominate the seas, trade in Alexandria ground to a halt and life there became miserable. There was no money or merchants or ships. Everything collapsed. The inn owner eventually had to close it down and sack everyone. I tried to find work, any work, and moved from city to city in Egypt to find my sustenance. At the same time, I was searching for Hussein, Suleiman's friend, who had become a pasha. Then I learned he had been murdered in Jeddah and I despaired. All I could do was try to find Suleiman, my last remaining friend who could rescue me from misery and penury.'

Jaafar gave the woman a pathetic look to elicit her sympathy. 'I came to Istanbul without a penny to my name! I worked as a porter in the markets. As I've got older, it has become difficult for me to continue this sort of work, so I decided to try to find the pasha at any cost!'

Jaafar shifted his eyes to his dirty and tattered clothes and then back to the woman, and continued. 'What else could I have done, madam? Each time I made queries about the pasha, I was ignored or, worse, insulted. No one knew who I was. They see my clothes and state and decide to look down on me immediately. That's life for you! I did try to make a decent living in a way that preserved my dignity, but I failed because of my injury!'

The woman's face had changed upon hearing Hussein's name. Now she was sure he was telling the truth. Hussein was indeed a friend of Suleiman Pasha. 'All right, don't worry. I am the pasha's wife. I will ask him to help you.'

The woman watched as a young man wearing an Ottoman officer's uniform entered the garden. She rose and embraced him. The young man looked at Jaafar in contempt. 'Who is this man, Mother? Another dervish?'

'A dervish, yes, but not just any one.'

The officer approached the dervish, who stood up in respect.

'This is my son Hussein, Jaafar. I named him after Hussein al-Kurdi, Suleiman Pasha's friend,' the woman said.

Jaafar examined young Hussein's face, trying to see if there was any trace of his old friend in him. 'I hope he doesn't take after Hussein, that man grumbled about everything.'

The woman laughed, saying, 'He did not grumble when I last saw him.'

Jaafar's expression changed. 'You've met him, madam? How? Where?'

The woman, who was still holding her son's hand, gestured to Jaafar to sit back down. 'Sit, Jaafar. The conversation might last a while.'

'I come from the kingdom of Hormuz, an island east of here. It used to be a splendid, wealthy kingdom before the Portuguese appeared on its shores. I married a man named Ghurair bin Rahhal, who was the vizier of Sultan Muqrin, an Arabian king in those parts. The sultan sent him to fight the Portuguese in India, where he met Hussein Pasha. They fought together but they unfortunately were defeated in battle, after which they returned in disguise to Bahrain, where I was living.'

The woman, who was none other than Halima, continued, 'Hussein did not stay with us for very long. He left for Jeddah, and I did not see him again after that. My late husband was killed months after Hussein left. Then I travelled to Jeddah for the Hajj, and there I met Suleiman who became my husband. He told me that Hussein al-Kurdi was killed in a rebellion in Jeddah.'

Pointing to the young man who was still standing near them, she said, 'I have three children with Suleiman. This is my eldest. We also have a girl whom we named Farah, after my best friend who died many years ago. Then we had another boy, Fekri, who is still in the military academy.' Halima now seemed more interested in the dervish, who knew a lot about her husband. She said, 'You have to wait until my husband comes. He will be back soon.'

Jaafar started eating from the food that was offered to him. Halima and her son Hussein, who was still not fully comfortable with this stranger, sat with him. Jaafar told them stories about Suleiman and Hussein when they were young officers in the Mamluk army.

They heard a noise outside the main door, and saw the pasha's wagon bearing the banners of the Ottoman navy stop outside. Guards from the Janissary regiment escorted him. The procession crossed the main gate and came up the path leading to the house, to the entrance decorated by beautiful carnations.

Halima and Hussein stood up and went to where the wagon had stopped. They spoke to the pasha before they returned to Jaafar. Halima had told Suleiman about his miserable state.

When the pasha came close to Jaafar, he opened his arms and said, 'Jaafar, you fatso! We miss the food you used to feed us. I see your belly has actually shrunk a little. Hopefully, you're less talkative too!'

'Pasha Suleiman! You survived the *atabeg* curse then. You murdered no one and no one murdered you in Cairo!'

They all sat in the garden and talked about every topic under the sun, until they got to the story of how Halima met Suleiman in Jeddah. Halima said, looking at her husband, 'Sheikh Tazi was very cunning when he asked me to wash my face with *zamzam* water in front of you, making up a *hadith*. He wanted you to see me and fall in love, so you could marry me before he left for Morocco.'

'The sheikh's trick worked. If he hadn't done what he did, I wouldn't have seen your face and married you,' Suleiman said happily.

Halima gave out a deep sigh, remembering the man and how much she owed him and his wife. She said in her usual gentle voice, 'I don't know what happened to him after he left Jeddah. May God have mercy on him if he passed away. His compassion, knowledge and intelligence have changed my life for the better.'

Jaafar continued to joke with Suleiman. 'Shall I call you Suleiman? Or shall I call you Suleiman Pasha? All these titles scare me a bit and I don't really understand their value. The highest rank I'd heard of was *atabeg*. May God have mercy on my mother, I wish she had named me "Atabeg Jaafar" so that the title would stick to me my whole life. People would say, "Atabeg Jaafar, bring us some meze and put on some extra olive oil."'

Everyone laughed. Halima looked at the faces around her and thought about how much her life had changed. She lifted her eyes to the sky and prayed for her father, whom she had heard nothing about for many years.

Her memory took her back to Bahrain, to the farmstead where she had lived some of the best days of her life. She tried to imagine the state of Farah's grave, isolated and forsaken in a strange land. She looked back at her husband and son and this odd dervish, and lifted her eyes back to the sky.

'Praise be to God for everything. Dear God, have mercy on my father!'

Massawa, East Africa

A CATHOLIC PRIEST FROM PORTUGAL disembarked from the ship that had brought him to Massawa. He scanned the people around him as if searching for a familiar face. The docks were teeming with people and goods being moved about. No one paid him any attention; many like him were seen coming and going every day.

He spotted a young man dragging a mule that lumbered heavily behind him. The priest approached him and asked whether he could take him to a place between the distant cloud-covered mountaintops that towered behind the port.

'Yes, I can take you there. But I will charge you by the day. It's very far as you can see.'

The priest shook his pocket so that the guide could hear the sound of the coins he carried. 'Very well, we shall do that. I will pay your wage when the sun sets every day, but my condition is that you must never leave me when we are on the road.'

The guide, stroking the neck of his mule, replied, 'I'm fine with that, sir.'

The two men headed west along a dirt road, where thin shepherds were herding their cows and sheep. The shepherds wore a length of fabric that wrapped around their waists and folded over their shoulders.

The guide asked the priest, 'Where to exactly, sir?'

'To the realm of Empress Eleni,' replied the Portuguese.

The guide trembled upon hearing the name. 'Are you sure, sir? People who go to her kingdom never come back. When I asked you at the port you said you were going to somewhere between those green mountains!'

'The place between the mountains *is* Empress Eleni's realm,' the priest replied mockingly. 'Do you remember my condition, which you agreed to before we set off?'

'I do, priest. But do you know you may never return?'

The priest wanted to put an end to the conversation. 'I know, friend. I know.'

The two-man convoy travelled without speaking through highlands, streams and valleys towards a plateau situated in the middle of the realm. After a few days, when the guide could no longer bear the priest's silence, he said, 'Father, we have been walking and eating together for days and yet you have not told me your name!'

'Francisco Álvares. I am a priest from Portugal. I am on my way to visit the empress to enquire about a man we lost in these parts many years ago.'

The guide pointed in the direction of the high mountains in front of them. 'It is a vast land, Father, full of predators and bandits. Anything could have happened to him. Why is he so important to you?'

'He's not important to me, but he is to my king. He sent him nearly thirty years ago to look for the kingdom of Prester John but the man vanished. We want to find out how and why.'

The guide tried to pull the mule, which did not seem to want to cross the narrow pass they were at now. The guide said,

'Empress Eleni is much better than her husband, who was a cruel man. He prohibited foreigners from leaving his kingdom once they entered, forcing them to stay with him. He believed all foreigners were spies who had come to scout out the kingdom's strengths and weaknesses. I heard the empress allows some to leave, however, thinking they could return with treasures and goods for trade, but I wouldn't trust that either. Those kings and queens change their mind every time they wake up. If I were you I would think twice before going there.'

The priest was surprised by the guide's advice. 'You speak like you are not one of the empress's subjects.'

The guide grunted at the animal, urging it to move. 'I am from the coast, sir. We don't see ourselves as her subjects. She rules the distant mountains in front of you, but her people know nothing about the sea. All I know is that she is a powerful queen who was able to return to the throne after being banished. Struggles for the throne in this country almost never stop.'

The pair encountered several tribes inhabiting the hills. Some were aggressive while others were peaceful. Each tribe had its own costumes and accessories. Some were completely naked. Some adorned their bodies with paint and tattoos. And others covered themselves with animal skins. But they all seem to have carved their faces with cuts and signs to distinguish themselves from others.

The priest had brought with him some leather goods, mirrors, hats, shoes and fabrics that he distributed to the tribal chiefs to gain their favour. 'The gifts work like a charm with these savages,' the priest told the guide.

Several days later, they reached a village high on a hill. The air was chilly. The people inhabiting the area seemed more civilised, wearing white wool garments and living in homes made from stones quarried from nearby hills. There were markets, domesticated animals and eateries.

They walked quietly in the middle of the village, trying to ignore people staring at them in amazement. The priest's black robes were especially unfamiliar in these isolated highlands, where people did not see many foreigners.

Álvares and his guide reached a stony plateau beautifully engraved near the entrance and on the sides. A group of men and women clad in white stood outside. The door was guarded by men carrying long spears and rudimentary straight swords. The guide exchanged a few words with them, after which they gave the priest a look of suspicion before allowing him to enter.

The priest walked through passageways carved into the rock. He could still see the sky above as they had no roof. The men reached another stone door. The guard asked him to remain there and wait for permission to enter.

A voice spoke from inside the hall. The guard then signalled for the priest to enter. The hall was lit by several torches placed strategically in the corners. It took the priest a few seconds to adjust to the dimmer light.

Álvares saw the empress sitting in front of him on a wooden throne adorned with intricate inscriptions. She wore a white robe that covered most of her body. Over it she wore a tiger cub skin stretching from her neck to her thighs, which was somehow affixed to her chest. She wore a crown of pure gold, and held a sceptre made of ivory with gold and silver engravings. A group of what looked like princes and dignitaries sat around her. Young girls wearing dyed woollen tunics with exquisite patterns sat behind her and at her feet.

The priest bowed before her in a show of respect. A voice told him to sit and he kneeled as though at the altar of a church. He started feeling pain in his knees but did not dare to stand up.

Someone addressed Álvares in Portuguese. The voice came from near the queen, and ordered him to sit on the ground and relieve his knees. The priest scanned the faces of the people present, his eyes now accustomed to the dim light in the hall. He noticed an elderly white man wearing a strange smile. The man asked him in perfect Portuguese, 'Who are you? Why have you come here?'

A broad smile appeared on the priest's face. He felt his mission was a success. He replied quickly, 'I am a Catholic priest from Portugal. My name is Francisco Álvares. I have come at the request of the king of Portugal in search of Covilhã, who disappeared in these lands.'

The old man translated what Álvares said to the queen, who shook her head and then gestured at him.

The elderly man stood up and bowed to the queen. He then asked the priest to leave the hall with him. Álvares followed the man outside, and walked towards a bullock cart. They rode it and headed outside the settlement in awkward silence.

The priest did not know the identity of this man, whom people treated with the utmost respect wherever he went. After the oxcart had travelled some distance to the west, he mustered up the courage to ask him, 'Who are you, sir?'

The old man smiled and answered, 'I was just about to ask you why you had come looking for Covilhã after all these years!'

Overjoyed, the priest said, 'You are Covilhã, aren't you?'

'Yes, I am Covilhã. But you haven't answered my question.'

The priest beamed with joy. He had achieved the first goal of his journey. 'Master Covilhã, I have braved many dangers and difficulties to get to you. Thanks to you and your friend Paiva, we managed to put our hands on the spice trade. The guide you drafted throughout your journey left almost nothing out. The wealth of information it contained led us to where we are and precipitated our victory, leading our ships to this part of the world.'

The priest shifted in his seat. The bare wooden planks he sat on were uncomfortable on the uneven road: each time the cart passed over a bump his bottom and back hit the wood painfully. Álvares continued, 'The king ordered for your report to be copied and given to every captain. After a few years, our captains were able to chart all those regions, and when your guide was no longer needed, it was returned for preservation at the Royal Library.'

Covilhã noticed that the priest was restless because of the pain in his back. 'Don't worry, we're almost at my farm. Carry on.'

'Very well, sir. After several years our trade flourished and Portugal became wealthy thanks to you, although people have forgotten about the report of your journey.'

Covilhã listened attentively to the priest. The peasants they passed on the road bowed to him in respect, and Covilhã returned their greeting.

The priest continued, 'One of the king's aides reminded him one day, thirty years after you set off, of your role in rescuing Portugal from financial hardship. The king requested for you to be found because he wanted to honour you as well as Paiva.'

Covilhã seemed surprised. 'Honour us? After all these years? Do you know what the Inquisition did shortly after we left

425

Lisbon? They drove our families out, burned Paiva's father alive and confiscated our properties. The king did not keep his promise. He was blinded by money.'

The priest made the sign of the cross. He had never heard anyone insult the king in this way.

Covilhã fell silent again, and looked ahead. Then he said, 'My friend Paiva disappeared in these mountains. I looked for him for many years but I found no trace of him whatsoever. Then I came to this kingdom. The previous king prevented me from leaving, but he granted me a large plot of land and heads of cattle, and gave me a wife too. I have been living here since, and had children.'

The cart reached a thoroughly cultivated terrace overlooking a plain littered with cows and sheep. At the top of the terrace there was a large house built of stone.

Covilhã pointed at the building and said, 'This is my home. I have lived here for a long time and I will die here. Go back to your king and tell him that Covilhã renounces all of the holy sails that he sent, bringing death and destruction to this part of the world. Our report opened the gates of hell on people who did not even know we existed!'

The priest looked at old Covilhã in shock. He was dismayed by his daring abuse of the king. But Covilhã continued speaking, like a scholar addressing a class. 'Happiness is not money and power, but being free to live away from the oppression of unjust kings who take pleasure in killing and torturing people!'

The priest made the sign of the cross again. This criticism of his great king was too harsh, he thought.

In the distance, the sun was about to set. A gentle, refreshing breeze blew across the two men's faces. The priest sighed when he caught a whiff of the fresh mountain air. 'It's very pleasant, isn't it, Father?' asked Covilhã.

The priest was too taken by the beauty of the place to answer.

The cart continued travelling until it stopped right outside the house.

Covilhã stumbled out of the cart, his old age having taken away all nimbleness in his body. He walked to his home followed by the priest, who tried to match his slow pace. A beautiful dark-skinned girl with fair hair came out of the house and bowed to Covilhã, then kissed his hand.

Covilhã looked at the priest and said, 'This is my daughter, Eleni. I named her after the queen. I also have a son who should be back in the evening. I will introduce you to him, he is very much like me.'

The sun went down and night fell. Around a large fire under a roasting carcass, Covilhã sat with his family and his guest. Laughter filled the air. The priest did not understand much of what was said that night, but he realised that Covilhã was never going back.

GLOSSARY

Ağ Qoyunlu: Turkic tribal federation that ruled present-day Azerbaijan, Armenia, Eastern Turkey, part of Iran and northern Iraq from 1378 to 1501.

Amir: In this context, Mamluk military officers of different ranks, including the rank of Amir of One Hundred and Amir of One Thousand.

Atabeg: In Mamluk Egypt, a military leader of the highest level.

Banyan: Banyan merchants is an expression used widely in the Indian Ocean trade to refer to Indian merchants who are clearly distinguished by their clothing, their religious and cultural dietary choices, and by the manner in which they conduct trade.

Bunder boat: A small boat used to transport people between large ships and harbours.

Caliph: A person considered a political and religious successor to the Prophet Muhammad and a leader to the entire Muslim community.

Caravel: A type of small ship used by the Spanish and Portuguese at the time.

Dawadar:	The bearer of the Sultan's inkwell, the equivalent of Chamberlain in the Mamluk hierarchy.
Dervish:	Member of a Sufi Muslim ascetic path (*Tariqa*), known for their extreme poverty and austerity. Dervishes focus on the universal values of love and service, deserting the illusions of ego in order to reach God.
Dhow:	A lateen-rigged ship with one or two masts, used chiefly in the Arabian region.
Dhul-Qarnayn:	A figure mentioned in the Quran, believed to have built a great barrier to hold Gog and Magog at bay.
Emir:	A prince or sovereign in the region.
Frankish:	A blanket medieval Muslim term for all Christian peoples of continental Europe and the British Isles.
Ghutra:	The traditional Arabian headdress fashioned from a square scarf (also known as *keffiyeh* or *hattah*).
Hadith:	Sayings of the Prophet Muhammad, separate from the Quran.
Haggadah:	The text recited at the Seder on the first two nights of the Jewish Passover.
Izar:	On the Arabian Peninsula, a large piece of cloth men wear around the waist, similar to a sarong.
Jabrid:	A tribal dynasty that ruled a large part of the western coast of the Arabian Gulf.
Jinn:	In Islamic theology, they are demons with free will made from smokeless fire.

Khasiki:	Bodyguards of the Sultans and high-ranking amirs.
Khawaja:	A title commonly used in the Middle East and Asia, meaning 'master' or 'lord'.
Majlis:	A room where rulers held council and received guests. In a private home, a room for receiving and entertaining guests.
Malabar:	Mercenaries from the Indian region of Malabar.
Mamluk Sultanate:	Militaristic medieval realm with its capital in Cairo that ruled over Egypt and Syria, initially formed by an aristocracy of slaves.
Palanquin:	A passenger conveyance, usually for one person, consisting of an enclosed litter and carried by means of poles on the shoulders of several people.
Pasha:	A title used in the Ottoman Empire for high-ranking military and political officials.
Qizilbash:	Shi'i militant groups that flourished in Azerbaijan, Anatolia and Kurdistan from the late thirteenth century onwards, some of whom contributed to the foundation of the Safavid dynasty of Iran.
Si:	A title meaning 'mister' or 'sir' in Tunisian Arabic.
Vizier:	A political adviser or minister of the highest rank. A Grand Vizier is similar in importance to a modern-day prime minister.
Zaidism:	An early sect which emerged in the eighth century out of Shi'a Islam.

BIBLIOGRAPHY

Green, Toby, *Inquisition: The Reign of Fear*, London, Pan Books, 2008

Hall, Richard, *Empires of the Monsoon: A History of the Indian Ocean and its Invaders*, New York, HarperCollins, 1998

Khalidi, Azzam bin Hamad & Khalidi, Iman bint Khaled, *The Jabrid Sultanate in Najd and Eastern Arabia*, Beirut, Al-Dar Al-Arabiya lil Mawsou'at, 2010

Khalil, Mohamed Mahmoud, *History of the Gulf and Eastern Arabia also known as the Bahrain Region under the Rule of Arab Statelets (469–963 AH/1076–1555 AD)*, Cairo, Al-Madbouli, 2006

Newitt, Malyn, *A History of Portuguese Overseas Expansion, 1400–1668*, London, Routledge, 2004

Al Omar, Said bin Omar, *The Arabian Gulf: Its Political History and its Relations with the Countries of the East and West*, Dammam, Maktabat Al-Mutannabi, 2008

Zine al-Abidine, Bashir, *Bahrain and her Foreign Relations in the Sixteenth Century*, Manama, Centre for Historical Studies, University of Bahrain, 2009